"IMAGINE A MIXTURE OF
TILL EULENSPIEGEL AND KEN KESEY

. . . and you've got the range of the merry pranksters who hot rod through Mr. Irving's book on a 700 cc Royal Enfield motorcycle, tossing flowers, stealing salt shakers, and planning the biggest caper of their young lives." —*The New York Times*

"When the great zoo bust finally comes through and some of the beasts run free, the drama encompasses the longings and agonies of youth. . . . A complex and moving novel" —*Time*

"SETTING FREE THE BEARS has much to recommend it. It moves rapidly from incident to incident in the best picaresque tradition. It is full of amusing dialogue. Its characters are depicted with love and skill." —*St. Louis Post-Dispatch*

Books by John Irving

The 158-Pound Marriage
Setting Free the Bears
The Water-Method Man
The World According to Garp

Published by POCKET BOOKS

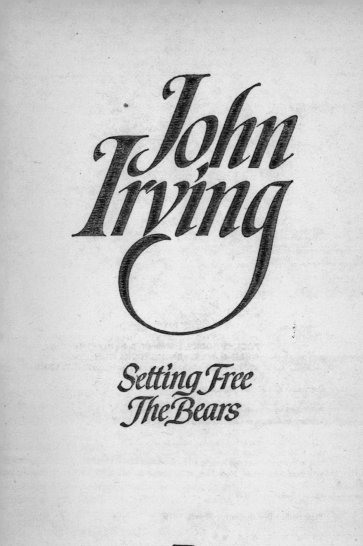

John Irving

Setting Free The Bears

PUBLISHED BY POCKET BOOKS NEW YORK

POCKET BOOKS, a Simon & Schuster division of
GULF & WESTERN CORPORATION
1230 Avenue of the Americas, New York, N.Y. 10020

This book is for

VIOLETTE *and* CO

in memory of

GEORGE

CONTENTS

Setting Free
The Bears

Part One

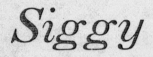

Siggy

A STEADY DIET
IN VIENNA

I could find him every noon, sitting on a bench in the Rathaus Park with a small, fat bag of hothouse radishes in his lap and a bottle of beer in one hand. He always brought his own saltshaker; he must have had a great number of them, because I can't recall a particular one from the lot. They were never very fancy saltshakers, though, and once he even threw one away; he just wrapped it up in the empty radishbag and tossed it in one of the park's trashcans.

Every noon, and always the same bench—the least splintery one, on the edge of the park nearest the university. Occasionally he had a notebook with him, but always the corduroy duckhunter's jacket with its side slash-pockets, and the great vent-pocket at the back. The radishes, the bottle of beer, a saltshaker, and sometimes the notebook—all of them from the long, bulging vent-pocket. He carried nothing in his hands when he walked. His tobacco and pipes went in the side slash-pockets of the jacket; he had at least three different pipes.

Although I assumed he was a student like myself, I hadn't seen him in any of the university buildings. Only in the Rathaus Park, every noon of the new spring days. Often I sat on the bench opposite him while he ate. I'd have my newspaper, and it was a fine spot to watch the girls come along the walk; you could peek at their pale, winter knees—the hardboned, blousy girls in their diaphanous silks. But he didn't watch them; he just perched as alertly as a squirrel over the bag of radishes. Through the bench slats, the sun zebra-striped his lap.

I'd had more than a week of such contact with him before I noticed another of his habits. He scribbled things on the radishbag, and he was always stashing little pieces of bag in his pockets, but more often he wrote in the notebook.

One day he did this: I saw him pocket a little note on a bag piece, walk away from the bench, and a bit down the path decide to have another look. He pulled out the bag

3

piece and read it. Then he threw it away, and this is what
I read:

The fanatical maintenance of good habits is necessary.

It was later, when I read his famous notebook—his Poetry, as he spoke of it—that I realized this note hadn't
been entirely thrown away. He'd simply cleaned it a little.

Good habits are worth being fanatical about.

But back in the Rathaus Park, with the little scrap from
the radishbag, I couldn't tell he was a poet and a maxim-
maker; I only thought he'd be an interesting fellow to
know.

HARD TIMES

There's a place on Josefsgasse, behind the Parliament Building, known for its fast, suspicious turnover of
secondhand motorcycles. I've Doktor Ficht to thank for
my discovery of the place. It was Doktor Ficht's exam I'd
just flunked, which put me in a mood to vary my usual
noon habit in the Rathaus Park.

I went off through a number of little arches with boggy
smells, past cellar stores with mildewy clothes and into a
section of garages—tire shops and auto-parts places,
where smudged men in overalls were clanking and rolling
things out on the sidewalk. I came on it suddenly, a dirty
showcase window with the cardboard sign FABER'S in a
corner of glass; nothing more in the way of advertising,
except the noise spuming from an open doorway. Fumes
dark as thunderclouds, an upstarting series of blatting
echo-shots, and through the showcase window I could
make out the two mechanics racing the throttles of two
motorcycles; there were more motorcycles on the platform
nearest the window, but these were shiny and still. Scattered about on the cement floor by the doorway, and
blurred in exhaust, were various tools and gas-tank caps
—pieces of spoke and wheel rim, fender and cable—and
these two intent mechanics bent over their cycles; playing

the throttles up and down, they looked as serious and ear-ready as any musicians tuning up for a show. I inhaled from the doorway.

Watching me, just inside, was a gray man with wide, oily lapels; the buttons were the dullest part of his suit. A great sprocket leaned against the doorway beside him—a fallen, sawtoothed moon, so heavy with grease it absorbed light and glowed at me.

"Herr Faber himself," the man said, prodding his chest with his thumb. And he ushered me out the doorway and back down the street. When we were away from the din, he studied me with a tiny, gold-capped smile.

"Ah!" he said. "The university?"

"God willing," I said, "but it's unlikely."

"Fallen in hard times?" said Herr Faber. "What sort of a motorcycle did you have in mind?"

"I don't have anything in mind," I told him.

"Oh," said Faber, "it's never easy to decide."

"It's staggering," I said.

"Oh, don't I know?" he said. "Some bikes are such animals beneath you, *really*—veritable beasts! And that's exactly what some have in mind. Just what they're looking for!"

"It's makes you giddy to think of it," I said.

"I agree, I agree," said Herr Faber. "I know just what you mean. You should talk with Herr Javotnik. He's a student—like yourself! And he'll be back from lunch presently. Herr Javotnik is a wonder at helping people make up their minds. A *virtuoso* with decisions!"

"Amazing," I said.

"And a joy and a comfort to me," he said. "You'll see." Herr Faber cocked his slippery head to one side and listened lovingly to the *burt, burt, burt* of the motorcycles within.

THE BEAST
BENEATH ME

I recognized Herr Javotnik by his corduroy duckhunter's jacket with the pipes protruding from the side slash-pockets. He looked like a young man coming from a lunch that had left his mouth salty and stinging.

"Ah!" said Herr Faber, and he took two little side steps as if he would do a dance for us. "Herr Javotnik," he said, "this young man has a decision to make."

"So that's it," said Javotnik, "—why you weren't in the park?"

"Ah! Ah?" Herr Faber squealed. "You know each other?"

"Very well," Javotnik said. "I should say, very well. This will be a most personal decision, I'm sure, Herr Faber. If you'd leave us."

"Well, yes," said Faber. "Very well, very well"—and he sidled away from us, returning to the exhaust in his doorway.

"A lout, of course," said Javotnik. "You've no mind to buy a thing, have you?"

"No," I said. "I just happened along."

"Strange not to see you in the park."

"I've fallen in hard times," I told him.

"Whose exam?" he asked.

"Ficht's."

"Well, Ficht. I can tell you a bit about him. He's got rotten gums, uses a little brush between his classes—swabs his gums with some gunk from a brown jar. His breath could wilt a weed. He's fallen in hard times himself."

"It's good to know," I said.

"But you've no interest in motorcycles?" he asked. "I've an interest myself, just to hop on one and leave this city. Vienna's no spot for the spring, really. But of course, I couldn't go more than half toward any bike in there."

"I couldn't either," I said.

"That so?" he said. "What's your name?"

"Graff," I told him. "Hannes Graff."

"Well, Graff, there's one especially nice motorcycle in there, if you've any thoughts toward a trip."

"Well," I said, "I couldn't go more than half, you know, and it seems you're tied up with a job."

"I'm never tied up," said Javotnik.

"But perhaps you've gotten in the habit," I told him. "Habits aren't to be scoffed at, you know." And he braced back on his heels a moment, brought up a pipe from his jacket and clacked it against his teeth.

"I'm all for a good whim too," he said. "My name's Siggy. Siegfried Javotnik."

And although he made no note of it at the time, he

would later add this idea to his notebook, under the revised line concerning habit and fanaticism—this new maxim also rephrased.

Be blissfully guided by the veritable urge!

But that afternoon on the sidewalk he was perhaps without his notebook or a scrap of radishbag, and he must have felt the prompting of Herr Faber, who peered so anxiously at us, his head darting like a snake's tongue out of the smoggy garage.

"Come with me, Graff," said Siggy. "I'm going to sit you on a beast."

So we crossed the slick floor of the garage to a door against the back wall, a door with a dartboard on it; both the door and the dartboard hung askew. The dartboard was all chewed up, the bull's-eye indistinguishable from the matted clots of cork all over—as if it had been attacked with wrenches instead of darts, or by mad mechanics with tearing mouths.

We went out into an alley behind the garage.

"Oh now, Herr Javotnik," said Faber. "Do you really think so?"

"Absolutely," said Siegfried Javotnik.

It was covered with a glossy black tarp and leaned against the wall of the garage. The rear fender was as thick as my finger, a heavy chunk of chrome, gray on the rim where it took some of the color from the mudcleats, deep-grooved on the rear tire—tire and fender and the perfect gap between. Siggy pulled the tarp off.

It was an old, cruel-looking motorcycle, missing the gentle lines and the filled-in places; it had spaces in between its parts, a gap where some clutterer might have tried to put a toolbox, a little open triangle between the engine and the gas tank too—the tank, a sleek teardrop of black, sat like a too small head on a bulky body; it was lovely like a gun is sometimes lovely—for the obvious, ugly function showing in its most prominent parts. It weighed, all right, and seemed to suck its belly in, like a lean, hunched dog in the tall grass.

"A virtuoso, this boy!" Herr Faber said. "A joy and a comfort."

"It's British," said Siggy. "Royal Enfield, some years ago when they made the pieces look like the way they worked. Seven hundred cubic centimeters. New tires and chains, and the clutch has been rebuilt. Like new."

"This boy, he loves this old one!" said Faber. "He worked on it all on his own time. It's like *new!*"

"It's new, all right," Siggy whispered. "I ordered from London—new clutch and sprocket, new pistons and rings—and he thought it was for his other bikes. The old thief doesn't know what it's worth."

"Sit on it!" Herr Faber said. "Oh, just sit, and feel the beast beneath you!"

"Half and half," whispered Siggy. "You pay it all now, and I'll pay you back with my wages."

"Start it up for me," I said.

"Ah well," said Faber. "Herr Javotnik, it's not quite ready to start up now, is it? Maybe it needs gas."

"Oh no," said Siggy. "It should start right up." And he came alongside me and pumped on the kick starter; there was very little fiddling—a tickle to the carburetor, the spark retard out and back. Then he rose up beside me and dropped his weight on the kicker. The engine sucked and gasped, and the stick flew back against him; but he tromped it again, and quickly again, and this time it caught— not with the *burring* of the motorcycles inside: with a lower, steadier *borp, borp, borp,* as rich as a tractor.

"Hear that?" cried Herr Faber, who suddenly listened himself—his head tilting a bit, and his hand slicking over his mouth—as if he'd expected to hear a valve tapping, but didn't; expected to hear a certain roughness in the idle, but couldn't—at least, not quite. And his head tilted more.

"A virtuoso," said Faber, who was beginning to sound as if he believed it.

HERR FABER'S BEAST

Herr Faber's office was on the second floor of the garage, which looked as if it couldn't have a second floor.

"A grim urinal of a place," said Siggy, whose manners were making Herr Faber nervous.

"Have we set a price on that one?" Faber asked.

"Oh, yes we have," said Siggy. "Twenty-one hundred schillings, it was, Herr Faber."

"Oh, a very good price," said Faber in an unwell voice.

I paid.

"And might I trouble you further, Herr Faber?" said Siggy.

"Oh?" Faber moaned.

"Might you give me my wages up to today?" said Siggy.

"Oh, Herr Javotnik!" Faber said.

"Oh, Herr Faber," said Siggy. "Could you manage it?"

"You're a cruel schemer after an old man's money," Faber said.

"Now, I've made some rare deals for you," said Siggy.

"You're a dirty young cheating scheming bastard," Herr Faber said.

"Do you see, Graff?" said Siggy. "Oh, Herr Faber," he said, "I believe there's a veritable beast at home in your gentle heart."

"Frotters!" Herr Faber shouted. "Thieving frotters everywhere I turn!"

"If you could manage my wages," said Siggy. "If you could just do that, I'd be off with Graff here. We've got some fine tuning to do."

"Ah!" Faber cried. "That motorcycle doesn't need a bath!"

FINE TUNING

So we sat in the evening at the Volksgarten Café and looked over the rock garden to the trees, and looked down in the pools of red and green water, reflecting the green and red lights strung over the terrace. The girls were all out; through the trees their voices came suddenly and thrillingly to us; like birds, girls in the city are always preceded by the noises they make—their heels on the walk, and their cock-sure voices confiding to each other.

"Well, Graff," said Siggy, "it's a blossom of a night."

"It is," I agreed—the first heavy night of the spring, with a damp, hard-to-remember heat in the air, and the girls with their arms bare again.

"We'll make it a *zounds!* of a trip," said Siggy. "I've thought about this for a long time, Graff, and I've got the way not to spoil it. No planning, Graff—that's the first thing. No mapping it out, no dates to get anywhere, no dates to get back. Just think of things! Think of mountains, say, or think of beaches. Think of rich widows and farm girls! Then just point to where you feel they'll be, and pick the roads the same way too—pick them for the curves and hills. That's the second thing—to pick roads that the beast will love.

"How do you like the motorcycle, Graff?" he asked.

"I love it," I said, although he'd driven me on it no more than a few blocks, from Faber's round the Schmerlingplatz and over to the Volksgarten. It was a fine, loud, throbbing thing under you—sprang off from the stops like a great wary cat; even when it idled, the loathsome pedestrians never took their eyes off it.

"You'll love it more," said Siggy. "Up in mountains. We'll go to Italy! We'll travel light—that's third, traveling light. I'll take my big rucksack, all our stuff in one pack and sleeping bags rolled on top. Nothing else. Just some fishing rods. We'll fish through the mountains to Italy!

"Frot Doktor Ficht!" he cried.

"Frot him," I said.

"May his teeth all fall out!"

"In the opera."

"Frot him good!" said Siggy. And then he said, "Graff? You're not sorry you flunked, are you? I mean, it doesn't matter so much."

"It couldn't matter," I said, and it really didn't—with the night air smelling like a young girl's hair. The tendrils of the heavy trees stooped and swooshed over the rock garden, and hushed the sounds of waterlap in the pools.

"Early in the morning," said Siggy, "we'll load up and slip away. You can just hear us! We'll be rumbling past the university before old Ficht has swabbed his gums! We'll be out of Vienna before he's uncorked his gunky jar.

"We'll go by the palace. We'll wake up everyone! They'll think it's a runaway *Strassenbahn*—or a hippopotamus!"

"A farting hippopotamus," I said.

"A whole army of them farting!" said Siggy. "And then we'll be out on the curvy roads. We'll have trees overhead and crickets smacking off our helmets."

"I don't have a helmet," I said.

"I've got one for you," said Siggy, who'd been getting ready for this trip.

"What else do I need?" I asked.

"Goggles," he said. "I've got them too. A World War One pilot's goggles—frog eyes, with yellow lenses. They're terrifying! And boots," said Siggy. "I've got real trompers for you."

"We should go pack," I said.

"Well, we should finish our beers."

"And then go."

"Go off in a roar!" said Siggy. "And tomorrow night we'll have a sip from a river in the mountains, or a drink of a lake. Sleep in the grass, let the sun wake us."

"With dew on our lips."

"With country girls beside us!" said Siggy. "Barring acts of God."

So we drank up. There was a murmur of voices on the terrace, faces from the tables round us swam and bobbed in our beers.

Then the pumping of the kick starter, and the faraway sucking sound of the pistons that seemed to be rising from miles beneath the engine. The grunt of it catching, and the slow, untroubled drumming of its even idle. Siggy let it warm, and I looked over the hedgerows to the tables on the terrace. The onlookers weren't irritated, but they stopped their murmuring and cocked their heads to us; the slow beat of our engine was in rhythm with the first buffs of the spring-heavy air.

And there was a new lump in the back vent-pocket of Siggy's duckhunter's jacket; when I looked again at our table, I saw that the saltshaker was gone.

THE FIRST ACT OF GOD

Siggy drove. We came through an arch into the Plaza of Heroes; I tipped back my head and watched the pigeons cross the tops of the buildings; the pudgy Baroque cupids peered at me from the government houses. The morning seemed more golden than it was, through the famous yellow tint of my World War One pilot's goggles.

A cheek-chewing old woman wheeled a pushcart full of flowers along the Mariahilferstrasse, and we pulled to the curb beside her to buy some saffron crocuses; we stuck them in the air holes of our crash helmets. "Boys up to no good," said the floppy-gummed hag.

We drove on, tossing our flowers to the girls who waited for buses. The girls had their scarves off their heads; the scarves flapped about their throats, and most of the girls had flowers already.

We were early; we met the horsecarts coming to the Naschmarkt with their vegetables and fruits, and more flowers. Once we passed a horse who'd been shell-shocked by the traffic, and who pranced at our motorcycle. The drivers were cheerful and shouting from their squealing wagonseats; some of the drivers had their wives and children with them, it was such a glorious day.

Schönbrunn Palace looked lonely; no tourist buses, no crowds with cameras. A cool mist hung over the palace grounds; a thin haze crept close to the trimmed hedgerows, stole turtlelike across the green, green lawns. We watched the country roll in and be pushed back.

In the suburb of Hietzing, on the country edge of the palace grounds, we smelled the first zoo whiffs from the Hietzinger Zoo.

We stopped for a traffic light, and an elephant trumpeted over our idle.

"We've time enough, haven't we?" said Siggy. "I mean, we've all the time in the world, as I see it."

"We shouldn't leave Vienna," I said, "without seeing how spring has struck the zoo."

Well, yes—the Hietzinger Zoo, gated by stone, admission granted by a jowled toad of a man with a gambler's green eyeshade. Siggy parked the motorcycle out of the sap drip, out from under the trees and flush to the gambler's booth—the ticket taker's domish stall—over which we saw the giraffe's head tottering on its neckpole. The shambly heap of the giraffe followed its neck; buckethooved, its legs tried to keep up. There was a raw, hairless spot on its thin chin, where it had scraped the high storm fence.

The giraffe looked down the fence line to the greenhouses of the botanical gardens; the plates of glass were still frosty with dew. It was too early for much sun, and there was no one else to watch the giraffe. Down the long cobbly alley, between the buildings and cages, there was no one but a cage-cleaner, who sagged with his mop.

Heitzinger Zoo hadn't been there long, but the buildings

were as old as Schönbrunn; a part of the palace grounds,
the buildings were all rubbled now—unroofed, three-walled,
with the open spaces filled in by bars or screens. The animals had inherited the ruins.

The zoo was waking up and making public sounds. The
walrus belched in his murky pool; we saw his old fish stiff
on the pool curb, where he'd nudged them out of his
water and left their scales on his mustache. The duck
pond was talking breakfast, and down the alley some animal hammered in its cage.

The Rare Birds Building made a din for us—little and
large ladies in costume hats with broken, choir voices; and
overlording the dull-clothed condors sat hugely on the toppled columns, perched on the fallen bust of some
Habsburg great. They took the statues' pedestals for their
own, and glared at the meshing pulled over the ruin above
them. A split carcass of sheep lay in the weeds of the
building's floor, and some South American with a terrifying wing-span had old meat in his breast feathers; the flies
zipped from sheep side to bird, and the condor snapped
his nicked, bone-colored beak at them.

"Our feathered friends," said Siggy, and we went on to
see what was thumping in its cage.

It was the Famous Asiatic Black Bear, crouched in a
back corner of his cage and rocking himself sideways to
slam his buttocks into the bars. There was a little printed
history of the bear, fixed to a map of the world, with the
species' roaming area shaded black and a red star to mark
the spot where he was taken—in the Himalayas—by a
man named Hinley Gouch. The Asiatic Black Bear, the
history explained, had his cage facing away from the other
bears because he was "enraged" when he saw them; he was
a particularly ferocious bear, the history said, and iron
bars enclosed him in his own three-sided ruin because he
was capable of digging through concrete.

"I wonder how old Gouch got him?" said Siggy.

"Nets, perhaps," I said.

"Or maybe he just talked him into coming to Vienna,"
said Siggy. But we didn't think Hinley Gouch was a Viennese. More likely he'd been one of those misplaced British-
ers, in league with a hundred brawny Sherpas who'd
routed the bear into a ready-dug pit.

"It would be fun getting him and Gouch together
again," said Siggy, and we didn't look at the other bears.

There were people coming down the alley behind us now, and a group watched the giraffe scrape its chin. The building in front of us was for small mammals; it was a restored ruin, with four more or less original walls, a roof and boarded windows. Inside, a sign told us, were the nocturnal beasts—"who are always asleep and anonymous in other zoos." But here they had infrared light in the thick-glassed cages, and the animals behaved as if it were night. We could see them in a purplish glow, but the world outside their glass was black for them; they went unsuspiciously about their nocturnal habits, never knowing they were watched.

There was an aardvark, or earth pig, sluffing off old bristles on a rough board hung over him for that purpose. There were giant anteaters licking bugs off the glass, and the arboreal rat of Mexico. There was a bat-eared fox and a ring-tailed lemur; and a two-toed sloth who seemed, up-sidedown, to catch our movements on the other side of the glass—whose dark little eyes, not so big as his nostrils, seemed to follow us dimly in the outside world, which wasn't quite dark for him. But for the others there was nothing; not for the flying phalanger, and not for the slow loris, was there anything beyond the infrared under glass. And maybe not for the sloth, either; maybe it was only dizziness from hanging upsidedown that made his eyes roam after us.

In the aisles between the cages it was dark, but our hands were tinted purple and our lips were green. There was a special sign on the giant anteaters' glasshouse; an arrow indicated a little trough on the bottom corner of the glass, leading into the anteaters' lair. When you put your fingers there, an anteater came to lick. The long tongue came through the maze that kept the world from getting in; there was a new look in the anteater's eye, upon finding a finger in the dark. But it licked like any tongue does, and made us feel a little closer to the nocturnal habits of the beasts.

"Oh, God!" said Siggy.

And people had found the Small Mammal House now. Children squealed through the infrared aisles; their mauve hair and bright pink eyes—their green tongues waggling.

So we took a dirt path off the alley; we'd had quite enough of ruins. And we came to an open area where the Miscellaneous Range Animals were—including the Assort-

ed Antelopes. Now this was better. There were zebras
nuzzling along the fence line, hipping up to each other and
blowing in each other's ears; their stripes ran cross-pattern
to the hexagons of the fence, and it made us giddy to see
them move.

Outside the fence and coming toward us was a wild-
haired little boy who wheezed and held his crotch as he
ran. The boy ran past us and stopped, bent over as if he'd
been kicked. He dropped his cupped palm down between
his knees. "Lord! Balls!" he hooted. Then he grabbed himself up again, and rabbited down the dirt path away from
us.

There was no question that he'd seen the oryx with the
rapierlike horns, very long and nearly straight, spiraled on
the basal half and sloped backward on the same plane
with the wrinkly forehead and the sleek black nose; no
question he'd seen the old oryx under his thin shade tree,
brindled by the sun- and shade-spots dappling his back—a
soft, lowing look in his large black eyes. A bull oryx too,
by his low, heavy chest and his thick-wrinkled neck. The
slope of his back ran downhill off the hump of his neck to
the base of his tail. And a bull from just under his buttocks, he was, all the way to the knots on his lean knees.

"God, Siggy," I said. "How big, do you think?"

"The biggest ever, Graff," said Siggy. They had to dan-
gle cock-eyed, just to fit in the oryx's narrow hind stance.

So we read the history of the oryx from East Africa,
"best-armed of all antelopes."

"Hinley Gouch," said Siggy, "never had the balls to be
responsible for this."

And quite true, so we read—this oryx had been born in
the Hietzinger Zoo, and that certainly made us glum.

So down the dirt path, back to the gate; we passed all
the signs for the pachyderms, and only gave a glance to
the little wallaroo—"the famous hill-living and very agile
kangaroo." It lolled on its side, propped on an elbow and
scratching its hip with a curled fist. It gave us a short look
with its long, bored face.

Then we were passing the sign for the Big Cats, and
passing the glint off the gambler's green eyeshade—his
ticket booth surrounded by an eager human covey—passing heads turned toward the groggy, waking caterwaul of
a lion; heads were turned upward to greet the giraffe.

Outside the zoo, there were two girls admiring our motorcycle. One of them admired it so much that she sat on it, hugging the gas tank between her knees; she was a thick, busty girl whose black sweater had ridden up over her paunch. And her hips jiggled taut each time she clamped that lovely teardrop of a tank.

The other girl stood in front of the bike, fingering the cables for the clutch and front brake; she was a very thin girl, with more ribs to show than breast. With a yellow hue to her face, she had a sad, wide mouth. Her eyes were as gentle as the oryx's.

"Well, Siggy," I said, "it's surely an act of God."

And it wasn't even ten in the morning.

GOD WORKS IN
STRANGE WAYS

"Graff," said Siggy, "that fat one's surely not for me."

But when we came closer, we saw how the thin girl's lips had a bluish tint, as if she'd been long immersed in water and had taken some chill.

And Siggy said, "That thin one's not too healthy-looking. Perhaps, Graff, you can set her straight."

When we were up to them, the fat girl said to her companion, "See now? I told you it was two boys taking a trip." She jounced on the seat of the motorcycle, flapping the gas tank between her thighs.

"Well," said Siggy. "Thinking of driving off with it, were you?"

"Was not," the fat girl said. "But I could drive this thing if I wanted to."

"Bet you could," said Siggy. He patted the gas tank and drummed his fingers over her knee.

"Watch out for him," the thin girl said. She had a strange spasm in her chin, and she wouldn't stop playing with the cables; looped under the handlebars, the cables were all atangle from her twisting them.

"Say, Graff," Siggy whispered. "Do you think that thin one's contagious? I don't mind if you want her. I'll just make do with the old fatty here."

And the fat one said, "Say, you boys. Would you buy us a beer?"

"There's a place for beer in the zoo," said the thin one.

"We've just been in the zoo," I said.

And Siggy whispered, "It's rabies, Graff. She's got rabies."

"You've not been in the zoo with a girl on your arm!" the fat one said. "And you've not gone through the Tiroler Garten, I'll bet. There's a mile of moss and ferns, and you can take off your shoes."

"Well, Graff," said Siggy. "What do you say?"

"He's wild for it!" the fat girl shouted.

"Graff?" said Siggy.

"Well, sure," I said. "We're in no hurry."

"Fate shapes our course," said Siggy.

So we went to the *Biergarten,* surrounded by bears— and all of them watched us, except the Famous Asiatic Black Bear, whose cage didn't allow him to face the *Biergarten,* or other bears.

The polar bears sat and panted in their swimming pool; now and then they took a slow, loud lap. The brown bears paced, brushing their thick coats against the bars; their heads swayed low to the ground, in rhythm with some ritual of stealth they were born knowing and pointlessly never forgot—no matter how out of place wariness was to them here.

Downwind from our table and Cinzano umbrella, squat and hot in their shared cage, was a reeking pair of Rare Spectacled Bears from the Andes—"the bears with the cartoon countenance." They looked like they'd been laughed right out of Ecuador.

And Siggy was unnerved to find no radishes in the *Biergarten.* The dark, fat girl was named Karlotta, and she had a pastry with her beer; but the thin one was Wanga, and she would have nothing but syrupy bock. Siggy touched his fat Karlotta under the table; my Wanga's hand was dry and cool.

"Oh, they should have more ice for the polar bears," said Wanga. And no more for you, I thought.

"Siggy," said Karlotta, "could use a little ice himself." And her arms went under the table, groping for him. She had dark little ringlets for bangs, glossy and damp on her forehead.

The Spectacled Bears had a blotch of white running forehead-to-nose and over their throats. Their squint-eyes were bandit-masked in shaggy black mats like the rest of their fur; their coats looked oddly slept on, like a series of cowlicks. They rapped their long claws on the cement.

Poor Wanga ran her tongue lightly over her lips, as if she were feeling out where she was chapped and hurt.

"Is this your first trip?" she asked.

"Oh, I've been all over," I said.

"To the Orient?" she asked.

"All over the Orient."

"In Japan?"

"Bangkok," I said.

"Where's Bangkok?" said Wanga, so softly I leaned near to her.

"India," I said. "Bangkok, India."

"Oh, India," she said. "The people are very poor there."

"Yes, very," I agreed, and watched her touch gently her broad mouth—hide her thin lips with her pale hand.

"You there!" said Karlotta to me. "Don't you hurt her. Wanga, tell me if he hurts you."

"We're talking," Wanga said.

"Oh, he's a nice boy," said Karlotta, and from under the table she gave me a slight goose with her wedging toe.

The Spectacled Bears slumped against each other, shoulder to shoulder; one dropped its head on the other's chest.

"Graff," said Siggy, "don't you think Karlotta would enjoy the oryx?"

"I want to see the hippo," Karlotta said. "The hippo and the rhino."

"Karlotta wants everything big," said Siggy. "Well, Karlotta, it's the oryx for you."

"We'll meet you behind the hippohouse," I said. Because I didn't want frail Wanga to see the oryx. Thus Siggy has it in his notebook:

You have to draw the line somewhere.

"Karlotta," said Siggy, "this oryx will give you some jolt." And Karlotta rubbed her paunch with the palm of her hand.

"Ha!" she said.

The Rare Spectacled Bears sat upright and stared.

THE HIPPOHOUSE

There was a moat around the rhino's field, and a fence on the outside of the moat. If the rhino tried to ram the fence, he'd break his legs falling into the moat; the kneepieces of the rhino's armor were cracked and open, like sun-splits in baked clay.

The field he jogged in was flat, and the grass was beaten to scruff. The field was somewhat elevated too—a hard, dry plateau surrounded by the hippohouse and the high, iron gates to the Tiroler Garten. If you lay flat on the ground just inside the Tiroler Garten, you could see under the boughs of the trees, through the gardens all the way to Maxing Park. If you sat up out of the ferns, you could see the rhino's back—the top of his driftwood head and the tip of his horn. The ground shook when the rhino ran.

Wanga and I lay in the ferns, peeking for Siggy and fat Karlotta.

"Where are you traveling now?" she asked.

"To the Arctic Circle," I said.

"Oh!" she said. "I'd love to come. I mean, if you were traveling alone, I'd ask to come with you."

"And I'd let you," I said. But when I nuzzled the down on her arm, she sat up and looked again for Siggy and Karlotta.

We heard Siggy trumpeting at the rhino; for a while I couldn't see him, but I knew Siggy's poetry voice. He bellowed somewhere along the rhino's field, and we could hear Karlotta tittering. When we saw them, they were arm in arm behind the hippohouse and coming for the gate of the Tiroler Garten.

From the wild eyes of Karlotta, it was easy to see that she would be one of us—marked for life; to remember always having seen the oryx.

"Let's hide from them," I said, and I tugged Wanga down in the ferns.

But her eyes were startled and she lay on her back, hugging herself. "Karlotta!" she called.

"You! Boy!" Karlotta shouted. "Are you hurting her?"

"We're talking," said Wanga, "but we're over here."

And they came along the fence line to us; Siggy slapped through the deep ferns, one hand up under Karlotta's sweater and cupped round her lumpy side.

"Well, Graff," said Siggy, "my Karlotta was properly impressed with the oryx."

"Who could fail to be?" I said.

"What?" asked Wanga. "With what?"

"Not for you, dear," Karlotta said. "You're a dear boy, you," she told me. "That was nothing for Wanga to see."

"It's for the world to see!" said Siggy.

"Stuff you," Karlotta said, and she went tugging him off to another fern patch.

When we were all lying down, we couldn't see each other. Close to the ground was an air trap, and the rich scent of some animal's dung settled over us.

"I believe that's rhino stuff!" Siggy called.

"Or hippo," I said.

"Something large and prolific," said Siggy.

"Hippos never leave the water," Karlotta said.

"Oh, they must!" said Siggy. "It's hard to imagine . . ."

And Wanga curled in the crook of my arm, knees up tight and a cool hand on my chest. We could hear the stirrings of Siggy and Karlotta; twice Siggy hooted like a wild bird.

Well, as the notebook wisely imparts:

Time passes, praise God.

And then we were hearing Karlotta. "You're not so funny *all* the time," she was saying. And when I looked, I saw Siggy's upstretched arm—waving above the ferns a mighty pair of black lace bloomers.

"You're just too much of a stuffing clown," said Karlotta, and I saw her bare, thick foot thrash upward through the ferns. "You can't ever be serious, you frotter!" she said. "Oh, there's something definitely wrong with you."

Then Siggy sat up and grinned toward our fern patch; he wore the thigh-wide bloomers for a hat. Karlotta swatted him with a clod of weeds, and Siggy danced over to us.

When Karlotta stalked after him, she swung at her side a black lace bra with a pink bow—one cup loaded with sod. It dangled from her wrist like a battler's sling.

"Here comes the giant-killer," said Siggy.

Karlotta's breasts sagged to her movable paunch. When her sweater rode up, I caught a peek of dark nipple-bit.

Then Wanga was out of my arms and running down the fence line to the gate; she ran in a buffeted way, like a leaf blown along by varying gusts—through the gate and back into the zoo.

"Hey!" I said. "Hey, Wanga!"

"Mine! Mine, Graff," said Siggy. "I'll get her." He flipped the bloomers to Karlotta and was off running himself.

"No!" I yelled. "Siggy, I'll go!" But Karlotta had moved alongside me; when I tried to stand, she threw her hip into me and knocked me down in the ferns.

"Oh, let *him* be the clown," she said, and she knelt beside me. "Dear boy," said Karlotta, "you've some *morality* about you. You're not a bit like him." And when I tried to sit up, she smothered my face in her bloomers and held me down. Then she peeked under the glorious panties and kissed me with her peach-sweet lips. "Hush, hush," she said, and she pressed me into the damp ground.

We rolled in the hidden and airless, dung-smelling patch; the sounds of the zoo merged and were lost in the lashing of ferns, and the rhino shook the ground.

And when we heard the birds again, their voices were raucous and demanding. The great cats were snarling for meat and revolution.

"Feeding time," said Karlotta. "And I've not yet seen the hippo."

So I tried walking, and she followed me, steering me into the hippohouse, a great vat sunk in the middle of a greenhouse, with a rail around the water so the children wouldn't fall in. At first, there was nothing but murk in the vat.

"Oh, he'll be coming up now, any time," said Karlotta. She scratched herself and showed me a leer. "My left boob's itchy," she whispered. "There's a truckload of ground in my bra." She squirmed and goosed me where I stood, and I watched the bilious pool with the fruit floating in it—and big, bobbing thatches of celery. Suddenly there were bubbles.

First we saw nostrils—two gaping holes, quite bottomless—and then came the thick-lidded eyes. Its head kept rising and rising, and its long pink mouth kept opening and opening; I saw the stump of an impossible epiglottis;

I smelled from its dank, empty mouth; a whole window-box of rotted geraniums. The children threw food to it, and it rested its chin on the pool curb; the children threw peanuts, marshmallows and caramel corn—they threw paper bags and souvenirs of the zoo, an old man's newspaper and a tiny pink sneaker. When the hippo had enough, he just rolled his head off the curb and made the pool a sea. He sprayed us and sank in his vat.

"He'll be up again now," said Karlotta. "God, he could swallow me whole!"

On the back of Karlotta's sturdy leg was the imprint of a fern—an accurate fossil on her dark, flexing calf. I slipped away from the vat rim unnoticed, and left Karlotta in the hippohouse.

DRAWING THE LINE

"I don't know how you could have done it," said Siggy. "You've such bad taste."

"Where did Wanga go?" I said.

"I lost her somewhere, Graff. I was just trying to get away from that fatty there."

"We went to the hippohouse," I said. "In a few hours it's going to be dark."

"Thank yourself for that, Graff. Honestly, I don't know how you could have! There's a point, you know, where a fellow should stop and think."

"If we left now," I said, "we'd be in the country before dark."

"Karlotta!" said Siggy. "I just can't imagine! Rich as mud, was it? I should think you'd feel contaminated."

"You're a crude oaf!" I said. "Wearing her bloomers for a hat, dancing around like a jester."

"But I draw the line somewhere, Graff. Oh yes." And he began to fiddle with the motorcycle.

"Well, how frotting grand of you that is!" I said. "It might interest you to know that it wasn't so bad. Not at all bad!"

"I've no doubt of that, Graff," he said. "Skill is more common than beauty." Well, stuffed and officious, that line reappears in his jottings:

Finesse is no substitute for love.

And at the zoo gate he was ignoring me, rising up on the kick starter and throwing down all his weight.

"You're a doctrinaire forker, Siggy," I said.

But the engine caught and he throttled it up and down, nodding his head to the music. I swung up behind him, and we buckled on our crash helmets. Then on with my World War One pilot's goggles, to tint my world yellow— to pinch and addle my mind.

"Siggy?" I said. But he didn't hear.

He turned us out of the Platz at the Hietzinger Zoo, while behind us the lions were roaring for freedom and food, and Karlotta, I could easily imagine, was in the process, both awkward and admiring, of feeding herself to the hippo.

NIGHT RIDERS

For several towns now, we hadn't seen a gasthaus lighted. There were farms with one tiny light still burning, most likely an attic light left burning always—a beacon to say: There's someone still up, if you've any plans to sneak about. There'd be a dog, too, who really was awake.

But the towns were all dark, and we roared through them, seeing no one; just once, we saw a man peeing in a fountain. We caught him suddenly in our headlight and in the clamor of our engine, and he dove to the ground, still fumbling himself, as if we'd been so many megatons dropped out of the night. That was in a place called Krumnussbaum; just before Blindenmarkt, Siggy stopped. He killed the engine and headlight, and the quiet of the woods sealed up the road.

"Did you see that man back there?" he said. "Have you looked at these towns? It must have been like this during the blackout." And we thought about that a minute, while the woods went cautiously about their night noises again, and *things* came out to watch.

When he turned on the headlight, the trees seemed to leap back out of the road; centuries of night-watchers scurried back in hiding—ferrets and owls, and the ghosts of Charlemagne's lookouts.

"Once," said Siggy, "I found a very old helmet in the woods. It had a spike and visor on it." And his voice hushed the night noises; we heard the river for the first time.

"Is that ahead of us?" I said.

So he worked the kick starter and got us moving slowly. We crossed the Ybbs just out of Blindenmarkt, and Siggy swung the bike sideways on the bridge. Just out of the headlight's beam the river was a black, rumpled sheet in the wind, but the spot where the light struck seemed waterless; the river was shallow and clear, and we saw the pebbles on the bottom as if there'd been no water to cover them.

A logger's road ran beside the river, and snow was still in the cool woods; patches of it were yellowed in our headlight and laced with dark needles from the firs. There were smudges of bright chalk-colors on the trees marked for lumber, and the road wound with the river.

When the river made a bend away from us, the bank widened; we jounced off the center crown and slithered over the wet grass to a flat place on the bank. There were frogs and mice in the grass.

I listened for dogs. If there'd been a farm very near, we'd surely have heard a dog. But instead there was only the river and the wind creaking the bridge out on the main road, the wind brushing through the tight forest—like silent city men creeping through coat closets; not the noises soldiers would make, with their iron parts clanking between the trees.

The Ybbs had a muted rattle and a thousand separate trickles. We unloaded the motorcycle in whispers, not missing a word of the night. When we laid the groundcloth down, we had to pinch the mice out from under it. We were still in sight of the bridge on the main road, but in all the time we stayed awake, there was nothing passing by. The bridge line across the sky made the only geometry above the riverbed; the only other shapes were the jagged ripples in the water and the black, uneven tree line against the brighter night. There were rock pools near the bridge pilings, and the waterlap tossed its phosphorescence to the moon.

Siggy was sitting up in his bag.

"What do you see?" I said.

"Giraffes, ducking under the bridge."

"That would be nice," I said.

"*How* nice!" said Siggy. "And the oryx! Can't you see him wading across the river, dipping those fantastic balls?"

"Freeze them off," I said.

"No!" said Siggy. "*Nothing* could damage that oryx!"

LIVING OFF THE LAND

There was a boulder under the bridge, and it made a tiny waterfall to clean our trout in; we let the water spill into their slit, flapping bellies, sluice about their lovely ribs and fill them up to their high, springy breastbones. You could clamp up their belly slits and pinch on the bulge; the water came out of their gills, first pink and then clear.

We took twelve trout between us and plunked down their innards on the bouldertop. Then we sat by the motorcycle and watched the crows swoop under the bridge, diving for the fish guts until the rock was picked bare. When the sun came off the water and hung level with the bridge, we thought we'd find a farm and make our deal for breakfast.

The road was soft and we slipped off the high crown into the ruts; Siggy drove slowly and we both leaned back to catch all the air smells, of pine pitch in the woods, and of clover and sweet hay beyond. The woods were thinning, fields swelled behind and beside them; the river was white-capped, running deeper and faster, and nudging a fine froth out to the cutaway banks.

Then the road climbed a little and the river ran down and away from us; we could see a village now—a squat church with an onion-shaped spire, and some solid buildings close together in a one-street town. But before the village was a farm, and Siggy turned in.

The driveway was a slough of mud, as plastic as dough, and our rear wheel sunk to the drive chain; we wallowed, caught in a sponge. There was a goat on the bank of the driveway and we aimed at it, posting on the foot pedals. The goat bolted when we made the bank; we thrummed past a pigpen, the little pigs springing like cats, and the big pigs running like fat ladies in spike heels. The mudcleats whacked themselves clean of the driveway slop; the mud-splatter pelted behind us. The bolting goat had roused the farmer and his wife.

A most jovial Herr Gippel and his Frau Freina looked quite eager to make the exchange—coffee and potatoes for half our trout, and the coffee was black-bean roast.

Frau Freina tried to say, with her pale, winking eyes: Oh, come see how pretty my kitchen is! She had a proud, motherly, grouselike swell to her breast.

And this Gippel appeared an expert in feeding.

"You're a fine fish eater," Siggy told him.

"Oh, we eat a lot of trout," he said. He'd pinch them up at the tails and coax the meat off neat. He kept a tidy stack of skeletons to one side of his plate.

"But so *many* trout!" Freina said.

"And we're just starting out at this business," said Siggy. "Living off the land, Graff! Back to the simple laws of nature."

"Oh, now," Gippel said, "you would have to go and re-mind me of *laws*."

"And we've had such a lovely meal," Frau Freina said.

"But the question of *laws* came up, dear," said Gippel. "And it was *twelve* trout they had between them."

"Oh, I know," Freina said. "But we wouldn't have had the same breakfast if there'd been just *ten*."

"Just five apiece," said Gippel. "What you're *allowed*, of course. But my Freina's right. It wouldn't have been the same breakfast at all."

"I think this is terrible," Freina said, and she went out on the porch.

"Herr Siggy," Gippel said, "I just wish you hadn't brought it up."

"What did I bring up?" said Siggy.

"Laws!" said Gippel. "You went and reminded me." And Freina came back in the screen door and gave Siggy a green piece of paper, face down.

"What's that?" I said.

"It's our fine!" said Siggy.

"Oh!" Gippel cried. "What manner of man am I?"

"Who in hell are you?" said Siggy.

"The fish-and-game warden," Gippel said.

"This is just terrible," said Freina, and she went out again.

"It's nice," said Siggy. "I always say it's nice to make a
friend of the local gamekeeper."

"Oh, that's something to be thankful for," said Gippel.
"That's why it's only fifty schillings."

"Fifty schillings?" I said.

"It was the least I could do," said Gippel, who moved
to the screen door himself now. "If you'll excuse me a
moment," he said. "I'm just so ashamed." And he went
very sadly out on the porch.

"The frotting thief!" I said. "How close is the bike
parked?"

"Well, Graff," said Siggy. "It's parked about a foot
from where Gippel's sitting, giving comfort to his gentle
wife."

"Fifty schillings, Sig!" I said.

But Siggy took the right note from his duckjacket. "You
go give them this comfort, Graff," he said. "I'll be just a
minute inside."

So I went to cheer up the kindly people; we all sat on
the porch and watched the witless goat squaring off with
the motorcycle, trying to get up the nerve for the initial
ram.

Then Siggy came out, quite choked up himself, and that
was enough to set off poor Freina again. "Oh, they're sure
lovely boys!" she wept.

"Oh, sweet, sweet," said Gippel. "The laws are just
vile!" he roared. "Allowances should be made for boys like
these."

But Siggy said, "Now, now"—with a forearm bolstering
up his belly. "It was such a feed we had, it was worth fifty
schillings." And that *did* surprise all of us—brought Freina
back to her senses and her alert, pale, winking eyes. Poor
Gippel was agog, with nothing more to say.

So they watched us climb on the motorcycle. We stood
off the goat and were careful this time to avoid the driveway. The pigs began their insane running.

"It's amazing," I said to Siggy, "the deals one can make
for breakfast." But I felt something hard against his belly,
under his duckjacket. "What have you got there?" I said.

"Frau Freina Gippel's fryingpan," said Siggy, "and one
flint, one bottleopener, one corkscrew and a saltshaker."

Well, we were pinched by the fence rows when we
came near the road, and we were forced into the driveway
for a moment. But this time we had the speed behind us

and we slurred out on the road. We could see Gippel waving both his arms like a madman; Frau Freina was swelling her breast and waving, kissing her fingers goodbye to us. The tires skidded us into the ruts, and again beat themselves clean of the driveway. The old mud flung madly after us; *thot, thot, thot* it went on the downhill road.

"There are certain investments required," said Siggy, "if one is to live off the land." And the fryingpan was still warm under his jacket.

WHERE THE WALRUSES ARE

As the notebook has it:

There are certain investments required.

And so. It was lunchtime when we rode into Ulmerfeld and bought two bottles of beer. We were nearly out of the village when Siggy saw the windowbox hung to a second-story window of a gasthaus.

"Radishes!" said Siggy. "I saw their little greens peeking over!"

We drove up under the window, and I steadied the motorcycle while Siggy stood on the gas tank; on his toes, he would just get his hands over the rim of the box.

"I can feel them," he said. "They were just watered— sweet snappy baby ones!"

He stuffed them in his duckjacket, and we drove through Ulmerfeld, still following the Ybbs. A mile or so out of the village, we cut through a meadowbank to the river.

"After all, Graff," said Siggy. "This day still owes us a piece of our fifty schillings."

And with that for grace, we opened our beers with Frau Freina's opener, and salted our radishes from Freina's shaker. Freina had a wondrously unclogged shaker. The radishes were crunchy and moist, and Siggy planted the greens.

"Do you think they'll grow?" he said.

"Well, anything's possible, Siggy."

"Yes, anything is," he said, and we flicked our close-nib-

bled stumps to the river, watching them bob under and
spin to the crest of the current again, like hats with pin-
wheels on the heads of drowning boys.

"Upstream," I said, "there's got to be a dam."

"Oh, a great falls in the mountains," said Siggy. "And
think of the fishing above the dam!"

"I'll bet there's grayling, Sig."

"And walruses, Graff."

We lay back in the meadow and tooted the bottlenecks
of our beers. Crows again, downstream, were circling the
radish stumps.

"Is there anything a crow won't eat, Sig?"

"Walruses," he said. "Couldn't possibly eat a walrus."

"Well, that's amazing," I said.

The spring-damp was still on the ground, but the thick
grass seemed to trap the sun and hold it against me; I was
warmed into closing my eyes. I could hear the crows telling off the river, and the crickets were sawing in the
fields. Siggy was chinking the bottleneck on his teeth.

"Graff," he said.

"Hm."

"Graff?"

"Here," I said.

"It was a terrible scene in that zoo," he said. "I think it
would be better if we had them out here."

"Those girls?" I said.

"Not the girls!" he cried. "I meant the animals!
Wouldn't they have a time out here?"

And I could see it with my eyes closed. The giraffes
were nipping the buds off the treetops; the anteaters gob-
bled waterbugs from the fine lace of foam on the shore.

"Those *girls!*" said Siggy. "God, Graff—what a frotting
ninny you can be."

So the sun and the beer settled our sleep; the Rare
Spectacled Bears were kissing in whispers, and the oryx
chased all the frotting ninnies out of the meadow. On the
bruise-purple Ybbs the walrus was rowing a boat with his
flippers, sunning his tusks and bleaching his mustache, and
he didn't see the hippo who lurked in the deep pool by the
bank—the disguised hippo in a veil of froth, mouth agape
for the walrus, rowboat and all.

I woke up to warn the walrus; the giraffes had munched
the meadow until they'd reached the sun and dragged it
down. The down sun glinted through the grass, caught the

motorcycle and stretched the shadow of wheels and engine over the river; the river raced under the motorcycle like a fast, bruised road.

"Siggy," I said. "It's time we moved."

"Gently, Graff," he said. "I'm watching them. They're stepping out of their cages, free as us."

So I let him watch awhile, and I watched the sun flattening the meadow out red, and the river running out of sun. I had a look upstream, but there was no peeking the mountains yet.

GOING NOWHERE

Out of the valley and the night bugs, the road turned to tar, then back to dirt, and always now the river was hidden from us in the thick tunnel of firs. The heavy gargle of the motorcycle beat against the forest, and our echo crashed alongside—as if other riders paced themselves to us and moved unseen through the woods.

Then we climbed out of the firs too, and the night was sharp enough to breathe in careful bits. We were aware of space again, and the sudden, looming things to fill it—a rocking black barn with great wind-swung doors, and triangular pieces of window casting a severed headlight back to us; something shuffling off the road, throwing its fierce eyes over its shoulder, hunched like a bear—or a bush; a farmhouse shuddering in its sleep, and a yapping dog who sprinted alongside us—over my shoulder, its eyes getting smaller and blinking out of the dancing-red taillight. And on the valley side, dropping below us, the little peaks of treetops were pitched like tents along the road.

"I think we've lost the river," said Siggy. He was shifting down to the upgrade; he went third to second and gave us a full throttle. We tossed a wake of soft dark dirt behind, and I leaned forward with my chest up on his back; I could feel him begin to lean before the bike would lay over, and I could lean through the corners—as perfectly with him as a rucksack on his back.

Then the road dropped out from under us, and our headlight darted straight out into the night, with the momentum of the motorcycle bearing us levelly into the sky;

when the front wheel touched the road again, we were
carried madly downhill to a wooden bridge. Siggy hit
first gear, but he still had to brake, and the rear wheel
moved up beside us; we skipped across the bridge planks
like a crab.

"It's the river," said Siggy, and we went back to peek.

He wrenched down the headlight and slanted the beam
to the river, but there wasn't any river. He pressed the kill
button on the engine, and we *heard* a river—we heard the
wind making the bridge planks groan—and we felt how
the bridge rails were damp from a rising spray. But in the
light's beam there was only a gorge falling into darkness;
and the tilted firs, holding to the gorge walls, reached for
help and didn't dare look down.

The river had taken a shortcut; it sawed the mountain
in two. We peered into the blank awhile. There'd be no
fish in the morning unless we dared some horrible pen-
dency before breakfast.

So we found a spot flat enough for the groundcloth, and
set back enough from the edge of the great gorge. It was
so cold we made a rumpus of undressing in our bags.

"Graff," said Siggy. "If you get up to pee, don't walk
the wrong way."

And later, our bladders must have remembered what he
said—or else, must have been listening too long to the
river-gush. Because we both had to get up. And oh, it was
cold, stepping naked and fearful across the field.

"How does the oryx keep his warm?" said Siggy.

"I've been thinking," I said. "Don't you think all of that
might have been a disease?"

"Oh, Graff!" said Siggy. "It's surely a case of over-
health."

"He must feel quite vulnerable," I said.

And we did a clutching, vulnerable dance back to our
bags. The bags had stayed warm for us; we curled, and
felt the mouseful field scurry. The night was so chilly I
think the mice crept up and slept warm against us.

"Graff," said Siggy. "I've been thinking too."

"Very good, Sig."

"No, really thinking, Graff."

"What, then?" I said.

"Do you think there's a nightwatchman at the Hietzinger Zoo—inside the grounds all night? Just peeking
around?"

"Communing with the oryx?" I said. "Asking him his secret?"

"No, just in there," said Siggy. "Do you think someone's in there at night?"

"Sure," I said.

"I think so too," he said.

I saw the guard muttering to the bears, waking up the oryx to ask the potent question; by the early dawn hours the guard walked hunched like an ape, swung from cage to cage, baiting the animals in their own languages.

"Graff?" said Siggy. "Do you remember any closed doors in the Small Mammal House? Was there anything that looked like a closet?"

"A closet in infrared?"

"A guard's got to have someplace to go, Graff. Someplace for sitting and having his coffee, and a spot to hang the keys."

"Why, Siggy!" I said. "Are you scheming a zoo bust?"

"Oh, wouldn't that be something, Graff? Wouldn't that be something rare? Just to let them go!"

"The rarest of fun!" I said.

And a veritable gaggle of bears went waddling out the main gate, carrying with them the ticket taker's booth, in which the man with the gambler's green eyeshade was crying for mercy.

But I said, "Except, of course, it wouldn't be any fun going back to Vienna. That's at the very *bottom* of things I'd like to do."

I opened my eyes and saw the lovely pale stars above me; the stunted, desperate firs were climbing out of the gorge. Siggy was sitting up.

"What's at the very *top* of things you'd like to do, Graff?"

"Have you ever seen the sea?" I said.

"Only in movies."

"Did you see *From Here to Eternity?*" I said. "It was an American film, with Deborah Kerr and Burt Lancaster. Burt was rolling Deborah in the surf."

"It wasn't the sea you were interested in, Graff."

"Wouldn't that be something, though?" I said. "Camped down on a beach somewhere—in Italy, maybe."

"I saw that movie too," said Siggy. "I felt that their crotches must have been sandy."

"Well, I'd like to see the sea," I said. "And fish some more, up in the mountains."

"And roll Deborah Kerr in the surf, Graff?"

"Why not?"

"And frot a whole herd of country girls, Graff?"

"Not a whole herd," I said.

"But one fine piece of a girl, Graff? Just one to make a world out of you awhile?"

"Suits me," I said.

"Suits you, indeed, Graff," he said. "You dreaming romantic ninny-ass bastard."

"Well, what do *you* want to do, then?" I said.

"Well, you can frot all you want," said Siggy, and he lay back down, his arms crossed outside the bag; his arms were all the bare, pale colors of the stars in the stinging night. "That zoo won't be going anywhere," he said.

I gave a glance to the firs in the gorge, but they hadn't climbed out yet. Siggy didn't move; his hair fell over his pillow of duckjacket and touched the shiny grass. I was sure that he slept, but before I slept myself, he mumbled me a groggy little bedtime song:

Frau Freina Gippel's lost her pan.
And never will she find it.
The Frau has teeth on her behind,
But Gippel doesn't mind it.

GOING SOMEWHERE

There was a frost in the morning, and the grass reflected a thousand different prism-shapes of sun; the meadowbank to the river gorge was like a ballroom floor, catching the patterns of an intricate chandelier. I lay on my side and squinted through the frost-furry grass to the gorge wall. The groundcloth was cool on my cheek, and the grass spears seemed bigger than the trees; the frost-melt lay in bright pools between the spears. There was a cricket coming along, using the grass for stilts to span the droplets—lake-sized, for a cricket; its joints were frosty, and it seemed to be thawing as it walked.

When you're level with it, a cricket can be fierce—a

giant anthropod come bending down the jungle, stepping
over oceans. I growled at it, and it stopped.

Then I heard bells, not far away.

"Cowbells!" said Siggy. "We're going to be trampled!
Oh, pushed down the gorge!"

"Church bells," I said. "We must be near a village."

"Well, frot me," said Siggy, and he peeked out of his
bag.

But my cricket was gone.

"What are you looking for, Graff?"

"A cricket."

"A cricket's quite harmless."

"This was an especially big one," I said. But it wasn't
under the groundcloth, so I got out of my bag and stepped
on the frost-stiff grass.

Well, the dew made me dance, and with that giddy
gorge close by, I got much more interested in dancing
than finding my cricket. But Siggy watched me coldly, and
not for long; he huffed himself out of his bag and began
stomping around the groundcloth—not at all the same sort
of dance I was doing.

"You don't have to get up yet," I said.

"Well, I don't recommend watching you in the nude,"
he said.

"Well, be careful with your stamping," I said. "You'll
get my cricket." But I stood oddly embarrassed in front of
him.

"Let's have some coffee and find a more fishable part of
this river," he said, like a frotting scoutmaster. And I forgot about my probable trodden cricket—watching him load
the motorcycle, like a frotting sergeant.

Se we left for the next town.

Hiesbach was less than a mile up the road; it was a
town piled against a hillside—old, rounded, gray-stone
buildings heaped like egg boxes, with the usual, outstanding, squat and onion-headed church that hunched beside the
road like an old, toothless lion who wouldn't attack any
more.

When we got there, Mass was over; stiff, crinkly
families milled on the church steps, creaking their once-a-
week shoes. The smaller boys bolted for a *Gasthof* opposite the Holy Onion Head: FRAU ERTL'S OLD GASTHOF.

Siggy rapped the sign as we went in. "Graff," he whispered, "Beware of the Ertl." So we came in agiggle.

"Well," said fat Frau Ertl, "you're very welcome."

"Oh, thank you," Siggy said.

"Coffee?" I asked the Ertl. "Is it hot?"

"And a place to wash our hands?" said Siggy.

"Oh, of course," she said, pointing us out the back door. "But the light bulb's burnt out, it seems."

If there ever could have been a light bulb. Because the *pissoir* was a dirt-floor stall in back of the *Gasthof* and next to a long, narrow pen for goats. The goats watched us work the pump. Siggy pumped the water over the back of his head; when he shook his head, the goats bleated and butted against the gate of the pen.

"My poor goats," said Siggy, and he went over to the pen to tug their chins. Oh, they loved him, it was easy to see. "Graff," he said, "step inside and see if anyone's coming."

Inside it was filling up—the families together with their coffees and sausages, the lone men together at a long table with their beers.

"Ah," said the Ertl. "I've your coffees by the window."

So when Siggy came in, we went to our table—next to a family with a cantankerous-looking grandfather for a leader. The family's youngest, a boy, watched us over his long sausage and roll, and his chin drooped in what he was gnawing.

"Gross little boy," Siggy whispered, and he made a face at him. The boy stopped eating and stared, so Siggy made a threatening gesture with his fork—stabbing air—and the boy pulled his grandfather's ear. When the old man looked at us, Siggy and I were just sipping our coffees; we saluted, and the grandfather pinched the boy under the table.

"Just eat, boy," the grandfather said.

So the boy looked out the window, and was the first to see the goats.

"Goats out!" he shouted, and the grandfather gave him another pinch. "Boys who keep seeing things should hold their tongues!" he said.

But others were looking now; the grandfather saw them too.

"I shut the gate," said Frau Ertl. "I shut them up before Mass."

Some older boys swaggered and shoved each other out of the *Gasthof;* the goats shyly herded by the church. And the pinching grandfather leaned over us. "Frau Ertl's a widow," he said. "She needs someone to keep her goat pen shut." Then he choked on whatever he was eating and had a little spasm over it.

The goats were nodding to each other, clattering off balance, up and down the church steps. The boys had herded them against the door, but no one dared to go up the steps after them, and mess one's Sunday clothes.

We went outside and watched, listening to the bells from another village—striking Sunday morning with insistent, hurry-up echo-shots that muted the end of each note.

"That's St. Leonhard's bells," said a woman. "We've got our own bells, and I'd like to know why they're not ringing on Sunday." And the issue was seized, taken up by other voices:

"But our bell ringer's eating his breakfast."

"Drinking his breakfast, you mean."

"The old swiller."

"And the children don't miss a thing."

"We've our own church and our own bells, and why should we have to listen to somebody else's?"

"Religious fanatics," Siggy whispered—but he was interested in the goats. The mob was trying to scare them off the steps.

"Go get that bell ringer," the woman said, but the bell ringer had been warned of the plot already; he stood on the steps of the *Gasthof*, a beer in his hand, wrinkling the veins on his nose to the sun.

"Now, ladies," he said. "Kindly ladies, I could never hope to attain"—and he swallowed a belch that made his eyes water—"to achieve," he said, "the mastery of bell-ringing that my competitor in St. Leonhard has"—and he let it come: a sharp, ringing belch. "Has attained," he said, and went back inside.

"Someone else," the woman said, "should learn how to ring the bells."

"Oh," said the pinching grandfather, "there's not much to it."

"Too much for you," the woman said, "or you'd be doing it, all right. You're just dying for something to do."

And a hardfaced girl flicked her saucy, hard butt at the grandfather; stepping in front of him, she brushed his chin with the down of her arm; she stretched herself away from him, almost leaving her leg behind—toe down, her

skirt tugged to mid-thigh. Her little calf leapt high above
her ankle and knotted like a fist.

"Too much for you," she said, and skipped away from
him, out into the street.

"Look at those goats, there!" said Siggy. "Why don't
they bolt? They should bolt right by those brats. Bolt!" he
hooted.

And the grandfather looked at us; he eased himself
down a step or two and sat on the stairs by us. "What did
you say, there?" the grandfather said.

"It's a goat call," said Siggy. "It works for some."

But the grandfather was staring too hard; he clicked his
teeth. "You're a queer rascal," he said, and he picked up
Siggy's hand. "I saw you," he whispered, and Siggy jerked
his hand away.

"Where's St. Leonhard and its famous bells?" I said.

"Over the mountain," said the grandfather. "And not
much of a mountain, either, but to hear this town talk,
you'd think it was Alps. Not much of a church, either, and
nobody who's much of anything living here—but to hear
this town talk. And there's nothing to ringing their damn
bells!"

"Go do it, then," said Siggy.

"I could!" the grandfather said.

"Do it, then," said Siggy. "Ring the piss out of them!
Get the whole town rolling in the street, holding their
ears!"

"I can't climb all those stairs," said the grandfather. "I'd
get winded halfway up."

"We'll *carry* you up," said Siggy.

"Who are you anyway?" the grandfather said. And he
whispered to me, "I saw him. He took the saltshaker off
the table—Frau Ertl's shaker—and he stuffed it in that
funny pocket."

"Oh, why don't they bolt, Graff?" said Siggy. And a
brat had the leg of one now; it bleated and kicked, but it
was slipping down the steps.

"You think you know so much about goats," said the
grandfather. "You let them out, didn't you? You're just
that sort of madman."

Then they had the one goat down.

"Let's go, Graff," said Siggy.

"I'm going to tell," the grandfather said, and he blushed.

"Widow Ertl thinks I'm just an old duffer who doesn't know anything."

"She'll think he's more of a duffer if he tells—won't she, Graff?"

"Oh," said the grandfather, "I'll let you get away before I tell."

"Ah, Graff," said Siggy, "the terrible chances old duffers will take!"

And when we were started, they had a second goat down. The first goat was on its feet, but a fat girl had it in a headlock and its beard was ratily plucked.

Its pink mouth was open for bleating, but we couldn't hear it calling us over the motorcycle.

As the notebook has it:

Goats won't bolt! But they aren't *wild* animals.
Take heart, you *wild* animals!

FAIRIES ALL AROUND

When we came into St. Leonhard, the bell ringer was still at it; he was trembling the church.

"What a racket!" said Siggy. "Bong! Bong! Bong!" he shouted at the belfry.

And a thin little girl with a licorice stick saw him shout. She looked up to the church as if she expected the clapper to break loose from the bell and fly at us.

"Bong!" Siggy said to her, and we went into a *Gasthof*.

Mass had been over some time, and the *Gasthof* was almost empty. A natty, quick-moving man stood staring out the window at our motorcycle. Every time he raised his beer he looked like he was going to toss it over his shoulder; he stood with one foot on top of the other, suddenly losing his balance and regaining it with a hop and two-step.

The tired bartender, the *Wirt*, was reading a newspaper spread on the counter. We bought two bottles of cold beer, a loaf of bread and a two-schilling butter pat.

And the tired *Wirt* asked, "All in one bag?"

"Oh, sure," I said.

"I'll have to give you two bags," he said. "I haven't a bag big enough for the whole works."

And the frisky man at the window turned round so suddenly he made us jump.

"Put the bottles up your asses!" he shouted. "Put the bread in another bag!"

"God!" said Siggy. "Frot you!"

"Eh?" the man cried, and he did his hop and two-step at us. "Frot me, eh? *Eh!*" he shrieked, as if something were caught in his throat.

"Better watch out for him," the *Wirt* said.

"I certainly will," said Siggy.

"Because he'll sue you," the *Wirt* said.

"Sue us?" I said.

"It's a profession with him," said the *Wirt*.

And the man who was going to sue said, "Put your asses in one bag."

"Now look out, you," said Siggy.

But the *Wirt* caught his arm. "Better for you to look out," he said. "He'll let you hit him and then he'll sue you. He'll say he can't breathe because of his jaw, he'll say he gets headaches when he eats. Oh, we don't get many strangers here, but he goes after every one."

"I'll give you the scrap of your life!" the suer yelled. He gave us the two-step again, cupping his beerglass in his palm and slopping his beer.

"I warn you, he won't fight," said the *Wirt*. "He just sues."

"I can't imagine," I said.

"It's amazing, I know," said the tired *Wirt*, as if he were falling asleep over it. "And he even gets away with it," he said.

"How can he get away with it?" said Siggy.

We three stood together and watched him, standing one foot on the other, tottering and squirming his knees like a child trying hard not to wet his pants. But there wasn't anything childish in the man's face. He opened his fly and poured his beer inside his pants.

"He's a bit queer too," said the *Wirt*.

And he gave us the two-step, but he was losing his nattiness fast; he flapped his pants fly open and closed, and the beer foam spit down his leg. He winked at Siggy. "You-you," he slobbered, "you-you!"

"He'll sue!" the *Wirt* cried, but he missed stopping Siggy's arm.

Because Siggy already had his helmet off the counter,

and he swung it twice-round by the chin strap, full circles of his arm, and swung it up under the surprised frisky man—caught him in the open crotch and tumbled his one-footed stance. The man howled over hind-end, his knees flinging up to his chest.

"Really," the *Wirt* said, "he'll sue you, I know it."

"You're an utter dope," said Siggy. "And you can tell him we went the other way."

"Well, sure I can," said the moping *Wirt*. "I don't mind at all, boys."

And we walked quickly out of there, with no bags at all for what we'd bought; we left the dullest *Wirt* I'd ever met—with his *Gasthof*, and with the other's singed-mouse howl.

At the motorcycle, I stuffed the things into Siggy's vent-pocket.

"Christ, Sig," I said. "Letting goats loose, bashing queers!"

"Well, frot me, then," said Siggy.

"Oh, we're quite a pair," I said, meaning nothing by it, and he turned on the seat; he stared at me.

His voice, then, came up so shrill it seemed to startle the motorcycle. "Are we now, Graff? Well, there's a butter pat for the pan, and bread for crumbs to roll the trout in. And there's beer for me to pour in my fly! And maybe I'll choke on a fish bone and let you botch the rest of the day by yourself!"

"Oh, frot," I said. "Oh, Jesus, Sig."

And just as he chunked the bike in gear, the thin little girl came up to us from nowhere and touched Siggy's hand with her licorice stick—touched him lightly and magically, as if her licorice were the Good Fairy's wand.

The notebook records it in poetry:

Oh, the things you want
Are very private—
Private, private,
Very private.
Oh, the only ways there are
To get them
Are very public—
Public, public,
Very ugly-public.

So God help us, Graff.
Great Bear, Big Dipper,
Help us both.

Which must be one of his worst poems.

THE SECOND SWEET
ACT OF GOD

From St. Leonhard the road turned steeply downhill, cutting high-banked and gravelly switchbacks to where the Ybbs would spill out of the mountain at Waidhofen. The gravel was soft and loose in the banks, and we tried to stay near the middle of the road; our rear wheel moved us all aslither, and we rode with our weight off the seat, pushed forward on the foot pedals.

The first of the orchards began less than a mile below St. Leonhard—apple orchards, the tree rows stretching on both sides of the road, the young trees snappy in the wind and the old twisties squatting immovable; the grass between the tree rows was mown and lumped, smelling sickish-sweet in the sun. The apple buds were coming to blossom.

Now we posted on the foot pedals and let the bike scatter under us like a horse; it was some road, all right, the way it dropped and bent, giving us a flash of trees on one side and then the other; the raspy grasshoppers snapping out of the ditches, and the blackbirds swooping to near-collision.

Then the girl's braid seemed to whip out at us as she flung her head round to our noise and skipped herself out of the road. It was a thick auburn braid, waist-length, with the end of it flicking her high, swinging rump, and there was more wind filling her skirt than hips. The gravel was too loose for braking, so we had just this flash of her—her long brown legs, and her long fingers flicking down to her knees, pinching her skirt safe around her. Then I was looking over my shoulder, and she was turning her face away—tossing her braid out beside her; it did a snake dance in the sun while the wind held it up. I could almost have reached it, but the wind dropped it on her shoulder and she tugged it roughly to her cheek; that was

all I saw of her, except for a laundry bag adangle from
one of her arms. She straightened her brown leather
jacket with a tug as rough as she gave to her braid. Then
we lost her in a switchback.

"Did you see her face, Sig?"

"You weren't looking at her face, either."

"When I turned around, I was. She hid it from me."

"Ah," said Siggy. "She feels guilty about it. An ill omen,
Graff."

But I looked for more of her along the road, as if girls
with braids so auburn and rich were as prolific as apple
buds and grasshoppers.

GREAT BEAR, BIG DIPPER,
THY WAYS ARE STRANGE
INDEED

Well, under the apple trees there was deadfall and
winter pruning that the firewood men had missed. The low
boughs with blossoms and buds; the bee boxes propped on
apple crates, the bee abodes painted white and set high up
so the tractors and horsecarts wouldn't bump them over
and spill the hives. It was all bees' work in the orchards
now; the bees were out opening the apple buds, from blossom to blossom—oh, the friend of the flower and fertilization, the polliniferous bee!

"Isn't fertilization grand?" said Siggy.

And the deadwood under the tree was easy to snap up
small—was making a quick-hot coal bed for us; we
sprinkled the coals with water to put the flame down. Then
we set the pan on the fired rocks and popped our butter
into the pan. Siggy crumbed the crust of the bread loaf, and
we rolled the wet trout until they were furry with crumbs.

The slim trickle of a trout stream crossed the road and
the orchards and leaned down the mountain—to where we
would go and see Waidhofen, after our lunch.

The stream was so tiny we'd almost missed it; the
bridge was so thin we'd almost been sifted through the
slats. But the trout here hadn't been shy about rising; now
they spattered in the pan and tuned their music to the bee
drone in the orchards.

And a bee flew a blossom over the stream; the air current dropped from under him, and the bee got his wings

wet, paddling an apple petal now. But he was better off floating air than water; the giant trout pulled out from the bank, rose and nosed bee and blossom down its throat— left barely a ripple mark in its descent.

"There's one we missed," I said.

"There's one who'd have eaten your whole rod," said Siggy.

We ate a bit messily ourselves, picking with jackknives until the trout were cool enough for our hands. And of course we had the beer cooling in the stream, waiting to go with an after-lunch pipe.

Belly-up to the sun, then, with the bee drone all around us; I couldn't see the road from the orchard, just the bridge rail underlining the treetops, the green-blotched bouquets of blossom and bud. This world is kind to itself, I thought. Well, the bees make honey for the beekeeper, the bees multiply the orchardman's apples; no one's hurt by that. And if oily Herr Faber were a beekeeper, and Gippel an orchardman, wouldn't they be all right too?

So I said, "Well, Sig, I could never tire of this."

"One day it rains," he said. "One day it snows."

And the notebook turns everything to poetry:

Fate waits.
While you hurry
Or while you wait,
It's all the same to Fate.

Then I saw her head moving gently above the bridge rail; she had one hand on the rail, and I think she was tippytoeing so she wouldn't rouse us. The red braid was pulled over her shoulder and tucked in the collar of her leather jacket; she tugged a thick knot of hair to her throat like a scarf, and her long face came down over it. The rail cut her off at the waist, so it was only a bit more than a bust of her that was sneaking by us.

I kept my eyes half closed, and I whispered, "Look there, Sig, but be easy—don't open your eyes. On the bridge, look."

"Frotting Graff!" said Siggy, and he bolted upright. "Look *where* without opening my eyes? Look *how?*"

And the girl gave a little cry; she nearly bobbed out of my sight. I had to sit up to see her skip off the bridge

and cross to the far side of the road. She was protecting
her legs with her laundry bag.

"It's the girl, Siggy."

"Oh, dandy," he said.

But the girl was still walking away.

"Here!" I called. "Can we give you a ride?"

"A ride with us?" said Siggy. "Three on our bike?"

"Where are you going?" I shouted. Now I had to stand
up to see her.

"She's running away from home, Graff. We won't be a
party to that."

"I'm not," said the girl, not looking back at us. But she
stopped.

"I didn't know she could hear, Graff. And anyway," he
whispered, "I know she's running away."

The girl turned a bit more to us, still keeping her legs
behind the laundry bag.

"Where are you going?" I asked.

"I've a new job in Waidhofen," she said, "and I'm going
to it."

"What was your old job?" said Siggy.

"I took care of an aunt," she said, "in St. Leonhard.
But I've another aunt in Waidhofen, and she owns a *Gasthof*. She's giving me wages and a room of my own."

"Did the other aunt die?" said Siggy.

"We were just leaving for Waidhofen," I said.

"We were just having a nap, Graff," said Siggy.

But the girl came back a little. She came kneeing her
laundry bag in front of her, keeping her face down—her
eyes under lashes and under the shadow of her hair. Her
face seemed to catch a blush-color from her braid. She
looked at the motorcycle.

"There's no room for me on that," she said. "Where
would I be?"

"Between us," I told her.

"Who drives?" she asked.

"I do," said Siggy. "And Graff would lovingly hold you
on."

"You could wear my helmet," I told her.

"Could I?" she said. "You wouldn't mind?"

"You'd have to leave your braid out," said Siggy.
"Wouldn't she, Graff?"

But I scurried him back to pick up the fishing stuff; we
cooled off the pan in the stream. The girl was tying the

laundry bag drawstrings round her waist, letting the bag
hang down in front of her.

"Can I just sit this on my lap?" she asked.

"Oh yes, yes," I said. And Siggy gouged the panhandle
into my belly.

"She's just a skinny baby one, Graff. She can't possibly
give you much of a ride."

"Oh, turn it off, Sig," I whispered. "Just turn it off a bit."

"Fate waits," he mumbled. "Great Bear, Big Dipper, how
you can wait!"

WHAT ALL OF US
WERE WAITING FOR

"Never done this before," she said.

And when she was on behind Siggy, I squeezed up behind her—sliding our rucksack back on the fender so I
could hang a bit of my rear over the seat.

"I don't need to be held," she said. "I'm in here tight
enough."

Then Siggy bucked the ditch up out of the orchard; he
raised the front wheel off the ground and brought it down
again so gently that it seemed to kiss the road. The rear
wheel went mushing out of the soft.

"Hold," said the girl; she was tossed back against me a
moment, and her braid hung to my lap. I caught her between my knees and pinched her to the seat. "Better," she
said. "That's enough." And we came down the pitch into
the switchbacks; the road was so worn and such a leathery
color, it looked like a razor strop. The trees seemed bent
by the sky, but we were the crooked ones—leaned-over
through the switchbacks, and barely out of one before we
were leaning into another.

"Hold," the girl said. "More." But I had no place to put
my feet; the girl hooked her sandal heels over my foot
pedals, and I held my feet up so they wouldn't be burned
on the exhaust pipes. I put my hands on her hips and
touched my thumbs together at her spine. "That's better,"
she said. "That's enough."

The wind took the tassel end of her braid and lashed it
upward at my chin, but the weight of her hair hung
against my chest in a wine-colored goblet-shape—coming

down loose and full from the helmet to her first braid
knot. I leaned a bit forward and pressed her braid against
my chest; and she pressed forward to Siggy.

Oh, girl, I thought, what lovely taut tendons hold your
ankle to your calf!

It was her laundry bag keeping her skirt in her lap, and
her elbows pinched her skirt to her thighs; she had her
hands tucked in the famous vent-pocket of Siggy's duckjacket, as if she were using it as a muff against the wind.

Her hair was sweeter than the mow-smells, richer than
the honeydrip hung from the bee boxes' little screen doors.

We were taking the switchbacks in slithers, plowing the
gravelmush out to the bank.

"Frot me," said Siggy. "There's some load pushing us
along."

"You've got the helmet on wrong," I said to her ear, so
soft it tickled my nose.

"Never mind now," she said. "Just hold."

I could peek how the helmet nearly covered her eyes
and rode high up on the back of her head; she gripped the
chin strap in her mouth, and it cut off the ends of her
words.

"It's the Ybbs, there," she said—and through the long-
falling orchard I had a glimpse of wide water, black as oil
in the shade firs at the meadow bottom.

At the next switchback we saw it again, only now it
was hammering over a falls. A mudstone town with rust-
colored roofs began where the black of the river fell to
foam—fell to a broth, bone-colored and bubbly. And there
were towers flying the canton flags, peep sights and gun
slits in the waterfront castles, and arching bridges of stone,
and little, swinging wood walks spanning the offshoots of
the river that ran through the streets. And garden plots
too, with the fading, fake colors of the city flower markets.

But Siggy had taken too much of a look; he'd gone too
high up on the bank of the switchback, and the crown of
the road was turned against us. Siggy was fighting the
gravel-mush on the fat lip of the bank. "Oh, frot!" he said.
"Oh, frot frot frot!"

One cheek of my rump wobbled down on the fender; I
was tipped, and there was no place for my poor feet.

So my thumbs slipped apart at the girl's spine; I plunged
my hands under her laundry bag and into her lap.

"Don't, you!" she said. And her elbows flew up under

my arms, like the startled winging of a grouse; her skirt
fluttered up to her thigh. I at least had a glimpse of that
hard, round leg before my other rump cheek sat on the
fender too; I was pushed between the seat and rucksack,
with no place for my poor feet, and with no way to steady
my slipping. My weight pushed the fender down; I was
warmed by the wheel rub. And I was slipping more. It
was my left leg that touched the pipe first, at mid-calf,
and I had no choice but to scissor the bike to stay on.

So the pipes received my calves like the griddle grabs
the bacon.

"Oh, he's burning!" the girl said.

"Is it Graff?" said Siggy. "God, I thought it was my
brakes!"

But there was no stopping quick in the gravel-mush at a
downhill pitch; of course he had to ride the bank out.
Siggy wedged us upright in an orchard ditch, and he lifted
me off—over the rucksack—though I was glued to the
pipes and needed yanking.

"Oh, we'll have to soak your pants off," he said.

"*Ai!*" I said. "Oh *ai, ai!*"

"Shut your mouth, Graff," he said, "or you'll lose all
dignity."

So I clamped on the hoots that were pelting up and
down my throat—I wouldn't let them out—and they sank
down to my poor calves: my sticky, gravel-spattered calves,
looking more melted than burnt.

"Oh, don't touch them!" said the girl. "Oh, look at
you!"

But I looked at her, with her cock-eyed helmet, and I
thought: How I'd like to bash you up good and hang you
by your frotting hair!

"Oh, you," she said. "When you grabbed, I didn't know
you were falling!"

"God," said Siggy, "doesn't he stink?"

"Oh, frot you!" I said.

"We'll need a bath to soak him in," said Siggy.

"There's my aunt's," the girl said. "Oh, her *Gasthof*
has baths and baths."

"That you could stand, Graff—baths and baths."

"So get him back on," said the girl. "I'll show you the
way."

And, oh, did the wind sting me—ice on my scorches. I
hugged the girl; she reached back one arm and wrapped

me around her. But the terrible hoots were rising within
me—I was going to be gagged, so I closed my mouth on
her neck, for the sake of my silence and bliss.

"What's your name, you?" she said through the chin
strap, and her neck blushed hot against my lips.

"Don't make him talk!" said Siggy. "He's Graff."

"I'm Gallen," the girl whispered. "My name's Gallen."

Gallen von St. Leonhard? I said to myself and her neck.

So three-up and wounded, we rode the beast through
town, blatting short echo-shots under the close arches,
booming over the high-walled bridge.

"It's your falls, Graff," said Siggy. "It's the Ybbs Falls."

But I was moving to a new spot of neck to kiss. We
dodged from sun to shade, with the stinging air first hot
and then cool—bellows to my flaming feet—and an or-
chestra of hoots wanted out of me.

"I'm sorry it hurts," Gallen said. "I'll take care of you."

But I couldn't squeeze her hard enough to stop the
stinging; I let my eyes be brushed by the falling goblet-
shape of her hair.

"Oh now," she said. "Now, all right."

The cobblestones were blurry; we seemed miles in the
air and rising. There were bears running below me, blowing on the coals that some fiend had left on my calves.

"It's a castle!" said Siggy. "Why, the *Gasthof*'s a castle!"

But I couldn't be so surprised. With Gallen von St. Leonhard taking care of me, I could expect a castle.

"Well," Gallen said. "It *was* a castle once."

"It's *still* a castle!" said Siggy, his voice miles away and
overrun by trampling bears. And from forty motorcycle
seats distant, he said, "A castle is always a castle."

And the last things I saw were the little boomerangs of
forsythia petals that littered our way and were flung con-
fettilike behind us, hurled in the terrible draft of the cycle's exhaust.

I shut my eyes and went giddy in my Gallen's lovely
hair.

CARED FOR

"Well now," Siggy was saying, "it's a piece of luck our Graff blinked out like that, or he'd have caused some stir, having his pants pulled off."

"You were gentle, though, weren't you?" said Gallen.

"Of course, girl," he was saying. "I put him in the bath with his pants on and did everything underwater." He was saying, "Then I drained the bath out from under him and let him lie."

But I still *felt* underwater, and I couldn't see anything. There were high, hard walls around me, and my legs were wrapped up in slime.

"Oh, help," I whispered, but not a pinprick of light broke my blackness.

And Siggy was saying, "Then I greased some towels with that gunk your auntie gave me, and I swaddled him up like Jesus."

"But where is he now?" Gallen said.

"Oh, where am I now?" I bellowed.

"In the bathtub!" said Siggy, and a harsh doorway of light swung over me; I looked down at myself, at the towels wrapped from shins to belly.

"He's had a fine nap," said Siggy.

"You didn't have to wrap up so much of him," Gallen said.

"Well, I thought you'd want a peek," said Siggy, "and the towels were easier than dressing him."

Their heads looked over the bathtub, but everything was all awhack—as if they were kneeling on the floor, because their chins barely made it to the tub rim.

"Stand up!" I shouted. "Why are you down there?"

"Oh, dear," said Gallen.

"Out of his head," Siggy told her.

It's a monster of a bathtub, I thought. But I said, "Let me down easy, up there!"

"God, Graff," said Siggy, and to Gallen he said, "He's ninny. He needs more sleep."

Then I watched their shadows bent over double and hinged at the ceiling and at the top of the wall; they were moving diagonally to the doorway, and their shadows grew jagged and huge.

"God!" I cried.

"Praise Him!" said Siggy, and they left me to my dark.

It wasn't a bad bit of dark, though; I had the tub walls, cool and smooth, to touch with my tongue, and I could latch hold of the tub rim with both hands, steering myself wherever I felt I must be going—whenever I shut my eyes.

In mad little swirls I was sledding about the bathroom when the doorway-shaped light came at me again, and a shadow unhinged itself, wall to ceiling—grew smaller, fled free-spirited down the other wall, just before the doorway of light closed.

"I saw you," I said to whatever hadn't gotten out. "I know very well you're in here, you frotter!"

"Be quiet, Graff," said Gallen.

"All right," I said, and I listened for her to come nearer; she sounded like she was under the bathtub. Then I felt the silky little shiver of her blouse across my hand on the tub rim.

"Hello, Gallen," I said.

"Are you all right, Graff?"

"I can't see you," I said.

"Well, that's good," said Gallen. "Because I've come to change your bandages and make them right."

"Oh, but Siggy can do that."

"He's got you wrapped too much."

"I feel fine," I said.

"You don't either. I'm just going to take off these old towels and put on a real bandage."

"It's nice that you work here," I said, and her braid end brushed my chest.

"Hush," she said.

"Why are you so far below me, Gallen?"

"I'm above you, silly," she said.

"Well, it must be a very deep tub."

"It's on a platform and seems so," she said.

Then I felt her hands find my chest and skitter down my hips.

"Arch your back, Graff."

One towel unwound, so lightly her hands never touched me.

"Again," she said, and I arched for another; I felt my-

self tubcool and naked to the knees. When she leaned to
catch my big toes for handles, her braid plopped in my
lap.

"Your hair tickles," I said.

"Where?"

"Tickles," I said, and caught the braid with both my
hands. I swished it over me, and she tugged it back.

"You stop, Graff."

"I want to see the back of your neck," I said.

She was unwinding from my ankles up, and when she
got to the hot, sticky places on my calves, she unwound
very slowly; they were the most congealed towels.

"Where have you hidden your braid?"

"Never mind," she said. All the towels were off now.

"Can you see in the dark, Gallen?"

"I can't!"

"If you could," I said, "you'd see me—"

"I would, all right."

"—all pink and scattered-hairy, like a baby ape."

"That's nice," she said. "Now stop."

But I was able to reach out and find her head, and slide
my hand under her chin, and run the backs of my knuckles across and down her throat to the first knot of her
braid, tucked into her blouse.

"I want to see the back of your neck," I said.

She was putting on the new bandages now; the gauze
wound lightly and fast. She bound only my calves, and she
didn't hobble my legs together; that was Siggy's sort of
work.

"I've a clean towel to cover you," she said.

"Is it a monstrous towel?"

"Arch," she said, and she whisked it around me so fast I
was fanned by the draft.

"Now give us some light," I said.

"I'm not supposed to be here, Graff. My aunt thinks I'm
turning down beds."

"I'll just have a look at your neck, Gallen," I said.

"And you won't grab me, will you?"

"No."

"Or pull off your towel?"

"Of course not!"

"Once a man did—in the hall, my aunt said. He just
pulled it off in front of her."

Then she danced the doorway's bright light across us,

and she leaned over me. I turned her face against my shoulder, and lifted her rich braid; I folded her ear down, and looked.

Why yes, in the down of her neck was the soft welt I'd given her.

"You're not unmarked yourself," I said, and I pecked her on the spot.

"You're not grabbing," she said, "are you?" And I let my hands lie on the tub floor; I pecked her twice more on the ear. And she touched my chest with her hand, just with the points of her fingers; she wouldn't let her palm lie flush. She kept her face turned against my shoulder; she touched me as stilly as she could. Her weight wasn't on me. She was like a long, lightly stunned fish—made to lie coolly atwitch, but airy in the hand.

"I'm going now," she said.

"Why do I have to stay in the bathtub?"

"I guess you don't."

"Where's Siggy?" I said.

"Getting you flowers."

"Getting me flowers?"

"Yes," said Gallen. "He's got a bowl of water, and he's going to fill it full of forsythia petals."

Then a wood-creek shuddered the walls and crept under the tub, and my Gallen flicked as noiselessly across the room as her shadow; the rectangle of bright doorway drew round its sides on itself, and my light disappeared like a water drop in a sponge.

OUT OF THE BATHTUB, LIFE GOES ON

Notorious Graff,
Lord of the Tub
Where nymphets come to water.
Grabby Graff,
Sly in the Tub,
Leads virgins to their slaughter.
Bottomless Graff,
Fiend of the Tub,
Wooer of beasts and nymphets.
Appalling Graff,

Stealthy in Tub,
Makes virgins into strumpets.

Oh, Graff!
Rotten Graff!
For your ass a briar staff,
To teach you to be kinder.

So writes Siegfried Javotnik, poet of the humdrum and
shell-shocked ear—bearer of forsythia petals afloat in a
borrowed bowl.

No one ever gave me a poem before, so I said, "I think
you cheat on your rhymes."

"You shouldn't have gotten out of the bathtub," said
Siggy. "You might have swooned and cracked your oafish
head."

"The flowers are great, Sig. I want to thank you for
them."

"Well, they're certainly not for you," he said. "They're
for our room in general."

"It's a nice room," I said.

We had a large, iron-grate window with a deep ledge;
the window swung out and let in the sound of the falls.
The old castle had a courtyard that our window opened
to; we could see the motorcycle parked by the fullest forsythia bush—a lovely, weaponlike hulk of such purposeful
machinery, misplaced in the yellows of the garden.

There were two beds, separated by a carved magazine
stand. One bed was turned down. The sheet lay back crisp-
ly unwrinkled; the pillow was punched up high and light.

"Did you fix my bed, Sig?"

"No, Graff, I did not. I'm sure it was your nymphet, or
perhaps her kindly aunt."

"Her aunt is kindly, is she?"

"A dear old babe, Graff—a loving old soul. Why, she
lent me this bowl for the flowers!"

"Well," I said.

"For a small price," said Siggy. "A pittance."

"Which was?" I said.

"My tolerance of her questions," said Siggy. "Where we
came from and how we came. And why we came. And
what is it we do for work?"

"Work?"

"Work, Graff. That's how we live."

"That's a question, isn't it?" I said.

"But not her best one, Graff. She wished to know which one of us had the eyes for Gallen."

"Well," I said, "a kindly aunt, she is."

"So I eased her mind on that score," said Siggy. "I told her we were both raving queers and she needn't worry."

"Frot you!" I said. "And what did she do then?"

"She lent me her bowl," said Siggy, "so I could pick flowers for you."

OFF THE SCENT

"I'm Frau Tratt," said Gallen's aunt. "We haven't met, as you were carried in."

"A disgrace to me, Frau Tratt," I said.

"How are your legs?" she asked.

"They've had the right sort of care," I told her.

"I take good care of my Graff," said Siggy.

"Oh yes, I can see," said Auntie Tratt, and she left us one menu to share.

The dining room of the Gasthof Schloss Wasserfall overlooked the dam, which added a woozy, bilious sensation to eating and drinking. The great falls spewed a froth on the windows, which made running, delta patterns down the glass. My stomach rolled over and gave me back an old taste.

"I've not seen that Gallen in a while," I said.

"She's probably in our bathtub, Graff. Waiting for you."

And the street lamps came on in the town, although the dark was another rusty evening-hour away. The lamplight flecked the water shot over the falls, filtered through it just at the arc where it bent to fall; the river held a million tiny shapes of dress-up colors reflected from the town.

Siggy was saying, "Unless, of course, she's heard from her auntie that you've no interest in girls."

"And thanks must go to you for that," I said. "I'll have to straighten it out."

"Ah, Graff. You'll find it's quite a mess, straightening out that sort of thing."

"She won't believe it anyway," I said.

And some of the shops blinked their lights across the

river; the towers bobbed downstream and toppled over the falls.

"Not hungry?" asked Auntie Tratt.

"I got very full, just sitting here," I said.

"Ah, Frau Tratt," said Siggy. "When you're in love, the other appetites suffer."

"Well, well," said Auntie Tratt, and she took our menu away.

"I don't think **you** need to carry this much farther, Sig."

"But, Graff! It's sure to put the old madam off your scent."

"And put us out of her *Gasthof* too."

"We can't afford it anyway," he said. "And your baby Gallen can't afford it either."

THE FOOT OF YOUR BED

My Gallen was not in the bathtub, so Siggy thought he'd have a bath.

"If you wouldn't mind," he said.

"I'd be happy for you," I told him. I sat on the window ledge while he splashed about and hummed in the tub; he was spanking the water with the flat of his hand, making sharp, beaverlike slaps.

Outside, the courtyard was full of soft yellows and greens; the evenings were taking longer and longer to come on. The falls brought a mist round the castle; I felt the wet of the air on my face.

"Come down here, Graff," said Gallen.

"Where are you?" I asked into the garden.

"On your motorcycle," Gallen said, but I could see the motorcycle looking gruff and shaggy like an old bull under the forsythia—lurking surly in the fairytale light of evening—and my Gallen was nowhere around it.

"No, you're not," I said. "I can see."

"All right, I'm under your window. I can see your chin."

"Step out, then," I said.

"I'm naked all over," said Gallen. "I haven't a thing on."

"You have so," I said.

"You come down here, Graff."

"I won't wear anything either," I said.

"Oh, you better," said Gallen, and she stepped out where I could see her, blousy in her long-sleeved ruffles and her apron full of frills. I thought: God, she can't be more than fourteen.

"Is your auntie with you?" I asked.

"Of course not," she said. "You come down."

So I danced down the prickly carpeted hall. The chandeliers swung overhead, giving me weary winks, as if they were tired of seeing such stealthy evening schemes go padding by underneath them. And the local soccer teams rebuked me from their framed, fixed poses on the lobby wall; year by year, their faces never changed. There was one year when they all shaved off their mustaches. There were the war years, when there'd been a girls' team—but righteous, athletic faces nonetheless. They were faces that had seen you before, had seen countless adventurers and lovers creeping through that lobby, and they'd rebuked them all. Impatient toes stirred their ready, soccer feet. They'd have left their photographs and kicked me, for sure, if only they hadn't seen so many secrets like mine.

The castle let me safely out, and Gallen said, "Who's there?"

"Bright pink Graff," I told her, "as shiny and nude as the Christ Child."

"You step out," she said.

I saw her in the vines along the castle wall; she ducked under the window ledges and waved me after her.

"Come around," she said. "Around here, Graff."

We turned the castle's cornerstone; the heavy spray from the falls met us. The rush of water silenced the crickets, and the gun slits of Waidhofen's towers, lit along the riverbank, were cutting light-slices in the creamy swirls of foam below the dam.

"It's been so long since I've seen you, Graff," said Gallen.

I sat down with her, our backs against the castle; her shoulder overlapped mine just a little. Her braid was coiled on top of her head, and she gave it a pat before she looked at me.

"How did I fix your legs?" she said.

"Oh, I'm fine now, Gallen. May I see your neck again?"

"Why can't you just talk?" she said.

"Words fail me," I told her.

"Well, you must try," said Gallen.

"I wish we had adjoining rooms," I tried.

"I'll never tell you where my room is," she said.

"Then I'll look in every one."

"Auntie has a dog sleep at the foot of her bed."

"Who sleeps at the foot of yours?"

"If I thought you were staying long, I'd have a lion. How long will you stay, Graff?" she said.

"Fate shapes our course," I told her.

"If I thought you were staying long, I'd tell you where my room is."

"Would your auntie give you a dowry?"

"I don't believe you're going to stay another day."

"Where would you go for your wedding trip?" I said.

"Where would you take me?"

"On a cruise in a bathtub!" I said. "A huge bathtub."

"And would Siggy come with us?" said Gallen.

"Well," I said, "I don't know how to drive the motorcycle."

"Here," she said. "See my neck? What you did is going away."

But it was getting too dark to see; I turned her shoulders and pulled her back against me. Oh, she never would give me all her weight; a part of her sat up away from me when I kissed her.

"You'll make it come back, Graff."

"Would you show me how your hair is when it's down and loose," I said.

And she reached up to uncoil her braid; under my fingers I felt the long, hard line of her collarbones, squared up to her shoulders when she raised her arms.

"What a lot of bones you have, Gallen," I said.

She brought her braid over her shoulder and undid the end knot. Then she tugged apart the thick-wound bands of her hair, combing her fingers through it, letting it crackle loose and dance like auburn milkweed in the spray gusts from the falls.

"There's nothing to cover my bones," said Gallen. "I haven't filled out in years."

"Oh, it's ages ago since you were fat," I said.

"Are you kissing or biting?" she asked.

"You're a little filled out," I said, and I put my arms round her waist, touched my fingertips to her long little belly. She seemed to draw herself from under me; I felt I was falling inside her.

"You're scaring me, Graff," she said. "You just want to scare me."

"I don't either."

"And that old Siggy-friend of yours," she said, "he just wants to scare Auntie."

"He does?"

"He did, and he meant to," she said, "because it's certainly not a bit true. And wouldn't I know it, if it were true of you?"

"Oh, you would," I said.

Her hair was wrinkled from the braiding and left a bare place behind her ear. So I kissed her there, and she moved a little more away, and came a little back, and pressed my hands down flush to her sides. "Feel the bones again," she whispered.

She relaxed, and then she didn't; she jounced away from me and stood up. "Oh, Graff," she said. "You mustn't think that I do anything I do on purpose. I don't know what I'm doing at all."

"Don't be frightened of what I might think," I said.

"Are you really pretty nice, Graff?" she asked. "Even though you scare me a little, aren't you really pretty good?"

"Bright pink Graff," I said, "to you."

And there were dramatic lightning flashes across the river, paling the yellows of the garden. The thunder was dry and splintery, far-off and in a world I didn't live in. Gallen's hair was bleached a brighter red in the lightning.

She skipped along the wall to the castle corner. When she got to the cornerstone, she let me come up to her; I put my arms round her waist again, and she leaned back into me. But she wouldn't turn; she just held my hands to her hips. "Oh my, Graff," she said.

"My, your bones," I whispered.

We looked into the courtyard. The few night-lit windows threw the bright squares and crosshatches of their grates over the lawn. Against the crosshatching I saw Siggy's shadow, arms over his head.

"What's that?" said Gallen.

"Siggy's touching his toes," I said. But, oh no, that wasn't it. He had ahold of the window grating; he'd reached over his head and had caught the weave of rungs and bars, and he seemed to press himself out into the courtyard—like some nocturnal enlivened beast, testing the strength of his cage.

"He's not touching his toes at all," said Gallen.

"It's just a stretching exercise," I said. And I hurried her along under the window ledges; I gave her a sudden blurry kiss at the monstrous castle door.

"We've got to watch out for your auntie," I said, and I went into the castle ahead of her.

And did the soccer players seem suddenly interested? Was there a light in their eyes that hadn't shone since the day they were fixed, framed and hung?

But there was no light coming under my own door, and for a long while I waited in the hall—listening to the perfect rhythm of my Siggy-friend's fake snores.

A BLURB FROM THE PROPHET

Will you ride with me?
The prison of the Sybarites
Is still fat and secure.

Will you always be such
Easy prey for sycophants?

Will you never admit
There are greater devotions?

Will you ride with me?
While the Sybarites take their sleep
We can set their prisoners free.

"You're a better snorer than a poet," I said. "I think you're more conscious about snoring."

"Did the thunder wake you, Graff?"

"I read your poem in the lightning."

"Ah," he said. "A veritable bolt lit your way."

"And did you summon it?" I asked.

"It was very officious of me," he admitted.

"From the window, Sig? Hanging on the grate, were you? Summoning wayward bolts?"

"Not at first," he said. "At first I was just watching, when old Fate happened along with the nightfall and gave me a second looking-over."

"Listen to that rain that's coming, Sig. Did you have a hand in that too?"

"Nothing to do with it, Graff. It's a slip-up, that rain. And all along the way, Graff, it's the slip-ups that have to be reckoned with."

"I wish I'd seen Fate too," I said. "It must make a fellow very knowing."

"Did you frot her yet, Graff?"

"I didn't," I said.

"You have a natural respect for youth," he said.

"When's leaving day, Sig?"

"Ah, the tearful departure! When can you whip yourself away?"

"You can be a prodding frotter, Siggy. I'd like to have some sleep now."

"So Graff would like to sleep!" he yelled, and he sat up with his pillow. "Sleep then," he said.

"Sleep yourself," I said.

"Like a volcano, Graff. This old Siggy sleeps like a volcano."

"I don't care how you sleep," I said.

"No, it's true you don't, Graff. You don't care a sweet frot!"

"Oh, Christ!" I said.

"He's in the bathroom, Graff," said Siggy, "cooking up what's next for you and me."

WHAT CHRIST COOKED
UP IN THE BATHROOM

The light was early in our room, even though the rain still puddled the courtyard; I could hear the fat drops *ping* on the pipes of the motorcycle. I propped myself up on my elbows and peered out the window through the grating; the wet cobblestones of the drive looked like a cluster of egg shapes, and I could see Auntie Tratt preparing for the milkman.

She seemed to come into the courtyard from under the

castle; she rolled two milkcans in front of her, prodding
them with her floppy galoshes. The pink hem of her robe
showed under her sacklike raingear; her hairnet slipped
down to her eyebrows and made her forehead look like
some puffy thing caught from the sea. The short shocks
of her calves peeked between her clog tops and the hem
of her robe; her flesh was as white as lard.

She set the milkcans on the cobblestones, just in front
of the castle door; then she hurried down to the courtyard
gate and opened it for the milkman. Only the milkman
wasn't there yet; Auntie Tratt looked both ways on the
street, and then she pelted back to the castle—flying her
soggy hem, leaving the gateway clear.

The rain now drummed on the milkcans; it *ponged* a
deeper sound than it made off the motorcycle pipes.

In a sudden, mad flurry, as doomed as dancing on ice,
the milkman arrived.

I saw the crooked-faced horse lurch into the gateway,
tilting his blinders against all the possible momentum of
the rickety cart and his own swaying body; the hitchmast
shunted up along his sagging spine, and the mass of
leathery harness and trappings leaned out against the corner this fool horse tried to cut. Then I saw the driver rein
and crank up the horse's maw; and the whole cart pick itself up and skitter after the horse, wrenching on the hitchmast and slinging its awkward weight to one side of the
animal's rump—as if a rider had flung himself off the
horse's back at full gallop, keeping the reins in hand, and
weighing as much as the horse.

The driver cried, "Jeee-*sus!*" and the cart hopped sideways on its two wheels, which locked and wouldn't spin.

The horse was waiting for all his legs to come down,
and for the cart to follow him. And I waited for the fool
driver to stop reining his poor horse's head so high up that
the animal saw only the tops of the forsythia bushes, and
not his own hooves landing on edge on the wet, egg-
smooth cobblestones.

The horse came down on his side, with the hitchmast
sliding along his spine and conking him in the ear; the little cart stopped high up on his rump. When his spongy
ribs whomped the cobbles, the horse said, *"Gnif!"*

The fool driver pitched out of his seat and landed on all
fours on the horse's neck, in a tangle of leather hitchings
and the jingling iron rings. The milkcans made a terrible

clamor in the slat-sided cart. The breeching slid up and lifted the horse's tail like a banner.

"What was that?" said Siggy.

And the milkman squatted on the horse's neck, jouncing like a spring just burst through an old bed.

"Jeee-*sus!* Horse!" he cried.

"God, Graff!" said Siggy. "What's going on?"

The milkman grabbed the sprawled horse by the ears and lifted the animal's head to his lap. He cradled the head and rocked back and forth on his haunches. *"Oh, sweet mother Jeee-sus, horse!"* he cried.

Then he pounded the horse's head on the cobblestones; he just tugged it up by the ears and flung it down again, leaning his weight after it. The horse's forehooves began to flay through the rain.

All the milkcan covers were tipped forward in the cart, and seemed like round, wet faces peering over the slatted sides. Auntie Tratt was stomping on the stoop to the main door, pushing her heels into her galoshes. She slopped crooked-footed along the drive to the milkman.

"Oh, here!" she said. "What can be the matter with you?"

The milkman, jockeying on the horse's neck, kept hold of the ears, laid his cheek in the hollow under the horse's jaw, and used his own head to batter the animal down. He was more expert at doing it now; he didn't try to lift the horse, he let the horse raise himself—just enough, to where the milkman was perfectly above the head, gripped on the ear handles. There he had the leverage; he could fling down so suddenly on the horse that its head would bounce a little before it lay on the cobbles—frothed over the bit, shook, bucked to raise itself again.

"Well, frotting Graff!" said Siggy. "If you won't tell me what's happening"—and he cloaked himself in the satiny pouf and hopped to the window ledge.

The horse was more frenzied now; the milkman was calm and terrible. The milkcart had ridden over the horse's rump, and the hitchmast bent like a great bow being strung on the horse's spine. And whenever the horse stopped churning, the hitchmast would spring back and over-straighten the unbelievable vertebrae.

But none of this bothered the milkman, he held so fiercely to the neck and ears, his cheek tucked in the jaw hollow.

"Oh my God," said Siggy.

"Berserk!" I said. "His brains must have muddled in the fall."

"*Aaah!*" said Siggy.

And Auntie Tratt moved gingerly about the scene, conscious of her pink hem in the rain.

And Siggy, the pouf cloaked over his shoulders and pinched to his throat—moving past me, one bare foot arched as a cat's back in wet grass—whooped over the magazine stand, was out the door and off down the hall. An utterly graceless pirouette round the stairwell, and his ballooning pouf snagged on the banister, just bending him backward as he took the steps; he let go of the pouf at his throat and went on. And he didn't come back for it. It gave me a satiny wave from the banister, fluffed by the draft from the main door opening wide and fast.

I ran back to my window.

And this is split-second seeing: someone new in the courtyard, a large man with pink knees and hairless legs below his lederhosen—an untucked ascot at the throat of his pajama tops, and very thick-soled sandals. He stood halfway between the main door and where Auntie Tratt was circling the fallen horse; stood with his hands on his hips, his hands stubbing suddenly at the ends of his arms—for he was a more or less wristless man, and a neckless, ankleless man besides.

He was saying, "Frau Tratt, what a terrible racket—it was very late when I got to bed"—and then he turned round to the castle and spread his arms as if someone were throwing him a bouquet from the door.

Siggy ran into him as dead-weight as a sandbag, and the man never closed his arms before he fell, or before Siggy's bare feet padded over his pajama chest.

Auntie Tratt was turning, a gesture beginning in her hands, the palms rolling up. Tiredly she said, "A fool, this driver—a crazy drunk." She just looked up and saw the puffy pink man pillowed on his ascot, his fingers twitching and his head moving very little. "It's going to rain all day," she said, and she caught a bit of Siggy flashing past her; she turned, her hands coming together.

Siggy's dazzling bottom was so sleek in the rain.

And the large, jointless man wet his ascot in a puddle, dabbed his mouth with it, lay just as he was on his back.

"No!" he shouted. "No, nothing! He had nothing on *all over, all over*."

And Siggy mounted the milkman; he worked his hands under the chin to a hold on the throat. Then he tucked his head down close to the milkman and bit into the back of his milky neck.

Down the prickly hall, I was hopping into my pants. Auntie Tratt came bobbing like a pigeon through the lobby; I saw her head jog by below me, just flit in and out of the slot in the stairwell.

Gallen had the pouf; she leaned against the banister, a touch of the satin to her cheek, and watched out the main door into the courtyard, where there were sounds of terrible suffering and pain—where the flaying horse jostled the milkcart about, and where the tumbled man sat up with his ascot hanging out of his mouth, gaping at the open castle door as if he expected a horde of naked men to come trampling him into the grooves of the cobblestones; and where Siggy rode the milkman through the garden, in and out of the forsythia.

"Graff," said Gallen, "my aunt's calling the police."

I took the pouf from her and nudged one of her small, upright breasts with my elbow. "Lovely little bosom," I said. "I'm afraid we'll be leaving you today."

"I couldn't sleep last night, Graff," she said.

But I had the pouf and I ran by her, into the courtyard.

The poor lopsided man made circles with his arms, tipped up his broad bottom and sat again. "He's all around," the man said. "Get nets and ropes." He gagged on his ascot. "Get dogs!" He choked, his arms still circling.

So in and out of the forsythia—the bell-shaped petals drooped with rain—in and out a strange figure was darting, bent over in the back bushes of the thicket, upright and charging by the motorcycle, here and there appearing, four-armed and two-headed; a terror-high, doglike wail marked the spot where I could expect it next to come in view.

The little needlepoints of rain fell icy on my back; I held the pouf like a bullfighter's cape, keeping it out from under my feet.

"Siggy?" I said.

In shiny raingear a hollow-eyed man with transparent ears came lurching between two fat forsythia bushes, spilling the rain from the burst cups of petals, showering the

boomerang pieces of flower with his thudding galoshes—
with a naked man on his back, fastened by teeth to the
milky neck.

"*Blaaah-rooo!*" the fool driver was screaming.

Two bushes away, I crossed between, after the next holler—the next peep of double-man to straighten up and
blunder on.

Then they were one bush away; I looked over a squat
shrub and could have touched the two heads with my
hand, if the shrub hadn't stabbed me when I reached.

"Siggy!" I said.

In the courtyard, on the stoop to the castle door, I
heard the tumbled man yelling, "Get the dogs on him!
Why aren't the dogs here?"

And now we ran in the same bush row; I followed the
wet-streaked, flexed bottom, the long toes bent back and
dragged behind the churning milkman, who was staggering
more headdown, more slowly now. I could catch them.

Then the milkman was three-headed; he couldn't run,
he swayed—his shoulders coming back—and his knees
quit.

"Oh, dear God," he moaned. And we were all in a pile
in the black garden-muck, the milkman groveling under
Siggy, skittering his hips out sideways and thrashing his
arms. I had Siggy's head, but he wouldn't come loose. I
got under his chin and tried to work open his mouth, but
he ground his jaw into my hands until my knuckles were
cracking. Then I biffed him in the ears and kneeled on his
spine; but he held. And the milkman began some chanting
wail, his hands digging back into Siggy's hair.

"Sig, let up," I said. "Let him go!" But he clenched his
teeth still, and kept the man from turning his hips.

So I broke a switch of forsythia off a bush, and lashed
it across Siggy's rear, and he writhed sideways; but I could
still catch him, and did. At the third fanny lash he rolled
free of the milkman and sat his smarting rump in the cool,
kind mud.

He put his hands under himself and slopped the mud
over his hips as if he were dressing himself in it; his mouth
made a little puckered *O*. I held out the pouf to him, and
he made whistling noises.

"The police are coming, Sig," I said.

And the milkman inched away from us; he scooped up

a great splot of mud to the mauve welt on his neck. He
made the whistling sounds too.

Siggy wrapped himself in the pouf. I caught him under
his arms and pushed him up in front of me—out of the
bushes and along the castle wall. Siggy began to march; he
took great strides that jogged his head up and down. His
feet left spread and terrible toe marks in the ooze.
"There's a mound of mud in my ass, Graff," he said; he
jiggled.

There was a mound of sorts in the lobby too. Auntie
Tratt, sponging, held the fat, dizzy man in a chair. She
tried to clean the mud off his lederhosen; my Gallen held
the water pail to dip the sponge.

"Well," the man said, "I heard someone coming and I
was turning around to see." And Siggy came up the stoop
with the pouf draped over one shoulder and down between his legs.

The dizzy man rocked in his chair; he made an odd,
fishy gurgle. He hammered his fists in his lap, where his
ascot lay puddled like a napkin over his bright knees; his
lower lip was as purple and fat as a beet.

"Frau Tratt," said Siggy. "It's raining up a flood, fit to
burst the dam. The end of the earth!" And he paraded by
her.

The pouf flared out as he swung on the banister, taking
the stairs on upward—rhythmically, with flourish, and two
at a time.

MASSING THE FORCES
OF JUSTICE

Now and then a clod of mud appeared in the air
above the forsythia, a long spitter of debris trailing behind
it. It was always flung nearly straight up, and followed by
unreasonable stamping sounds and violent shakings of the
bushes. The milkman was composing himself in the garden.

The poor horse was only making his lot worse. He'd
managed to turn himself, still on his side, so that he now
lay perpendicular to the hitchmast, and under it; he'd twisted himself so tightly in his breeching that he hadn't room
to move any more. A lump the size of a tennis ball swelled

on the ridge of his eyebrow and closed one eye. The other eye blinked into the rain, and the horse lay back and wheezed—his tail switching.

"Is it still raining, Graff?" said Siggy.

"Harder now."

"But it's not an electrical storm, is it?"

"No," I said, "not any more."

"Well," he said, "it's not a good idea to have a bath during an electrical storm."

"You're safe," I said.

"It's an enormous bathtub, Graff. I can see how you managed it."

"The milkman's still in the bushes," I said.

"Are you taking a bath after me, Graff?"

"I didn't get that muddy," I said.

"How fussy of you," said Siggy.

"The police are here, Sig," I told him.

The green Volkswagen with the bar of blue lights had some trouble getting through the gate and past the milk-cart. There were two policemen, high-booted and in immaculate uniform, the collars of their rain slickers identically curled to a sneer; and perhaps there was a third one, out of uniform—in a long coat of black leather, belted, and under a jaunty black beret.

"They've brought an assassin," I said.

"The police?"

"With a secret agent."

"It's probably the mayor," said Siggy. "A small town, a rainy day—what has a mayor got to do?"

The three went into the castle; I could hear the man who was being sponged, creaking his chair and raising his voice to greet them.

"Siggy?" I said. "How many kicks would it take to start that good motorcycle?"

But he gave me a bathtub song:

Disaster, disaster,
We're having a
Disaster.
If we try to
Get away,
Disaster
Will run faster.

"Oh, frot your damn rhyming," I said.

"You should have a bath, Graff," said Siggy. He splashed for me.

And one of the uniformed policemen came out in the courtyard, carrying some large hedge-trimming shears. He straddled the horse and squatted on the poor animal's back; then he snipped along the hitchmast, freeing the harness. But the horse just lay there, dizzy, with his old blinky one-eye; the policeman hissed and turned back for the castle.

It was then he saw a mudclot come spinning out of the forsythia, and heard the stamping, battering sounds of the milkman in the garden.

"Hello?" said the policeman. "You! Hello!"

And the milkman spattered handfuls of mud and sticks in the air.

"You!" the policeman shouted. And he advanced on the garden, with the hedge trimmers held in front of him like a water douser's rod.

I could see the milkman darting from bush to bush— crouching, scooping mud and twigs and hurtling them in the air; he lurked, watching his little bombs fall; and with cartoon stealth, he darted on.

"Sig, the milkman's lost his head," I said. And the policeman tiptoed into the forsythia, the great, vicious beak of the hedge trimmers held before him.

Then I heard them gathering in the hall outside our door. The light slot under the door was patched and blurred by sneaking feet; an elbow, a hip or a belly brushed the wood. They were milling, their voices thin and whispery—now and then a word, a phrase, would stand out clearly and be hissed, be hushed:

"as the day he was born"
"there should be"
"live together"
"hoe"
"must be"
"laws"
"dogs"
"unnatural"
"God knows"

And everything else—as if someone were speaking through a fan, and only the quickest speech-pieces made it between the blades—was chopped and whished into a single voice, indistinguishable from the rub of clothes and human weight against the walls and door.

"Sig," I said. "They're out in the hall."

"Massing the forces of justice?" he asked.

"Are you staying in the tub?"

"Why, hello!" he cried. "Look here!" And there was a lot of splashing. "Lash marks!" he said. "Whippings! Pink as your tongue, Graff. You did some job with your switch, you should see."

"I couldn't get you off him," I said.

"My ass is remarkable!" he said. "Veritable grooves!" And I heard him plunking and skidding in the tub.

Then there was a tiny knocking on the door, and the hall was very quiet; there were only two feet taking up the light slot now.

"Graff?" said my Gallen.

"Have they made you our Judas?" I said.

"Oh, Graff," she said.

Then weight came against the door, and someone was trying a key.

"Stand back!" said Auntie Tratt.

"It's unlocked," I told them.

A uniformed policeman booted the door open, springing the knob; he came sideways into the room, and the doorway filled behind him. Anxious Auntie Tratt, her arms crossed; the newly sponged man, pushing his shiny knees into the room; between them was the assassin, or the mayor. And nowhere was my Gallen now.

"Where's the other one?" said the sponged man, walking his knees forward.

And Siggy said, "You should see, Graff," and opened the bathroom door.

He flashed to all of us his stinging, washed bottom. The pink scars glowed across his rump like the tilted smiles of new moons.

"There!" said Auntie Tratt. "Do you see?"

And it was the mayor, all right—the formidable *Bürgermeister,* who hadn't removed his beret for Auntie Tratt, but who removed it now with a precise nod to the fanny poised in the bathroom doorway. A perfect job of doffing, quick enough to catch the fanny before Siggy leapt his hind end back in the bathroom and whomped shut the door.

"I see, Frau Tratt," said the mayor. "We all see, I'm

sure." And he barely raised his voice. "Herr Javotnik?" he
called. "Herr Siegfried Javotnik."

But we could hear Siggy padding across the bathroom
floor; he thumped up on the platform and plunked back in
the tub.

THE REVEALING OF CRIMES

He wouldn't unlock the bathroom door, so we all
waited in the lobby downstairs—all of us except one policeman, who was left behind to search our room.

The very upset pink man said, *"Herr Bürgermeister,* I
can't understand why we just don't smash down the door."
But the mayor was watching his other policeman, leading
the milkman through the courtyard and up the castle
stoop.

"Drunk again, Josef Köller?" the mayor said. "Having
wrecks and beating your horse?"

The milkman was so muddy it was hard to see his fabulous neck-welt. But the mayor moved closer and examined.

"Taught a small lesson?" he said; he poked around the
welt, and the milkman drew himself in like a turtle. "Perhaps a bit more than you had coming," the mayor said.

"And my milk is all froth," said Auntie Tratt.

"Then, Josef," the mayor said, "you'll leave an extra
can?"

The milkman tried to nod, but his jowls knotted and he
made a winced-up face.

"He's a madman," I told the mayor.

"Bitten on the neck," the mayor said, "and bitten hard
enough to break the skin and raise a welt the size of my
fist! And *who's* a madman? Running nude in the courtyard! Riding a man! Biting a man! And dallying about in
a bathtub, locked in! An exhibitionist and a flagellant!"
roared the mayor.

"Worse!" Auntie Tratt said. "A pervert!"

"A screwdriver!" bellowed the pink man. "Just a screwdriver would get you in that bathroom. And if you'd only
gotten the dogs here on time, there'd be no mess now."

Then the upstairs policeman appeared on the stairs—the

toes of his boots so perfectly together he looked as if he would fall.

"He's still in there," the policeman said. "He sang me a song."

"What did you find?" the mayor asked.

"Saltshakers," said the policeman.

"Saltshakers?" the mayor said—his voice like the high-pitched gnaw of the rain on the castle's hollow-tiled roof.

"Fourteen," said the policeman. "Fourteen saltshakers."

"My God," the mayor said. "A pervert, for sure."

FETCHING THE DETAILS

What's going on? These interruptions! They're what happens when you stand still long enough to let the real and unreasonable world catch up with you. And listen, Graff—that's not standing still very long.

My father Vratno, Vratno Javotnik, born in Jesenje before there were wheels in that part of Yugoslavia, moved to Slovenjgradec, where he fell in with the Germans—who were doing things with wheels no one had seen before; and with them rolled to Maribor, where a good road ran him straight across the border into Austria. And by himself, for he was sly.

Young Vratno followed the tank-trodden way to Vienna, where my mother was starving stoically and beautifully, and waiting to fall in with someone as sly as him—and not expecting, I'm sure, to play a part in the conception of anyone as born to wheels as me.

Young Vratno, who said across his soup to me, "Harder and harder it's getting, to have a thing going for yourself that isn't somehow the apprenticeship to something that's gone before; and not yours and never will be. And never a thing to make you happy." That's just what the poor fart said, I'm told.

Oh, my father was a splendid, melodramatic troll for mischief all his own; and so am I. And so are you,

Graff. And so this world might yet be spared the cool, old drudge of death-by-dullness.

But these interruptions! Digressions. Oh, it's repetitive death every time you let the world catch up with you!

Young Vratno, the ladling spoon a part of his lip and the soup becoming a part of his speech—he said, "Listen, you've got to move in the split-second interim between the time they find you out and the time they decide what to do with you. Just a hop ahead, and you're a cut above!" So he said, or so I'm told.

Siggy's note. Pinned to the bottom sheet of my bed, where my bottom found it—a starchy crumple to make me grope for the light. And I hadn't seen him leave any note.

In fact, when the mayor had me try my hand at getting him out of the bath, and when I'd come into the room again, Siggy was tub-slicked and dressed—all except the duckjacket, to which he was applying the last, thick rubs of saddle soap.

And the mayor's voice came up from the lobby: "If you can't get him out of there, he'll have to pay for the door!"

Siggy had the raingear out of the rucksack, the plastic bags to cover his boots, the rubber bands to wrap the bags tight to his calves, and the saddle soap. The duckjacket took a candle gloss and looked like a thing melted over him. "Don't worry," he whispered. "You draw them off, and I'll be back for you."

"They're down in the lobby, Sig. They'll hear you."

"Then get them up here. I'll be back, Graff—a day, two nights, at the most. You've got the pack and all the money I don't need for gas."

"Sig," I said.

But he opened the window and swung out on the ledge. He put on the goggles and helmet—a parachutist tightening his flyaway parts. Then he stepped his boots into the bags; they ballooned; he looked like a man with his feet in glass pots.

"Siggy?"

"Graff," he said, "we're in need of *details!* After all, Graff, we didn't really have much of a look at the place—what with your sporting with that hippo of a girl, and with the offense we took to it right away—now did we?"

And I thought: What? How your mind can leap—to something the spanning of is beyond me.

He jumped.

And I thought: What a show! You could have climbed down the vines.

He made a *splotz* sound in the garden-muck.

I heard the mayor's voice again. "Herr Graff! Is he making up his mind?"

"Oh, I think he'll talk," I called, and I went out in the hall. "Come up now!" I yelled, and I could hear them thudding the stairs.

I could hear the damp-chilled motorcycle too; it made short and enginelike sucks—caught and faltered once, like a bull-voiced man who started a shout, but gagged in mid-holler. Those rounding the stairwell, they heard it all too; we faced each other with the safe length of the hall between us.

Then I ran back to my room and the window; I could hear the stairs being swung down upon to the lobby. The mayor, though, came alongside me; his eager face spasmed from cheek to ear.

Siggy had caught it and held it; thick balls of gray were lobbed from the tailpipes, as weightless and wispy as dust kittens. They seemed like flimsy wads of hair, so tangled that we'd later find them in the garden, strung from the forsythia like mangled pieces of wigs.

Siggy smoothed the engine in one throttling, up and down—and lined up with the gateway, still narrowed by the strewn milkcart.

So it was *before* the policemen were off the castle stoop—and *before* the shoving milkman, the pink-washed man and Auntie Tratt had all shouted themselves out the castle door—that Siggy sped through the gap, posting on the foot pedals. The hunched, waxy duckjacket gleamed like a beetle's back. And even through the rain, I could hear him hit three of his gears.

Oh, a lover of ill weather and of the overall, precarious condition! This was—why yes, the trial marathon to Vienna—Siggy's reconnaissance mission to the Hietzinger Zoo.

THE REAL AND
UNREASONABLE WORLD

So I read the note more than once, and Gallen saw
the light under my door. I saw her foot shadows, creepy
and soft.

"Gallen?" I said. "I'm unlocked"—because no one had
fixed the knob that the policeman had sprung.

And I expected her in nightgown, unblushing black lace,
and sleekly unfrilled.

But she had her apron on; she jingled into my room,
hands stuck in the flowery pocket for coins.

"I know," I said. "You want to sleep with me."

"Stop it," she said. "I can't stay a second."

"It'll take hours," I told her.

"Oh, Graff," she said. "They're talking about you."

"Do they like me?"

"You helped him get away," she said. "No one knows
what to do."

"They'll think of something," I said.

"Graff, they said you don't have much money."

"So you don't want to marry me, Gallen?"

"Graff! They really mean to get you."

"Come and sit, Gallen," I said. "I really mean to get
you too."

But she sat on Siggy's bed; it was so soft and had such a
sag in it that her knees were tipped face-up to me—lovely
little chin-sized knees.

"Stop blushing, Gallen."

"What are you doing in bed like that?" she said.

"I was reading."

"I'll bet you've nothing on," she said. "Underneath the
covers, I'll bet you sleep without a stitch."

"Does it drive you wild to guess?" I asked.

"They're going to get you, Graff," she said. "I just saw
your light, so I knew you were up. I thought you'd be
dressed."

"Well, I'm hidden," I said. "Come sit on my bed."

"Graff—the mayor and my aunt, they're cooking something up."

"Well, what?" I said.

"They've looked through your stuff, you know. They saw what your money was like."

"I've enough to pay for this room," I said.

"And there's not much left after that, Graff. They can arrest you for not having money."

"I'm a loiterer," I said. "I always knew someone would find it out."

"And you helped him get away, Graff. They can get you for that."

"I can't wait to see what they'll do," I told her.

"They're going to make you get a job," she said.

Well, that was something, all right—a frotting job. Of course, I could just scram, make off for the mountains and fish, and tell Gallen where Siggy could find me when he came back looking; leave the money with her for the *Gasthof* bill.

Now I thought that, but Gallen had her eyes on me— and that one lovely line making the fine, sharp jut to her jaw, putting the slope off her shoulder that ran long to her wrist and the angle her hand made; her fingers were as sensitive as a Braille reader's, I was sure; and her dark lip-color, the rust blush-color on her cheek, and her pale, high-freckled forehead. She went as well together as the different ripe- and sun-spots of a peach.

So I said, "What kind of a job?"

"Just a little job," she said. "Just another way to have someone keeping an eye on you so they'll know when he's coming back."

"So they think he'll be back?"

"I think so too," she said. "Will he be back, Graff?"

"Are you a Judas, Gallen?"

"Oh, Graff," she said. "I'm just warning you what they're thinking they'll do." And she made her braid hide her face from me. "And I've got to know when you'll be leaving. I want to know where you're going so I can write you. And I want you to keep writing that you'll come back."

"Come sit here," I said, but she shook her head.

"They think he'll come back, Graff, because Auntie said you were lovers."

"What sort of a job is it?" I said.

"You've got to bring in the bees," she said.

"What bees?" I said.

"The bee boxes in the apple orchards," said Gallen.

"The hives are full and ready to be brought in. It's a job you do at night, and they think that's the most likely time you'd be trying to leave with him."

"And if I won't take the job, Gallen?"

"Then they arrest you," she said. "You're a vagrant, they'll say, and they'll lock you up. You helped him escape, and they can get you for that."

"I could skip out tonight," I said.

"Could you?" she said, and she went round to the other side of Siggy's bed; she sat with her back to me. "If you think you could do that," she whispered, "I could help you do it."

Well, I thought: Is it forsythia that turns the moon so yellow and sends it through my window to your hair—hues the air vemilion above your small, lovely head? "I couldn't do that, Gallen," I said.

She jingled her pocket of coins. "I've got to go now, Graff," she said.

"Would you come and tuck me in?" I asked.

She turned quick and smiled. Oh yes. Oh my.

"Don't you grab," she said. And she came round to my bedside, put off my light. "Get your arms under," she said to the dark.

She tucked once and came round to my other side. I was wriggling an arm out, but she tucked too fast. Then she pounced her hands down on my shoulders; her braid fell in my face.

"Oh, I'm so clumsy," she said, but she didn't let me go.

"Where's your room, Gallen?" I asked.

But by the time I'd untucked myself, she was out the door. Her foot shadows crept out from under the light slot, and I couldn't hear a thing amove in the hall.

I got up and opened the door just a bit, and peeked round the jamb; there she was, just waiting for me—not so angry that she couldn't blush.

"You never mind where my room is, Graff," she said.

So I went back to my sad, saggy bed; I rumpled around a bit, trying to second-guess the world. Well, I thought, the bees are done with their pollinating now; the honey's come full and the hive's fat for tapping. Oh, look out.

LOOKING OUT

I woke up with a sun smell on my pillow. So I thought:
Siggy is leaving Vienna now; he's had time to fetch his details, time to skulk in the zoo all night.

I saw him saying goodbye to the animals, trying to
cheer them up.

"Bless you, Siggy!" said the fraught giraffe.

And the wallaroo cradled a tear in its fist.

"Graff," said Gallen, under my door. "They're down in
the dining room."

Well, I didn't feel very good about any of it; their conspiracy weighed in the air of the hall. It was like they'd left
a door open to the cellar-dungeon; I could smell the foul,
dank mildew of thoughts left down there to ripen and go
moldy, but I couldn't find the door, to close it.

They had a table in the dining room, near to mine: the
wily *Herr Bürgermeister*, dear Auntie Tratt, and the
cider-smelling one—Herr Windisch, appleman and em-
ployer of the needy. He had withered blossoms caught in
the cuffs of his pants.

There was another they hadn't let sit with them; he
slumped in the dining-room doorway—Keff the tractor
driver. Windisch's man. He was burly enough, descended
pure from the Java stock, and his leathers smelt fresh
from the goat.

And how would they attempt it? Watching me butter
my *Brötchen*. Would Keff block my escape at the door?
Mush my spine with the meat of his knee?

But, yes, Siggy had written it:

Just a hop ahead, and you're a cut above!

So I dashed off the breakfast that my Gallen had served
me. And I went right up to their table.

"Forgive me if I'm interrupting," I said, "but I thought
all of you could advise me. Since I'll be staying awhile, I'd
like a job. Oh, just a little something at night, I'd prefer.
If you know of anything," I said.

And I heard it all! The dungeon door closing with terri-

ble wrenching clanks; and deep in my ears, sounding all
the way from Vienna, the Rare Spectacled Bears were
stamping their feet and shaking their heads with a fury
that flapped their jowls.

"Oh my," said Auntie Tratt. "Isn't that a fine idea?"

And that had their tableful wondering.

But behind my eyes, and making them water, Siggy was
riding faster and faster. The motorcycle screamed beneath
him like an animal in pain.

SPECULATIONS

I took some beers out in the garden and sat where I
could see round the castle to the falls. I found a spot
where the motorcycle had dripped oil and clotted the
grass. In a while the forsythia would all be gone by; the
garden would turn brown- and green-weedy, tropical and
over-thick. The river spray made everything a little wet,
and the garden made ominous growing sounds in the wind.
Only the soil smudge resisted; the spray was as beaded as
sweat on the little black clot.

And I thought: He's just stopped for lunch. The pipes
are *ping*ing with heat; he's been pushing it. If you spat on
the pipes, your spittle would ball up and bounce like
waterdrops off a ready griddle. He's had an early start and
he's really been pushing it. He's a long way out of the
Danube Valley; he may even be following the Ybbs by
now. And of course he'll have it all written out in that
frotting notebook, with little maps of the cages, and all
the details you'd ever need to know.

Eighteen minutes from behind the bush in Maxing Park
to the outskirts of Hietzing; eighteen minutes, four up-
and down-shifts, two skids, one *Strassenbahn*-crossing and
a blinking-yellow light.

And behind you, the din of escaping aardvarks.

Well, I thought, he probably won't even stop for lunch.

And there was Auntie Tratt in my room, airing me out;
she shot a smile down to me when she opened my window
and beat my pillow.

Well, you old gob, Auntie—he's not going to ride that

motorcycle in here for you to see. No, blobby Auntie—my
Siggy-friend's brighter than your old fishy eyes.

And there was my Gallen in my window too. Trimming
off the corners of my bed, no doubt, just as innocent as
milk.

Now which bed does that Graff sleep in? the sly Tratt
says.

Well, I don't know, Auntie, but this one looks most re-
cently used.

"Herr Graff?" the Tratt called. "Which bed are you
sleeping in?"

"Nearest the bathtub, Frau Tratt," I said. And Gallen
breezed past the window without looking down at me.

Well, you're right, Gallen dear, the Tratt is saying—
thinking every minute.

And I was thinking too, all right. Frau Tratt on the
poke in my room; someone sent to fix my doorknob,
secretly, while I was getting a job—so they could lock me
in? And those hazy clouds, stealing the yellow from the
last, fallen forsythia, squatted like bomb smog in the sky.

And where was Siggy? Out of Ulmerfeld by now? Hiesbach, maybe, or even on the road to St. Leonhard? If he's
coming that way. Was he taking a roundabout route?

How many hours away is that Siggy? And what will my
Gallen be wearing when she visits my room tonight?

The spray put such a wet weight in the air—and the
garden going on with its damn growing, getting all out of
hand. Well, as the Old Oaf, Fate—the Great Lout—could
tell you: look out, look out.

It's the kind of thing Siggy might have written a poem
about. In fact, there's a rough beginning in the notebook:

Ah, Life—fat bubble fit to burst!
Fate's got the veritable pin.

But it would have made a terrible poem. One of his
worst.

THE APPROACH OF
THE VERITABLE PIN

The fat sun, very low, turned everything the color of forsythia—yellowed the squares of last night to fall through my window's grating, blotched my bed and my resting toes.

"He's coming, isn't he?" said Gallen.

"Anytime now," I told her.

"Graff," she said, "if he comes from St. Leonhard, they'll see him. If he takes the road by the orchards, Graff, there's Windisch and Keff who'll be looking."

"Well, he won't just come rolling in on the bike, will he?"

"I'll bet he drives it into town," she said. "Oh, he won't bring it right to the courtyard, but he's not going to walk from St. Leonhard either—if he's fool enough to come from St. Leonhard, and not pick a new way."

"You figure it out, then," I said. "You think of the road he'll take in."

"Graff, you're not even going to say goodbye, are you?"

"Come and sit with me, Gallen," I said. But she shook her head and wouldn't budge from the window ledge. From down on the bed I could peek past her knees; there was a roundness to her leg where the ledge pinched her.

"Stop looking up my skirt!" she said; she drew her legs up and swung herself back-to me. She gave a look out the window. "Someone just ran out of the garden," she said.

Then she got on her knees and leaned out the window.

"Someone's up against the wall," she said. "Someone's scratching the vines, but I can't see."

So I came up beside her on the ledge; we knelt together, leaning out. Her braid slid up her back and over her shoulder; it shaded her face from me. I put my arm round her waist, and she straightened a little. On all fours we were, I draped on her back.

"Oh, damn you, Graff!" she said, and gave me her elbow in my throat. It choked me up so, I had to sit and water my eyes. She sat cross-legged on the ledge in front of me.

"Oh, you Graff!" she said. "Goodbye, you! You just go on and go."

She was getting teary; I had to look away from her. I peeked out the window, but there was nobody there. I was still gagging; it was like swimming, my eyes were so watery.

"Oh, Graff," she said, "don't you cry too." And she pitched forward at me, burrowing round me with her arms. Her face was wet against my cheek. "I could meet you somewhere, Graff. Couldn't I? I've got wages coming, and I never buy anything."

My Adam's apple was so fat in my throat I couldn't talk; I think she'd given it a bat that had turned it around.

"*Gak,*" I said.

And she dissolved; she bit her braid end and shivered herself up small against me.

"Gallen," I managed, "there's nobody out there."

But she wouldn't hear it. She was still shaking when the two strange elbows and the fist-shape of chin came wriggling up on the window ledge, together with animal pants and groans, and followed by the Great Greek Face of Comedy without a hair on his head—which all bore a bald resemblance to my previous Siggy-friend.

"God, give me a hand!" he said. "My foot's caught in this frotting ivy."

So I had to slide Gallen off my lap and drag the terribly disguised Siggy into the room.

"I'm back!" he said.

And he flopped down next to the heap my Gallen made on the floor.

FATE'S DISGUISE

Poor crumpled Gallen couldn't look at him again; and one look was enough—I agree, I agree.

"Siggy?" I said.

"Right you are, Graff! But I know, you didn't recognize me?"

"Not right away, without the duckjacket," I said, although I meant: Without any hair! How could I recognize you when you don't have any hair?

"And the new shave, Graff?" he said. "That was the trick!"

"But your whole head, Siggy?"

"Eyebrows too, Graff. Did you notice?"

"You look awful," I said.

"A walking dome, Graff! A solid pate from chin to uppermost cranial lump. Did you ever know there were such dents in a skull?"

"In *your* skull," I said. "Mine doesn't look like that." But maybe it did—little grooves and knots all over, like a bleached peach pit.

He said, "I walked through town, across the bridge. No one knew me, Graff. I saw the mayor, and he passed me by as if I were a war relic."

A barber's relic, his head was icy to the touch; I jumped. His relic was spattered with mosquitoes, and with larger more smearing flyers who'd run into his hurtling dome; there was a wing-mash above one ear that might have been a crow. Of course, he'd ridden here helmetless, letting the wind cool the barber's mistakes.

I said, "Siggy, you're hideous to behold."

"Of course, Graff. Of course," he said, "and I'm parked in hiding across the town. Get your stuff."

"Well, Siggy."

"Get it packed and we'll wait for dark," he said. "It's all set, Graff. It's just perfect."

And my crumpled Gallen huddled on the floor, a fetus dropped madly into this world and shrouded in a servant's clothes.

"Gallen?" I said.

"It looks like you got her," said Siggy.

"Don't," I said.

"Pack," he said. "I've found the spot."

"What spot?"

"To stash the guard!"

"Siggy."

"I was there all night, Graff. It's all planned."

"I knew it would be," I said.

"I didn't know you had such faith, Graff."

"Faith!" said Gallen.

"Is she going to scream?" said Siggy.

"Faith," Gallen said. "Did he come by the orchard road?" Oh, she wouldn't look at him. "Then they saw his motorcycle!" she wailed. "Oh, everyone's been told to look for it!"

"Why does she care?" said Siggy.

"Did you come from St. Leonhard, Sig?" I asked him.

"Graff," he said. "Look at me and tell me if you see an amateur."

FAITH

Well, I heard the first of the wood-creaks edge down the hallway from the stairs—and the sound of the top step being squeaked, the banister being leaned on.

"Who's that?" Gallen whispered.

"It's not about me," said Siggy. "No one's seen me."

So I peeked out in the hall. It was the old Tratt, sagged on the banister, winded from her climb.

"Herr Graff!" she called. "Herr Graff?"

I came out in the hall where she could see me.

"It's Keff," she said. "It's Keff, come to take you to your job."

"Job?" Siggy whispered.

"He's much too early," I told the Tratt. "Tell him he's early."

"He knows he's early," she said. "and he's waiting." And the terrible Tratt and I understood each other for a moment; then she swayed back down the stairs.

But bald Siggy was bent over my Gallen. He had her braid in his fist, and she bit her lip.

"He's got a *job?*" said Siggy. "Has he got a *job,* you damn girl?"

"Siggy," I said.

"Faith!" he said. "You never thought I'd be back, did you? Got yourself a job and a frotting *girl!*"

"They were going to arrest him," Gallen said over her lip.

"I set it all up," said Siggy. "Did you think I'd run out?"

"I knew you were setting it up," I said. "But, Siggy, they were figuring me as a vagrant. They were setting things up, too."

"Keff's waiting," said Gallen. "Oh, it's all fixed, Graff! If you don't go down, he'll come up."

"Sig," I said, "where can I meet you after work?"

"Oh, sure!" he said. "You're telling me you've not frotted this sweet rag of a girl?"

"Siggy, don't," I said.

"You're telling me!" he shouted. "Telling me you're coming with me? But *after* your frotting job! Oh, sure."

"This Keff," I said. "He's looking out for me." And I heard woody little spasms down the hallway: somebody heavy, mounting two at a time.

"Sig, get out!" I said. "You're going to get caught. Say a place where we'll meet."

"Say a place to meet *me*," Gallen said to him. "Graff's got to go."

"Meet *you*?" said Siggy. "Meet Graff's little raggy drab! Meet you for *what*?"

And big steps were taking up the hallway, huffs like tractor breath stirred the doorway air.

"Get out, Siggy," I said.

"I want my sleeping bag and my toothbrush, Graff. Please can I have my things back?"

"Oh, Christ, Sig!" I said. "Get out of here!"

And *thump!* said Keff to the door. *Thump.*

"Oh! Enter the heavy!" said Siggy. "Enter the crusher of spines!"

Keff thumped.

"I'm coming back for my things," said Siggy.

"Oh, you're crazy!" said Gallen. "You bald goon," she said. "You mean terrible queer!"

"Oh, Graff," he said—he was backing between the beds—"oh, Graff, I had this beautiful plan."

"Siggy, listen," I said.

"Oh, damn you, Graff," he said so softly—he was on the sunset on the window ledge.

"Sig, I'm really going to meet you," I said.

"Oh, Keff!" said Gallen. "Keff!" He was thumping very hard.

"Sig, say where you'll meet me."

"Where *did* I meet you, Graff? You watched girls in the Rathaus Park," he said. "You watched me too."

"Siggy," I said.

"You've had a good laugh over me," he said. "You and this tender young slip-in you've made the whole trip for."

And the hinge pins sprouted from the door. Oh, how Keff could thump!

"You got a *job!*" said Siggy. And he jumped, *splotz* in the awful garden-muck.

The sunset struck his terrible, hairless dome. Shadows deepened his skull dents, and the skeleton gape of his mouth—scooped the life from his eyes.

"Graff?" said Gallen.

"You shut up," I said. "You tell me when he comes back, Gallen—if you have to walk the orchards to St. Leonhard, you find me and tell me when he's come back."

"Oh damn, Graff!" she cried. Then she said, "Oh, Keff"—who now appeared round the hinge side of the door, swinging the door with him until the knob side snapped free of the jamb. Surprised, he still held the door —not knowing where to lay it down.

"Oh, Christ!" I said.

But no one spoke up.

DENYING THE ANIMAL

As the notebooks say:

Hinley Gouch hated animals on the loose, having so long and selfrighteously denied the animal in himself.

But Keff was not one to deny the animal. Not when he carried my kicking Gallen downstairs to her auntie; not when he lifted the hitch end of the iron flatbed and clamped trailer to tractor with one mighty Keff-heff.

I balanced on the flatbed while Keff drove; the iron sang under my feet, and the trailer end swung with the switchbacks. We climbed the orchard road, and for a while the evening grew lighter; we were catching the day's end-glow, which the mountain held last.

When we reached the top of the orchards, near St. Leonhard, Keff waited for a more final dark.

"Been in the bee business long, Keff?" I asked.

"You're a smarty, for sure," he said.

And the scarce neon from Waidhofen, the pale lights along the river, winked at us way below. The fresh white paint on the bee boxes took a greenish cheese-color; the boxes dotted the orchards like gypsy tents—living a secret life.

Keff slumped on the tractor seat, crouched among hand clutch and foot brakes, gearshifts, gauges and iron parts; he sprawled using the great wheels as armrests in some warlike easy chair.

"It's dark, Keff," I told him.

"It'll get darker," he said. "You're the one who's picking up the hives. Don't you want it darker?"

"So the bees will be faster asleep?"

"That's the idea, smarty," said Keff. "So you can sneak up and close the screen door on them. So when you start juggling them awake, they can't get out."

So we waited until the mountaintop was just another sky-shape, until the moon was the only color, and far-off, blinking Waidhofen gave the only signs of night people awake under lantern and bulb.

Keff would do it this way: I balanced on the trailer, and he drove through the tree rows of one orchard and then another. He'd stop at a bee box and I'd creep up to it easy. They had a little entrance the size of a letter slot in a door. There'd be a few sleepy bees on the ledge outside; I'd nudge them into their house, extra gently, and then I'd pull the screening down over their entranceway, and exit.

When you picked up the box, the hive woke up. They hummed inside; like distant electricity, they vibrated your arms.

The boxes were very heavy; honey leaked between the bottom slats when I lifted them up to the flatbed.

Keff said, "If you drop one, smarty, it'll split for sure. If it splits, smarty, I'll drive off and leave you."

So I didn't drop any. When they were on the flatbed, six or so, I had to brace my back against them so they wouldn't slide. First they'd slide toward the tractor on a downhill pitch, then they'd slide to the rear end when we climbed.

"Scramble, smarty," said Keff.

They fitted, fourteen on the flatbed floor; that was the first tier. Then I had to stack. With a second tier on, they didn't slide as easily; there was too much weighing them down. But I had to leave one space off the second tier so that I could load a third tier. I had to stand on a bee box with another bee box in my arms. Then I had to crawl over the second tier to fill out the corners.

"Three tiers is enough, huh, Keff?"

"Don't let your feet fall through," said Keff. "You'll be stuck, for sure."

"For sure I would, Keff." Honey-mucked, knee-deep, a prowler crashed into the home at night.

Keff would do this: I braced the hives and he crossed the road, working one side and then the other, moving down the mountain. He kept the orchards even on each side, but crossing the road was the problem. Coming up out of one ditch and down into the other, the flatbed would tilt enough to rock the second-tier boxes on edge. I braced, and Keff would do this: kill the engine, turn off the headlight, let all the groans and snaps of his tractor part cease and be quiet. Then he listened for cars on the road; if he heard anything, he'd wait.

Well, it took such a long time for the tractor and trailer to cross, and the road was too winding to be safely spotting headlights. So Keff would listen for engine sounds.

"Is that a car, smarty?"

"I don't hear anything, Keff."

"Listen," he said. "Do you want to get broadside in the road and have somebody drive through the hives?"

So I'd listen. To the tractor's manifold singing its heat. To the talkative bees.

I was stung just once. A bee I'd brushed off the door-stoop ledge, and who hadn't gone into the house, got caught in my shirt cuff and got my wrist. It made just a little burn, but my wrist got fat.

And we were four or five bee boxes away from a full third tier, when Keff stopped the tractor to check the pressure in the trailer tires. "I think they've got him by now, smarty," he said.

"Who?" I said.

"Your queer friend, smarty. He got in to see you, but he won't get out."

"Just voices you were hearing, Keff. Just Gallen and I were in that room."

"Oh, smarty," he said. "There's footprints in the garden, and there's everyone who heard the yelling. See? It makes you dumb to be a queer, smarty."

He read his tire gauge. How many pounds of air does it

take to hold a single-axle trailer, two tires a side, carrying what must be tons of honey and bees?

Keff stooped near the space I'd left for standing on the second tier. I could have just hopped up and shoved a whole row of third-tier boxes on him; I hopped up on the second tier.

"What were you doing with that little Gallen, smarty?" He wasn't looking up. "I've been waiting for her to get old enough," he said. "And a little bigger." And his squat, neckless head spun his face up to me, grinning.

"What are you doing up there?" he said. And his feet moved back under his haunches, like a sprinter getting set.

I said, "Why don't we have bee suits, Keff? Why don't we have masks and all that?"

But he was backing up, not taking his eyes off that third-tier row of hives.

"Why don't we have what?" he said.

"Bee suits," I said. "Protection, if there's an accident."

"Beekeeper's idea," said Keff, standing up now. "When you're protected, you're careless, smarty. When you're careless, you have accidents."

"Why doesn't the beekeeper get the hives himself, Keff?"

But Keff was still oogling at the third-tier row. "Third tier's almost full," he said. "Once more across the road, and we'll go back to the barns."

"Well, let's do it then," I said.

"Think he'll still be there, do you, smarty? We'll take another load after this one, and you think he'll still be around, fancy-free?"

"Well, Keff," I said, thinking: You almost weren't so fancy-free yourself, Keff—you almost weren't around any more. Eager bees are in those hives, Keff, and you were almost mired in honey-muck; with bee stings swelling your fat head fatter.

Keff was listening for anything coming.

Well no, of course, I thought. You were always there, safe all along, Keff. And don't you see, Siggy, how I'm drawing the line? And what in hell is it you expect of me, Siggy?

"Someone's coming," said Keff. He kept the engine killed.

Well, even the bees were quieted, listening too.

"Someone's running," said Keff, and he opened the tool-box.

I could hear the breathing down the road; gravel-scuff and the sounds of panting.

"Someone you know, smarty?" said Keff, the open-end wrench in his paw.

Then he twisted the housing round the headlight, opened the face of the light down the road; but he kept the light off. He was just getting ready.

Hush, bees, I thought. Those are little, short steps; those are quick, little breaths.

And Keff turned the light on my Gallen, hair loose and fanning the night as she ran.

HOW MANY BEES
WOULD DO FOR YOU?

Coming with the news, she was—rubber-legged from running uphill since Waidhofen. Gallen brought the news of Siggy's great return for his toothbrush, how he swung apelike from ivy vine to the window's grate to gain another entrance, how he bleated down the hall, rode the banister to the lobby, spoke the epitaphs for them all—for Auntie Tratt, who clucked like a tupping hen in her nook under the stairwell; and for my Gallen too, he gave some screaming metaphor of shattered maidenhood. And for me, he had also spoken for me—Gallen told—a diatribe, a prophecy of my eventual castration.

"Oh, crazy!" she gasped. "Oh he was, Graff. And he pawed up the garden, he threw mud on the castle walls!"

Well, the bees heard it all; they hummed against her where she slumped against them—the bee boxes propping her up all along her long, slight back.

"Don't let her lean too heavy," said Keff. "Don't have her tip a hive, smarty."

Oh, enough of you, Keff. Isn't it entirely enough now? I thought.

"They'll get him for sure," said Keff.

"Oh, he's wild," Gallen said. "Graff, the whole town is out for him. I don't know where he's gone."

"They should box him in," said Keff—and down the road behind him the crazy-twisted headlight startled the

trees crouched against the switchbacks. The town blinked
noiselessly beyond the dentshapes and reliefs of round tree
clumps balled against the night sky.

"Oh, Graff," said Gallen. "I'm so sorry. Please, I am
sorry, Graff—if he's your friend," she said.

"Listen," said Keff, but I heard nothing. "Listen,
smarty"—down in the town, winding up our way but just
a murmur yet—"do you hear the car?"

And some of the tree clumps caught the blinking-blue
light, flashing above the road and changing sides with the
turn of the switchbacks.

"Listen," said Keff. "That's a Volkswagen. That's the
police, for sure."

For sure. Sirenless and stealthy.

There were two in the car, and they didn't stay long.

"We're making a roadblock at the top!" said one, and a
black glove snapped its fingers.

"At St. Leonhard!" said the other. "If he comes this
way."

And the bees heard; the diminishing blue blinked away
from their box houses; they stirred against my poor,
propped Gallen, who for the second time this evening had
been reduced to a heap on account of me.

And I could only think: For sure, he's not going to try
riding that bike out of town. Oh, for sure—at least—he
won't be coming *this* way.

And Keff said, "Smarty, we can't just be gawking here
all night. If the girl won't fall off, I'd like to get across the
road."

"I'll be all right," said Gallen, but her voice shivered as
if some kind of wind down the mountains had blown all
the way from the Raxalpe, all the way from last January,
and caught her warm and precious and vulnerable, just
waking up in the morning, coverless. She was so hurt,
really, and there was nothing I could think clearly.

"Let's listen, then," said Keff, mounting the great
spring-back seat, settling among his iron-clanking parts.
We listened and he wrenched the housing for the headlight
around, so we were pointed and lit straight across the
road. Then he came up with a heavy foot on each wheel
brake; he rocked and struggled the tractor out of gear.
The trailer shifted; the bees sang.

"I don't hear anything," I said.

"No, nothing," said Keff, and he reached for the start-rod.

He was reaching; I said, "Keff?"

"Smarty?" he said, and his hand stopped in air.

"Listen," I said. "Do you hear?"

And he froze himself still, not squeaking the tractor's parts, not gusting his own breath.

"Oh yes," he said.

Maybe not even out of the town yet, but coming—and maybe not even coming our way. In those close arches, maybe—maybe that's what brought on the sound and then suddenly shut it off. Off and on again.

"Why, smarty," said Keff. "That's real good listening."

And now it was out of the town; it took our road. A hoarse man clearing his throat, many closed rooms away—clearing a great hoarse throat, not momentarily but eternally; going on forever, coming toward us forever.

"Oh yes!" said Keff.

Oh yes, I would have known it from a million others. Oh, the good sounds of the throggy beast my Siggy rode!

"Ha!" said Keff. "It's *him*, smarty. It's him, the queer!"

And, Keff, you were almost done then. A third-tier bee box for you, Keff, right where your neckless head looms almost level with the humming stack; right where you lurk on your high seat, Keff, a bee box for you. And perhaps another, perhaps a whole toppling row come down on you, thick Keff. If I dared, Keff, and if I thought it would make any difference or do any good.

How many bees would do for you, Keff? A strapping fellow like yourself—how many bee stings could you take? What's your quota, rotten Keff?

UPHILL AND DOWNHILL, HITHER AND YON

And was it Gallen's cold hand that brought me back? That crouched me by the trailer end, thinking: What now, Siggy? How do I stop you from meeting the mountaintop with the blinking-blue Volkswagen, and the snapping, black-gloved fingers therein, therein?

Up the mountain, where Keff and I had wound down from, the gravelly switchbacks are sharper; three S-curves above the bee-wagon was the very best S-curve of them all. It was as sharp as a Z. Well, I thought, he'll have to slow down for that one—even Siggy, even the beast, will have to come down a gear or two for that one. Maybe even first gear; he'd be going slow enough to stop, or at least slow enough so he'd have to see me in the road.

I ran, and I didn't decipher Keff's shouting; no, I didn't heed his woolly voice.

You always think you run so fast at night, even uphill; you can't see how slowly the road slips under you or the trees come by. The old night-shapes loomed and hovered; I could hear the beast rage louder.

Is it looking back that makes me fill in all the pieces, and make the facts come out so tight? Or did I really hear them then? The bees. Their million, double-, triple-million voices, urgent and impatient and abuzz.

But *this* I'm sure of: it was three S-curves up the tumbling mountain, and then the Z. Was it so perfectly worked out that I saw the headlight hit the tree clumps around me, precisely when I turned the Z? Or was it really somewhere in the last S, approaching the Z? Or did I really have to wait in ambush, long before the *throg* and *thump* of valve and tire slap bent into the Z itself?

At least I was there; I saw his rider shape come slithering out of the S below me—could hear that his gear was third—and saw the jerking headlight wash me a moon color and fix me forever to that spot on the road.

Then, hearing the gears come down to first. Into the elbow of the Z—was he coming at me sideways? Was the headlight jogging along all by itself?

"Frotting Graff!" he said, and the beast coughed itself out.

"Oh, Siggy!" I said, and I could have kissed his shining helmet—only it wasn't his helmet. It was his bare dome, bald as the moon and bared for the night of his escape. Cold as a gun.

"Frotting Graff!" he said, and he struggled to kick the bike out of gear. He lifted his foot for the kick starter.

"Sig, they've a roadblock for you at St. Leonhard!"

"You've a roadblock in your brain," he said. "Let me go."

"Siggy, you can't drive out. You'll have to hide."

But he got his foot back again; I joggled him off balance so he needed both legs to hold the bike up.

"Frotting Graff! Messing things up, you ninny-assed lover of that *girl!*"

And he wrestled the bike up steady, kicked back with his starting foot. But I wouldn't let him.

"Siggy, they're laying for you. You can't go."

"Have you a plan, Graff?" he said. "I'd like to hear your plan, frotting Graff!"

Why no, there wasn't any plan. Of course, there wasn't.

But I said, "You've got to stash the bike. Drive off in the orchards, lay low till the morning."

"Is that a *plan?*" he said. "Is there any good plan coming from you, Graff? Until every maidenhead on earth is taken, will you ever have a worthwhile plan?"

And he wrenched the handlebars out of my grip, but I pinned his legs against the bike and he couldn't kick.

"Never a plan from you, frotting Graff! Never a scheme of any greatness from you—not while there are any young upright unfondled diddies left in the world!"

And he shunted the bike around, jerking up on the handlebars, digging in with his heels. But I still had his starting foot trapped.

"Small-minded, immediate Graff!" he roared. "All the unbounced boobies of the world are in your brain!"

And he woggled the front wheel to point downhill. He started his beast rolling; I caught the vent-pocket of his duckjacket and ran close alongside.

"Hysteria for hymen!" he shouted. "You Graff, Graff you!"

Oh, he was rare, he was gone by, all right. And the bike moved along now; he tried to find a gear, he was pulling in the clutch to jump-start his beast on the glide.

"You'll always throw everything away, Graff," he said, strangely gentle.

And I couldn't keep up. I jockeyed on behind him, and the bike wobbled. I flung myself to his back, but he had folded up the foot pedals for the rear rider. He'd thoroughly planned this trip alone.

I felt him find the gear with a chunk.

But I did this: I leaned over his shoulder and dropped the heel of my hand on the kill button. The bike never caught. It made a muted, airy farting behind us, but the gear pull slowed us fast. I was slammed up against him, and he skipped over the gas tank astraddle, his knees

wedging up under the handlebars; his feet came off his
own foot pedals, and he couldn't reach back for the gears.

And whatever gear we were in didn't hold. The old
rampaging, momentum-bent beast slipped into neutral. We
were wheeling free, the headlight jogging down the road in
front of us; we floated engineless, coasting—the soft whir
of gravel-mush sprayed out beside us; the whispering
hum-slap of tires jounced us down. We weren't making a
sound.

Did even the bees hear us coming?

This S-curve and that one, blurring by faster than the
night bolting alongside.

"Move back on the seat!" said Siggy. "I've got to get in
gear."

But the pitch was too steep; my weight was fallen forward, on him, on the gas tank. And just when I tried to
move, another S-curve was coming at us hard.

"Shift, Graff!" he yelled. "You can reach it, you ninny!"

And he snapped in on the clutch handle; I dug my toes
under the foreign little lever, but it wouldn't budge.

The jostling headlight threw us pieces and juts of the
broken road, a scare of tree clump and bottomless
ditch—of cold, peaceful night sky and the shimmering angelic town, countless switchbacks below. Everything came
at us on jagged mirror-sections set askew.

Almost carelessly he said, "Graff, you've got to work
it."

My toes ground in pain, but the gear lever made a sudden, ratcheting sound; the engine blatted, cannonlike and
horse-whinnying, and I felt myself pelting up Siggy's back,
and clawing to get myself down. The front shocks hissed;
the bike bent forward.

Siggy's weight was too far front for good leaning; we
lumbered heavily and wobbly round the top of an endless
S, but we were slowing, a little.

"That's second," said Siggy. "Find me first, slow us
down."

The bottom of the S bent in front of us; the bike picked
itself up and hopped the crown sideways, but we stayed
with the road. We held, and Siggy said, "First gear, Graff.
Now *first.*" And my toes were digging again, prying the
lever; I thought I could feel it begin to move. And Siggy
said, "Don't miss the gear, Graff. Get it all the way in,
Graff." And I thought: Almost now, it's almost over—

we're coming clean out of this mad little ride. And we came shunting out of the S. I thought: That's it, it's all right, for sure.

But what was Keff doing, just ahead? What were his tractor and beewagon doing there, broadside in the road?

And didn't they look surprised? Keff holding the great steering wheel like a world slipping out of his grasp, and Gallen perched on the trailer end, steadying those third-tier bee boxes.

Keff, the great listener, who of course hadn't heard the beginning of our engineless descent. And just what are you going to do, Keff, broadside and taking up all the life in the road?

"Oh," said Siggy, so softly it was either a whisper or a complaint spoken straight into the rush of the wind.

THE NUMBER OF BEES
THAT WILL DO

The headlight was dancing over them; the squat, alive boxes, three tiers high, looming in front of and fast above us. The humming iron bottom of the flatbed—sagging under honey and level with our coming headlight—reflected our unfair arrival back to us.

Siggy's elbow pumped twice, whumped me in the chest and rocked me off his shoulders. But I was already helping him; my hands were already knuckling into the tight squeeze of seat and gas tank between us. I pushed up and off from my wrists, snapped my arms out straight and felt myself move away from Siggy and the beast, very slowly, it seemed—for a hundred miles of down-hill-flying road I was pushing myself up and off; for a hundred miles, I was floating behind and away from the beast, who was still in second gear and would never find first.

The jogging-red taillight pranced below and in front of me. And I thought: I'm going to sit in the air and float this road down to Waidhofen. I'm going to clear these bees by a mile; for a hundred miles I will never come down.

And the taillight moved away from me, sidestepped, tried to make up its mind and direction—had, of course, no place to go.

The longest hundred miles I was ever in the air strangely took no time at all. Not even time enough for the indefatigable Siggy to free his knees from under the handlebars, though time enough for me to see him trying—his dome snapping back and catching all the weird reflections of headlight, taillight, edges and faces of bee box, flatbed, hulking tractor-fender and the iron parts of Keff's open mouth.

The taillight, doing the damnedest dance, fell down on the road and spattered patterns of red-light, white-light pieces—did its dance out and went dark. Siggy, tucking his dome in the shadows, and in his duckjacket, put the old beast on its side.

The headlight pierced under the flatbed to the safe road beyond. The bike, on its side, was taking that route, flowering sparks from the drag of the tailpipe searing along—of foot pedal and kickstand, of handlebar and wheel hub, biting off chunks of the falling-down road.

And won't it surprise you, Keff, to see me fly over the whole damn mess and meet up with Siggy when he ducks out from under the far side of your terrible cargo?

But what did you do, Keff? Just what precisely did you think you were doing—when you lurched forward, Keff, and stalled; when you stalled and then lurched, or whatever the order was? What were you trying to do, Keff? What in your too-late brain could you ever have been thinking? Keff, why did you think you could ever get out of the way?

Why did you move, Keff—so that Siggy slid under the flatbed, but *not* out the other side?

Oh, you didn't move much, Keff, but just enough so that something caught a part of Siggy or his beast—an axle? an inch of tire? the outjutting edge of the flatbed's bottom? God, something said THANG!—a hollow, iron ringing that shook the moon.

You didn't move much, Keff, but you lurched.

Just as I was about to fly over your awesome cargo, you lurched, Keff! And Siggy, or a part of his beast, said THANG! up under the flatbed's bottom; and Gallen, her long, loveless arms only pretending to steady the terrible third-tier bee boxes, jumped! Knew the game was up and that the hives were moving beyond her control. She jumped clear; just as I was about to buzz over your bees, Keff—just then. You lurched, stalled, choked—whatever it is you do, and did, behind your gauges, gears, and ominous iron parts.

And the third-tier bee boxes hung on edge for as long as it had taken me to travel my hundred miles in the air; they fell in slow motion, feathered down to the powder-soft road and the waiting iron edge of the flatbed. The bees and I fell in slow motion, Keff.

Did I decide to put in a landing when I saw them fall? I came down mushy in the road, which was harder than it looked, and chewed all the skin off the heels of my hands.

But the bee boxes fell harder than I did. They were as heavy and vulnerable as water balloons. Their frail sides split, and they spilled their running, spongy hives.

God, what did they say? What did the bees say? Was it "Who's mashed my home in the middle of night?" Or was it "Who's woken me up—crashed into the hive, crushed my babies in their waxy little cells of sleep! *And who blinds me now with this light?*"

Because the beast wouldn't die, would not put out its headlight; it shone up under the trailer, so beautifully amber, on the great gobs of honey that drooled down over the flatbed's edge.

Well, the light caught you too, Keff—coming up the road to me, loping bearlike and swinging your great arms round your head, smacking your pants cuffs and leaping, Keff—yes, leaping—and turning around in the air, hugging yourself, Keff; and bending low; and again loping on toward me.

Did Gallen get to me before you did, Keff? Or did I only imagine her there for a second before you scooped me up like a ball and half carried, half rolled me up the mountain, out of the light that was showing the bees the way?

And did the stinging begin then? I don't remember feeling a thing. I remember hearing a quieted, much duller repetition of the original THANG! the beast, or something, had made against the trailer. I remember it, *thang-whump, thang-whump,* up under the flatbed's bottom.

Siggy, were you trying to lift the trailer off you—still trying to get your poor, wedged knees out from under the handlebars? Your fist, or forearm—your dome?—*thang-whump* and *thang-shump* again; did you know I'd hear you and come running?

I heard you. I came running. And I would have gotten

there if the bees hadn't closed my eyes, filled my ears and
slowed me to a crawl. Even then I might have gotten
there, if Keff hadn't come lumbering down on me, taking
me over his hip and up under his arm and bumbling me
back up the road.

If I screamed, it was to hear a human sound; to drown
out the bee drone—what was it they were saying?

"Here is the breaker of homes, the masher of baby
bees! And he can't get away if we follow his light!"

And after that, what was the true order of things?

There was Keff, telling me what I already knew: "Oh,
smarty, I *listened*. I *listened!* I heard your engine die, and
I listened for it to start up, but it didn't. I didn't hear it,
smarty! I said to the girl, 'Just you steady those boxes and
we'll finally get across this road.' Oh, smarty, ask her! We
both listened, and you *weren't* coming. Nobody was coming. How did you get here so fast that I never heard?"

And before that, or during that, or even after that, the
blinking-blue Volkswagen came down from St. Leonhard,
having heard, they said, the THANG!—even up there.

I was trying to open my eyes, sometime in all of that.
But they wouldn't open, and Gallen put her mouth to
them and wetted them cool for me.

And again Keff assured me that he had listened.

Then I'm really not sure what I listened for and heard;
if there was another *thang-whump* or two, or if I asked
Keff, "How many bees, would you guess?" And whether
Keff and I had a highly technical discussion on the number of bees per box and the number of boxes that had
toppled off—whether it was just the third-tier rows on the
trailer's uphill, hind-end side, or was it more or less. And
did it matter how many?

And whether Keff answered or guessed; if all of this
had happened on the spot, or if my counting of bees
hadn't really been later, semi-conscious and semi-sunk in
an Epsom salts bath. If any of this was three minutes after the last *thang-whump* I really heard, or three days after—three Epsom salts baths away.

And did the faces of the only true mourners crouch
about me there on that down-falling road, in that bee-con-
spiring night? Did the animals accuse me then, mourn him
then? Or was that soaked out of me in Epsom salts too?

The weeping wallaroo, the shaken oryx, the despairing

Rare Spectacled Bears. When did I see them mourning him?

Was it there, with my eyes still puffed shut? Or was it countless cathartic baths away, and long after Siggy had reached and surpassed his quota of bee stings?

Part Two

The Notebook

The First Zoo Watch:
Monday, June 5, 1967, @ 1:20 p.m.

I won't actually go inside until midafternoon. Another hour or so in this sun won't hurt me a bit; I might even dry out. As you certainly know, Graff, I left Waidhofen in a considerable downpour. And the roads were slick almost all the way to Hietzing, even though the rain stopped once I was out of the mountains.

I wasn't at all sure of the time when I left. When was it that the milkman first arrived? Everything happened very fast and early; I'm sure I was away by nine, and I've been at this café just long enough to order—a tea with rum, because the rain gave me some chill. So then, if I left at nine and it's one-twenty now, we can figure on four hours—Waidhofen to the Heitzinger Zoo. And that's with a wet road.

You know the café I'm at? On the Platz, off Maxing Strasse, across from the main zoo gate. I'm simply resting up and drying out. I'll just saunter over to the zoo about midafternoon, browse a bit, and find myself a spot to hide by the time they start ushering customers out and locking up for the night. That way I'll be inside to see the changing of the guard, if they have such a thing, and I'll be in a position to observe the habits of the nightwatchman. I hope I'll have the opportunity to talk with some of the animals, too, and let them know they've got nothing to fear from me. I'll stay until the zoo reopens; when there's enough of a crowd I'll just meander out, as if I've been an early-morning, paying customer.

Right now, the café's very nice. My waiter rolled back the awning for me, and I've got a tableful of sun; the sidewalk's warm to my feet. A pretty nice waiter, as waiters in the outer districts go. He's got a Balkan look, and his accent's as light as the chinking of wineglasses.

"Come here after the war?" I asked him.

"Oh, I missed the whole bit," he said.

"What did you miss?" I asked.

"The whole damn war," he said.

I couldn't tell if he was disappointed about it, or if it was at all true. It's true of you, isn't it, Graff? You were

103

all Salzburg people, weren't you? And moved yourselves
well west of Zürich before the war, you've said. I'd guess
that Switzerland was as well off as any place on the continent. And you had Salzburg to come back to. The Americans occupied Salzburg, didn't they? And from all I've
heard, they kept things pretty clean.

My waiter just brought me my tea with rum. I asked
him, "The Americans are a marvelously clean people,
aren't they?"

"I never met one," he said.

Sly, these Balkans. He's just the right age for the war,
and I'll bet he didn't miss a thing. But if you take me, for
example, I'm just the wrong age. I was in the right place
for the war, all right, but it passed me by when I was in
the womb, and on my way there—and again too fresh
from the womb to even take part in the post-mortem.
That's a bit of what you live with if you're twenty-one in
1967, in Austria; you don't have a history, really, and no
immediate future that you can see. What I mean is, we're
at an interim age in an interim time; we're alive between
two times of monstrous decisions—one past, the other
coming. We're taking up the lag in history, for who knows
how long. What I mean is, I have only a pre-history—a
womb and pre-womb existence at a time when great popular decisions with terrible consequences were being made.
We may be fifty before it happens again; anyway, now
science has seen to it that monstrous decisions don't need
popular support. You see, Graff, in our case, it's the pre-
history that made us and mattered to what we'd become.
My *vita* begins with my grandparents and is almost over
on the day I was born.

My waiter just brought me the Frankfurt newspaper.
He opened it to page three and let it fall in my lap.
There's a photo from America of a German shepherd dog
eating the dress off a Negress. There's an unmistakably
white policeman standing by, truncheon raised; he's going
to whop the Negress, it looks like, just as soon as the dog
gets off her. Quite blurry in the background, there's a line
of black people plastered against a storefront by an incredible stream from a fire hose. Didn't I say how these
Balkans were sly? My waiter just walked off and left this
in my lap. Marvelously clean people, the Americans; they
wash their black folk with fire hoses.

I guess if you're twenty-one in 1967, in America, you

needn't glut yourself with pre-history; in America I understand that there are crusades every day. But I'm not in America. I'm in the Old World, and what makes it old isn't that it's had a head start. Any place that's lagging, waiting again for The National Crisis—that's an Old World, and it's often a pity to be young in it.

I guess if I cared very profoundly I'd go to America, join the blackest extreme and wash white people with fire hoses. But it's only an idea that pops up every now and then, and I don't really give it much thought.

My waiter came to take his newspaper back.

"All done with it, sir?" he asked, and held out his hand. He's missing an index finger, down to the base knuckle. I gave him back his paper, spreading my thumb on the white policeman's face.

"Well, it's a German paper," I said. "Don't you think it must give some old Germans a kick to see a little racism in America?" Just to nudge him, I said that.

"I couldn't venture a guess," he told me, sly as he could be. Extra spiffy waiters, these Balkans. Half of them appear to have been full professors, before taking up their humble trade.

Vienna puzzles you that way. It's all pre-history—smug and secretive. It leaves me out, every time. But if we're supposed to be the generation that's to profit from our elders' mistakes, I feel I ought to know everyone's error.

My tea's cold, but it's heavy on the rum. A good waiter, no matter what else I say of him. But how did he lose that finger? If you asked him, he'd tell you—as a little boy, he was run over by a tram. Only there weren't any trams in far-eastern, small-town Yugoslavia when he was a little boy; there may not even be trams there now. But I guess if you were in America and asked a fingerless man how he lost it—probably a man who'd slashed it to the bone in a bottleneck—he'd tell you how a red-hot trigger burned it off while he was shooting the enemy in Manchuria.

Some people are proud, and some have their doubts.

And I can look at how left out of these times I feel—how I rely on pre-history for any sense and influence—and I can simplify this aforementioned garble. I can say: all *anyone* has is a pre-history. Feeling that you live at an interim time is something in the nature of being born and all the things that never happen to you after birth.

And once in a rare sometime, there's a grand scheme that comes along and changes all of that.

So I'll tip this good waiter fairly, and be getting myself across the street. There's many an animal I'd like to have a word with.

(BEGINNING)

THE HIGHLY SELECTIVE AUTOBIOGRAPHY OF
SIEGFRIED JAVOTNIK: PRE-HISTORY I

May 30, 1935: Hilke Marter, my mother-to-be, celebrates her fifteenth birthday. Her back against a naked trellis, she lolls in a Grinzing wine garden; some miles below her, the sun is melting its way to the snow's last, Baroque hiding places in downtown Vienna; above her, the meltwater trickles through the Vienna Woods, and the treetops are bobbing in a ground fog as intricate as the lacework in the downtown lingerie. Melt, says the day, and my mother melts.

Zahn Glanz, Hilke's first boyfriend, has such soft and blurry, mudpuddly eves. But what my mother most admires are the few threads of cornsilk he wears on his bright chin. And Zahn can make his wineglass hum by skidding his tongue round the rim; he can change to an octave higher by the force of his grip on the stem. In 1935, art is still common in glassware, even in public places, and talents as graceful as Zahn's develop, simply, to greatness.

So Zahn thinks he'll be a journalist, or a politician. And he'll never take Hilke to places where the radio doesn't work—or isn't always on, and loud enough—just so he'll be up with the current events.

"Watch you don't jar the trellis," says Zahn, and my mother leans forward, fingers on the table, looks over her shoulder and up to the speaker box wedged in the latticework above her head.

Even the waiter is careful he doesn't disturb Zahn's contact with the world outside the wine garden; he tiptoes—a gingerbread man crumbling softly over the terrace.

And Radio Johannesgasse complies with Zahn's readiness. Hitler is quoted as saying that Germany has neither the intention nor desire to interfere with internal affairs of Austria, or to annex or incorporate Austria.

"I'll cut off my trunk," says Zahn Glanz, "if a bit of that's true."

Oh, your what? Hilke thinks. No, you wouldn't. Oh, don't.

The Second Zoo Watch:
Monday, June 5, 1967, @ 4:30 p.m.

Shortly after I came in, I watched them feed the Big Cats. Everyone in the zoo seemed to have been waiting all day for that.

At the time, I was having a look at Bennet's cassowary, a wingless bird, related to emus and ostriches. It has enormous feet, which are said to be dangerous. But what I thought was interesting is that the bird has a bony casque on top of its head, and the information sheet speculated that this was to protect it—"as it bolts through dense undergrowth at amazing speeds." Now why would cassowaries be bolting through dense undergrowth at amazing speeds? They don't look especially stupid. My own theory on the evolution of that head armor is that the cassowaries only grew such helmets after people started trapping them in dense undergrowth, and chasing them at amazing speeds. Perhaps a worry gland produced it. It certainly is nothing they'd need if they were left alone.

Anyway, I was having a look at Bennet's cassowary when the Big Cats started their caterwauling. Well, everyone around me was hopping, and shoving, just dying to get to the spectacle.

Inside the Cat House, it smells very strong. People were remarking on that, all right. And I saw two terrible things.

First, this keeper came and flipped a horse steak through the bars to the lioness; the keeper flipped it right in a puddle of her pee. Everyone snickered, and waited for the lioness to make some derisive expression.

Second, the keeper was more professional with the cheetah; he slid the meat in on a little tray, shook it off, and the cheetah pounced on it, snapping it around in his mouth. Just the way a house cat breaks a mouse's neck. Great roars from everyone. But the cheetah shook his meat too hard; a big hunk flew off and plopped on the ledge outside the bars. Everyone was hysterical. You see, the cheetah couldn't quite reach it, and being afraid some-

one would steal it, the poor animal set up this roar. Some
children had to be taken outside the Cat House when all
the other Big Cats started roaring too. They thought, you
see, that this cheetah was threatening their own food. All
of them were crouched down over their meat hunks,
eating much too fast. All down the cage row, the tails
were swishing—flanks flexed and twitching. And naturally,
the people started hollering too. Someone pranced in front
of the cheetah, pretending to make a grab for the meat on
the ledge. The cheetah, must have lost his mind, trying to
jam his head between the bars. Then the keeper came
back with a long pole that had a sort of gaffing hook on
the end of it. The keeper snared the meat and flung it
through the bars like a jai-alai ball. The cheetah reeled to
the rear of his cage, the meat caught in his mouth. God,
he ate up that meat in two terrible bites and swallows—
not one bit of chewing—and sure enough, he gagged, finally spewing it all back up.

And when I left the Cat House, the cheetah was bolting
down his vomit. The other Big Cats were padding in circles, envious that someone had a bit left to eat.

And even now, at four-thirty, I don't see any signs of
the zoo getting ready to close. I'm under an umbrella in
the *Biergarten*. You remember? The Rare Spectacled
Bears. They've surely not bathed since the last time we
were here; they're reeking worse than ever; they seem
very nice, though; they're very gentle with each other. We
should decide: either we let both of them out, or we leave
them both. It wouldn't do to break them up. That's where
the viciousness would come in.

Of course, I don't believe we can do anything for the
Big Cats. I'm afraid they'll have to stay. Although I hate
to admit it, we do have a responsibility to the *people* of
this world.

(CONTINUING:)

THE HIGHLY SELECTIVE AUTOBIOGRAPHY OF
SIEGFRIED JAVOTNIK: PRE-HISTORY I

February 22, 1938: morning in the Rathaus Park. Hilke
Marter and Zahn Glanz are sharing a bag of assorted
Spanish nuts. They're taking a chilly, head-down walk,
and they've kept a tally of how many different, following

squirrels have begged and received a nut from the bag.
Hilke and Zahn have counted four: one with a thin face,
one with a tooth gone, one with a bitten ear, and one who
limps. Zahn makes squirrel-summoning sounds. And Hilke
says to the thin-faced one, "No, you've had yours. One
apiece. Isn't there anyone else?"

"Just four squirrels in the whole park," says Zahn.

But my mother thinks she spots a fifth; they count
again.

"Just four," says Zahn.

"No," says Hilke. "The one with the limp is gone." But
Zahn believes it's the same, fourth squirrel who's given up
limping for leaping.

"That's a different one," Hilke insists, and they approach a squirrel chasing its shadow. But the shadow-
chaser isn't after its shadow at all. Zahn kneels, blocks off
the squirrel's sun, and Hilke offers it an almond. And the
squirrel goes right on unreasonably leaping, in circles.

"Some sort of calisthenics," says Zahn, and Hilke holds
the almond closer. The squirrel reels, draws back, leaps—
spinning and directionless, like a bronco tossing off its
rider.

"It might be a trained squirrel," Hilke says, and sees the
pink on its head.

"It's bald," says Zahn, and he reaches. The squirrel
spins; its only course is around. And when Zahn has it in
his lap, he sees that the baldness has a shape; there's an
etching on the squirrel's head. The squirrel shuts its eyes
and bites the air; Zahn stops breathing to unfog his view.
The squirrel has a pink and perfect, hairless swastika carved
on its head.

"My God," says Zahn.

"Poor thing," my mother says, and offers the almond
again. But the squirrel appears dizzy and near to fainting.
Maybe it was an almond that set the trap before. The scar
is edged with blue; it pulses—signals that this squirrel
wants nothing more to do with nuts. Zahn lets it go; it
goes around.

Then my mother feels like bundling. Zahn tucks her
head in the great fur collar of his cavalry coat, which is in
style with students of politics and journalism; on snowy
days there's such a wet-fur reek in the classrooms that the
university smells like a rabbitry.

A line of tramcars comes down Stadiongasse at a tilting

jog: the cars wince and tip along, like heavy men with cold, brittle feet. Hands are rubbing the steam from the windows, a few gay hats are waved; some fingertips are spread on the glass and pointed at the couple bundling in the Rathaus Park.

A wind blows up; the squirrels crouch when their fur gets tufted. Mindless of the wind, and of all else, the fifth squirrel goes his own way: around—leaping, maybe, to catch up with the hat it's lost, or to regain whatever sense is only skin-deep for squirrels.

"Someplace warm?" says Zahn, and feels Hilke Marter catch her breath against him. My mother gives a nod that bumps Zahn Glanz's bright, smooth chin.

The Third Zoo Watch:
Monday, June 5, 1967, @ 7:30 p.m.

I confess I've not seen any evidence of actual atrocities being performed on these animals, either by the guards or by the customers. Unhappy arrangements, I've seen, but actual atrocities, no. Of course I'll keep looking, but right now it's best if I don't come out of hiding. It will be dark very soon, and I can investigate more thoroughly.

I had plenty of time to get myself hidden. A little before five a janitorial fellow came through the *Biergarten*, sweeping across the flagstones with a great push broom. Well, I got up and strolled. All over the zoo I could hear the brushing sounds. When you passed a sweeper, he'd say, "The zoo's about to close."

I even saw some people *trotting* for the gates—panicked, it seemed, at the thought of spending the night.

I thought it best not to try and hide with any of the animals; that is, I felt if I got inside a pen with one of the safe creatures, I might be discovered by some after-hours guard whose job it is to come and wash the animals, or give them a bed check—read them a story, or even beat them.

I did consider the lofty shed of the Yukon dall sheep, which sits on top of a fake mountain—a man-made pile of ruins, knit together in cement. The Yukon dall sheep have the best view of the zoo, but I was worried by this after-hours-guard idea, and I also thought the animals might have an alarm system.

So I'm hiding between a high hedgerow and the fence line for the Assorted Antelopes. It's a long, thick hedgerow, but at root level I can find spaces to look through. I can watch down one path to the Cat House, I can see the roofs of the Small Mammal House and the House of Pachyderms; I can look up another path, past the great oryx's private shed and yard, all the way to where the Australian creatures dwell. I can move behind the cover of this hedge, almost fifty yards in two directions.

As far as guards go, they won't be any problem. The sweepers passed my way several times after the official closing. They came brooming along, chanting, "The zoo is closed. Is there anyone in the zoo?" They make a game of it.

After them, I saw what you'd call an official guard—actually two guards, or the same guard twice. He, or they, took more than an hour testing cages; giving a tug here, a clank there, jingling a very large keyring; and then seemed to leave by the main gate. That is, I can't see the main gate from here, but an hour after my last glimpse of anybody, I heard the main gate open and snap shut.

I've seen no one since then. It was a quarter to seven when I heard the gate. The animals are quieting down; someone with a large voice has a cold. And I'll be a while yet behind this hedgerow. I don't think it's going to be as dark a night as I'd like to have, and although it's been almost an hour since I've seen or heard another human being, I know someone's here.

(CONTINUING:)

THE HIGHLY SELECTIVE AUTOBIOGRAPHY OF
SIEGFRIED JAVOTNIK: PRE-HISTORY I

February 22, 1938: afternoon in a *Kaffeehaus* on Schauflergasse. My mother and Zahn rub steam off the window and look out at the Chancellery on the Ballhausplatz. But Chancellor Kurt von Schuschnigg isn't going to come and stand in an open window today.

The guard at the Chancellery stamps his boots and takes a wishful peek at the *Kaffeehaus*, which seems to be thawing; the snow is building ledges on the guard's mustache, and even his bayonet is blue. Zahn thinks the rifle bore is full of snow and no defense at all.

It's only a guard of honor, after all, which was certainly known well enough in 1934, when Otto Planetta walked past the honorable, unloaded gun, and with his own, dishonorable weapon shot and killed the previous Chancellor, little Engelbert Dollfuss.

But Otto's choice for a replacement didn't fare well; Nazi Doktor Rintelen attempted suicide by inaccurately shooting himself in a room at the Imperial Hotel. And Kurt von Schuschnigg, friend of Dollfuss, moved his slow feet to fill his shoes.

"Does the guard of honor load his gun now?" says Zahn.

And Hilke squeaks her mitten over the window; she touches her nose to the glass. "It looks like it's loaded," she says.

"Guns are supposed to look loaded," says Zahn. "But that one just looks heavy."

"Student," the waiter says. "Why don't you charge the guard, and see?"

"I can't hear your radio," says Zahn, uneasy to be here—a new place with an untested volume, but the nearest warmth to the Rathaus Park.

The radio goes loud enough; it catches the guard's attention, and his boots start to waltz.

A taxi stops outside, and whoever is the taxi's fare dashes into the Chancellery, giving a hand signal to the guard. The driver comes and mashes his face against the *Kaffeehaus* window, fish-nostriled, appearing to have swum a snowy ocean to the farthest, glass end of his aquarium-world; he comes inside.

"Well, something's happening," he says.

But the waiter only asks, "A cognac? A tea with rum?"

"I've got a fare," the driver says, and comes to Zahn's table. He rubs himself a peep sight on the window above my mother's head.

"A cognac's quicker," the waiter says.

And the driver nods to Zahn, compliments him on the elegance of my mother's neck.

"It's not every day I get a fare like this," he says.

Zahn and Hilke make peep sights for themselves. The taxi stands chugging in its own exhaust; the windshield is icing and the wipers slip and rasp.

"Lennhoff," says the driver. "And he was in a hurry."

"You could have finished a cognac by now," the waiter says.

"Editor Lennhoff?" says Zahn.

"Of the *Telegraph*," the driver says, and wipes his own breath from the window—peers down Hilke's neckline.

"Lennhoff's the best there is," says Zahn.

"He puts it straight," the driver says.

"He sticks his neck out," says the waiter.

The driver breathes like his standing taxi, short huffs and a long gust. "I'll have a cognac," he says.

"You won't have time," says the waiter, who's already got it poured.

And Hilke asks the driver, "Do you get a lot of important fares?"

"Well," he says, "important people like the taxi all right. And you get used to it after a while. You learn how to put them at their ease."

"How?" the waiter asks, and sets the driver's cognac on Zahn's table.

But the driver's eyes and mind are far down my mother's neckline; he takes a while to get back. He reaches over Hilke's shoulder for his cognac, tilts the glass and twirls to coat the rim around. "Well," he says, "you've got to be at ease yourself. You've got to be relaxed with them. Let them know you've seen something of the world too. Now, for example, Lennhoff there—you wouldn't want to say to him, 'Oh, I cut out all your editorials and save them!' But you want to let him know you're bright enough to recognize him; for example, I said just now, 'Good afternoon, Herr Lennhoff, but it's a cold one, isn't it?' Called him by name, you see, and he said, 'It's a cold one, all right, but it's nice and warm in here.' And right away he's at home with you."

"Well, they're just like anyone else," says the waiter.

And just like anyone else, Lennhoff stoops in the cold; his scarf flourishes and drags him off balance; he's flurried out of the Chancellery and swept into the surprised guard of honor, who's been scratching his back with his bayonet and has his rifle upsidedown above his head. The guard avoids stabbing himself by a batonlike brandish of his weapon. Lennhoff cringes before the spinning rifle; the guard begins a slow salute, stops it midway—remembering that newspaper editors aren't saluted—and offers a handshake instead. Lennhoff moves to accept the hand, then remembers that this isn't part of his own protocol. The two scuff their feet, and Lennhoff allows himself to be buffeted out to the curb; he crosses the Ballhausplatz to the shuddering taxi.

The driver fires his cognac down, swallowing most of it through his nose; his eyes blear. He swims his way up Hilke's neckline, clears his head, and steadies himself with a touch of Hilke's shoulder. "Oh, excuse me," he says, and gives another complimentary nod to Zahn. Zahn rubs the window.

Lennhoff pounds on the taxitop; he opens the driver's-side door and blares on the horn.

With a miraculous, run-on fumble, the driver finds the right change for the waiter—touches my mother's shoulder again, and gets his chin tucked under his scarf. The waiter holds the door; the snow scoots over the driver's boots and flies up his pants. He slaps his knees together, spreads himself out thin and knifes into the flurry. At the sight of him, the horn blares again.

Lennhoff still must be in a hurry. The taxi reels round the Ballhausplatz, drifts to a curb and caroms off. Then the snow makes the taxi's straightaway journey seem so slow and soft.

"I'd like to drive a taxi," says Zahn.

"It's easy enough to do," the waiter says. "You just have to know how to drive."

And Zahn orders a bowl of hot wine soup. One bowl with two spoons. Hilke is fussy about the spicing; Zahn sprinkles not enough cinnamon and too much clove. The waiter watches the spoons compete.

"I could have given you two bowls," he says.

And Zahn hears the signal blip he knows so well—newstime, Radio Johannesgasse. He pins down my mother's spoon with his own and wishes the waves in the soup to be still.

Worldwide: French chargé d'affaires in Rome, M. Blondel, is rumored to have suffered some unspeakable insult from Count Ciano; and Anthony Eden has resigned from whatever he's been doing.

Austria: Chancellor Kurt von Schuschnigg has confirmed his new appointments to the Cabinet—Seyss-Inquart and four other Nazis.

Local: there's been a tram accident in the first district,

at the intersection of Gumpendorfer Strasse and Nibelungengasse. A driver on Strassenbahn Line 57, Klag Brahms, says he was creeping down Gumpendorfer when a man came running out of Nibelungen. The tram tracks were iced, of course, and the driver didn't want to risk a derailment. Klag Brahms says the man was running very fast, or was caught in a gale. But a woman in the second tramcar says the man was being chased by a gang of youths. Another passenger in the same tramcar refutes the woman's theory; the unidentified source says that this woman is always seeing look-alike gangs of youths. The victim himself is as yet unidentified; anyone who thinks he knows him may call Radio Johannesgasse. The man is described as old and small.

"And dead," the waiter says, while Hilke tries to remember all the old, small men she knows. No one she can think of was ever in the habit of running on Nibelungengasse.

But Zahn was counting up his fingers. "How many days ago was it," he asks, "when Schuschnigg went to Berchtesgaden and visited with Hitler?" And the waiter starts counting his own fingers.

"Ten," says Zahn, with fingers enough. "Just ten days, and now we've got five Nazis on the Cabinet."

"Half a Nazi a day," says the waiter, and spread-eagles a handful of fingers.

"Little old Herr Baum." my mother says, "isn't his shoeshop on some street like Nibelungen?"

And the waiter asks Zahn, "Don't you think the man was chased? I've seen those gangs around myself."

And Hilke's seen them too, she remembers. In trams, or in the theater, they sprawl their legs in the aisles; arm in arm, they shoulder you off the sidewalks. Sometimes they march in step, and they're great at following you home.

"Zahn?" my mother asks. "Would you like to come home for supper?"

But Zahn is looking out the window. When the wind drops, the guard of honor looms clear and motionless; then the snow gusts him over. A totem-soldier, turned to ice—if you bashed his face, his cheek would break off bloodless in the snow.

"That's no defense at all," says Zahn, and adds, "Now the trouble starts."

"*Now?*" the waiter says. "It started four years ago.

Four years ago this July, when you weren't even much of a student. He came in here and had a cup of mocha. He sat just where you're sitting. I'll never forget him."

"Who?" says Zahn.

"Otto Planetta," the waiter says. "Had his cup of mocha, watching out the window, the smug pig. Then a whole truckful of them unloaded outside. SS Standarte Eighty-nine, but they *looked* like Army Regulars. This Otto Planetta—he had his change all counted—he said, 'Why, there's my brother.' And out he went, marched right in with the rest of them, and killed poor Dollfuss; he shot him twice."

"Well, it didn't work," says Zahn.

"If I'd known who he was," the waiter says, "I'd have had him where he sat—right where you're sitting." And the waiter fumbles in his apron pocket, comes up with a pair of meat shears. "These would have done him, all right," he says.

"But Schuschnigg took over," says my mother. "And didn't Dollfuss want Schuschnigg?"

"In fact," Zahn says, "when Dollfuss was dying, he asked that Schuschnigg be the new Chancellor."

"He asked for a priest," the waiter says, "and they let him die without one."

My mother can remember more; these are the sad, family pieces of history she remembers over the rest. "His wife and children were in Italy," she says. "His children sent him flowers on the day he was killed, so he never got them."

"Schuschnigg's half of what Dollfuss was," says the waiter, "and you know what's amazing? Dollfuss was such a *little* man. I used to watch him going out and coming in, you know. I mean, he was a *tiny* one—with all his clothes too big for him. Really, he was almost an *elf*. But it didn't matter at all, did it?"

"How do you know?" says Zahn, "that it was Otto Planetta who came in here?" Then Zahn notices the waiter's size. He's a very small waiter. And the hand that holds the meat shears is more fragile than my mother's.

The Fourth Zoo Watch:
Monday, June 5, 1967, @ 9:00 p.m.

There's a nightwatchman, all right. But as far as I know, there's just one.

I waited an hour after dark, and I didn't see anyone. Nevertheless, I promised myself I wouldn't come out from behind the hedgerow until I knew the whereabouts of the guard. And a half-hour ago I saw a light I knew was inside the zoo. It was a glow, coming from the Small Mammal House. The light had probably been on since nightfall, but I hadn't noticed it as being actually inside the zoo— and not a reflection from Hietzing. At first I was frightened; I thought the Small Mammal House might be on fire. But the light didn't flicker. I went along my hedgerow to the corner of the fence line that gave me the best view. Trees in my way, a cage looming up here and there; I couldn't see the doorway, but I could see the eaves under the tiled roof, taking on a glow that had to come from the ground in front of the building. It had to be that; after all, there are no windows in the Small Mammal House.

I may have been sure of myself, but I was careful. Inching along stooped over—at times on all fours—against the cages and pens. I startled something. Something got up right next to me and thrashed into a gallop; snorted or whinnied or harumphed. I went down along the ponds of Various Aquatic Birds—all with fairly high pool curbs and signposts here and there: histories and bird legends. I had good cover round the ponds, and I found a spot with a clear view of the Small Mammal House's door. It was open; there was a light coming down the long hall and landing outside, thrown back up against the building. I think the light comes from an open room round the corner at the end of the hall. You remember the Small Mammal House—all those corridors winding round and round, in the fake night of infrared?

I did some thinking while I waited. It might not have been the nightwatchman's room at all; it might have been a light left on to give the nocturnal beasts a chance to sleep—in a daylight as illusory as their infrared night.

I nested in a shrub and leaned my arms on a pool curb. I read the nearest bird legend in the moonlight. It had to do with auks. The Hietzinger Zoo has only one member of the auk family. It is the least auklet, described as small and wizen-faced, and rather stupid; it has been known to wander down the paths, where it can easily get stepped on. In fact, the king of the auk family was such a stupid bird it became extinct. The great auk was last seen alive in 1844, and the last dead great auk, to be seen, was washed ashore at Trinity Bay, Ireland, in 1853. The great auk was both inquisitive and gullible, the legend says. If quietly approached, it would stand its ground. It was a favorite to provision fishing vessels; fishermen stalked the shorelines, approaching quietly and beating the auks with clubs.

Pretentious bird legend! Do they mean that the great auk was stupid—or that stupid men extinguished the great auk?

I looked about for the great auk's surviving kin, but I found no silly least auklet—not wandering down the paths, either, or dolting underfoot.

I was watched for awhile. Something webfooted tottered down the pool curb to me, stopped a few feet away and garbled softly—wishing to know whom I came to see at such an odd hour. It flopped down in the water and paddled past below me, gurgling—perhaps complaining; I believe, from its backswept head, it was an eared grebe, and I'd like to think it was encouraging me.

I got a little stiff and damp among the ponds, but I got to see the guard. He came out in the hallway of light and squinted out the door. Uniformed, holstered, and although I couldn't really see—certainly armed; he took his flashlight for a walk down the dim hall and through the dark zoo—not as dark as I would wish it; there's too much moon.

But, oh, it's oh
so easy!—
Watching
Watchmen.

(CONTINUING:)

THE HIGHLY SELECTIVE AUTOBIOGRAPHY OF
SIEGFRIED JAVOTNIK: PRE-HISTORY I

March 9, 1938—and every Wednesday teatime—my Grandmother Marter straightens fork tines. Grandfather Marter is impatient with the Pflaumenkuchen; the plum skins are blistered from the oven, and anyone can see the cake's too hot to eat. But my grandfather always burns his tongue. Then he paces in the kitchen; he sneaks more rum in his tea.

"I hate this waiting for the damn cake to cool," he says. "If the cake were started earlier, we'd have it ready with the tea."

And Grandmother aims a fork at him. "Then you'd want to have tea sooner," she says. "Then you'd start your waiting sooner, and move everything up so we'd be having our tea on top of lunch."

Zahn keeps his teacup in his lap; so he's ready when Grandfather comes round the table, sneaking rum. Grandfather tilts the bottle from his hip.

"Watch out for my Hilke, Zahn," he says. "Watch out she's not a know-it-all like her Muttie."

"Muttie's right," says Hilke. "You'd fuss around and burn yourself, no matter when the cake came out of the oven."

"You see, Zahn?" says Grandfather.

"The forks are all straight," Grandmother announces. "Nobody's going to stab a lip now!" she crows. "Real silver, you know, Zahn—it's so soft it bends easy."

"Muttie," says Hilke, "Zahn's got a job now."

"But you're in school, Zahn," says Grandfather.

"He's driving a taxi," Hilke says. "He can drive me around."

"It's just a part-time job," says Zahn. "I'm still in school."

"I like riding taxis," Grandmother says.

"And just when do you do all your taxi-riding?" says Grandfather. "You always take the trams when you're out with me."

Grandmother prods the plum cake with one of her forks. "It's cool enough now," she announces.

"Know-it-alls," says Grandfather. "Everyone's a know-it-all today." And before he draws a chair up to the kitchen table, he feels obliged—for Zahn's happiness—to jar the static out of the radio.

Zahn is pleased. Here's Radio Johannesgasse, clear for tea, and he anticipates the newstime signal blip. Time is that dependable on Wednesdays; when the forks are straight and the cake's cool, it's time for news.

Worldwide: Steenockerzeel Castle, Belgium, where the Habsburg Pretender lives. Legitimist leader Freiherr von Wiesner calls on all Austrian monarchists to resist Nazi Germany's continued pressure to incorporate Austria into the Reich. Von Wiesner appealed to Chancellor Schuschnigg that a return of the monarchy would offer the best resistance to Germany.

Austria: Tyrolean-born Kurt von Schuschnigg, at a mass meeting in Innsbruck, announced to his native province, and to the world, that in four days' time, on Sunday, the country will hold a plebiscite. The voters may decide for themselves—an independent Austria, or the Anschluss with Germany. Chancellor Schuschnigg ended his speech by shouting in Tyrolean dialect to the twenty thousand assembled in the Maria-Theresien-Platz: "Men, the time has come!" In Innsbruck this had special significance, of course, because one hundred and thirty years ago the peasant hero Andreas Hofer had with the same cry impassioned his countrymen to resist Napoleon.

Local: a young woman identified as Mara Madoff, daughter of clothier Sigismund Madoff, was found this morning hanging in her coat on a coat hook in the second-balcony wardrobe closet of the Vienna State Opera House. Opera custodian Odilo Linz, who discovered the body, says he's sure this particular closet is never used, and at least wasn't being used at last night's performance of *Lohengrin*. Odilo checked the closet sometime during the Prelude; he says nothing was hanging there then. Authorities attribute the cause of death to a star-shaped series of fine-pointed stab wounds in the heart, and estimate the time of death as well toward the end of the opera. The authorities say that the young woman was in no way assaulted; however, her stockings were missing and her shoes had been put back on. Late last night, someone claims to have seen a group of young men at the Haarhof Keller; allegedly, one of them wore a pair of women's stockings for a scarf. But among the young men, these days, this is a common way of showing off.

Also local: spokesmen for several anti-Nazi groups have already pledged their endorsement of Schuschnigg's proposed plebiscite. Karl Mittler has promised the support of the underground Socialists; Colonel Wolff has spoken for the monarchists; Doktor Friedmann for the Jewish community; Cardinal Innitzer for the Catholics. Chancellor Schuschnigg will be taking the overnight train from the Alps and is scheduled to arrive in Vienna by early morning. Some welcome is expected for him.

"Some welcome, for sure!" says Zahn. "He's done something, anyway, to show we're not just Hitler's backyard."

"Know-it-all," says Grandfather. "Just who does he think he is? Another Andreas Hofer, standing up to Napoleon. Cheers in the Tyrol—*that* I believe. But what do they say about Schuschnigg in Berlin? We're not standing up to a Frenchman this time."

"God," says Zahn. "Give him some credit. The vote's a sure thing. Nobody wants Germany in Austria."

"You're thinking like a taxi driver now, all right," Grandfather says. "*Nobody*, you say—and what does it matter?—*wants*, you say. I'll tell you what *I* want, and how little it matters. I want a man who'll do what he says he'll do. And that was Dollfuss, and he got murdered by some of those *nobodies* you mention. And now we've got Schuschnigg, that's what we've got."

"But he's called for an open vote," Zahn says.

"And it's four days away," says Grandfather, scornfully—and notices the cake crumbs he's sprayed about the table. He grows a bit muttery, and his ears blush. "I'm telling you, student or taxi driver or whatnot," he says, careful of cake, "it's a good thing the world's not flat, or Schuschnigg would have backed off long ago."

"You're such an old pessimist," Hilke says.

"Yes you are," says Grandmother, herding crumbs off the tablecloth with one of her forks, "and you're the biggest know-it-all there is, too. And got the worst eating manners I've seen, for someone of your colossal age."

"Of my what?" shouts Grandfather, and showers cake. "Where'd you ever learn to say a thing like that?"

And Grandmother, haughtily, moistens a fingertip, dabs at a cake crumb on Grandfather's tie. "I read it in a book you brought home," she says proudly, "and I thought it was very poetical. And you're always telling me I don't read enough, you *know-it-all*."

"Just show me the book," says Grandfather, "so I won't make the mistake of reading it."

Zahn makes faces at Grandfather, to show his tea is weak on rum. "Well, there's going to be some celebrating tomorrow," he says. "I could make a pile of fares, all right."

And Hilke is deciding what she'll wear. The one-piece, red wool jersey with the big roll collar. If it doesn't snow.

The Fifth Zoo Watch:
Monday, June 5, 1967, @ 11:45 p.m.

The watchman starts his first round at a quarter to nine and returns to the Small Mammal House at a quarter past. He made another round from quarter to eleven till quarter past. It was just the same.

The second time, I stayed behind the hedgerow and let him pass by close to me. I can tell you what he looks like from the waist down. A military snap-flap holster on a skinny ammunition belt that holds twelve rounds; I don't know how many rounds his snubnose revolver holds. The keyring loops through the ammunition belt; it would be too heavy for a belt loop. The flashlight has a wrist thong and is cased in metal; it may make up for the fact that he doesn't carry a truncheon. Gray twill uniform pants, wide at the ankle, and cuffless. The socks are funny; they have a squiggly design, and one of them keeps slipping into the heel of his shoe; he's always stopping to tug it up. The shoes are just black shoes, sort of everyday shoes. He doesn't take his uniform very seriously.

I was in no danger of being spotted. He shone his light along the hedges, but they're too thick to penetrate. Maybe if he'd been down on all fours, shining at root level—and if his eyesight had been very keen to begin with—he might have seen through to me. But you can tell what a good place to hide I've got.

This watchman doesn't seem so bad. He's sometimes inconsiderate as to where he shines his flashlight. He just flashes it around to every little cough or stir, and you'd think by now he'd know the dreaming prattle of his charges, and wouldn't have to be checking up on every little snore. Still, he doesn't seem to be malicious about it. He may be nervous, or bored—and trying to find as much to look at as he can.

He even seems to have his favorites. I watched him call a zebra over to the fence line. "Fancy horse," he said. "Come here, fancy horse." And one of the zebras, who must have been awake and waiting, came alongside him, shoving its muzzle over the fence. The watchman fed it something—certainly, against the rules—and gave its ears a tug or two. Now, any man who likes zebras can't be all bad.

He also has an interesting relationship with one of the lesser kangaroos. I think it's the wallaby, or perhaps the wallaroo; they're rather similar, at the distance I was from them. It wasn't the great gray boomer, certainly; I could have noted the size of that monster, the whole length of the path. Anyway, the watchman called somebody over. "Hey, you Australian," he said. "Hey, you dandy, come over here and box." And somebody thumped; a long, sharp ear sprang up—a stiff tail thwacked the ground. Maybe the guard's tone was a little taunting, and it may have been rude of him to be waking up the Australian's neighbors. But this watchman is a pretty gentle type, I feel. If it turns out that he's the guard we have to nab and stash, I'd want to do the job as politely as possible.

Something strange just happened. A little bell rang in the Small Mammal House; very clearly, I heard it ring. The animals heard it too. There was a tossing, a general turn-over—coughs, grunts, startled snorts; a lot of short, wary breathing. There are a number of those noises things make when they're trying to keep quiet; joints snap, stomachs rumble, swallowing is loud.

First the bell rang, then the watchman came out of the Small Mammal House. I saw his flashlight nodding. Then I saw this flashing down one of the paths; I think it came from the main zoo gate, and I think the watchman flashed back to it.

Along the fence line, behind my hedgerow, the Assorted Antelopes are shuffling their hooves. Something's up, all right. I mean it; it's midnight and this zoo is wide-awake.

(CONTINUING:)
THE HIGHLY SELECTIVE AUTOBIOGRAPHY OF
SIEGFRIED JAVOTNIK: PRE-HISTORY I

March 10, 1938: a warm, unsnowy Thursday, perfect for
Hilke's one-piece, red wool jersey with the big roll collar.

In the early morning, about the time Chancellor
Schuschnigg's train from Innsbruck is arriving at the West-
bahnhof—and just after Zahn Glanz has chalked JA!
SCHUSCHNIGG! on the black hood of his taxi—a chicken
farmer in the outskirting countryside of Hacking begins
getting dressed for the celebrations anticipated in the city.
Ernst Watzek-Trummer has neglected the eggs this morning and collected the feathers instead. Which is no less
strange than the work that kept him up all night—punctur-
ing and wiring together tin pieplates to make a suit of
mock chainmail, and then larding the suit to make the sur-
face sticky enough to hold the chicken feathers he now
rolls in. Anyone watching Ernst Watzek-Trummer getting
dressed would never buy a single egg from him again. But
no one sees, except the chickens who squabble out of his
way as he rolls back and forth through his feather pile on
the henhouse floor. And, moreover, no one could accuse
Ernst Watzek-Trummer of being extravagant; this costume
hasn't cost him a thing. The pieplates he has plenty of,
and they can still be used for selling eggs in; and this is
more use than he's ever got out of the feathers before.
Why, even the head of his costume is pieplates, a helmet
of pieplates, two for the earflaps, one for the top, and one
bent to fit his face—with eyeholes, and a breathing hole,
and two tiny punctured holes for the wire which fastens
on the hammered tin of his beak. A beak sharp enough to
lance a man through. And between the eyeholes is a decal
of the Austrian eagle, steamed off the bumper of Ernst
Watzek-Trummer's truck and reaffixed with lard. So that
hasn't cost him either. And it is undeniably an eaglesuit of
frightening authenticity—or if not authentic, at least
strong. The feathered chainmail hangs to his knees, and
the pieplate sleeves are made loose enough for flapping.
He leaves the head unfeathered, but lards it anyway—not
only to make the decal stick, but to make his whole dome
gleam. Ernst Watzek-Trummer, for this day an eagle—

and the Austrian eagle in particular—finishes dressing in his henhouse, and clanks fiercely toward the outlying district of the city, hoping he will be permitted to ride on the tram.

And Zahn Glanz, en route to my mother's street, has stopped once, just to let a little air out of his tires to make them squeal, and is now practicing the noise of his cornering in the rotary between the technical high school and Karl's Church.

And Grandfather Marter has decided not to go to work this morning, because no one will be reading in the foreign-language reading room of the International Student House anyway, and so the head librarian won't be missed. Grandfather watches for Zahn's taxi because he can at least indulge the young their optimism, Grandmother has said, and he can certainly indulge himself whatever drink is due a day of celebration.

And Zahn, on his fourth trip around the rotary, sees an early Mass letting out of Karl's Church. Only slightly money-minded, Zahn thinks an early fare would nicely preface his arrival at my mother's. He idles his taxi at the curb in front of Karl's Church, and reads his *Telegraph* spread over the wheel. Lennhoff's editorial praises Schuschnigg's plebiscite, expresses snide curiosity concerning Germany's reaction.

While at the Hütteldorf-Hacking Station for Strassenbahn Line 49, a sour tram driver refuses a ride to a man in an eaglesuit. Ernst Watzek-Trummer adjusts his beak, thumps his breast feathers and struts on.

And on the Ballhausplatz, Chancellor Kurt von Schuschnigg peers from a Chancellery window and spots a banner stretched from the balustrade of St. Michael's, across the Michaelerplatz, to a balustrade of the Hofburg showrooms. The banner is bed sheets stitched together, the lettering is neat and enormous: SCHUSCHNIGG, FOR A FREE AUSTRIA. And the Chancellor guesses that, in order for him to be able to see it at this distance, the comma must be the size of a man's head. It warms him to the tip of his Tyrolean, to know that beyond the banner, down Augustinerstrasse, to the Albertinaplatz and still beyond—throughout the Inner City—the throng is toasting him.

It would warm him even more to see the determination of Ernst Watzek-Trummer, who is suffering the humiliation of being thrown from a tramcar at the St. Veit Station—in full view of the children who've been collected along the way from Hacking, and who've been following at a steady, taunting distance. The eagle leaves a few untidy larded feathers; he struts on. But Chancellor Kurt von Schuschnigg can't see over five city districts to witness this unique, patriotic demonstration.

Grandfather Marter would say that the Chancellor has never been particularly far-sighted. My grandfather fancies himself as having a monopoly on far-sightedness. For example, he says to my mother, "Hilke, get your coat, it's Zahn"—while Zahn is still three blocks away, and only now, thinking that early Mass-goers must be walking types, decides to abandon the curb at Karl's Church. But whether it's far-sightedness or plain impatience, Grandfather and Hilke have their coats on when Zahn turns down their street.

"Don't get in any scuffles," says my grandmother.

"You just read a good book," Grandfather tells her.

And it's midafternoon before Grandfather Marter has a vision through a smeary window of the Augustiner Keller; he sloshes his beer and hides his face against Zahn's collar. He giggles.

"Father!" says Hilke, embarrassed.

"Are you going to be sick?" Zahn asks, and my grandfather snaps his face around to the window again; he still keeps hold of Zahn's lapel, ready to dive back in hiding if the creature of his vision reappears.

"It's the biggest bird I ever saw," he mutters, and then his vision looms round the revolving door—is flown into the *Keller* with staggering, tinny wing flaps, alarming a counter row of men munching sausage; they stumble backward in a wave; a thick slice of meat flaps to the floor, and they all stare at it as if it were someone's heart or hand.

"Jesus!" says Grandfather, and dives for Zahn's lapel again.

The vision with the terrifying wingspan clatters its feathered pieplate breast. *"Cawk!"* it cries. *"Cawk! Cawk!* Austria is free!" And very slowly, after an awesome silence, drinkers, one by one, rush to embrace the national symbol.

"Cawk!" says Grandfather, with dignity again, and Zahn catches hold of the eagle's chainmail, dragging him to

their table; his beak nearly stabs my grandfather, who greets the great bird with a bear hug.

"Oh, *look* at you," says Grandfather. "What a *fine* eagle!"

"I came all the way to Europe Platz on foot," the eagle says, "before I was allowed on the tram."

"Who put you off?" shouts Grandfather, furious.

"Drivers, here and there," Ernst Watzek-Trummer says.

"There's very little patriotism in the outer districts," my grandfather tells him.

"I made it all myself too," the eagle says. "I'm just an egg man, really. I've got chickens"—touching his feathers, and tapping the tin underneath—"and I've got these little pans around, for selling eggs in."

"Marvelous!" says Zahn.

"You're beautiful," Hilke tells the eagle, and pokes his downy parts, where the feathers are all wadded up and stuck on the thickest—under his tin-jutting chin, wild across his breast and gathered in his wing pits.

"Take off your head," says Zahn. "You can't drink with your head on."

And a wave of jostling men surges up behind the eagle. "Yes! Take off your head!" they shout, and reach and slosh their way nearer the bird.

"Don't crowd! Show some respect!" Grandfather says.

A violinist skitters to the balcony above their table—a cellist, stooping and grunting, follows. They refold their handkerchiefs.

"Music!" says Grandfather, lording over the *Keller* now.

The violinist tweaks his bow. The cellist creaks a string of finger-thickness; everyone clutches his spine, as if the cellist had struck a vertebra.

"Now quiet!" says Grandfather, still in charge. The eagle spreads his wings.

"Take off your head," Zahn whispers, and the music begins—a *Volkslied* to make the mighty blubber.

Hilke helps the eagle off with his head. Ernst Watzek-Trummer crinkles his old elfish face and sinks a dimple deep in his chin. My mother wants to kiss him; my grandfather does—out of second-joy, perhaps, to find so many gray hairs fringing the eagle's ears. Only a man of my grandfather's generation could be the Austrian eagle.

Ernst Watzek-Trummer is overcome—toasted and kissed by a man of some education, he can tell. He keeps ago-nized time with the *Volkslied*. His head is reverently passed around; it skids from hand to hand, losing lard and some of its gleam.

The windows frost. Someone suggests they devise a plan to fly the eagle—to hang him and swing him from the balustrade of St. Michael's. If they did it at St. Michael's, then Schuschnigg could see. Suspenders are offered. The eagle seems willing, but my grandfather is stern.

"Sirs," he says, and hands back a broad pair of red suspenders. "Please, sirs." And surveys the puzzled, blurry faces of the men holding up their pants with their thumbs. "My daughter is with us," says Grandfather, and he gently lifts my mother's face to the crowd. They retreat, admonished, and the eagle survives a near-swinging—what might have been a most elastic flight, with the combined snap-and-stretch of strong and weak suspenders.

Ernst Watzek-Trummer makes it safely to Zahn's taxi. At Grandfather's suggestion, the eagle blunts his beak with a wine cork—so he won't give injury on his way through the throng to the door. With beak corked—and a little bit bent, getting into the taxi—he enfolds my mother and grandfather in the backseat, while Zahn reels them through the Michaelerplatz, under the rumpling bed sheets that bless Schuschnigg, and down the *Kaffeehaus* alleys off the Graben.

Zahn announces, with shouts and his horn, the deliverance of Austria. *"Cawk! Cawk!"* he cries. "The country's free!" And the by now weary observers, sobering in coffee and behind hand-rubbed peep sights on steamy windows, pay little attention. They're already tired of miracles. This is only some large bird in a flying taxi's backseat.

And waiting up for them, is my grandmother—book open, tea cold. When she sees the eagle led into her kitchen, she turns to Grandfather as if he's brought home a pet they can't afford to feed. "Lord, look at you!" she says to him. "And your daughter with you all the while."

"Cawk!" the eagle says.

"What does it want, Zahn?" Grandmother asks. And to Grandfather: "You haven't bought it, have you? Or signed anything?"

"It's the Austrian eagle!" says Grandfather. "Show some respect!"

And Grandmother looks, not quite respectfully; she peers past the corked beak, into the eyeholes.

"Frau Marter," says the eagle. "I'm Ernst Watzek-Trummer, from Hacking."

"A patriot!" Grandfather shouts, and clomps the eagle's shoulder. A feather falls; it appears to go on falling forever.

"Muttie," says Hilke. "He made the suit himself."

And Grandmother makes a wary reach, touching the plumage on the eagle's breast.

Grandfather gently says, "It's just a little last fling I was having, Muttie. Our daughter's been properly looked after."

"Oh, indeed she has!" says Zahn, and thumps the eagle.

And Grandfather very sadly says, "Oh, it's Austria's last fling too, Muttie." And he genuflects before the eagle.

Ernst Watzek-Trummer covers his eyeholes, trembles his feathers and starts to cry—a grinding whimper into his beak.

"Cawk! Cawk!" says Zahn, still gay, but the eagle's helmet is rattling with sobs.

"Oh, there," Grandfather says. "Here now, you're a fine patriot, aren't you? There, there—and didn't we have some evening, though? And Zahn's going to drive you home, you know."

"Oh, the poor thing," says Grandmother.

And together, all of them, they get the eagle to the taxi.

"You'll have the whole backseat to yourself," says Zahn.

"Get his head off," Grandfather says. "He could drown."

And Hilke says to her father: "It's all your fault, you pessimist."

"You know-it-all!" says Grandmother.

But Grandfather is slamming doors and directing imaginary traffic on the empty street. He signals to Zahn that it's safe to pull away.

Zahn drives through the cemetery stillness of the outer districts—Hadik and St. Veit and Hütteldorf-Hacking—where, Zahn can only guess, the ghosts and present dwellers seem as ready or not to welcome the Holy Roman Empire as Hitler.

While the eagle takes himself apart in the backseat. And when Zahn finds the dark farm hiding outside the glow from the night-laying henhouse, there's a disheveled old man in his rear-view mirror, weeping—and feathers are floating all over the taxi.

"Come on," says Zahn, but Ernst Watzek-Trummer is attacking the empty eagle, shouldering it against the front-seat. He's trying to break its back, but the eagle is surprisingly well made; it slumps in a half-sit position, its weave of pieplates stronger than a spine.

"All right, all right now," says Zahn. "Just look at what you're doing to your suit." But Ernst Watzek-Trummer punches, snatches handfuls of feathers and gropes his kicking-foot along the floor—trying to find and squash the fallen head.

Zahn crawls in the backseat after him and wrestles him out the door. Ernst Watzek-Trummer flaps his arms. Zahn shuts the door and steers the egg man.

"Oh, please," says Zahn. "You'll have a good sleep, won't you? And I'll drive out and bring you to the polls myself."

The egg man buckles; Zahn lets him stumble forward but comes round in front of him to hold up his head. They kneel, facing each other.

"Can you remember?" says Zahn. "I'll pick you up for the plebiscite. I'll drive you to the polls. All right?"

Ernst Watzek-Trummer stares hard and lifts his fanny like a sprinter poising up on the blocks; he jerks his head as if to charge, draws Zahn off and scampers round him—on all fours, but running himself upright. He stops and looks back at Zahn. Zahn plots a move.

"Come on," says Zahn. "You'll go to bed, won't you? You won't get in any trouble, will you?"

Ernst Watzek-Trummer lets his arms hang. "There won't be any vote," he says. "They'll never get away with it, you young fool." And he breaks for his henhouse; Zahn starts after him, but stops. A doorway of light opens on Zahn's horizon, and then Ernst Watzek-Trummer closes it after him. The henhouse stoops under its own roof and groans; there's a moment, Zahn is sure, when eggs are caught in the act, half laid. Then there's some squabbling; Zahn sees a hen go winging or falling past a window; the light inside dances or is swung. Another hen, or even the same one, shrieks. Then the light goes out; there won't be any eggs laid tonight. Zahn waits until he's sure that Ernst Watzek-Trummer has found a berth—has put someone off his roost. But whoever is put out is at least being quiet about it.

Zahn wobbles back to the taxi, sits on the running

board and has a pull from the cognac bottle Grandfather
has left with him. He tries to smoke, but he can't keep lit.
And he's almost behind the wheel and driving off when he
spots the eagle, uninhabited, leaning over the frontseat.
Zahn sits the eagle beside him, but it keeps slumping over;
Zahn finds the eagle's head, sits it in the eagle's lap—offers
it some of my grandfather's cognac.

"You'll have quite a head in the morning," Zahn tells it,
and begins a giggle that turns into a sneezing bout, a fit—
a seizure loud enough to cause some clucking in the henhouse. Zahn can't stop; hysterical, he sees himself in the
eaglesuit suddenly looming into the henhouse, switching on
the light and *cawk*ing till the frenzied hens begin a binge
of laying eggs—or never lay an egg again; *cawk*ing so
loudly that Ernst Watzek-Trummer lays the greatest egg
of all.

But Zahn just offers the eagle's head another drink;
when it fails to respond, he pours a shot down the head
hole.

It seems to Zahn that they talk for hours, passing the
bottle, keeping watch over the darkened henhouse,
guarding the sleep of Ernst Watzek-Trummer on his lordly
roost.

"Drink up, brave eagle!" says Zahn, and watches the
head hole quaffing down the upended bottle.

The Sixth Zoo Watch:
Tuesday, June 6, 1967, @ 1:30 a.m.

The changing of the guard happened at midnight, and
things haven't been the same since. Everyone is still
awake. Really—this zoo is one restless stir and scuff; no
one is asleep. A general insomnia arrived at midnight.

At first, I thought they were on to me. I thought the
first-shift guard told the second-shift guard that someone
was prowling about. Or, perhaps, the animals passed the
word around; along some universal grapevine of tapped
hooves, twitters, grunts and such, they told each other
about me. And now they're waiting to see what I'll do.

But I don't think that's really why the zoo's awake. It's
because of the new nightwatchman. The little bell-ringing
prepared everyone; the animals were expecting him.
There's some difference in the guards, I can tell you.

He walked by me. This one's got a truncheon; he sticks

it in a sheath that's stitched inside his left boot. They're above-ankle, modified combat boots, laced loosely at the calf. The gray twills tuck in the boots. He wears an open holster, cowboy-style, and the barrel of his clip-load handgun is at least six inches long. He does an interesting thing with the key ring. He puts his arm through it and hikes it up on his shoulder; he fastens it under an epaulette—his uniform still has both epaulettes too. All the keys hang under his armpit and jangle against him. It seems awkward to me; if you've a bunch of keys in your armpit, you carry your arm funny. It's his right arm, though, and maybe that puts him in a better position for going at the open holster, which is worn rather high on his right hip. I think, although he looks a bit off balance, he has his hardware fairly well understood. Of course, he's got a flashlight too. He carries that left-handed, and it's on a wrist thong—so it wouldn't interfere if he reached for the truncheon. That's reasonable: if you're close enough to use a truncheon, you don't need a flashlight to see; if you're far enough away to use a gun, you want a flashlight steady in your other hand. I think this watchman takes his job seriously.

He walked the length of my hedgerow. When he'd passed me, I leaned out through a root gap—just enough to see him from the waist up: the key ring, the epaulettes, the crook in his right arm. But I only saw the whole of him back-to, and it had to be a quick look. He's very sudden with his flashlight. He'll be nodding the light out on his boot toes, and then he'll whirl and paint a circle of light around himself.

It's been an hour and a half, and he's still out in the zoo, whirling his light. Perhaps he thinks the first-shift guard is careless. Perhaps, before he settles down to a normal watch, he has to make the place safe in his mind.

It must make the animals very nervous to have this disturbance every night. I see the watchman's sudden circles of light—often three or four times in the same area. And he's very aggressive about checking the locks. Just a tug won't do for him—he trembles the cages.

It's no wonder everyone's awake.

(CONTINUING:)
THE HIGHLY SELECTIVE AUTOBIOGRAPHY OF
SIEGFRIED JAVOTNIK: PRE-HISTORY I

Black Friday, March 11, 1938: at a little after half past five, the early morning priests are setting up the side altars in St. Stephen's and Kurt von Schuschnigg ducks in for a very brief, clear prayer. He's been up and en route to the Chancellery ever since Secretary of Security Skubl phoned him about the Germans closing the border at Salzburg and withdrawing all customs officials. Skubl also mentioned a German troop build-up from Reichenhall to Passau. And at the Chancellery, Schuschnigg finds the sour telegram from Austria's consulate general in Munich: LEO IS READY TO TRAVEL. All this before it's light outside, and before all of the morning's German press has been telegraphed to Vienna for Kurt von Schuschnigg's perusal. They have just a smattering of German sentiment to go on, though it should be enough. The Nazi news agency, D.N.B., claims that hammer-and-sickle flags have been hoisted in Vienna, and that the frenzied citizens have been yelling, "Heil Schuschnigg! Heil Moskau!" in the same breath. D.N.B. says that the Führer might be forced to make an "anti-Bolshevik crusade," on Austria's behalf. Poor Kurt von Schuschnigg must confess that this is particularly creative reporting of his plebiscite. He gets off an urgency phonecall to the British minister, who in turn cables Lord Halifax in London—to inquire if Britain will choose sides. Then Schuschnigg watches the first light, glancing through the sooty windows of the Hofburg showrooms—seeking out the rare old jewels and gold within.

The slow March light is lifting windowshades in drowsy St. Veit, and Zahn Glanz is crowing a welcome to the dawn. It's good for Zahn that it's early, and there's little traffic, because he's not being very consistent at the intersections. The cobblestones are giving him a headache, so he drives in the tram tracks wherever that's possible; he doesn't quite get the taxi to fit in the tracks, but he can usually manage to have one wheel side unjarred.

He's approaching the Inner City on Währinger Strasse when he stops to pick up a fare. A head-down man, nodding out of an early Mass in the Votivkirche, steps into the backseat. Zahn is off with him before the man can properly close the door.

"Cawk! Cawk!" says Zahn. "Where to?"

And the man, smacking chicken feathers off his trousers, says, "Is this a taxi or a barnyard?" And looks up at Zahn's bent beak in the rear-view mirror, and sees the spotty-feathered shoulders hunched over the wheel. And rolls out the door he hasn't quite closed.

"Better not leave the door open," says Zahn, but he's looking at an empty backseat awhirl with feathers.

Zahn turns up Kolingasse and stops; he shambles out of the taxi and struts back to the corner of Währinger, where he sees the man limping to the curb. The man must think he's seen a seraph, being so fresh out of Mass.

So Zahn springs back to his taxi, startles a café-owner rolling up his awning to watch whatever weak sun there is. The man lets go of the awning crank; the awning comes rumpling down over him, and the crank spins madly, cracking the backs of his hands.

"Oh, I'm sure up early this morning," says Zahn, and gives a fierce cock call from his taxi's running board. Somehow Zahn's got chicken feathers, cocks' crowing and eagles all confused.

Zahn does feel something is amiss, and decides it's that he's clawless. Whatever bird he is, he should have claws. So he stops at a butcher shop in the Kohlmarkt and buys a whole chicken. Then he crunches the legs off and fastens them in the mesh of his chainmail, just under the wide, forearm-length cuffs. The claws curl over his own hands; as he drives, they scratch him.

But butchers are notoriously unimaginative types, and the Kohlmarkt butcher is no exception. He calls Radio Johannesgasse to report a man in a birdsuit, inexpertly driving a taxi.

"What sort of man, you tell me," says the butcher, "would buy a whole chicken and crunch off the legs on the edge of his taxi's door? Just so—opening and shutting the door on his poor chicken's legs until he had them sawed through. And he threw away the chicken!" says the butcher, who thinks the people should be warned.

But Radio Johannesgasse already has been informed of something feathery—from a worried cab-company man, who phoned after someone was arrested on Währinger Strasse for blasphemous rantings and general disturbances concerning a possible seraph. So the word is out on Zahn, all right. The only one who's heard it on the radio and isn't interested is Kurt von Schuschnigg, for whom this day has too much time.

The next thing to befall poor Kurt is Nazi Cabinet member Seyss-Inquart, reporting a most unreasonable phonecall from a diatribing Goebbels in Munich. Seyss has been told to seize control of the Cabinet and see to it that Schuschnigg calls off the plebiscite. Seyss-Inquart is almost apologetic about it; perhaps he's not sure if things aren't happening a bit too fast. He and Schuschnigg go along to find President Miklas, after Schuschnigg—or someone near him—has sent a Chancellery pageboy to pick up the fallen mass of bed sheets that is interfering with traffic in the Michaelerplatz.

And Grandfather Marter has again decided that the head librarian will stay at home; in fact, since he heard the first radio report of the taxi-driving, birdlike creature, my grandfather has not left the window. Grandmother brings him his coffee, and Hilke watches the Schwindgasse with him. The sun isn't down on the street yet. It's an occasional sun, anyway, and it strikes, when it does, only the topmost stories and roofs across the street—and is impressive only when it catches the brass ball cupped in the palms of a cupid atop the Bulgarian embassy. There are cupids all over, but only the Bulgarians gave theirs a brass ball to hold; or someone else gave it, perhaps to insult the Bulgarians. Anyway, it's the only embassy building on the Schwindgasse, and it's given Grandfather something to watch while he's waiting for Zahn. Grandfather has noticed that even the Bulgarians are making and receiving phonecalls today. A short, heavy man, who must have hair all over himself, has been stooped at the phone in the front-office window, all the while that Grandfather has been standing watch.

When Grandfather hears the latest news brief of the Kohlmarkt butcher's experience, he asks Grandmother for a tea with rum. The Kohlmarkt butcher has an eye for detail. Radio Johannesgasse broadcasts a picture of a madman in a birdsuit, reeking of cognac, driving a taxi with JA! SCHUSCHNIGG! chalked on the hood.

If Schuschnigg pays any attention to this local affair now, it's only because he has enough imagination to see what the Nazi news agency could do with such an item: A secret Bolshevik society of terrorists disguised as birds, taking over the city's public transportation systems to prevent voters from participating in Schuschnigg's rigged plebiscite. But local disturbances can't seem very important to Schuschnigg now. He's having trouble enough convincing old President Miklas that Germany's demands for Seyss-Inquart should probably be carried out. And old Miklas, so long inactive, is picking this occasion to offer resistance.

Perhaps Schuschnigg has read the writing on the wall, on his early-morning stroll through the dark-paneled offices of the Chancellery; Maria Theresia and Aehrenthal, and the small wood-carved Madonna for the murdered Dollfuss: a gallery of Austria's deciders—always for or against Germany.

No such heavy thoughts are weighing down Zahn Glanz. He's a bird, and flying. He's coming up Goethegasse and almost doesn't stop for the tram coming round the Opernring. It's unfortunate that Zahn makes such a display of last-minute stopping; the squeals attract the attention of some rowdy street workers, waiting for a drill-bit replacement. One of them must have just been near a radio, because the JA! SCHUSCHNIGG! on the hood appears to have special significance. It's lucky for Zahn, though, that they don't conceal their excitement and approach the taxi with stealth. Instead, they raise an awful cry and charge, and Zahn has time enough to feel quite threatened. He shoots the intersection with only one of the workers making it to the running board. And if that worker was pleased with himself—if he's been leering in the window at Zahn—he's not very happy when Zahn reaches the Schillerplatz and startles a drove of pigeons, dung-dropping their terror in flight.

"Cawk!" Zahn screams to them, birds of a feather. And the worker is convinced he should be waiting for the drill bit with his friends, and not hanging on to the handle of the locked door, and beating his head on the rolled-up window—receiving, only once and briefly, a terrible glance from the empty eyeholes of the armored eagle.

Round the Schillerplatz and through a close arch of the Academy of Graphic Arts, the worker flattens himself against the taxi and hears the echo of some awful wail he doesn't recognize as his own.

Zahn Glanz, in the clear for a moment, kindly slows his

taxi and aims for the last archway of the Academy of Graphic Arts. Then he opens his door. Not too hard; he just lets it swing out, carrying the surprised, clutching worker off the running board. The worker dangles, watching the arch approach; then he lets go of the handle, and Zahn closes the door. In his rear-view mirror, he can see the worker back-pedaling and almost catching up with his own momentum. But he topples over a little foolishly, and somersaults out of Zahn's mirror.

Zahn decides that alley travel is advisable, since he's not sure who's after him. But he runs out of gas in the alley alongside the Atelier Theater. His taxi comes to rest just under the billboard portrait of dark-eyed Katrina Marek, who's been a sensational Antigone for the past two weeks.

"Pardon me," says Zahn, because he bumps Katrina when he opens the door. If it even crosses his mind that it's strange of the actress Katrina Marek to be dressed in a sheet for hailing taxis, Zahn doesn't give it much thought. He's dressed none too smartly himself.

And once again my grandfather is troubled by what he calls his far-sightedness.

"Hilke," he says. "Would you bring me my coat? I think I'll be going out." And although there are two possible entrances to the Schwindgasse, Grandfather settles his gaze on one.

Meanwhile, the eagle is still preferring alley travel; he swoops along the garbage routes, and it's not until he emerges in the Rilke Platz that he realizes he's in my mother's neighborhood. Zahn feels a little weighed down from all his swooping under chainmail. He boards the hindmost platform of a Gusshausstrasse tram, just starting up from behind the technical high school. Zahn thinks it's wise to stay outside the tramcar, but the tram picks up a little speed, and the eagle's pieplates begin to clap. The conductor squints down the aisle; he thinks a piece of the tram is loose and flapping. Zahn hangs back on the handrail and takes one step down the platform stairs. Someone points at him from a pastry-shop window. Zahn rides the platform stairs alone; his tail feathers learn to fly.

And he'd have been all right that way, for at least the block or two farther he had to go, except that a throng of technical-high-school students, sitting in the last car, decide to come out on the platform for a smoke.

"Morning, boys," the eagle says, and they don't say a

word. So Zahn asks, "You haven't seen Katrina Marek this morning, have you? She's wearing her sheet, you know."

And one of the student mechanics says, "You wouldn't be that birdman, would you?"

"What birdman?" says another.

"What birdman?" says Zahn.

"The one who's terrorizing people," the student says, stepping a little closer, and one of his friends remembers, then; he steps up closer too.

Zahn is wishing he had his head off so he'd have better peripheral vision—and know, if he were to jump, whether he'd hit a hitching post or a litter basket.

"It looks like my stop coming up," says Zahn, only the tram isn't slowing any. He puts one foot down another platform step, and leans out on the handrail.

"Get him!" shouts the closest student, and brings a lunch pail down on Zahn's hand. But the eagle flies off backwards, losing one of his claws.

Zahn makes an awful clatter, and his pieplates spark on the sidewalk; several little fastening wires gouge the eagle's back. But he is less than a block away from my mother's, and hasn't time to grieve over the pieplates spinning and rolling free down the sidewalk and along the curb.

My grandfather says, "You can shut off the damn radio, Hilke"—having just heard the news brief of the birdman's brutal kidnapping of a worker from an Opernring street crew.

Hilke already has her coat, and she puts her scarf on— loose around her neck. She follows Grandfather to the staircase landing outside the apartment. Grandfather looks up the marble and iron-spiral stairs, tuning his ear to the opening of letter slots and doors. Then he leads Hilke downstairs and through the long lobby to the great door with the foot-length crank-open handle. Hilke peers up and down the street, but my grandfather looks only left— to the corner at Argentinierstrasse. He watches a man who's tamping his pipe bowl with his thumb and standing back-to Argentinier.

Then the man turns round to the corner and ducks his head, thinking he hears the approaching wing beat of a hundred pigeons. And Zahn Glanz, banking on the corner, topples the man and jars himself off balance down a short flight of steps and against the door of someone's cellar

cubby. So that Zahn is below sidewalk level and altogether
out of sight when the man picks himself up and shakes the
pipe tobacco out of his hair; and looks both ways along
the street—and seeing nothing at all, bolts down Argentinierstrasse with a wing beat all his own.

Grandfather waves. Zahn is crawling up to the sidewalk
when a bustling little laundress opens the cellar-cubby
door. She jousts the eagle with a sock stretcher, and
prances lively up to the sidewalk; she's going to give the
bird a clout, but Zahn lays his limp, cold remaining claw
against her indignant bosom. The laundress drops to her
knees, convinced the thing is real.

Zahn is winging to my mother. He chooses to fly the
last few yards and nearly clears a parked car, getting his
beak caught on the aerial and ripping off his whole head.
Grandfather gets a grip under the pieplates and clatters
Zahn through the great lobby door. Hilke scoops the eagle's head under her arm and covers it with her scarf.
Downstreet, the laundress still kneels on the sidewalk, hiding her face in her hands; fanny-up, she seems to be expecting some ungentlemanly visit from a god.

My mother picks up feathers and bits of down; fussily
she gets them all, from the parked car to Grandmother's
kitchen. Where Zahn slumps against the oven—an almost-
plucked bird, wrapped in tinfoil and ready to bake.

"Zahn," says Grandfather. "Where did you leave the
taxi?"

"With Katrina Marek," Zahn says.

"Where?" asks Grandfather.

"I ran out of gas right under her nose," Zahn says.

"How far from here, Zahn?" says Grandfather.

"She was wearing her sheet," Zahn says.

"Did anyone see you leave the taxi?" Grandfather asks.

"The proletariat," says Zahn, "they're rising up to de-
stroy the city."

"Did anyone see where you left it, Zahn?" Grandfather
shouts.

"Katrina Marek," says Zahn. "I should go back for
her."

"Put the poor boy to bed," says Grandmother. "He's totally addled. Get him out of that costume and put him to
bed."

"Jesus," says Zahn. "It's been one long day." But my

mother is too kind to tell him that the morning's just beginning.

And although I'm sure that Schuschnigg already has
guessed the outcome, the day must seem long to him too.
It's only nine-thirty when Hitler makes a phonecall and
delivers a personal ultimatum to the poor Chancellor: the
plebiscite must be postponed for at least two weeks, or
Germany will invade Austria this evening. So Schuschnigg
and the faithful Skubl confer: the class of 1915 Austrian
reservists are called to colors, supposedly to keep order on
the upcoming election day; the Socony Vacuum Oil Company of Austria is asked to supply extra fuel to motorize
possible troop movements. And Chancellor Schuschnigg
gloomily notices that by noontime the city is preparing a
second day of celebrations for Schuschnigg's Austria.
Leaflets for the plebiscite are floating down the streets.
The sun is very warm and bright at noon. The people don't
seem to notice the increase of militia on the fringe of every little fest. And the militia, too, are tapping their boots
to waltzes and patriotic marches, from radios pointed out
the open windows.

Schuschnigg makes his third phone call to Mussolini, but
the Duce is still *unavailable*. Someone sends another message to France.

The noontime report on Radio Johannesgasse is somewhat vague with the worldwide news. It's about the
Salzburg border being closed, and the uncounted troop
build-up; a rhino assembly of tanks inching forward in the
night, a daze of headlights peering across the border, and
in the morning, a screen of smoke hanging above the German forests—from a million cigarettes lit and puffed once
and put out on signal. And something about how Radio
Berlin is broadcasting the news of yesterday's and today's
Bolshevik riots in Vienna, where there haven't been any rioting Bolsheviks since the great siege and capture of the
Schlingerhof Palace in 1934.

The local news is more detailed. The kidnapped worker
has been found; he was beaten off the birdman's speeding
taxi and miraculously escaped with scratches. The birdman, the worker estimates, is at least seven feet tall. That
was in the Schillerplatz. The birdman was then spotted on
a Gusshausstrasse tram; a brave group of technical-high-
school students tried to capture him but were overpow-
ered. And lastly, in the Schwindgasse, the birdman assault-

ed Frau Drexa Neff, laundress. Frau Neff maintains the creature is most certainly not human, and she didn't see which way it went after it attacked her. Authorities in the nearby Belvedere Gardens are searching the shrubs and trees. And there is still no sign of the apparently abandoned taxi, with JA! SCHUSCHNIGG! on the hood.

But my grandfather knows where to look. By checking the theater listings and discovering where Katrina Marek has been astounding as Antigone, and by realizing that the Atelier Theater is neatly between the castaway worker at the Schillerplatz and the eagle's first taxiless appearance on the Gusshausstrasse tram. So Grandfather empties a two-quarter cookie crock and dampens a sponge; he puts a funnel in his overcoat pocket. Zahn doesn't have a key on him, so Grandfather hopes the eagle left it in the ignition. Then Hilke puts the sponge in her pocketbook, and Grandfather carries the cookie crock under his arm, hefting it up as if it were full; they leave the Schwindgasse apartment, trusting my grandmother will tend to the undisturbed sleep of Zahn Glanz, laid to rest in Hilke's bed.

It's unfortunate that Kurt von Schuschnigg is of a more compromising nature than my grandfather. At a little after two-thirty, Schuschnigg bows to one of Germany's ultimatums. He asks that Seyss-Inquart phone Göring in Berlin and convey the Chancellor's decision to postpone the plebiscite; Seyss-Inquart also tells Göring that Schuschnigg has not resigned his Chancellorship. Grandfather, of course, could tell Kurt a thing or two about the insatiable nature of Field Marshal Göring's appetite.

But my grandfather isn't available for consultation. He's walking my mother out of the *Tankstelle* on the Karlsplatz, with a cookie crock of gasoline under his arm—just three-quarters full, so he can walk without slopping. My mother is smiling more than a family-outing smile, because Grandfather has told the *Tankstelle* man that the cookie crock is a surprise for an uncle, who eats too much and is always running out of gas.

They cross the Getreidemarkt, whispering family secrets; they slow down to look at the billboards on the Atelier Theater.

"Oh, look," says Grandfather, reading matinee times.

And Hilke says, "I think there's more around the side." And turns up the alley, trying not to be startled by the taxi squatting under Katrina Marek's nose. "Come on,"

she says to Grandfather. "It's really the best picture I've
seen of her."

"Just a minute," says Grandfather, still staring at the
matinee schedule. But he moves along, reading, and darts
a look up and down the street; he sticks his hand round
the corner of the alley and waggles a finger at my mother.
She takes the damp sponge out of her pocketbook and
rubs JA! SCHUSCHNIGG! off the taxi's hood. Then she stands
back to look at Katrina Marek, and moves casually round
the taxi, here and there whisking away a flake of chalk.
Then she comes back out of the alley and tugs my grandfather's arm.

"Come on, go look," she says. "It's a wonderful picture
of her."

"You read this," says Grandfather. "Would you just
read this? Isn't that amazing?" And he moves around the
corner, pointing back to the matinee schedule. Hilke tosses
her head, gets a look both ways; she shakes her bracelet
for Grandfather.

From the alley, Grandfather says, "A real beauty,
you're right." And removes the gas cap his first trip round
the taxi; inserts the funnel while leaning against a fender,
gazing fondly at Katrina Marek. "What do you think of
that schedule?" he calls, and my mother jingles her
bracelet again. Grandfather empties the cookie crock into
the gas tank. On his way out of the alley, he passes the
driver's-side window and is delighted to see the key in the
ignition.

"This is truly incredible," says Hilke, pointing to the
schedule. She takes Grandfather's arm, and together they
walk on, past the alley and up a block. Then Grandfather
makes her a bow, kisses her cheek and hands her the
cookie crock. My mother returns the kiss and goes straight
on, while Grandfather turns up a side block. He comes
out behind the theater and waltzes into the alley, facing
the taxi head-on.

My mother tosses herself along, throwing back her hair
for the storefront windows to see; she cuddles the cookie
crock against her high, light bosom; she sees herself,
transparent, passing through racks of dresses, rows of
shoes, swivel displays of cakes and pastries; through the
Kaffeehaus windows too, she sees herself lift faces from
the rims of cups—and pass indelibly, even if transparent,
through the mind of everyone who's looking out when my

mother looks in. She imagines Zahn Glanz is watching her too, in his dreams brought on by her girlishly perfumed bed. But she's not in such a trance that she forgets her street corners; she slows at Faulmanngasse and Mühl, and hesitates until she recognizes the driver before she hails the taxi coming along.

"Where to?" says Grandfather, chin on chest, and waits until they're under way before he says, "Pretty damn slick father you've got, haven't you? Went all the way down Elisabethstrasse for a full tank of gas, and picked you off this corner just as you got here. I could see you coming. You didn't even have to wait. Some sense of timing, I have."

Hilke tugs her hair around her ears; she laughs a bright, adoring laugh, and Grandfather, nodding his head, laughs along. "Pretty slick, pretty slick—a flawless job, I must say."

Anyone watching them, bobbing up and down in the getaway taxi, must be thinking: Now what could an old man like that have to say, to make such a pretty girl laugh?

My grandfather gets things done—delicately, and with fanfare.

So does Göring—but with much less fanfare, and no delicacy at all. Just twenty minutes after receiving the phonecall of Schuschnigg's first concession, Göring phones back. He tells Seyss-Inquart that Schuschnigg's behavior is unacceptable and that the Chancellor and his Cabinet are asked to resign; that President Miklas is asked to nominate Seyss-Inquart for the Chancellorship. Göring has such an odd way of putting things. He promises that Austria will have German military *aid*, if the Schuschnigg government cannot change itself promptly.

It's a most embarrassed Seyss-Inquart who breaks this news to Kurt von Schuschnigg, and Schuschnigg takes his next-to-last step backward. At three-thirty, or only half an hour after Göring's phonecall, Schuschnigg simply places the resignation of his entire government in President Miklas' hands. And here's an arbitrary matter: it would have looked so much nicer, after the war, if Schuschnigg had held out an hour longer—until Lord Halifax's message was conveyed from the British embassy in Vienna; how His Majesty's government wouldn't want to be taking the responsibility of advising the Chancellor to expose his country to dangers against which His Majesty's government would be unable to guarantee protection.

It's a matter of giving in when you're abandoned, or abandoning yourself when you know you're going to be abandoned. But after the fact, fine hairs are indeed split.

At three-thirty, Schuschnigg doesn't need anything formal to know he's been abandoned. He can anticipate: that Lord Halifax will evade; that French chargé d'affaires in Rome, M. Blondel, will be told by Count Ciano's private secretary that if the reason for his visit is Austria, he needn't bother to come; and that Mussolini will never be reached by phone—that he's hiding somewhere, listening to it ring and ring.

So Schuschnigg leaves Federal President Miklas with the decision for a new Chancellor. Old Miklas has been this route before. Under the Nazi *Putsch* of four years ago—poor Dollfuss murdered in the sanctity of his Chancellery office, and a courtyard of toughs below, waiting to sway the crowd whichever way the limbo turned; then Miklas turned to Kurt von Schuschnigg. Now Miklas has until seven-thirty. So the old President goes looking for a Chancellor.

There's faithful police head Skubl, but Skubl declines; he's known in Berlin, and his nomination would be a further irritation to Hitler. There's Doktor Ender, authority on constitutional law, who feels his need to be Chancellor already has been satisfied, as leader of a previous government. And General Schilhawsky, Inspector General of the Armed Forces, says he's an officer, not a politician. So Miklas finds no takers.

Pity that he didn't know my grandfather, who would probably enjoy another intrigue.

Grandfather—who's parked and locked the taxi in the lot at Karl's Church—walks Hilke and the cookie crock home. Ignoring Grandmother's protest, they peek in on Zahn Glanz. Peeled out of his pieplates, disarmed of his last claw, the eagle's feet protrude from the little girl's bed. A chicken feather laces his ear, a pink pouf makes him cozy; he sleeps midst the knickknackery and troll kingdom of my mother's room. Hilke tucks him in again, and he sleeps through supper; he sleeps right up to the seven o'clock report on Radio Johannesgasse. Grandfather can't let Zahn miss the news.

The postponement of the plebiscite is announced, and

the resignation of the entire Cabinet—all except Seyss-In-quart, who's staying on in his office as Minister of Interior.

Zahn Glanz is not fully recovered; when he goes word-lessly back to bed, old Miklas is sitting all alone in his of-fice of the Federal President, watching the clock run by seven-thirty. Field Marshal Göring's ultimatum time has expired, and Seyss-Inquart is still not Chancellor of Austria. Miklas refuses to make it *official*.

Then Kurt von Schuschnigg performs the last and most conclusive leap backward of his career—an executive or-der to General Schilhawsky to withdraw the Austrian Army from the German border; to offer no resistance; to watch, or perhaps wave, from behind the River Enns. The Austrian Army has only forty-eight hours of steady-fire ammunition anyway. What would be the point of so much blood? Someone phones from Salzburg to say the Germans are crossing the border; it's not true, it's a false alarm, but it's another fine hair to be split and Schusch-nigg doesn't wait for verification. He steps back.

At eight o'clock, he asks Radio Johannesgasse for a na-tionwide broadcasting privilege. The microphone wires are strung up the banister of the grand staircase in the Ball-hausplatz. And Grandfather wakes up Zahn again.

Schuschnigg is all sadness and no reproach. He speaks of yielding to force; he begs no resistance. He does say there's no truth to the Berlin radio reports of worker revo-lutions terrorizing Austria. Kurt von Schuschnigg's Austria isn't terrorized; it's forced to be sad. And in the whole show, the only sentiment that touches Grandfather's skulk-ing heart is the rude outburst of the Commissioner for Cultural Propaganda—the old cripple Hammerstein-Equord, who grabs the microphone when the Chancellor is finished, but before the technicians can pull the contact plug. "Long live Austria!" he burbles. "Today I am ashamed to be German."

It's a sad thing for Grandfather to hear. Even tough old cripples like Hammerstein-Equord consider *German* as something in the blood, and look at Germans as a *race* to which Austria must belong.

But my grandfather has never looked at things that way. "Pack, Muttie," he says. "There's a taxi full of gas just around the corner."

And my mother takes the arm of Zahn Glanz; she holds

to it tighter than she's ever held a thing alive, and waits
for Zahn to raise his eyes to hers; her fingers on his arm
are talking: Hilke Marter will not let go, will not pack
herself or any of her things, until this eagle can unfuddle
enough to make up his mind and speak it clear.

While Miklas, with his mind made up and all alone, refuses to accept Schuschnigg's personal resignation and is
still speaking of resistance—without a single soldier of the
Austrian Army between the German border and the River
Enns. In the Federal President's office, Lieutenant General
Muff, German military attaché to Vienna, is explaining
that the reported border-crossing by German troops is a
false alarm. But the troops *will* cross, says Muff, if Miklas
doesn't make Seyss-Inquart the Chancellor. Perhaps old
Miklas is less futile in his resistance than it appears; he
may even recognize Hitler's apparent need to legalize the
takeover. But the patient Muff keeps after him: Does the
Federal President know that all the provinces are now in
the hands of local Austrian Nazi officials? Does the President know that Salzburg and Linz have given the seals of
office to Nazi party members there? Has the President
even looked in the corridor outside his office, where the
Vienna Nazi youth are lighting cigarettes and jeering over
the balcony of the grand staircase; they're curling smoke
rings round the head of the wood-carved Madonna in
mourning for poor Dollfuss.

At eleven o'clock the patient Muff is still conjuring
images. Seyss-Inquart has revised his list for his proposed
Cabinet; Miklas, in his tenth hour of resistance, is telling
an anecdote about Maria Theresia.

At eleven o'clock my grandfather is arbitrating the matter of silver or china. The china is breakable, and less
salable. It's the china that stays in Vienna, the silver that
goes. And whether Zahn Glanz will go or stay is still being
perceived through my mother's touch.

"It doesn't necessarily mean they'll come marching in,"
says Zahn. "And where can you go in my taxi anyway?"

"It *does* mean they'll come marching in," Grandfather
says, "and we'll take your taxi to my brother's. He's the
postmaster of Kaprun."

"That's still Austria," says Zahn.

"It's the cities that won't be safe," Grandfather says.
"The Kitzbühler Alps are very rural."

"Rural enough to starve, is it?" asks Zahn.

"Librarians put away *some* money," Grandfather tells him.

"And how will you get it out of your bank," Zahn asks, "in the middle of the night?"

Grandfather says, "If you decide to stay awhile, Zahn, I could endorse my bankbook to you and have you post a draft."

"To your brother the postmaster," says Zahn. "Of course."

"Why can't we just leave in the morning?" Hilke asks. "Why can't Zahn come with us?"

"He can, if he wants to," says Grandfather. "Then I'd stay until morning, and Zahn can drive you."

"Why can't we *all* go in the morning?" Grandmother asks. "Maybe in the morning, we'll find it's going to be all right."

"A lot of people will be leaving in the morning," says Grandfather. "And Zahn hasn't checked in his taxi for a while. Do you think they might start missing your taxi, Zahn?"

"The taxi better go tonight," Zahn says.

"But if Zahn stays," says Hilke, "how can he get to Kaprun?"

"Zahn doesn't have to stay if he doesn't want to," Grandfather says.

"And why would he want to?" Hilke asks.

"Oh, I don't know," says Zahn. "Maybe to watch what happens for a day or so."

And my mother keeps taking the pulse in his arm. Hilke Marter is speaking through her fingers again: Oh, Zahn, there's nobody outside, there's nobody there at all.

But a little before midnight, in the Ballhaus courtyard, there are forty toughs from SS Standarte 89, of which the assassin Otto Planetta was a member. Perhaps it's then—when Miklas sees them—that the old President shares a bit of Schuschnigg's vision for the slaughter that could be Vienna's. Perhaps it's then that Miklas droops down his chins to Muff the middleman.

Zahn Glanz must feel like a middleman now, with my grandfather's bankbook fat in his pocket. He makes the walk from Schwindgasse to Karl's Church, my mother still fastened to his arm. At the Gusshausstrasse corner they're forced to hop off the curb.

Arms locked, in step, five boys from an alphabetized

meeting of Vienna's Nazi youth come shouldering along.
It must have been a meeting of the S's from the fourth
district. Freshly sewn, their nametags glow: P. Schnell,
perhaps, and G. Schritt, with F. Samt, J. Spalt, R. Steg
and O. Schrutt—just to name some ordinary names.

Zahn doesn't say a word to them; my mother has shut
off his pulse. He unlocks the taxi in the Karl's Church lot
and drives back to the Schwindgasse another way. It
wouldn't do to have the cruising youth club see them so
suddenly motorized. Zahn drives lights-out up the
Schwindgasse. My grandfather opens both sides of the
great lever-handled lobby door, and Zahn backs over the
sidewalk and inside the apartment building.

It's late, but the upstairs apartments can't be sleeping
very soundly tonight. They certainly must hear the motor
before Zahn shuts it off. The garbage truck—do they
think?—making some awful collection that can't keep till
morning? But no one brings their garbage downstairs.
There are no frightened faces over the spiraling banister—only juts of light, from letter slots and doors ajar.
Grandfather waits for the last, stealthy ray to leave the
stairs; then he stations my grandmother by the banister,
and has her listen for the cranking of a phone.

It's one o'clock Saturday morning when they begin to
load the taxi.

The Seventh Zoo Watch:
Tuesday, June 6, 1967, @ 2:15 a.m.

Some of the animals are dropping off to sleep. A certain
nervous element is still in this zoo, all right, but the watchman's gone back to the Small Mammal house, and some
of us feel like sleeping.

When the watchman first went inside, I felt like a short
nap myself. I heard the Assorted Antelopes lying down in
soft collapses. I really thought I'd sleep awhile, and I was
snuggling myself around the roots when the Small Mammal House changed color. That's just the way it happened.
Over the tops of cages, the glow was white and it changed
to blood-purple. The watchman had switched on the infrared.

There they all are again, with the putting-out of one
light and the switching-on of one they can't see; there they

are, with their distorted view of how quickly the night falls.

So I went lurking along my hedges, and even out of cover, for a moment, to where I could see the door.

Why did the watchman do it? Does he like looking at them when they're awake? Then it's a bit selfish of him to end their sleep to please himself; he should come during the regular zoo hours, if it matters so much to him. But I don't think that's it.

Especially now that I've had a better look at this watchman, I don't think that's his reasoning at all. What I mean is, I went to have a closer look. I wanted a look at that little room.

I was all set up behind a cage. I couldn't see very far into the cage; the moonlight caught just the outer edges. But I was sure it was a part of the indoor-outdoor Monkey Complex. I was peering down the violet corridor of the Small Mammal House when two very rough hands grabbed my head and jerked me against the bars. I couldn't get free, but I was able to turn my head in the thing's hands. I faced the hairless, bright red chest of the male gelada baboon—powerful, savage bandit from the highland plains of Abyssinia.

"I'm here to help you," I whispered. But it sneered.

"No noise now," I pleaded, but its thumbs sank in the hollows behind my ears; the thing was putting me to sleep with its grip. I reached into my jacket and handed it my meerschaum.

"Would you like to try a pipe?" I asked. It looked. One forearm went a little limp on my shoulder.

"Go on, take it," I whispered, hoping I wouldn't be forced to ram the pipestem up one of its flaring nostrils.

It took; one hand peeled off my neck and covered my fist, pipe and all. Then its other hand came delicately poking for the pipe between my fingers. I lunged my head back, but I couldn't free my fist; the gelada baboon shoved the pipe in its mouth and grabbed hold of my arm with both hands. I wasn't a match for it, but I got my feet against the bars and pushed back with all my weight. I fell out of its reach, away from the cage, and the gelada baboon, munching my meerschaum and spitting it out on the cage floor, knew it had been fooled. It made enormous noises.

It whooped and raced round the cage, leaping off the

bars and stamping in the water trough. The indoor-outdoor Monkey Complex understood: a baboon had been
outwitted by a lower-species creature.

If there had been animals finally dropping off to sleep, I
apologize. They awoke to a clamor of general primate
noisemaking; the Big Cats roared back; bears grumbled;
all over the zoo was a skitter of hooves, dashing from
fence line to fence line. And I was stumbling backward
down the path, heading for my hedges again, when I saw
the watchman round the end of his lavender hallway.

It surprised me. I expected the infrared to go out; I expected the guard, camouflaged and crawling belly-down,
combat-style, to sneak up on me from behind with his
truncheon. But he stood and gaped down the blood-col-
ored aisle, frozen and aghast; he would have made an easy
target.

I was safe behind my hedgerow before I saw his light
come whirling down the path; when his light began to
whirl, the zoo was suddenly hushed. He spun from bush to
bush, and cage to cage. When he passed the spot where
I'd been assaulted, I expected trouble. But the gelada baboon must have gathered together the bits of my pipe and
slinked through the back-wall door, losing itself in the
parapets and split-level avenues of the Monkey Complex.

The guard seemed to know that this was where it started, though. He stopped and shone his light, from the corners of the cages to the treetops all around him. He
timidly kicked the cage where the gelada baboon had
been. "Was it you?" he cried, in a high lisping voice.

The zoo was wide-awake and silent; a hundred breaths
were being held, and lost in little pieces.

On past the Monkey Complex the watchman skittered—and stopped again at the corner of my hedgerow,
the diluted blood-light from the Small Mammal House
faintly reaching him on the path. He whirled for us, shaking his light. "What happened?" he shouted.

Something with hooves took a false step, caught itself
and held its ground. The watchman's light leapt down to
the Australians' area, struck across the sky. The guard
fired his light up a nearby tree, seeking leopards or ocelots
that might have been lurking there, ready to pounce. "All
of you!" he screamed. "You go to sleep now!"

His own flashlight, tilted from his hip and pointed overhead, illuminated him for me. The watchman was lighting up himself.

I saw him head-on, his old face lightly tinged by infrared—with a rich magenta scar, sharp and thin, from the top of his gray crew-cut head, past his ear to his left nostril, where it plunges through the gum. A part of his upper lip is tucked in by it, and appears as a slightly raised hackle—baring all the scarlet of his upper left gum. It was no proper duel that caused it. Perhaps a foil gone berserk.

Head-on, I saw him—that face, and that remarkable uniform-front. It's not only that he hasn't, somehow, lost his epaulettes; his uniform still has a nametag. O Schrutt, he is—or was once. And if it's not still O. Schrutt, inside that old uniform, why would he have left the nametag on? O. SCHRUTT, with the period very faded. What an edge it seems to give you—to find out someone's name before they've even seen your face. This watchman is O. Schrutt.

Strange, but that's a name I've used before; I've had O. Schrutt on my lips before. It's possible I knew an O. Schrutt; surely I've known one Schrutt or another in my time. Vienna is full of Schrutt families. And I also believe I've used this name in one fiction or another. That's it, I'm sure; I've made up an O. Schrutt before.

But this O. Schrutt is real; he searches the upper tree limbs for ocelots and such. Animals don't sleep when O. Schrutt is on the prowl, and neither do I.

I can't sleep now, although O Schrutt's gone back to his Small Mammal House. He retreated from my hedges, pretending lack of interest; casually backing down the path—he would then erupt, in circles, exposing each lurking bit of the darkness around him. O. Schrutt makes vowel sounds when he whirls his light. "*Aah!*" he cries, and "*Oooh!*"—surprising the shapes that hide just out of his beam.

Now the animals are dropping off; groans, stretches, sighs, slumps; a brief, shrill-voiced argument in the Monkey Complex, and someone swings a trapeze against an echoing wall. But I can't sleep.

When O. Schrutt emerges for another round, I want to get inside his blood-lit den and see just what it is that makes old O. turn on the infrared. One reason, I can guess: O. Schrutt is not a man who likes to be seen. Even by animals.

(CONTINUING:)

THE HIGHLY SELECTIVE AUTOBIOGRAPHY OF
SIEGFRIED JAVOTNIK: PRE-HISTORY I

Saturday, March 12, 1938: 1:00 A.M. at the Chancellery on the Ballhausplatz. Miklas has given in. Seyss-Inquart is Chancellor of Austria.

Seyss is in conference with Lieutenant General Muff. They want to make certain that Berlin knows everything is in control, and that the German border troops no longer think of crossing.

Poor Seyss-Inquart, he should know better:

If you bring lions to your home,
They'll want to stay for dinner.

But about two o'clock, it's Muff who phones Berlin and attempts the put-off. Perhaps he says, "It's all right, you can take your armies home now; it's all right, we've got our politics just like yours now; you don't have to hang around our border now, because it's really all right here."

And at two-thirty, after a frantic bicker between the War Office, the Foreign Office and the Reich Chancellery, Hitler's personal adjutant is asked to wake up the Führer.

Wake up any man at two-thirty in the morning, says Grandfather—even a reasonable man—and see what you get.

At two-thirty, Zahn Glanz is pressing my mother against the great lobby door, and Grandmother still hasn't heard anyone cranking a phone. Grandfather is bringing out the little things now: a crate of kitchenware, a carton of food and wine, a box of winter scarves and hats, and the crocheted bedspreads.

"If not *all* the china," says Grandmother, "maybe just the gravyboat?"

"No, Muttie," says Grandfather, "just what we need"—and makes the last check of Hilke's room. He packs the eaglesuit in the bottom of a winter army duffel.

In the kitchen, Grandfather empties the spice rack and tumbles all the little jars into the duffel, thinking that anything with enough spice can taste like food; then the radio.

Grandmother whispers from the staircase, "I just looked

in that car, and you're going to have a whole seat left empty."

"I know it," says Grandfather, thinking that there's room for one more who's leaving Vienna this morning before light.

It's not Schuschnigg. He leaves the Ballhausplatz, shakes hands with a tearful guard, ignores the Nazi salute from the file of citizens with swastika armbands.

The apologetic Seyss-Inquart drives Schuschnigg home —to ten weeks of house arrest and seven years in Gestapo prisons. All because Kurt von Schuschnigg has claimed he's committed no crime, and has refused the protection of the Hungarian embassy—has not joined the lines of monarchists, Jews, and some Catholics, who've been jamming up the Czech and Hungarian customs posts since midnight.

Grandfather finds the traffic is all going the other way. East. But Grandfather seems to feel that the Czechs and Hungarians will be next, and he doesn't want to have to move again; especially since then there would be no choice of moving east or west, but only east again—and that would be Russia. My grandfather has a picture of himself in nightmares: driven to the Black Sea, hunted by Cossacks and wild-haired Turks.

So driving west, he has no traffic going his way. St. Veit is dark, Hacking is darker. Only the lighted trams are still going in my grandfather's direction; the conductors wave swastika flags; at the stations, men with armbands and nametags are singing; someone *bloops* a one-note tuba.

"Is this the fastest route west?" my grandmother asks.

But Grandfather finds his way. He stops at the only unlighted henhouse in the outskirts of Hacking.

Ernst Watzek-Trummer has plucked and spitted three anonymous chickens over a low-coal fire on the henhouse floor. He gnaws at a bone on his roost. Grandfather and the patriot gather a pail of eggs and water, and hard-boil the eggs. Watzek-Trummer slaughters and plucks his best capon; it's thrown in the pail to boil. Then they hobble four prime hens and a stud champion rooster. Hilke bundles them violently together in a blanket; they go berserk on the floor under the backseat, against the long duffel which separates my mother from my grandmother. Ernst Watzek-Trummer takes the frontseat by Grandfather, each to his own side of the kitchenware crate—the egg

pail on the floor between them. Before they leave, Watzek-
Trummer sets his chickens loose and lights the henhouse
afire. In the glove compartment, he stows his best slaying-
cleaver.

The three anonymous chickens, spitted and charred, and
the freshly boiled capon, a bit underdone, are hacked and
ripped apart by Watzek-Trummer while Grandfather
drives. Ernst distributes chicken parts and hard-boiled eggs
while Grandfather turns south, through Gloggnitz and
Brück an der Mur, then west, and even a little north—
skirting mountains. He settles straight-ahead west at St.
Martin.

That's a long way from Vienna; that puts them almost
due south of Linz and nearly out of gas. The Mercedes,
used to taxi-living, bubbles up its radiator once—even
though it's March—and Ernst Watzek-Trummer has to cool
it off with lukewarm water from the egg pail.

My mother, in the backseat, doesn't say a word. She
feels she's still pinching Zahn Glanz's knee between her
own, and feels Zahn's despairing weight—making her back
take on the grain of the wood in the great lobby door.

Grandmother says, "The live chickens are smelling."

"We need gas," says Grandfather.

And in Pruggern they find there's still a celebration
going on. Grandfather rolls down his window and slows
for a policeman with his coat uniform open down his
chest—and somehow, a swastika armband stretched
enough to slip over his head and collar his neck. It's hard
to tell whether he put it on himself or had his head held
while someone else did the fitting.

Watzek-Trummer sets the glove compartment ajar and
holds it half shut with his knee; the slaying-cleaver winks
at him. My grandfather shoves a Nazi salute out the window. "I'm glad to see the whole country's not gone to bed
on such a night!" he says. But the policeman peers inside,
suspicious of the egg pail and scattered chickens.

Ernst Watzek-Trummer clomps my grandfather's back.
"His brother's got a seal of office in Salzburg now!" he
says. "You should see Vienna, and all the Bolsheviks we've
passed along the way—running east."

"Your brother's got a seal?" the policeman says.

"I may be sent to Munich!" says Grandfather gayly.

"Well, bless you," the policeman says. Watzek-Trummer
passes him a hard-boiled egg.

"Keep it up!" says Grandfather. "Keep the whole town up till dawn!"

"I wish I knew what was going on," the policeman says. "I mean, really, you know."

"Just keep it up," says Grandfather, and starts to pull ahead, then stops. "You wouldn't have any gas for us, would you?" he asks.

"There's things we could siphon," says the policeman. "You wouldn't have a hose?"

"Just happen to," Watzek-Trummer says.

They find a mail truck in the back buildings of a dark post-office lot. The policeman even does the sucking to get the siphon hose started, so they give him one of the capon's legs.

And my mother bears down on the imagined knee between her own; she rubs the window with the heel of her hand, as if it were a crystal ball to show her every safe, unfoolish move Zahn Glanz will make to get himself out of Vienna.

And the rest is mostly hearsay. That Hilke assumes Zahn finds out—almost as soon as befuddled Muff—the German border troops are crossing anyway. That, as a fact among few, Zahn does forward the draft of Grandfather's endorsed bankbook to the postmaster of Kaprun. That Zahn may have been reading Lennhoff's editorial about the German *Putsch* as late as noon, and then heard of the warm welcome Hitler was receiving in Linz—where the Führer marched to from the border to Passau, with soldiers and tanks, "to visit his mother's grave." And that Zahn, or someone like him, was the one who borrowed or stole the taxi which drove the criminal editor Lennhoff across the Hungarian border at Kittsee—having been turned away by the Czechs. If Zahn Glanz wasn't the driver, why did he never meet my mother in Kaprun? So he must have been the driver. And carried with him half of what I was at that time, because then I was, at best, only an idea of my mother's—half of which, if it didn't cross the Hungarian border at Kittsee, went wherever Zahn Glanz went.

And the rest is simply the seven-year affair of living in the protective shadow of my grandfather's brother, the postmaster of Kaprun, who kept his official post by joining the Nazi party, and because Kaprun was so small then, found the post not demanding, and the Nazi guise quite easy to maintain, except in the presence of the one youth club he supervised—some member of which suspected the postmaster's sincerity and caught him off guard in a poorly insulated latrine stall of the Hitler Youth's barracks, and roasted him with a lightweight SS flamethrower the postmaster had demonstrated just that morning. But that was when the war was almost over, and I don't think my mother or my grandparents suffered or starved so very much, especially owing to the food-hoarding genius of Ernst Watzek-Trummer, and the spices my grandfather wisely added to the last duffel packed in Vienna.

And the rest is all in Göring's telegram to Hitler in Linz, because Göring at his radio in Berlin heard of the Führer's triumphant welcome in that first city. Göring asked, "If the enthusiasm is so great, why not go the whole hog?" And Hitler certainly went ahead and did that. In Vienna alone, the first wave of Gestapo arrests took seventy-six thousand. (And if Zahn Glanz wasn't the driver of the editor's getaway taxi, wouldn't he have been one of these seventy-six thousand? So he must have been the driver.)

And the rest, as far as I was concerned, had to wait for my mother's second suitor. I wouldn't want to say, exactly, that he was a suitor less worthy than the first—or that I've condemned my mother for not letting Zahn Glanz father me. Because even if it wasn't carried in the genes, something of Zahn Glanz certainly got into me. I only want to show how Zahn Glanz put an idea of me in my mother. Even if he put nothing else there.

The Eighth Zoo Watch:
Tuesday, June 6, 1967, @ 3:00 a.m.

Almost everyone is asleep. One of the Various Aquatic Birds is garbling, prophecies or indigestion. I'm certainly awake, and I don't believe that sleep ever comes to O. Schrutt. But everyone else has finally dropped off.

I've been thinking: How do they know the last great auk is dead? The Irishmen at Trinity Bay—did they hear the great auk's final murmur? Did it actually say, "I am the last, there are no more"?

I've heard that Irishmen are always drunk. How could they be sure this great auk washed ashore was the last? It

might have been a plot. The great auks might have anticipated their own extinction, and sent a martyr—instructed
to identify itself as final. And somewhere, maybe in deserted coastal cottages in Wales, a tribe of great auks are
living still, multiplying, and teaching their young about
the martyr who washed itself ashore that they might live—
and be not gullible.

I wonder if the great auk is a bitter bird. I wonder if
their young are warlike, if they're organized in diving
teams, scuttling small fishing boats, spreading rumors as
old and unbelievable as sea serpents and mermaids—working up to the day when the Great Auk Navy will rule the
waterways of the world. *Human* history happens that way.
I wonder: do the surviving great auks bear grudges?

I've also been thinking about O. Schrutt. Curious that I
should have created his namesake. I thumbed back
through my various fictions, true and false, and found the
other O. Schrutt. A decidedly more tender-aged O. Schrutt
than this nightwatchman. Curious that my invented O.
Schrutt should be a bit character, a walk-on part, an alphabetized member of Vienna's Nazi youth. It's *very* curious, isn't it?

Just imagine: if my invented O. Schrutt had lived
through all the walk-on parts I anticipated him to play,
what would that O. Schrutt be doing now? What more
perfect thing could he be than this second-shift nightwatchman at the Hietzinger Zoo?

(CONTINUING:)

THE HIGHLY SELECTIVE AUTOBIOGRAPHY OF
SIEGFRIED JAVOTNIK: PRE-HISTORY II

I can't make my father fit the ethnographic maps of Yugoslavia. He was born in Jesenje in 1919, which at least
made him a Croat, and possibly a Slovene. He was certainly not a Serb, although Vratno Javotnik was such a
worldly sort of Yugoslav, I believe he was the only Yugoslav to whom being a Serb instead of a Croat wouldn't
have made any difference—and splitting the hair between
Croats and Slovenes would have been absurd for him. His
politics were strictly personal.

By that I mean he had no affiliations. If he was born in
Jesenje, it's likely he was baptized a Roman Catholic. If

not, it's at least certain he was in no way near enough Serbia to be Eastern Orthodox. But it couldn't have mattered
to Vratno, one way or the other.

One thing seems to have mattered, though. My father
was something of a linguist, and Jesenje is less than fifty
miles from the University of Zagreb, where my father
studied languages. This may have been a premonition on
his part—pessimism at a tender age: to master the speech
of several occupying armies before they came to occupy.

Whatever the motives, Vratno was in Zagreb on the
twenty-fourth of March, 1941, when Foreign Minister
Tsintsar-Markovich left Berlin for Vienna, and when the
students at the University of Belgrade demonstrated on
that Serbian campus—burning German textbooks and
picketing all the German classes.

The Croatian reaction in Zagreb was probably sullen—
the feeling that the Serbs were sure to get everyone killed
by their lunatic defiance of Germany. Vratno only thought
they'd missed the point. It didn't matter whose side you
were going to be on; when Germany came into Yugoslavia, one day it could save your skin to speak German.
Burning your textbooks was certainly unwise.

So the next day my father left Zagreb for Jesenje. It's
my belief that he traveled light.

That day the Tripartite Pact was signed in Vienna;
Vratno was probably en route to Jesenje when he heard
the news. I'm sure he guessed that various Serbian zealots
wouldn't accept this welcome to Germany. And I'm sure
Vratno turned to practicing his German idioms.

All the way into Jesenje, I can hear him practicing.

In fact, on the next night, while in Belgrade the General
Staff of the revolution was in its final, deciding session,
Vratno was probably perfecting his irregular verbs. When
the bold takeover was in process, and plans for the impossible resistance against Germany were being made, Vratno
was making umlaut sounds.

In Belgrade, the quisling government was overthrown;
Prime Minister Tsvetkovich was arrested at 2:30 A.M.
And Prince Paul was caught later aboard a train in
Zagreb; he was exiled to Greece. In Belgrade there were
heroes: Lieutenant Colonel Danilo Zobenitsa, tank corps
commander and the rescuer of young King Peter; Profes-
sor Radoye Knezevich, King Peter's former tutor; Ilya
Trifunovich Birchanin, commander of Chetniks, those

diehard Serb guerrillas of World War One—the only warriors, they say, who can fight hand to hand with the Turks.

And in Jesenje was my father, making himself universally fluent, preparing for his sly survival.

The Ninth Zoo Watch:
Tuesday, June 6, 1967, @ 3:15 a.m.

A few minutes ago I had this urge to make a bed check on the elephants. I'm sure at one time or another everyone has heard, as I have, that elephants never sleep. So I decided to go check on the elephants, even at the risk of disturbing the other, finally sleeping animals—or even at the risk of catching the awful attention of O. Schrutt, professional insomniac. After all, there aren't many opportunities in this world for testing myths. And the myth of the never-sleeping elephant is one that I've often thought needed testing.

I can tell you, I already had my doubts about the myth. What I expected to find in the House of Pachyderms was a boulder field of heavily sleeping elephants—cages of elephant mounds. I pictured them heaped together, circled like a Western wagon train—their trunks draped over each other, like great pythons sunning on bouldertops.

But if you take this night's example, the myth was substantiated. The elephant quarters were uncannily awake. The elephants stood in a perfect row, and hung their great heads over the fronts of their stalls like restless horses in an ordinary barn. They nodded, and waved their trunks; they breathed in slow motion.

When I walked in front of their stalls, they reached their trunks out to me—they opened and closed their nostrils to me. Their trunks kissed my hands. One of them had a cold—a runny trunk that rattled.

"When I come back for the real thing," I whispered, "I'll bring some medicated cough drops for you."

It nodded: All right, if you can remember. But I've had colds before.

The bored elephants nodded: Bring a lot of cough drops. We'll probably all have colds by then. Everything's very catching here.

It's puzzling to me. Perhaps there's some connection be-

tween their sleeplessness and how long they live. Seventy
years without a snooze? Although it seems unlikely, perhaps there's a myth snorted trunk to trunk among the elephants—that if you fall asleep, you die.

Someone should find a way to tell them it's perfectly
healthy to sleep.

I'll bet there's no one, though, who could convince O.
Schrutt of that.

I heard him when I stalked back to my hedgerow from
the House of Pachyderms. I heard him taking chances
with the animals' sleep. Doors in the Small Mammal
House were creaked, and sliding glass was slid.

O. Schrutt, creeping around in the residue of infrared.
O. Schrutt is up to no good, I'll bet. But so long as he
chooses to stay inside the Small Mammal House, I'll just
have to wait my chance.

Or maybe go back and ask the sleep-suspicious elephants, who must be wise: what prompts O. Schrutt to indulge himself with infrared? And: more than twenty years
or so ago, just what did old O. Schrutt do?

(CONTINUING:)
THE HIGHLY SELECTIVE AUTOBIOGRAPHY OF
SIEGFRIED JAVOTNIK: PRE-HISTORY II

I wonder where my stealthy father was when the
Luftwaffe bombed the open city of Belgrade, without a
declaration of war. I feel certain that Vratno wasn't observing any protocol either.

On April 6, 1941, Heinkels and Stukas were used simul-
taneously. The Wehrmacht pushed into Yugoslavia with
thirty-three divisions, six of which were panzers and four
of which were motorized. The aim was to march on Russia in mid-May, in the dry-weather season—when the
roads would still be hard. So the German onslaught
against this upstart revolution was fierce. So fierce that on
May 4 Germany announced that the Yugoslav State was
nonexistent. But on May 10, Colonel Drazha Mihailovich
and his band of wild Chetniks hoisted the Yugoslav flag on
the mountain of Ravna Gora. Mihailovich and his freedom fanatics went on doing that kind of thing all summer.

Oh, stories got told, you know, how Croat quislings and
other Yugoslav capitulators marched with the Germans,

hunting down Chetniks. How the Chetniks would disguise
themselves as Croat quislings and appear to be hunting
for themselves. How Mihailovich was a magician in the
mountains—potting Germans throughout Serbia. In fact,
in watchful America, *Time* magazine voted Drazha
Mihailovich Man of the Year. And the Communist press
was most praiseworthy too. After all, the Germans didn't
get to march on Russia in mid-May. They were delayed
five weeks, and they sloughed in on soggy roads. And they
were no longer thirty-three divisions strong; between ten
and twenty divisions were left behind as an occupying
force—still hunting down those fanatical Chetniks.

But those were heroes, and I'm wondering where my father was. I suspect he summered in Jesenje, mastering the
languages of likely victors—even learning the names of
foreign wines and soups, brands of cigarettes and movie
stars. Regardless, his whereabouts were unknown to me
until the fall of '41, when Vratno Javotnik appeared in
Slovenjgradec.

The city was full of capitulating Slovenes and Croats
who felt reasonably secure to be occupied by Germany,
and who resented the wildly resisting Serbs to the
southeast. The only people my father had to fear in
Slovenjgradec were a few uprooted Serbs. These called attention to themselves on October 21, 1941, by protesting
the somewhat conflicting reports of the massacre at
Kraguyevats, where—one broadcast said—2,300 Serbian
men and boys were machine-gunned in retaliation for 10
German soldiers killed by Chetniks, and 26 Germans also
sniped but only wounded; another broadcast said that at
least 3,400 Serbs were shot, which would have been in ex-
cess of the retaliation number promised by Germany to
combat Chetnik sniping—that is, 100 Serbs per German
killed, and 50 Serbs per German wounded.

Whichever broadcast was correct, the womenfolk of
Kraguyevats were digging graves from Wednesday to Sunday, and Slovenjgradec, at least, was generally pacified to
learn that the Germans had presented the Kraguyevats
Town Council with 380,000 dinars for the poor. Who
were just about everyone after the massacre. Oddly, the
amount of the German donation was estimated to be
slightly less than half of what 2,000 to 3,000 dead Serbian
men and boys might have had in their pockets.

But the Kraguyevats massacre had all of Slovenjgradec

outdoors anyway. Just to hear the conflicting broadcasts and to catch the sentiment of the city from sidewalk talk. In fact, the massacre brought people out in public who might otherwise have stayed aloof.

Namely, my father—out listening to dialects of his native Serbo-Croat, and picking up various German colloquialisms from café to café.

And namely, the entire Slivnica family horde, as they were known—dreaded fiends, all of them, enlisted in the service of the Ustashi terrorist organization, supposedly headed by the fascist Ante Pavelich. It was a hireling of Pavelich's, we're all told, who assassinated King Alexander and French Foreign Minister Barthou in Marseilles in '34.

Fascist Italy was reportedly behind the Ustashi end of this organization; Yugoslavia's neighbors were known to take advantage of the endless tiff between Serbs and Croats. But the Slivnica family horde were Ustashi terrorists of a special kind. Oh, the terror they waged wasn't in the least political; they were simply well fed for their work. In fact, they were feeding when Vratno encountered them, although it was only the lovely Dabrinka who first caught my father's eye.

The Slivnicas were at a long table at an outdoor terrace restaurant above the Mislinja River. Fair Dabrinka was pouring the wine for her two sisters and four brothers. Her sisters were nothing to what Vratno saw in Dabrinka. Only squat, circle-mouthed Baba, and the sulky, melon-round Julka. Dabrinka was a creature with lines and bones—more features than flesh, my father was fond of saying. Dabrinka was a cool, slim trickle—more the green stem than the flower. My father thought she was a waitress, and never guessed her to be a member of that most thick family she served.

One table away, Vratno raised his empty glass to her. "My girl," he said. "Would you fill me up?" And Dabrinka hugged the wine decanter; she turned away. The Slivnica menfolk turned to my father the linguist, now speaking Serbo-Croat. My father felt the wrath. Oh yes. Four of them: the sturdy twins, Gavro and Lutvo; Bijelo, the eldest—and leader—and terrible Todor, body-awesome.

"What shall we fill you up with?" Bijelo asked.

"Nails?" said Todor. "Or ground glass?"

"Oh, you're all one family," my father cried. "Oh yes, I see."

For the resemblance was striking among them all, excluding Dabrinka. She had their olive-black and -green color only in her eyes, but not their quickly sloping-away foreheads and nothing of the family swarth. Not the flat, pounded cheeks—which even Baba and Julka had—and not the twins' close-together eye slits. Not the exaggerated dimples of Bijelo the eldest; not a bit of the bulk of her big brother Todor, and not his cleft chin, either—the imagined tool work of hours with a rat's-tail file.

"Seven of you!" said my father. "My, what a big family!" Thinking: What inconceivable twosome could ever have mated and conceived them?

"Do you know us?" Bijelo asked. The twins sat mum and shook their heads; Baba and Julka licked their lips, trying to remember; Dabrinka blushed through her blouse; Todor hulked.

"I'd be honored," my father said, in ordinary Serbo-Croat; he faltered to his feet. Then in German he said, "It would be my pleasure." And in English: "Happy to know you, I'm sure." And in the Mother Russian tongue, hoping to arouse possible pan-Slav sympathies: "Extraordinarily glad!"

"He's a languist!" said Todor.

"A linguist," Bijelo said.

"He's sort of nice," said Baba.

"Just a youngster," Julka breathed, while Lutvo and Gavro still sat mum.

"And you don't know us from somewhere?" said the leader Bijelo.

"But I hope to," my father said, in his straightest Serbo-Croat.

"Bring your wineglass over," Bijelo commanded.

"Perhaps," said Todor, "we could powder the rim of your glass into the finest possible bits, and let you sip the glass dust down?"

"That's enough humor, Todor," Bijelo said.

"I only wondered," said Todor, "what language he would speak with glass dust in his larynx."

Bijelo cuffed a twin. "Give the linguist your chair and get another," he said. Both Gavro and Lutvo went looking.

When my father sat down, Baba said, "Oh, get him!"

"Go on, if you want," said Julka.

Gavro and Lutvo came back with a chair each.

"They're dumb," Baba said.

"Dummies," said Julka.

"They share one brain between them," Todor said. "It's a small allowance to live on."

"Enough humor, Todor," Bijelo said, and Todor sat mum with the twins, who sat puzzling over the extra chair.

When the young Dabrinka turned around, my father felt his wineglass was too heavy to lift.

And that was how Vratno Javotnik met the Slivnica family horde, odd-job artists for the Ustashi terrorists—who had use for a linguist.

The Ustashi had touchy sort of work in mind. In fact, this job was so delicate that the Slivnicas had been surprisingly inactive for the past two weeks, pending the discovery of just the *right* man. The Slivnicas were probably quite restless for work—or for work less random than linguist-looking. Their last job had called on the services of the entire family and had gratified everyone. A French newspaperman, unauthorized in Yugoslavia, had sought a home experience with a typical Slovenjgradec family—to learn for himself the degree of fascism and Italo-German sentiments in the average Slovene or Croat. The Ustashi were not interested in this sort of publicity, feeling that the French were soreheaded enough about Minister Barthou's assassination. So the Ustashi selected the Slivnicas as the typical family for the French newspaperman.

But this Monsieur Pecile didn't think the Slivnicas were average, or wished, at least, to live with a family that *didn't* have twin mutes and *did* have a living mother and father. Perhaps he doubted, as Vratno had, the possibility of natural genitors; or perhaps he made a pass at Dabrinka—and with Baba and Julka offering it so freely, the Slivnica family feelings were hurt. At any rate, the gleeful twins, Gavro and Lutvo, described in drawings, on the dusty hood of the Frenchman's car, the spectacular rocklike plummeting of Monsieur Pecile into the Mislinja River.

Now there was a job that had involved them all—a real family project. But this linguist hunt had been something else. Todor confessed it to be so tedious that he feared his humor had soured.

Oh yes, the job that Ustashi terrorists had for Vratno was indeed more delicate than the mere disposal of an unauthorized Frenchman. This new subject was a German named Gottlob Wut, as authorized in Yugoslavia as the rest of his horde, and the particular job asked of Vratno—for the moment, at least—was not a disposal. Gottlob Wut was scout-outfit leader of Motorcycle Unit Balkan 4, and the Ustashi weren't looking for any trouble with the Germans. Chiefly, they wanted my father to make a fast friend of Gottlob Wut.

The Slivnicas were to prepare my father for this considerable task; Gottlob Wut, as far as anyone knew, had never had a friend.

Poor Wut had been uprooted by the war, which isn't a thing you could say for all Germans. Gottlob had left an art for a service, and the Ustashi were interested in what Gottlob Wut might reveal of his mysterious past, to a friend, in his presently low-key, nostalgic condition.

It's not clear what the Ustashi had against Gottlob, but I suspect it was an issue of wounded pride. Gottlob Wut had been a racing mechanic for the NSU motorcycle factory at Neckarsulm before the war. The motorcycle world was always saying that Wut had a mystical touch. The Ustashi also thought he had a violent touch, even a certain criminal touch—because a new-model NSU racer surprisingly won the Grand Prix of Italy in 1930, with Britisher Freddy Harrell doing the driving, and the Ustashi figured that Gottlob had more of a hand in the victory than his precise genius with valve control. The Italian counterpart of the Ustashi produced some evidence that Gottlob Wut had tinkered effectively with more than hairpin valve springs. Allegedly, Gottlob Wut had tinkered with the head of the Italian favorite, Guido Maggiacomo, whose body was found after the race in the Grand Prix body shop—lying peacefully beside his highly touted Velocette, which had missed the race. Guido Maggiacomo's temple was severely dented, authorities claimed, by an Amal racing carburetor found at the scene of the crime. It was said of Gottlob Wut, in those days, that he was never without an Amal racing carburetor. The new NSU racer had attained a new speed by successfully tilting these carburetors at a slightly downdraft angle.

Unfortunately, the Italian counterpart of the Ustashi had backed a number of syndicates who put their money on Guido Maggiacomo and his highly touted Velocette. When the betting turnover was tabulated, it appeared that

the NSU team of Britisher Freddy Harrell and German
Klaus Worfer had made a killing. But the record has it
that all the betting was done by the mystical mechanic
Gottlob Wut. It was Wut who took away the booty.

But that was in 1930, and if the Ustashi were to reveal
this crime to Wut's Nazi superiors, the Germans certainly
wouldn't care. Gottlob Wut was a valuable scout-outfit
leader of Motorcycle Unit Balkan 4.

This unit itself didn't seem to be very valuable at the
moment. The Germans had found their motorcycle scouts
rather obsolete in the Yugoslav campaign. They were easy
targets to pot off in the Serbian mountains; the way those
Chetniks hid and fought, motorcycles were easy to spot.
But to keep Gottlob Wut's unit in Slovenjgradec wasn't
very vital either. There wasn't a real war in Slovenia or
Croatia—just an easy occupation; for police work, there
were better means than motorcycles available.

Gottlob's rough riders looked a bit silly in a quiet city.

Of course, the Ustashi had more in mind about Gottlob
than an old financial grudge. They thought it would be
nice to catch the old mystic at a new crime, and one
which could be presented as anti-German. They already
knew of a small scandal. If Gottlob Wut didn't have a
friend, he did have a woman—a Serbian woman, who was
something of a political outlaw in Slovenjgradec. Gottlob
Wut, it might be shown, was taking his German blood
rather lightly. In fact, he didn't seem to give a damn for
the whole war.

All of which was how the get-the-goods-on-Wut campaign began, with my father studying motorcycle memorabilia on the Slivnicas' kitchen table. Vratno learned the
names of racers and the dates of races; Vratno learned
the bores and strokes, and the significant compression ra-
tios; Vratno distinguished the side-valve model from the
supercharged double-overhead-cam twin in sizes 350 and
500 cc. My father had never been on a motorcycle before,
so the Slivnicas helped where they could.

Broad Todor went down on all fours, and my father
mounted. Todor gave his elbows for handlebars; he
demonstrated cornering. Bijelo called out the road conditions.

"Corner sharp right," Bijelo said.

"Lean from your spine," said Todor. "Don't move those
elbows, you never want to steer a bike, the handles are

just for holding on. You got to lean a bike, hips and head. Now tip me a little right."

"Corner sharp left," Bijelo said, and watched my father gingerly lean left off the broad back, his knees slipping.

"You wouldn't have made that one," said Todor. "You'd have gone wild, Vratno, my boy. Let's feel those knees, now, give me a squeeze."

And Baba giggled. "I'll be the bike," she said. "Let me."

"Todor makes a fine motorcycle," said Bijelo the eldest; he had an eye for bikes, all right. He'd stolen some Italian's Norton, over the border in Tarviso—oh, before he was a responsible head of a family—and had ridden the great chugger over the mountains, back to Yugoslavia, crossing where there wasn't a customs checkpoint because he crossed where there wasn't a road. But he was so carried away to be back in his homeland with it, and finally driving on a real road, that he drove it into the Sava River on the outskirts of Bled. Climbed out wet but wildly happy, knowing how he'd do it again if he had the chance—and this time, make it all the way to Slovenjgradec. So he said.

He was a good teacher for my father, at least. My father rode Todor Slivnica under Bijelo's critical eye, for hours every evening—with Baba offering her own broad back, should Todor give out, and Julka claiming that she could clamp a gas tank on her brother's rib cage tighter than Vratno could.

My father, riding long hours through the nighttime kitchen, would see his shy Dabrinka maybe once or twice. She poured the wine, she served the coffee, she was pinched by her sisters and she never met my father's eyes. Once, on a corner sharp left, Vratno held a smile up for Dabrinka; he would have waited forever to catch her eyes. But Todor turned his head, the back of which usually pretended to be the headlight and necessary gauges. Todor dumped my father on the corner sharp left.

"You must have leaned too far, Vratno," he said, then leaned himself closer to where my father sat. "I think it should be grownup ladies for you," he said. "You don't have to go outside this house to get it, and you don't have to kill yourself looking for it, either." And Todor made a scissors of his index and middle finger, thick as garden shears, and he snipped his finger scissors just above my father's lap.

Oh, now that the linguist hunt was over, Todor
Slivnica's humor was brightening, you could tell.

The Tenth Zoo Watch:
Tuesday, June 6, 1967, @ 3:45 a.m.

Seeing those elephants has made me sleepy, but if they
can be insomniacs for seventy years or more, I can hold
out for a few more hours. It's just because of the lull in
here; for a moment, I was bored.

When I came back from the House of Pachyderms, it
was so quiet that I went on by my hedgerow. I went down
the path to the oryx's pen. For no good reason, I realized,
I'd been putting off visiting the oryx.

It was easy, climbing the pen, but I saw as soon as I set
foot inside that the oryx was in his shed. His hind hooves
were splayed out the shed door, over the ramp; silky white
hairs lay over his fetlocks. He looked like someone who'd
been felled with a sledge as he came in his house—ambushed in his doorway. But when I gingerly came up behind him, he raised his head and shoved his face out the
doorway into the moonlight; I touched his wet black nose;
he sort of mooed. It was a little disappointing, he was so
docile; I'd expected to be challenged—to be backed
against his shed wall, threatened with horn and hoof, until
I proved to him I was the sort he could trust. But the oryx
needed no proof; he lay back again, stretched, raised up
again, sliding his great hip out from under himself—kneeling, actually! His great ballocks bumped the boards of the
ramp. He stood up tiredly, as if to say: All right, I'll *show*
you where the bathroom is. You probably can't find it by
yourself.

He invited me into his shed; that is, he backed up,
completely off the ramp, and with his nodding head, he
showed me about his room: This is where I sleep when it's
cold—when it's warmer, as you saw, I hang a piece of me
out the shed door. And this is where I take my brunch, by
the glassless window. And this is where I sit to read.

He knocked about the shed (expecting, I think, that I
was going to feed him something), and when I showed him
I didn't have anything, he somewhat indignantly walked
out of his house. The moonlight bounced off the ramp; his

balls wobbled and were shot through by the strobe-light effect of the reflecting moon.

Something more definite should be said for the size. Not basketballs—that's exaggerating, of course. But they're bigger than softballs and—really!—bigger than the elephant balls I saw standing at attention just a while ago. They're volleyball-sized, only too heavy to be perfectly round. They're volleyballs that look sat on, or with the air let out—little dents where the ball collapsed for lack of air. That's as close as I can come, other than to point out that they're dangled in long, loose leather moneybags, and also, that they're a little crusty—owing, I'm sure, to the muck in the poor oryx's slum.

Imagine: the oryx was born in the Hietzinger Zoo! Brainwashed! He thinks his balls are just for lugging around. They never told him; he probably wouldn't know what to make of a lady.

And that's when I got to thinking: Why isn't there an antelope of sorts, a mountain goat or experienced gnu, who could show this poor oryx what his volleyballs are for?

I'm convinced: it's abstinence that's given them their size!

So I made a check of the surrounding pens, looking for a lady who might enlighten the naïve and apathetic oryx. Now this was hard. The blesbok was too small and skittish—would only teach our oryx frustration. I felt the white-tailed gnu was far too hairy; Mrs. Gray's waterbuck looked absurdly virginal; the lesser kudu had little to offer; the hartebeest had too thin a back; and the only female wildebeest had a beard. There was nothing in all of the Hietzinger Zoo as perfect for the oryx as a gentle old madam cow.

So I decided. Rather than corrupt the oryx with a lascivious llama, I'd hope for the best on the day of the bust; that our oryx would escape forever to the Wachau pasture lands along the Danube, plundering queenly cows and lording over the awe-struck herds.

And thus encouraged, I skulked past the Small Mammal House. O. Schrutt was off somewhere in the back streets of the Small Mammal Maze—still creaking doors, I could hear, and sliding the sliding glass.

But along with O. Schrutt's sounds of clumsiness, I could hear something new from my stand just outside the open door. O. Schrutt had woken up his charges; there were shuffles, scratching, claws clacking on the glass. And just as I began to think of this waking as a preface to O. Schrutt's own sudden emergence in the aisle, and his striking out for the open door—just as I'd turned a bit down the path, and was retreating to my hedgerow—I heard a wail from some lost aisle of the Small Mammal Maze. A cry cut off at full force, as if O. Schrutt had flung open a door on some poor beast's nightmare and slammed the door shut again as quickly as he'd opened it—fearing, perhaps, he'd be involved in the beastly dream.

But the wail was contagious. The Small Mammal House whimpered and moaned. Oh, the screams blared and were cut off again, muffled but not altogether gone. As if a certain zoo train had passed you somewhere, going fast, and the frightened animals' cries had slashed out at you like a passing buggy driver's whip; and the cries hung for a moment all around, like the sting of the whip lingering on your neck after the buggy driver had slashed and passed on.

So I pawed my way through the nearest root gap and crawled under and behind my hedge. Holding my breath.

It wasn't until I exhaled, and heard a thousand exhalations round me, that I realized the rest of the zoo was awake again too.

(CONTINUING:)
THE HIGHLY SELECTIVE AUTOBIOGRAPHY OF
SIEGFRIED JAVOTNIK: PRE-HISTORY II

On Sunday the twenty-sixth of October, 1941, Vratno Javotnik was judged by the Slivnicas as being prepared to meet Gottlob Wut, who had Sunday habits convenient for a meeting.

The scout outfit had Sundays off. There was no guard at the Balkan 4 barracks on Smartin Street, and no guard at the motorcycle unit's garage—a nearby block down Smartin Street, flush to the Mislinja riverbank.

Sunday was Wut's day for a leisurely breakfast with his Serbian mistress, whom he'd openly moved to a Smartin Street apartment, halfway between the Balkan 4 barracks and the garage. Wut would cross Smartin Street every Sunday morning, briskly out of the barracks, wearing his bathrobe and unlaced dress shoes, carrying his uniform under his arm; it was the only day of the week he wasn't wearing or carrying his crash helmet. Wut had his own key to the Serbian woman's apartment. All Smartin Street watched Wut let himself in.

Occasionally, one of the scout outfit's members would have stand-by messenger duty on Sundays. In which case, one of the 600 cc. NSU side-valve sidecar models would be parked in front of the barracks. Otherwise, all the bikes were locked up, downstreet at the garage.

Wut had a key for the garage too. He'd leave his mistress in the late afternoon and go down to his motorcycles, letting himself in again, neat in his uniform—this time—his bathrobe under his arm. Then he'd fiddle with the bikes until dark. He'd start them, adjust them, tighten them, bounce on them, leave little tickets tied to several handlebars—stating the nature of maladies he'd discovered, noting ill effects of maladies left uncorrected, sometimes suggesting punishments for the more careless of his drivers.

When fussing, he left the garage door open to vent the exhaust—and to admit his audience; mostly children, they'd stand in the doorway and make revving sounds of their own. Wut let them sit on the sidecar models, but never on the ones that could tip off their kickstands and crush a child. Gottlob brought pastries from the Serbian woman and had a snack with the children before he closed up. But the children who stole—even so little as an insignia—he never let come back. Wut always knew who stole what too.

Gottlob Wut was a stringy, hipless and rumpless man, bent-backed, and stiff in all his twitchy motions; he had a wincing walk, as if it hurt him to unbend his joints. It probably did hurt too. At one time or another, Gottlob Wut had broken all his fingers and half his toes, both wrists and both ankles, one leg and the other elbow, all but the highest rib on his left side, once his jaw, twice his nose, and three times his sunken left cheek—though never his right. Wut had never driven in a race, but he'd tested all the racers before the flaws were gone. NSU discovered flaws through Gottlob Wut. Poor Wut, pinned under one test model or another, his hand lanced through by a front brake handle, fuel sloshing over his chest, the old hand gearshift of a Tourensport stuck in his thigh—while hirelings pull the monster off him, Wut is speaking: *"Ja,* I'd say there is clearly no rear suspension, and we'll have to retain the girder fork in front if we're to have any suspension at all. Because I certainly was totally lacking suspension of any kind, in that corner I missed back there."

But now Wut had a dull job, writing tickets: Bronsky, your tires are forever soft; Gortz, tissue paper will not stop your leak, you've lost a seal in your transmission, and don't you ever put such gunk as tissue in there again; Wallner, you've been laying over too much on your corners, you've skinned your tailpipes and bent your kickstand—such hot-rodding will get you just nothing but a sidecar attached, to slow you down, you fool; Vatch, your tail fender Iron Cross is gone, and don't you tell me it was my children who took it, for I watch them and I know it's some girl that has it or you sent it home and said it was a medal you never got—it's got screw holes in it, you won't be fooling anyone—so get it back on that tail fender; Metz, your sparkplugs are filthy, and I don't scrape carbon for anyone, that unskilled labor like you can do—Monday, instead of your lunch.

Yes, Gottlob Wut had a dull job—survived adventures to be bored to death. He would have liked to tell his best driver, Wallner, how he could skin his tailpipes down to dust, how he could lay over on a corner and really grind his tailpipes down to nothing—only watch out for the kickstand, it can snag you up, which is why you don't put one on a bike you're racing, and often no tailpipes either. But Gottlob wrote tickets on Sunday, and had to write tickets that kept Scout Outfit Balkan 4 intact, even if obsolete; parts and drivers weren't so easily replaced in Slovenjgradec as they were in the old Neckarsulm factory.

Certainly the Sunday of October 26, 1941, was a fine Slivnica sort of choice for a day when my father could attempt to bring some excitement into the dull life of Gottlob Wut.

It was also the fifth and last day of gravedigging for the shovel-sore and weary widows of Kraguyevats.

And it was probably a day of sneaky fighting, like many other days, for the Chetniks of Mihailovich and for the Communist partisans who at this time were supporting the Chetnik forces against the Germans—the Communist partisans being led by a little-known son of a Croatian blacksmith from the village of Klanyets, The blacksmith's son had gone to the Russian front with the Austro-Hungarian Army, but he went over to the Russians and fought with the Red Army through the civil war; then returned home as a leader of the Yugoslav Communist party; then was arrested as a Communist in 1928 and served five years in prison; then allegedly was in charge of the Yugoslav Communist party through the period of illegality, although those involved with the Balkan underground centers in Vienna, at the time, swear they never once heard of this blacksmith's son. Certain members of the Balkan underground claim that the blacksmith's son was actually a member of the Russian secret service, and that he was in Russia until the Germans' delayed invasion got under way. Whatever his real history is, the blacksmith's son was the mystery-man leader of the Communist partisans, who were fighting along with the Chetniks against the Germans—when they weren't fighting against the Chetniks. He was a Communist; he had a large and handsome Slavic head; he was fighting along with Mihailovich before he turned against Mihailovich; he was indeed mysterious.

At the time my father was on his way to meet Gottlob Wut, very few people had ever heard of Josip Broz Tito, the blacksmith's son.

My father certainly hadn't heard of him, but, as I've said, Vratno paid little attention to politics. He was attentive to more constant details: the various uses of Amal carburetors, the advantages of the double-overhead cam, umlaut sounds and verb endings. In fact, by the Sunday of October 26, 1941, my father had learned his introductory lines by heart.

Vratno spoke his German softly to himself; he even spoke made-up lines for Wut. Then he strolled through the open doors of the motorcycle unit's garage, an indigo-blue racing helmet with a red-tinted visor cocked a bit back on his head, chin strap loose and jaunty; and over the ear hole of the helmet, a crossed pair of checkered racing flags with a halo printed above them, reading: AMAL CARBURETORS FINISH FIRST—AND LAST!

"Herr Commander Wut," he said. "Well, yes, I'd still recognize you. You're older, of course. I was only eleven, so of course I'm older too. That wonderful Wut!" Vratno crowed. "If only my poor uncle had lived to meet you."

"What?" said Wut, strewing tools and children. "Who?" said Wut, a socket wrench firm in his puffy old hand—the dirtiest, most knuckle-cut hands that my father had ever seen.

"Javotnik here," my father said. "Vratno Javotnik."

"You speak German," said Wut. "And what are you doing in leathers?"

"Wut," said Vratno, "I've come to join your team."

"My what?" said Wut.

"I've come to learn all over again, Wut—now that I've found the master."

"I don't have any teams," said Wut. "I don't know any Javotniks."

"Remember the Grand Prix of Italy, 1930?" Vratno asked. "Ah, Wut, you really made a killing."

Gottlob Wut unsnapped his sidearm holster.

Vratno said, "My poor dead uncle took me, Wut. I was only eleven. Uncle said you were the very best."

"At what?" said Wut, holster open.

"Motorcycles, of course, Wut. Fixing them and driving them, testing them and coaching drivers. A genius, Uncle said. Politics got in the way, of course, or my uncle would have joined your team."

"But I don't have any *team*," said Wut.

"Look," my father said, "I've got a real problem."

"I'm very sorry," said Gottlob Wut, sincerely.

"I was just coming along as a driver," Vratno said, "when my uncle was killed—drove his Norton into the Sava outside the Bled. It ruined me, Wut. I haven't sat on a bike since."

"I don't know what you want," Gottlob said.

"You can teach me, Wut. I've got to learn all over—how to ride. I was good, Wut, but I lost my nerve when poor Uncle sank in the Sava. Uncle said you were the very best."

"How did your uncle know me?" Wut asked.

"The world knew you, Wut! The Grand Prix of Italy, 1930. What a killing!"

"You said that before," Wut complained.

"My uncle was teaching me, Wut. My uncle said I had all the moves. But I lost my nerve, you see. It would take a master to have me riding again."

"There's a war now, you fool," said Wut. "What are you anyway?"

"Croat, I guess—if it matters," Vratno said. "But motorcycles are international!"

"But there's a *war* now," said Wut. "I'm the scout-outfit leader of Motorcycle Unit Balkan 4."

"That's the team I want!" my father said.

"It's not a *team!*" said Wut. "It's a *war!*"

"Are you really in the war, Wut?" Vratno asked. "What will the war do to NSU?"

"Set us back ten years," said Wut. "There won't be any racers made, there won't be any improvements made. There might not be a factory to go back to, and all my drivers could lose their legs. Everything will come back, covered with camouflage paint."

"Oh, you're surely right that these politics have no place with motorcycles," my father said. "Wut, is there any way I can overcome my fear?"

"My God!" said Wut. "You can't have anything to do with a German military unit."

"You can help me, Wut, I know you can. You could make me a driver again."

"Why are you speaking German?" said Wut.

"Do you speak Serbo-Croat?" my father asked.

"Of course not," Gottlob said.

"Then I'd better speak German, don't you think? I was driving all over the continent, you see—mostly amateur events, sure. But I was an alternate for the 1939 Grand Prix races. Pity that NSU wasn't a winner in '39—a bit heavy, your racer model that year, wasn't it? But I picked up some languages when I was touring."

"Before you lost your nerve?" said Wut, who was lost.

"Yes, before poor Uncle drowned with the Norton."

"And you were only eleven at the 1930 Grand Prix of Italy?"

"Eleven, Wut. Merely an admiring child."

"And you found out I was here?"

"I found out, Wut."

"How did you ever find that out?" Gottlob said.

"The world knows you, Wut—the motorcycle world."

"Yes, you said so before," Wut agreed.

"How would you go about overcoming such a fear?" my father asked.

"You're crazy," said Wut. "And you'll frighten the children."

"Please, Wut," Vratno said. "I had all the right impulses, and now I'm frozen."

"You must be out of your head," said Wut, and my father cast a wild eye around the garage.

"Lots of sidecars," he said, "but they're not motorcycles, really. And side-valvers," he said, "lots of low-speed torque, which is all right for the war, I guess, but you don't win races with them, do you?"

"Just a minute," said Wut. "I've got two six hundred cc. overhead valves. They move along all right."

"No rear suspension, though," Vratno said. "Center of gravity was too high, and hurt the handling—if I remember '38."

"Remarkably, you remember," said Wut. "And how old were you then, boy?"

"Just two '38 models, the side-valvers and the sidecar tanks," my father counted scornfully. "I'm sorry, Wut," he said, "I was mistaken. You don't have anything for me here." And he started for the door. "By the end of this war," he added, "NSU will be back to making nothing but mopeds."

"And they don't even send me where the real driving is!" said Wut.

My father walked out into Smartin Street, with Gottlob Wut wincing behind, socket wrench stuck in his boot.

"Maybe," said Vratno, "they thought you were too old for the front. Maybe, Wut, they figured you had your action behind you. Lost your zip, you know?"

"You didn't see the racer in there," said Wut, shyly. "I keep it under a tarp."

"What racer?" Vratno asked.

"Grand Prix racer of '39," said Wut, and stood unbalanced with his feet too close together—his hands locking and unlocking behind his back.

"The one that was too heavy?" Vratno said.

"I can make it lighter," said Wut. "Of course, I had to put some trimmings on it so they'd think it was just a workhorse machine like the others. But I take them off for a run, now and then. You know—the kickstand, toolbox, pack rack, radio mounts and that saddlebag crap; I had to fill it in a little, for the war look, but it's still the '39 Grand Prix racer, five hundred cc. model."

My father came suspiciously back to the doorway. "That's the twin, right?" he said. "The supercharged double-overhead-cam twin? Got the duplex cradle frame, and the boxed plunger rear suspension?"

"Want to see it, huh?" said Wut, and he blushed.

But under the tarp was the racer disguised as a war bike, the camouflage paint a somewhat darker tone because of the black enamel layers underneath.

"What can she hit?" Vratno asked.

"Strip her down and she'll hit one-fifty," said Wut. "Her weight's still high at four eighty-six, but a lot of that's fuel. She puts it away; she's under four hundred when she's dry."

"Roadability?" said Vratno, giving conspicuous little jounces to the front end, as if he knew all about the shocks.

"Oh, still a bit rough," Wut said. "Handles hard, maybe, but the power never fails you."

"I can imagine," said Vratno, and Gottlob Wut looked at the racing flags crossed over my father's ear hole. Then he sent one of the children to the barracks for his helmet.

"Javotnik, wasn't it?" he asked.

"Vratno. Vratno Javotnik."

And Gottlob said, "Well, Vratno, about this fear of yours . . ."

"Overcoming it's the problem, Wut."

"I think, Vratno," Gottlob said, "that good drivers have to transfer their fears."

"To what, Wut?"

And Gottlob said, "Pretend it's a different fear, boy. Pretend it's like the fear when you first learn to ride."

"Pretend?" said Vratno.

"If it's not too hard," said Wut, "you should try to pretend that you've never driven a motorcycle before."

"That shouldn't be too hard," Vratno said, and watched Gottlob Wut doing knee bends—limbering up the old sticky joints before mounting the monster Grand Prix racer, '39.

If you're careless with the spark retard, the kickstarter can kick you back hard enough to slide your ankle joint flush to your knee joint—shove the whole shaft of your thighbone screaming up under your lungs.

Or so claimed Gottlob Wut, the motorcycle master and secret keeper of a Grand Prix racer, '39, who was as unconcerned with politics as my father was; who hadn't yet heard of Josip Broz Tito, either.

The Eleventh Zoo Watch:
Tuesday, June 6, 1967, @ 4:15 a.m.

I can't imagine what O. Schrutt could be doing to them.
I still hear them; the whole zoo is listening. Now and then
there's a door that opens suddenly on some awful animal
music, and just as suddenly closes—muffles the cry.

I can only guess: O. Schrutt is beating them, one by
one.

It's clearly anguish. Whenever the cries blare full force,
there's an answer for the rest of the zoo. A monkey
scolds, a large cat coughs, the Various Aquatic Birds are
practicing takeoffs and landings; bears pace; the great gray
boomer is viciously shadow-boxing; more subtly, in the
Reptile House, the great snakes twine and untwine. Everyone seems in angry mourning for the creatures under infrared.

I can only guess: O. Schrutt is mating with them, one
by one.

There's a herd of Miscellaneous Range Animals just behind my hedgerow; they're huddled round each other, con-
spiring. I can guess what they're saying, nipping each
other's ears with their strange, herbivorous teeth: Schrutt's
at it again. Did you hear the last one? Brannick's giant
rat. I know its terrible bark anywhere.

Oh, the zoo is full of gossip.

A moment ago, I crept out of my hedgerow and down
to the empty *Biergarten* to have a word with the bears.
They were all in a stew. The most fierce and famous Asiatic Black Bear squatted and roared himself upright, lunging into the bars as I scurried past his cage. I saw his
shaggy arms still groping out for me when I was half a
zoo block away. The Famous Asiatic Black Bear must
have been thinking of his captor, Hinley Gouch—and was
interpreting the nameless diabolics of O. Schrutt as no
more than another capture of that deceiving Hinley
Gouch's kind. For the terrible Asiatic Black Bear, all men
must be Hinley Gouch—especially O. Schrutt.

I tried to calm them all, but the Asiatic Black Bear was
unfit for reason. I did whisper to the polar bears that they
shouldn't take it out on each other, and they floated,
though uneasily, thereafter; I did beg the grizzly to have a

seat and collect his thoughts, which, after a half-blind
charge at me, he begrudgingly did; my gentle pair of Rare
Spectacled Bears were so very worried that they hugged
each other upright.

Oh, I can only guess: O. Schrutt—mad fetishist!—what
is your evil indulgence that frenzies the whole zoo?

But no one can tell me, I'm in some haunted bazaar in
someplace more scheming than Istanbul; in their cages
and behind their fences, the animals are gossiping in a language more violent and foreign than Turkish.

I even tried a little Serbo-Croat with a Slavic-looking
great brown bear. But no one can tell me a thing.

I can only guess what the last shriek meant: O. Schrutt,
with ritual slowness, is strangling the coati-mundi. The cry
pushes thickly through the lavender maze; now it's cut off
like all the rest.

Now sliding glass is slid. And the zoo gives me a Turkish explanation.

(CONTINUING:)

THE HIGHLY SELECTIVE AUTOBIOGRAPHY OF
SIEGFRIED JAVOTNIK: PRE-HISTORY II

The ritual of Vratno learning to drive the 1939 Grand
Prix racer was limited to Sundays. My father would wait
for Gottlob Wut on the Smartin Street sidewalk in front
of the Serbian woman's door. Wut was punctual, bath-
robed, helmeted, shoed but unlaced—uniform under his
arm. My father, in Bijelo Slivnica's leathers, would polish
his indigo-blue helmet while waiting for Wut.

Gottlob Wut required a two-hour bath Sunday mornings. The tub had a ledge for his pastries and coffee. My
father ate his breakfast on the hopper, lid down. They
talked around and occasionally through the passing bulk
of Wut's Serbian mistress, who refreshed the coffee and
Wut's bath water—who at times simply squatted between
tub and hopper, watching the changing colors of Gottlob
Wut's many scars underwater.

Zivanna Slobod was about as effortless a mistress as
anyone could come by. Middle-aged, heavy in the jaw and
hips, she had a shiny, black-haired, gypsy strength to her.
She never spoke a word with Wut, and when my father
would compliment her services in Serbo-Croat, she would

raise her head a little and show him the fine rippling vein in her neck and all her bright, heavy teeth.

Zivanna took Wut away from my father after the bath; she returned him in half an hour. This was the rubbing-down session, wherein the thoroughly bath-limp Wut would be bundled in towels and escorted from the bathroom by strong Zivanna. Vratno turned up the radio and loudly drained the bath so he wouldn't hear Gottlob Wut's joints being loosened beyond imagination on the great airless mound of bed things in Zivanna's only room with a door that closed. Vratno saw the mound once—the door had been left ajar as he followed Wut to the bathroom one morning. It would have been like sleeping on a ball, because Zivanna's bed, if that's what really was beneath the bed things, was strewn with silks and pelts, fur pillows and large, shiny scarves; a tippy bowl of fruit perched on top of the mound.

God bless Gottlob Wut for his indulgent Sundays. The man knew how to break up the weeks.

And he knew everything about his 1939 Grand Prix racer. He could strip it in ten minutes. It was to Wut's unending sorrow, however, that he hadn't the time to do anything about the camouflage paint. Some appearances had to be maintained. Wut was fortunate enough to have a most agreeable motorcycle unit; they never reported the racer's presence to the overseers of the German scout command. Gottlob kept them happy by giving each his turn on the racer, although this pained him a good deal. Wallner was too cocky with it—had no respect for the power; Vatch was afraid of it and never shifted out of second; Gortz ground gears; Bronsky floated corners, one gear too high; Metz was an utter dolt about the overuse of brakes—he brought the racer back smoking. Even out of Slovenjgradec on a very open road, Gottlob was nervous about anyone else riding his racer. But certain sacrifices had to be made.

With my father, Wut was very cautious. They began by riding the racer double—Wut driving, of course, and carrying steady instructions back to his passenger. "Now see?" said Wut, and would corner neat, with a whining, flawless down shift at the break of the turn. My father's eyes were shut tight, the wind screamed in his ear holes and moved his helmet up and down. "You can even take it up a gear when the curve is banked," said Wut. "Now

see?" And would never break the steady, increasing pace
when he changed his gears; and would never miss a gear,
either. "Never miss," said Wut. "There's too much weight
behind you to miss a gear and hold the road." And would
give an example: he'd pull in the clutch and freewheel the
racer into a turn. "Do you feel?" Wut asked. "You'd never
hold this corner out of gear, would you?"

"Oh, my God no!" my father answered, to show as
quickly as possible that he felt very surely they wouldn't
hold the curve. And Wut would ease the clutch out; they'd
feel the sweet and heavy gear pull drawing them back to
the crown of the road.

If you were deaf, you would never know when Gottlob
Wut was shifting; he was much smoother than an auto-
matic transmission.

"Do you *feel* it, Vratno?" Wut was always asking.

"A conditioned reflex," my father would answer.
"You're pure Pavlov, Wut."

But they didn't get far into November of '41 before it
snowed, so my father had to wait awhile before going
beyond the passenger stage. Wut let Vratno get the feel of
the gears on the big side-valve model 600 with the sidecar,
but he refused to let my father drive a straight bike until
the ice was off the roads.

Wut himself was not so cautious. In fact, one Sunday in
February of '42, he took one of the straight 600 over-
heads, 1938, and with Vratno as passenger, drove north
of Slovenjgradec to the village of Bucovska Vas, where an
elbow of the Mislinja River was reportedly frozen the
thickest. My father stood shaking in the pine grove on
the edge of the bank while Wut gingerly drove the '38
out on the ice. "Now see?" said Wut, and began to move
slowly from my father's left to my father's right—very
slowly, with steady first-gear work, Wut cornered and
came back, right to left; then he cornered again and came
back, left to right—this time hitting second gear. When he
cornered in second, his rear wheel slipped and he touched
one tailpipe down to the ice; then righted the bike, slipped
to the other tailpipe and righted it again. And came back,
right to left—now hitting third. "Now see?" he cried, and
swung his leg over from the side of the bike that was
going down, this time, all the way to the rear wheel hub;
he stood two-footed on one pedal and held the throttle
steady while the bike righted itself. He remounted and

came back, carrying a little farther in both directions each
time he turned, so that my father had to come gaping out
of the pine grove and stand with his toes on the river's ice
heave—just to see the farthest reaches of Wut's fantastic
turns. Again and again, the bike rocked over a tailpipe
and touched down the rear wheel hub, and Wut swung a
stiff leg to right the machine. "Now see?" Wut screamed,
and made the frozen river twang and sing beneath him.
Back and forth, faster and faster, in a wider and wider ra-
dius—letting the bike almost lie flat on the ice, with the
wheel hub trying to eat its way down to the running
water. In a flourish, Wut tapped his rear brake very
lightly—let the bike slip out from under him while he
swung his leg; let the bike rest at last, laying it down
gently—standing on its gas tank until it had stopped spinning.

Then the only thing Wut had trouble with was getting
the heavy old '38 back up on its wheels. Gottlob's feet
kept slipping on the ice when he tried to lift. My father
came off the bank, and together they righted it, and wiped
off the tank where some fuel had sloshed.

"Of course," said Wut, "you've got to feel that just
right. But that's how it's done."

"Driving on rivers?" my father said.

"No, you fool," said Wut. "That's how you handle tar
or an oil slick. You hold your throttle steady, you get your
leg out from under, and if you don't touch the brake, she
should come back up on her own."

Then they minced along the ice, walking the old '38 to
where the bank was flattest. And from the bank on the far
side of the river came a shouting foursome of ice fishermen on a sled with droning runners; out from wherever
they'd watched the performance, they brought their
strange, mittened applause.

Gottlob Wut, perhaps, had never had such a public audience before; he seemed wholly stunned. He took his helmet off and held it under one arm, waiting for the wreath
or trophy, maybe, or for no more than a bearded ice
fisherman's kiss. He was bashful, suddenly self-conscious. But when the sledful of fishermen arrived, my
father saw that the Slovenians were hopelessly drunk and
oblivious to Wut's uniform. They nudged their sled up to
Gottlob's left boot; one of the fishermen used his mitten

for a megaphone and shouted up to Wut, in Serbo-Croat, "You must be the craziest man in the world!"

Then they all laughed and clapped their mittens. Wut smiled; his kindly eyes begged my father for a translation.

"He said you must be the best in the world," Vratno told Gottlob Wut, but to the drunks on the sled, my father said, in cheerful Serbo-Croat, "Keep smiling, oafs, and bow a little as you leave. The man's a German commander, and he'll shoot your bladders if you say another word."

Vratno had them smiling foolishly up from the sled, their heels slipping on the ice as they backed. The beefiest of them went down on his knees on the river and grunted against the runners. They straddled the sled and hugged each other, hip-to-thigh, looking like children who'd ridden their sled into a place where sleds were absurd, or not permitted.

My father held the motorcycle up for Wut, who waved after his departing fans. Poor, gullible Gottlob Wut, standing helmet-in-armpit, chin-up and vulnerable on the creaking ice.

"That was really great, Wut," my father said. "You were just fine."

The Twelfth Zoo Watch:
Tuesday, June 6, 1967, @ 4:30 a.m.

I was thoroughly chilled and was burrowed down in the roots of my hedge when old O. Schrutt came jangling his keys down the center-doorway aisle; for a second, I came crouching and duck-walking out from my hedge and peered down the path at him. He staggered out of the Small Mammal House and down the blood-glowing stairs.

O. Schrutt drinks on the job! Smokes pot, takes acid or pep pills. O. Schrutt pushes heroin—to the animals! Perhaps.

God, he was awful. He looked ravished. One pant leg was untucked from one combat boot; one epaulette was unbuttoned and flapped; his flashlight was jittery; he carried the keyring like a great mace.

Perhaps his mind is stretched and torn and then mushed back in shape by dark and tidal, almost lunar forces. Perhaps O. Schrutt averages three transformations a night.

But whatever cycle his insanity goes through—whatever phase this was—his effect on me was hypnotic. I crouched almost too long on the path; I would have been dumbstruck at his feet, if he hadn't sent me scrambling back to the cover of my hedge with his sudden barking at the Monkey Complex.

"*Rauf!*" he barked—perhaps still remembering the gelada baboon. "*Raa-ow-ff!*" But all the primates kept very still, hating or pitying him.

And when he came on down the path again, he was making growls.

"*Aaaaarr,*" he said softly. "*Uuuuurr.*"

While the Parliament meeting of Miscellaneous Range Animals tried to look casual about herding and milling together. But O. Schrutt walked the length of my hedgerow with his eye on them. When he turned down the path to the *Biergarten*, I ran scootched-over behind the hedge —all the way to the far corner, where I could see him move on. Sauntering, a changed man in a minute—cocky, I tell you—he whirled back to face the Miscellaneous Range Animals.

"Awake, eh?" he cried—so shrilly that the tiny kiang, the wild ass of Tibet, bolted out of the herd.

And virtually swaggering then, O. Schrutt walked on to the *Biergarten*—as far as I could see. He stopped a few feet before the Famous Asiatic Black Bear; then O. Schrutt leaned out toward the bear's cage and rang his keyring like a gong against the bars.

"You don't fool me!" cried old O. Schrutt, "crouching there like you're asleep and not planning an ambush!" While the Asiatic Black Bear threw and threw himself against his cage—roaring like I've never heard, alarming the Big Cats so much that they didn't dare to roar a challenge back, but only coughed in little rasps, and unbefitting mewing noises: Oh, feed me or forget to—I'll eat old O. Schrutt or anyone else. But whatever you do, God, don't you let that Oriental bear out. Oh please, no.

But O. Schrutt boldly taunted; exhausted, the Asiatic Black Bear slumped against the front of his cage, his great forepaws dragging through the peanut shells on the path, on the cage side of the safety rope—as far as he could reach and still six inches short of old O.

O. Schrutt went on, continuing what must be the aggressive phase of his zoo watch. I heard him plunk a rock in the polar bears' pool.

He's not quite far enough away to suit me yet; I would guess he's only at the ponds of Various Aquatic Birds. I believe that's him I hear, skipping stones across the ponds—bonking, now and then, a rare and outraged Aquatic Bird.

Let O. Schrutt get a little farther off. Let him get to the House of Pachyderms, let him rouse the rhino or echo his keys in the hippohouse. When he's a whole zoo away from me, I'll be in that Small Mammal Maze to see what's what.

And if there's time, old O., I've something else in mind. It's easy enough to do. Just move that safety rope six inches or a foot nearer the Famous Asiatic Black Bear's cage. It wouldn't be hard at all. There's just a rope strung between those posts; they have an awkward, concrete base, but they're certainly not immovable.

How would that fix you, O. Schrutt? Just change your safety line a foot or so—move you closer than you think you are, old O., and when you waggle your taunting head, we'll all watch it get lopped off.

And now, if that's him I hear, O. Schrutt is braying his empathy with the elephants' paranoia concerning sleep. Now he's far enough away.

(CONTINUING:)

THE HIGHLY SELECTIVE AUTOBIOGRAPHY OF
SIEGFRIED JAVOTNIK: PRE-HISTORY II

The 1939 Grand Prix racer 500 cc. could summon 90 h.p. at 8,000 r.p.m., and hit 150 m.p.h. when stripped of unnecessary parts, but my father was allowed no more than 80 m.p.h. when he took to driving the racer in the spring of '42. Vratno carried a necessary part. Namely, Gottlob Wut as passenger—the constant, correcting voice in my father's indigo-blue ear hole.

"You should be in third now. You steered us through that last one more than you leaned. You're much too nervous; you're tight, your hands will cramp. And never use your rear brake on the downhills. Front-brake work, if you've got to brake at all. Use that rear brake again and I'll disconnect it. You're very nervous, you know."

But Gottlob Wut never said a thing about what a good job my father was doing at pretending he'd never driven before. And only after Wut had been forced to disconnect the rear brake did he ask Vratno where he lived and what he did for food. Clerical work, my father told him—occasional translations for pro-German Slovenes and Croats in a subgovernment position. Whatever that meant. Wut never asked again.

Although it wasn't exactly fair to call the Ustashi pro-German, they were pro-winning—and in the spring of '42, the Germans were still winning. There was even a Ustashi militia who wore Wehrmacht uniforms. In fact, the Slivnica twins, Gavro and Lutvo, had Wehrmacht uniforms of their own, which they wore only for dress-up, or for going out at night. The twins weren't part of any unit Vratno knew of, and once Bijelo scolded them on their manner of acquiring the uniforms; it seems they had several changes. The Ustashi overseer for the Slivnicas was alarmed, and called the twins a "relationship risk."

"Our family," said Todor, "has never been afraid to risk relationships of any kind."

But Todor was often snappish in the spring of '42. After all the work, the Ustashi had either lost interest or given up their hope that Gottlob Wut would betray anything vital enough to make him touchable. At least, as long as the Germans were winners—and as long as the Ustashi were pro-winning—Wut seemed quite safe from revenge. About all Wut was guilty of was the keeping and disguising of a Grand Prix racer in a motorcycle unit meant to have slower and less delicate war models. And Zivanna Slobod, Wut's ritual-minded Serbian mistress, turned out to be a Serb more by accident than inclination—and a "political outlaw," as she was called on record, only because her list of lovers included every political or apolitical type imaginable. So they couldn't very well incriminate Wut on her account either. And Sundays were free; what Wut did with the racer and my father, he did on his own time. It could even be argued that Wut's Sundays demonstrated extra effort on the part of the motorcycle unit's leader—a kind of keeping-in-shape exercise. The Ustashi simply had nothing they could ever make stick on Gottlob Wut.

"We could steal his pet racer," Bijelo suggested. "That might make him do something foolish."

"We could steal the Serbian woman," said Todor.

"Great cow of a woman," grumped jealous Baba, a titter-minded toad of a girl—as my father has described her. "You'd need a van to move her."

"I seems to me," said Julka, "that Wut is more fond of the motorcycle."

"Certainly," my father agreed. "But stealing it would do nothing. He'd have perfectly good military means for recovering it, or at least for looking. And I'm not so sure that the German command would even mind him having a racer."

"We'll just kill him, then," said Todor.

"The Ustashi," Bijelo said, "are in need of being legal, to a point."

"The Ustashi are boring me to death," said Todor.

"They have to stay on the right side," Bijelo said. "Wut is a German, and the Ustashi are siding with the Germans now. The idea is to make Wut be a bad German."

"Impossible," said Vratno. "He doesn't think one way or the other about being a German, so how could he be a bad one?"

"Well," Bijelo said, "I don't think the Ustashi are so very much interested in Wut any more. People are changing sides all the time, and the Ustashi have to come out with the winner. That's no longer so easy."

Because there were too many side wars within the war; whole sides were changing sides. In the spring of '42, the worldwide Communist press suddenly changed its mind about the Chetnik colonel Drazha Mihailovich—who was now a general. A suspiciously Russian-located station called Radio Free Yugoslavia was reporting that Drazha Mihailovich and his Chetniks were siding with the Germans. Radio Free Yugoslavia—and through them, even the B.B.C.—was saying that a certain blacksmith's son had been the only freedom fighter all along. Josip Broz Tito was the leader of the real resistance, and the defenders of Yugoslavia were Communist partisans, not hairy Chetniks. It seemed that Russia was looking ahead; with remarkable optimism, they appeared to be looking past the Germans to a more crucial issue in Yugloslavia.

Who would run the country when the war was over?

"Communists," said Bijelo Slivnica. "It's quite obvious, really. The Chetniks fight the Germans, the partisans fight the Germans, and in a little while the whole Red Army will be here—fighting Germans. In between Germans and after Germans, partisans and the Red Army will fight Chetniks—claiming that Chetniks side with the Germans. Good propaganda is what counts."

"A divine scheme," said Todor.

"Publicity's the thing," Bijelo said. "Look: the Chetniks beat the Germans in Bosnia, right? But Radio Free Yugoslavia broadcasts that it was partisans who did the beating, and that they discovered Chetniks in Wehrmacht uniforms."

At the mere mention of which, Gavro and Lutvo went to change into their uniforms.

"Utter dummies," said Julka; while in the kitchen, fine Dabrinka washed wineglasses. My father didn't dare to watch her any more.

"Which brings us back to Wut," Bijelo Slivnica said.

"I don't at all see how," said Todor.

"Because the Ustashi need to be sure," Bijelo said. "Wut is a German. Germans kill Chetnik-Serbs, and lately, partisans. Partisans kill Chetnik-Serbs, and lately, Germans. The Ustashi will kill whatever the Germans want killed, but they don't want to kill partisans, if they can help it."

"Why not?" my father asked.

"Because," said Bijelo, "the Ustashi will soon enough be killing Germans *for* the partisans, because in the end the partisans will win."

"So what?" said Todor.

"So who does just about everyone want to kill?" Bijelo asked.

"Serbs!" said Todor.

And Bijelo Slivnica finally said, "Then a Serb should kill Gottlob Wut. Because the Ustashi will support the German percentage proclamation and kill one hundred Serbs for the one German, Wut. So the Germans are appeased, and when the Red Army and the partisans team up and drive the Germans from Yugoslavia—there's the Ustashi, having a good reputation for killing Serbs, nasty Chetniktypes. So the partisans are happy to have the Ustashi along. And the Ustashi stay happy; they pick winners. And, of course, they get to settle the score with old Gottlob Wut. Now I ask you," said Bijelo, "how's that for thinking?"

"What *Serb* is ever going to kill Wut?" my father asked.

"You," said Bijelo, "only you make it look like the job

was done by Zivanna Slobod, who really is a Serb. Then
you'll have to kill her too. So the Ustashi and the Germans will round up ninety-nine other Serbs and bump
them—to make the forewarned ratio come out right. One
hundred to one, see?"

"Bijelo has a touch for making everyone happy," said
Todor.

But my father said, "I don't think I want to kill Gottlob
Wut."

Julka brought her thighs together. *Flap!* they said. In
the kitchen, Dabrinka broke a wineglass.

"Oh, dear," said Baba.

And my father said to Bijelo, "Well, if it happens like
you say, the war will get old Wut anyway, won't it? And
the Ustashi aren't so very interested in Wut, you said so
yourself, anyway."

The twins came in, in their uniforms, and paraded for
everyone.

Bijelo, very calmly, said, "Look, it would be on a Sunday. See the twins' uniforms? You carry one with you in a
paper bag. Wut's having his endless bath, you see. And the
lid on the flush box behind the toilet? It's porcelain, right?
And very, very heavy. So when Zivanna goes to get her
pastries from the oven, you drop the flush-box lid on the
bathing, unsuspecting Wut. Should submerge him quite
handily. And where's Wut's sidearm holster? Hung on
the bathroom mirror, isn't it? So you take the gun and
shoot Zivanna when she brings back the pastries. Then
you put on Gavro's or Lutvo's uniform, and call the
German scout command. It's Sunday, remember; the
motorcycle unit has the day off. It's spring, remember;
they won't be sweating inside their barracks, either. German command takes you for one of Wut's regular drivers
—you know their names, so give one. Just watch your
irregular verbs. You tell a few tales about the Serbian
woman—how you heard of a plot to kill Wut but you
arrived too late. There are more than two million Serbs
in Slovenia and Croatia. Surely the Ustashi and the Germans can round up ninety-nine in downtown Slovenjgradec. Shoot them all the same day too—I wouldn't be
surprised."

But Vratno said, "I *like* Gottlob Wut."

"Sure," said Bijelo. "I like him too."

"We all like Gottlob Wut," Todor said. "But you like your job with us, don't you, Vratno?"

"Of course he does," said Bijelo. "Now why don't you try on a uniform, Vratno?"

But my father backed into the kitchen doorway; over his shoulder he could hear the squeak of a dishtowel on glass—the high, nervous sounds of Dabrinka's fast finger work.

"Why don't you try one on, now?" Todor said, and grabbed Lutvo, the nearest twin, and snatched down Lutvo's pants to his ankles, jerked up and dumped poor Lutvo on the floor.

Webfooted Baba prodded her still-uniformed brother Gavro toward the upturned face of the naked Lutvo— where Gavro behaved as a perfect twin and undressed himself. Todor then gathered the uniforms and flung them to my father in the kitchen doorway.

"Pick a uniform," he said. "Either one should do."

My father, backing into the kitchen, heard the gentle Dabrinka break another wineglass, and was turning to lend assistance when Dabrinka's slim wrists skated over his shoulders; her fine, girlish fingers lightly pricked my father's jugular with the needlepoint of the wineglass's splintered stem.

"You try on one of those uniforms, please," she said in Vratno's blushing ear. Which marked the first and only time there were ever words between them.

The Thirteenth Zoo Watch:
Tuesday, June 6, 1967, @ 4:45 a.m.

There's something funny going on here, all right.

When O. Schrutt was teasing the insomniacs in the House of Pachyderms, I went inside the Small Mammal House. Very spooky in there—with those infrared-exposed animals, thinking they live in a world with a twenty-hour night. They were all wakeful, most of them sort of shifty in their glasshouses—crouched or even pacing in the corners of their cages.

But I couldn't see that anything in particular was wrong! There wasn't any blood, and no one looked beaten or ravished or at Death's Door. They were just watchful, suspicious, and too alert for nocturnal creatures supposedly put at ease in nocturnal surroundings. Take, for example, the spotted civet cat—who was panting on its belly, its hind legs spread out behind it like a seal's tail-flipper. It swished its tail, waiting for the mouse or mad-man who would any second now burst through the closed back door of its cage.

The back doors of these cages, I found, lead into alleys that divide and are shared by the two opposing faces of cages in each block of the Small Mammal Maze. The al-leys are more like chutes for coal—a guard would have to kneel to make his way between and behind the cages, checking each labeled door. It is very nifty. A guard or feeder or cage-cleaner could creep along this passageway and know which animal's house he was invading, just by reading the tags on the door. Very wise. You wouldn't want to be unprepared—to carelessly dart your head in-side a cage, expecting the wee Brazilian pygmy marmoset and finding instead the great curved fighting claws of the giant anteaters, or a brash, ill-tempered mongoose.

From the alley, you can get some idea of what the out-side looks like to the animals. I opened the back door of the ratel's cage, thinking that a ratel must be a wee sort of rat, and to my surprise, discovered that the ratel is a fierce, badgerlike creature of Afro-Indian heritage, silky-furred and long-clawed; but before I slammed the door in his snarling face, I got a peek at how he saw the world. Darker than dark, like a solid rectangle of black, blacker than the entrance to a cave, there was a void drawn down like a shade beyond his front window glass.

When I closed the door, I had the awful feeling that if O. Schrutt had sneaked back to his lair, he could have been watching the ratel, and would have seen me suddenly loom in the ratel's back doorway and quickly slam the door on my own frightened face. I crept out of the chute, expecting at any moment to meet—if not O. Schrutt grunting on all fours—an ape specially trained for routing things out of the alleyways.

So when I got out in the main maze again, I went straight ahead with my business, with no more dallying. I went to O. Schrutt's room, the nightwatchman's layover spot. A percolator coffeepot, a cup with dregs, a ledger on the messy desk—the master sheet for the zoo animals, with columns for special entries, things to be on the look-out for. Like:

The giant forest hog has ingrown tusk; is caused some pain. Give aspirinated salt cubes (2), if suffering.

The ocelot is expecting, any day now.

The binturong (bearcat of Borneo) has rare disease; better watch out for it.

The bandicoot is dying.

And each animal had a number; on the master plan of the zoo, the cages were numbered in an orderly, clockwise fashion.

My God. A *rare disease!* Is that all—just watch out for a rare disease? The binturong has nameless, incurable suffering. And the bandicoot is dying! Just like that—dying; the rare little leaper. Keep an eye on it, sweep it out when it's through.

Into a world like this, the ocelot is giving birth. My God. Stop the whole process.

O. Schrutt's den. This ledger, this murky percolator, and hanging by a leather thong to a hook just inside the door—an electric cattle prod; beside it was a pole with a gaffinglike hook on the end.

For the life of me, I can't tell what O. Schrutt has done in here.

I looked around as long as I dared. And then I heard him coming by the bears again. I heard the famous frustration of the Asiatic Black Bear, lunging just short of O. Schrutt's combat boots. I realized I'd missed my chance, this time, for moving the safety rope about a foot in the unsafe direction. I made my break then, down by the Monkey Complex.

This time, I didn't come too close. I saw the frotter, this time. The gelada baboon, waiting for me, crouched motionless on the dark, outside terrace of his cage—hoping I'd come too close to the bars again. And when he saw I saw him, and that I wasn't coming anywhere near him, he leapt to the nearest trapeze and swung himself howling through the half-dark, landing high up on the bars, facing me. He just screamed, and the scheming Monkey Complex broke out in unison, in a banter that got all the zoo heated and talking again.

O. Schrutt came, bobbing his flashlight along, but I was

easily ahead of him and under my hedge before he'd even got to the Monkey Complex.

And again, when he arrived, there wasn't so much as a spider monkey on the outside terrace. They were all swinging silently within the complex; once or twice, a thump of a trapeze, or dry slaps—as if an ape were rolling over and over, beating his chest and knees, aping laughter in a pantomime of loud and huge delight.

"You did it again!" O. Schrutt screamed. "What are you up to?" And he lost a shade of his aggressiveness; he began again to back away, darting his flashlight through the treetops, jerking his head back from imagined, claw-carrying shapes he saw hurtling down on him. "What's out here?" cried old O. Schrutt. And backing farther off, leaning toward the security of the Small Mammal House, he shouted, "You damn baboon, you can't fool me! I'm not monkey enough to fall for your games!"

Then he turned and ran for the door of the Small Mammal House, looking back over his shoulder as he stumbled headlong up the stairs.

I thought: If ony at this moment, *there* was the Asiatic Black Bear, or a mere vision of him, in the doorway—if just for a second, precisely as O. Schrutt gave a last look over his shoulder before going inside, there would be the terrible Oriental bear laying a gruff paw on the back of O. Schrutt's neck—old O. would die of fright, without a word.

But he got back inside. I heard him swearing. Then I heard doors being creaked, and at least I knew now what doors they were, and where they led. And I again heard sliding glass being slid. I thought: What glass? There was no glass I saw that slid.

But it was very soon thereafter that the cries and snarls reached me in their piecemeal fashion again, and I knew that I simply had to see the Small Mammal House while O. Schrutt was still *inside* and up to his dirty work.

I feel I have to risk it. If only because the bandicoot is dying—and the glossy ocelot is expecting, any day now.

(CONTINUING:)
THE HIGHLY SELECTIVE AUTOBIOGRAPHY OF
SIEGFRIED JAVOTNIK: PRE-HISTORY II

The Slivnicas were a rare family for foresight. The plan
for sinking Gottlob Wut in his bathtub was approved by
the Ustashi. And the penalty of one hundred to one being
carried out on Serbs for the death of a German was not
unfamiliar with the Ustashi either. They'd been setting up
Serbian massacres since the middle months of '41. There
had been some countermassacres as well, but the Ustashi
were numerically far ahead; they had a percentage proclamation just like the Germans'—one hundred Serbs for
each Ustashi killed. If anything was accomplished by this,
by the summer of '42, it was the feeling among Serbs that
all Slovenes and Croats were Ustashi terrorists—among
Slovenes and Croats, that all Serbs were hairy Chetniks. A
fine muddle was made, as Bijelo Slivnica wisely foresaw,
and Tito's partisans were growing stronger on the fringes
of every mess. The Germans were spread out thin, from
Slovenjgradec en route to Moscow, and the Italians now
held the Dalmatian coast of Yugoslavia and royally sup-
ported the Ustashi.

"Wut is nicely settled," said Bijelo Slivnica through a
huge sandwich.

But my father had a bit of foresight himself.

On a Sunday morning in August, known as Wut Sunday
among the Slivnicas, my father sat in the bathroom while
Gottlob Wut soaked. When Zivanna Slobod went to check
her oven, Vratno said, "There's a strange car across the
street from us, Wut—a strange, large family on some sort
of outing."

"That so?" said Wut.

My father lifted up the flush-box lid and held it in his
lap.

"Need exercise?" said Wut.

"I'm supposed to kill you," Vratno said. "I'm supposed
to sink you under this toilet top and shoot your lady when
she brings in the pastries."

"Why's that?" said Wut.

"Oh, it's a real mess," my father said.

"Are you a Chetnik," Gottlob asked, "or a partisan?"

"I'm presently employed by the Ustashi," my father said.

"But they're on our side, now," said Wut.

My father explained: "They were also on the side of Guido Maggiacomo at the Grand Prix of Italy in 1930. So I imagine it's awkward for them too."

"Oh, dear, I see," said Wut. "Of course, it must be very difficult for them, I'm sure." He stood up, embarrassed in his tub; his countless, indented scars held the bath water and dripped like wounds still open.

When Zivanna Slobod came back to the bathroom, she noticed that her ritual had been upset and she dropped her pastries in Gottlob's abandoned bath. Wut himself was putting the toilet top back in place, and Vratno was getting into a Slivnica Wehrmacht uniform. Wut then uniformed himself, while the blubbering Zivanna was fishing a nut loaf out of the bath water. Surprises did not become her.

Surprises weren't very becoming to the Slivnicas, either. When Gottlob Wut, all alone, came out on Smartin Street and wandered leisurely toward the motorcycle unit's garage, Bijelo Slivnica simply must have said: sit tight. Because the carload of the whole family sat there, watching Wut and waiting for Vratno to make a dash.

They waited all the while it took Wut to start one of the 600 cc. sidecar models and roll it into the open doorway, pointed out—to go. Then Wut took the carburetors out of all the remaining motorcycles in the garage, except the 1939 Grand Prix racer. Wut put all the carburetors into the waiting sidecar—along with a toolbox, points, plugs, cables, assorted engine parts, a primary and a drive chain, topographical maps of Slovenia and Croatia, and two dozen grenades; he cupped one grenade in his hand and started up his racer.

The Slivnicas were still waiting when Gottlob Wut came back up Smartin Street on the Grand Prix racer, stripped of trimmings, and they must have thought Wut was having trouble with his bike, because he was riding bent over and had one hand cupped under his gas tank—where his fuel line might have come loose. The Slivnicas watched Wut weave up the street toward them, head down and fumbling under the gas tank, and quite possibly they never saw him roll the unpinned grenade under their car.

I believe that Bijelo Slivnica and his unpleasant family were still sitting tight when the car blew up.

The noise of which brought my father bolting out on Smartin Street and up behind Wut on the racer. Gottlob turned back to the garage and established Vratno on the running, warmed-up sidecar model 600.

"Why'd you do it, Wut?" my father asked.

"For some time now," said Gottlob Wut, "I've wanted to be on the road again."

But whatever the reason Wut gave, there was this understood: they were even. My father had not submerged Gottlob Wut, and Gottlob had not abandoned my father.

They weren't followed. Scout Outfit Balkan 4 was hard to find on Sundays, and when found, they were hard to mobilize—owing to a lack of caburetors.

When they got to Dravograd, Wut and my father heard the carefully censored news. A well-liked Ustashi family of six had been killed—sabotaged on Smartin Street, Slovenjgradec. Ustashi and German troops seized Zivanna Slobod, notorious Serbian prostitute—and the murderess responsible for this crime. In accordance with German and Ustashi proclamations, one hundred Serbs will be shot for each German or Ustashi murdered. In Slovenjgradec, Serbs were being sought to answer for the crime. Six Slivnicas equals six hundred Serbs—Zivanna Slobod and five hundred and ninety-nine others.

And in Dravograd my father was thinking: But there were *seven* Slivnicas. Bijelo, Todor, Gavro, Lutvo, Baba, Julka, and Dabrinka makes seven. Whichever one escaped saved the lives of one hundred Serbs, but my father, who was unconcerned with politics, wasn't comforted by that thought.

"I think it was Dabrinka who wasn't blown up," Vratno told Wut. "She had the least flesh to get in the way of flying stuff."

"Doubtful," said Wut. "It must have been the driver. He was the only one who might possibly have seen it coming, and he had the wheel to hold on to—to keep himself from going through the roof."

They discussed it further over a urinal in a Dravograd dive.

"Who would have been the driver?" asked Wut.

"Todor always drove," said Vratno. "But he also had

the most flesh to get in the way of flying stuff, if you go by my theory."

"I don't go by any theories," said Gottlob Wut. "It's just very pleasant to be on the road again."

The Fourteenth Zoo Watch:
Tuesday, June 6, 1967, @ 5:00 a.m.

I'm stalling. But I have my reasons!

One thing, it's beginning to get light out—as if this moon hasn't been light enough. And foremost, I don't see how I can get into the Small Mammal House without O. Schrutt seeing me. If I were inside and O. Schrutt came in, that would be a different matter; then I could listen to where he was and avoid him in the maze. But I don't like the idea of making a dash up those stairs and coming through that doorway, when I can't be sure what part of the maze O. Schrutt is in.

So I've decided: I have to wait for the plotting gelada baboon to come outside again. Now that it's getting light, I can see the outside terrace of the Monkey Complex from the end of my hedgerow. When that gelada baboon comes out, I'll make my move.

It's simple. I'll station myself behind the children's drinking fountain, near the entrance to the Small Mammal House. Then I'll get that baboon's attention; I'll lob rocks at him; I'll leap out from behind the fountain and make rude, insulting gestures. That will set him off, I know. And when he's raging, O. Schrutt will come pelting down those stairs, fit to kill. And when O. Schrutt is going through his paranoiac ritual at the Monkey Complex, I'll streak silent and barefoot into the Small Mammal House; I'll get myself well back in the maze. O. Schrutt may come out so fast that he'll leave the bloody evidence this time. And if not, then at least I'll be in there when he starts up again.

At least, there's been no indication that he'll let up. The fiend seems bent on keeping everyone up till the zoo opens. No wonder the animals always look so drowsy.

You may think, Graff, that I sound extreme. But if there's an ulterior motive behind this zoo bust, it would certainly be the exposing of old O.—even if I don't know exactly what he is, yet.

I know where he's come from, though. Twenty or more

years ago—it's common history what various O. Schrutts
were up to. I know the route O. Schrutt has been, and I'll
bet there are those along that route who'd be surprised to
hear of O. Schrutt again. At least, there are those who'd
be more than interested to find an O. Schrutt who still
wears his nametag and has kept both epaulettes.

Ha! After how many atrocities to previous small mammals, how very fitting that old O. should end up here.

(CONTINUING:)
THE HIGHLY SELECTIVE AUTOBIOGRAPHY OF
SIEGFRIED JAVOTNIK: PRE-HISTORY II

My father and Gottlob Wut spent two years in the mountains of northern Slovenia. Twice they were lonesome and
planned trips. The first one, to Austria, ended at the Radel
Pass along the mountain border. The Austrian Army
guards appeared very formal and thorough with their rifles
and paper work at the checkpoint. Wut decided that
they'd have to abandon the motorcycles to make a crossing feasible, so they drove back into the Slovenian mountains that same night. And the second trip, to Turkey, ended just southeast of Maribor at the Drava River, where
the Ustashi had accomplished another massacre of Serbs
the night before; an elbow of the Drava was clogged with
corpses. My father would always remember a raft snagged
in some deadfall along the bank. The raft was neatly piled
with heads; the architect had attempted a pyramid. It was
almost perfect. But one head near the peak had slipped
out of place; its hair was caught between other heads, and
it swung from face to face in the river wind; some faces
watched the swinging, and some looked away. My father
and Gottlob again drove back to the Slovenian mountains,
near the village of Rogla, and that night slept in each
other's arms.

In Rogla, an old peasant named Borsfa Durd kept them
alive for the privilege of having rides on the sidecar model
600. Borsfa Durd was scared of the racer—he never understood what kept it upright—but he loved to sit toothless in the sidecar while my father bumped him over the
mountains. Borsfa Durd got them fuel and food; he raided
the Ustashi depot at Vitanje—until the August of '44,
when he was returned to Rogla in a fellow-villager's

mulch wagon. The terrified villager said the Ustashi had
stood the kicking old Durd on his head on the wagon floor
and shovel-packed mulch all around him; only the soles of
his shoes were visible at the peak of the mulch mound,
when everyone tried to extricate him for a proper burial
in Rogla. But the mulch was too wet and heavy, too hard-
packed, so a certain mass of mulch was chopped and
rolled off the wagon into a hole; the hole was circle-shaped
because that was the appropriate cut of the mulch mass,
which was said to contain Borsfa Durd. Although no one
really saw more of him than the soles of his shoes, the fel-
ow-villager who'd brought him back, in his reeking
wagon, testified that it was Borsfa Durd without a
doubt—and Gottlob Wut said he recognized the shoes.

So Borsfa Durd was buried coffinless in a chunk of
mulch, which ended the fuel-and-food supply for the runaway motorcycles and their keepers. My father and Gottlob Wut thought they'd better move; if the Ustashi at the
depot in Vitanje were at all curious as to why Borsfa Durd
had been raiding their supplies, Vratno and Gottlob could
be expecting a visit. So they left, taking what Borsfa Durd
had owned for clothes.

Relying on the topographical maps, they went over a
route in the daytime, dressed as peasants and scouting on
foot—the motorcycles were always stashed in brush;
they'd walk five miles down the mountains, spotting the
villages for small armies of any kind, and then five miles
back to the motorcycles—out again on the bikes at night,
this time in their Wehrmacht uniforms. By checking the
route in the daytime, they not only knew how far away
they were from villages, but they could drive most of the
time with their headlights out and be reasonably confident
of where they were going. They had some fuel left over
from Borsfa Durd's next to last raid at Vitanje, but there's
no doubt it would have been safer to abandon the motorcycles; they'd have run little risk, dressed as peasants and
traveling on foot. This alternative, however, was never
mentioned; it must be understood that the scout-outfit
leader of Motorcycle Unit Balkan 4 had deserted the war
in order to devote his time to motorcycles, not to escape
anything in particular—especially on foot.

In fact, Gottlob Wut was such a bad walker that they
couldn't for long keep up their routine of five miles out
and back in one day. Wut developed shin splints, or water

on the spine, or an ailment stemming from early
childhhood—when he had somehow cheated on his learn-
ing-to-walk responsibilities, and depended, even at that
time, on wheels. Actually, he confessed to Vratno, it was
just one wheel at first. Wut had been the unicycle champion of Neckarsulm Technical High School for three
straight years. As far as Gottlob knew, he still held the
school record for the unicycle: three hours and thirty-one
minutes of steady wheeling and balancing with no rest and
without touching the ground with heel or toe. This performance was recorded on Parents' Night too, on the
speaker's platform—when hundreds of weary elders
drooped and shifted on hard benches, praying for three
hours and thirty-one minutes that Wut would fall and
break his boring neck.

But Gottlob Wut simply needed a wheel or two under
his spine, in order to stay even moderately upright for any
length of time.

They were a long time in the mountains, with only one
incident. They were in the habit of fishing for food, or
raiding, at night, the villages they'd spotted in the daytime.
But on the third of September, 1944, they'd been two days
with nothing but berries and water when they fell in with
an odd crew. Croats, they were—a ragged peasant
army—on their long way to join Mihailovich and his
diehard Chetniks. Gottlob and my father, fortunately in
Borsfa Durd's old clothes, were ambushed by them in a
valley below Sv. Areh. The ambush was all shouts, a stick
or two, and a very old gun fired in the air. The Croats
were, among other things, lost, and they offered Vratno
and Gottlob safe passage for good directions out of where
they were. It was a very odd crew—Croats wanting to
join up with Serbs! They had apparently all been un-
willingly involved in a recent partisan-Ustashi massacre of
Serbs, and had seen for themselves how the Serbs were
abused. Of course, their position was hopeless; there
couldn't have been any organized Chetniks of any account
in Slovenia. But my father and Gottlob spent a day and an
evening with them, eating off a captured cow and drinking
a wine so new it was pulpy. Vratno told the Croats how
Gottlob hadn't been able to talk since he was shot in the
brain. Which excused old Wut from the Serbo-Croat.

The Croats said the Germans were losing the war.

The Croats also had a radio, which was how Vratno

and Gottlob discovered the date was September 3—and were able to confirm their guess that the year was '44. And that evening they heard a Communist communiqué on Radio Free Yugoslavia, concerning a partisan victory over the Germans at Lazarevats. The Croats wildly protested, saying they'd had it from Serb sources that the Chetniks were surrounding Lazarevats and therefore must have been responsible for the victory and the capture of some two hundred Germans. The Croats insisted there were no partisans within miles of Lazarevats; then one of them asked where Lazarevats was, and the poor, befuddled Croats bemoaned again how lost they were.

That same evening, Vratno excused Gottlob and himself. And plodded back to the motorcycles. He explained to the Croats how Gottlob's muteness caused him pain, and they had to find a doctor. The poor Croats were so hopeless; not one of them even had the sense to notice that my father and Gottlob went off in the opposite direction from how they'd been headed at the ambush.

Vratno gave Wut a translation of the radio broadcast.

"Mihailovich is a goner," Wut said. "The trouble with the Chetniks and all those fool Serbs is that they've got no idea of propaganda. They don't even have a party line—not so much as a slogan! There's nothing to grab on to. Now these partisans," said Wut, "they've got the radio controls, and a simple, unswerving line: defend Russia; communism is anti-Nazi; and the Chetniks really side with the Germans. Does it matter if it's true?" Wut asked. "It's repeated and repeated, and it's very simply principled. The very essence," said Wut, "of effective propaganda."

"I didn't know you had any ideas," my father said.

"It's all in *Mein Kampf*," said Wut, "and you certainly have to agree. Adolf Hitler is the greatest propaganda artist of all time."

"But Germany's losing the war," my father said.

"Win or lose," said Gottlob Wut, "look at how much that little fart got going. Look at how far the fart has gone!"

The Fifteenth Zoo Watch:
Tuesday, June 6, 1967, @ 5:15 a.m.

O. Schrutt has gone too far!

Oh, my part was easy. When that sulking baboon came out on the prowl again, I tore around the Monkey Complex and broke cover—for a moment—going full-tilt for the children's drinking fountain. I didn't even have to cause a stir; the old gelada saw me coming before I got behind the fountain. He brayed, he barked, he crowed; in a frenzy, he chomped the chain of his trapeze. And, of course, the zoo joined in again.

And, of course, O. Schrutt left some small mammals in the midst of their various agonies and stormed out the door.

He went off the deep end this time; this time, he went inside the Monkey Complex. I waited only a second, horrified at the din O. Schrutt and the monkeys made; it all squeezed out a small, open skylight in the Monkey Complex, like one tremendous lungful blown in a flute and squeezed out through only one shrill finger hole. And before O. Schrutt came outside again, I dashed up the stairs and into the Small Mammal House.

I didn't stop to look in the cages. I pelted down the nearest aisle, took a left and then a narrower right—considered entering a chute, but thought against it—and finally stopped where I felt it quite safe; I was within listening distance of the main door, and I was around several corners from whatever way O. Schrutt might come; there were corners and turnoffs enough between us, so that I could hear him coming and have time to plot my next, avoiding move.

I saw briefly that I'd stopped alongside the aardvark's glasshouse. But it wasn't until I'd made an effort to control my panting that I realized the aardvark wasn't alone.

There was a stand-off! In one corner of his home, the aardvark backed himself up on the root of his tail—balancing, and holding his foreclaws out like boxing gloves; in the opposite, diagonal corner, facing the aardvark, was the small but vicious Indo-Chinese fishing cat—a nasty little item, hackles up and back arched high. They hardly moved. It didn't appear that either one would attack, but each time the aardvark would slightly lose and then catch his balance on the root of his tail, the fishing cat would snarl and hiss and lower its chin to the sawdust floor. And the aardvark—old sluggish earth pig—would snort a low sort of snort. I was trying to weigh all the odds in my mind when I heard O. Schrutt.

He sounded like he was just outside the Monkey Complex, but his bullying voice was coming my way. "There's nothing here, you fake of a baboon! You try me once more, and I'll have you go a round with my little jaguarundi! I'll give you something to scream about, I will!"

While beside me the fishing cat yowled, faked a spring; and the aardvark grunted, stiffened up on his hind legs and the thick root of his tail. They stood off each other—my God, for how long?

O. Schrutt! He makes his own theater! He creates a late show all for himself!

O. Schrutt came roaring into the Small Mammal House. I heard him taunt someone; and then I heard the combat boots walking round a corner closer to me, one aisle to my left and one up; I traced an aisle to my right, padding coolly barefoot on the cement. I waited for O. Schrutt's next move.

Only twice did I actually see O. Schrutt in the maze.

Once, when I was crouched flush to a cage wall, but below a cage window—out of the infrared reflected through the glass, I think, and a whole aisle-length away—I saw old O. approach one of his productions. He slid back the glass to the cage! That's the glass that slides, the whole damn window face slides back. O. Schrutt's got a little key that lets him unlock the sliding glass—it makes sense; if someone heavy died, or someone vicious was sick and wouldn't come out, you wouldn't want to fool around with that little back door off the chute—but O. Schrutt opens the glass to urge his gladiators on! If he thinks a stand-off is much too calm, he slips his cattle prod inside and touches off one of his contestants. And, of course, they can't see him, standing in the void—inserting his electric arm; it comes groping at them out of the dark, and jolts them neatly, once or twice.

I saw him conduct the vocal levels up, then slide the glass back—cutting off the complaints. Then he watched, with interest, the Tasmanian devil skittering side to side and yelling as if it were running over hot coals—kept at bay by the surly ratel. O. Schrutt watched quite calmly, I thought—his raving mind at ease, or drugged.

And once more I saw O. Schrutt. This time, I was perfectly safe in observing him. He'd gone in one of the chutes, so I just watched a whole glassy row of animals, looking for which cage would suddenly exhibit old O. at the back door—from where, I knew, he had the animals' perspective, and couldn't see a thing beyond the front glass.

I watched him break up a stand-off that looked like it had been running over-long. Two tired giant anteaters looked as if they had taken all they could stand from a wildly pacing, panting jaguarundi—long, low, lean, little tropical cat. O. Schrutt is sly! He doesn't want any blood. O. Schrutt's overseers would be suspicious of mangled small mammals. O. Schrutt is a careful director; he keeps the matches at an exhausting standstill; he's there with his cattle prod to break up anything that gets out of hand.

I saw enough, I'll tell you. O. Schrutt operates on all scales.

The slow loris exchanges terrified glances with a lemur. The Malayan tree shrew is aghast at the startled leaps of the kangaroo rat. I was so ashamed to see: even the dying bandicoot is forced to endure the antics of the flying phalanger. And the expectant mother ocelot lies haggard in her cage corner, listening to the grunts and scuffles in the chute behind her back door.

O. Schrutt knows no bounds.

I waited until he was off in one end of the maze, and then I fled his house of organized horror.

I lay back in my hedgerow, thinking: Whatever gave him the idea? Where did O. Schrutt first develop his perverse habit of playing small mammals off against each other?

It's getting lighter all around me now, and I'm still without an overall scheme. But I can tell you, I have plans for old O. Schrutt.

(CONTINUING:)

THE HIGHLY SELECTIVE AUTOBIOGRAPHY OF
SIEGFRIED JAVOTNIK: PRE-HISTORY II

On the fourteenth of October, 1944, the Red Army entered Belgrade, with ex-quisling Marko Mesich leading the Yugoslav contingent. Well, times change; it was a hard war to go through if you stayed on the same side you began with.

On the twenty-fourth of October, 1944, a Russian partisan group were surprised to find Chetniks engaging a force of twenty thousand Germans at Chachak. While the Russians and Chetniks were making a pincer attack on the Germans, a Russian officer observed that the partisans were attacking the Chetniks from behind. After the battle, the Chetniks turned over forty-five hundred German prisoners to the Russians; the following day, the Russians and partisans disarmed the Chetniks and arrested them. Chetnik Captain Rakovich escaped, and the partisans made a most sincere hunt for him throughout the Chachak area.

My father and Gottlob Wut were still in the Slovenian mountains, west of Maribor, when the hunt for Chetnik Captain Rakovich began.

There was no hunting at all in the Slovenian mountains. The Germans were on the defensive now, and the Ustashi were biding their time, middle-of-the-road. The Red Army wasn't as far west as Slovenia, and the partisan forces weren't at their strongest; the Ustashi weren't really fighting *for* the Germans any more—not wanting to turn the partisans against them—but it wasn't quite safe enough for the Ustashi to fight *against* the Germans either. At least not in Slovenia.

And Gottlob Wut was getting depressed. His legs and back and general walking apparatus were pitifully shot, and there were very few roads in the mountains where Gottlob could wheel his motorcycle peacefully and freely. And by November the mountains were very cold; the motorcycles needed a lighter oil.

It was some time in mid-November that the staff radio in the 600 sidecar model began to burble; up to that time, Vratno and Gottlob had figured the radio was dead, or that any mobilized German effort was out of broadcasting range. Gottlob eavesdropped over his radio; for two days the burble grew louder, but it was all some sort of number code. On the third day, however, Gottlob Wut recognized a voice from Motorcycle Unit Balkan 4.

"That's Wallner!" Gottlob said. "That hot-rodding punk, he's got my old job!" And before my father could knock him away from the radio, poor Wut flipped on the transmit switch and shouted, "Piglet! Incompetent piglet!" Then Vratno tackled him off the seat, scrambled back to the radio and flipped off the transmit switch, leaving the dial at listen-in. Where they heard a motorcycle idling, almost stalling.

Then Wallner's voice whispered or gasped, "Wut! Herr Commander Wut?" While Wut tore the grass on the ground. "Commander Wut?" the voice said again.

There was only the rough idle coming over the radio when Gottlob said, "Listen to that engine! It's so far out of tune, it would burn up if you ever had to push it."

But the transmit switch was left off; Wallner was given no opportunity to confirm what he thought he heard. Radio Wallner said, "Bronsky, are you switched on? Come in, come in." And there was nothing, so Wallner said, "Gortz, listen in! Listen in, Metz! It's the commander, didn't you hear him?" And then he shouted, "Vatch, are you there, Vatch?" Then the motorcycle stalled and Wallner grunted some untender oath. Vratno and Gottlob could hear him jumping on the kick starter.

"He's got the choke full on," said Wut. "Listen to him draw the air."

And they heard the kick starter ratcheting up and down; far away from catching, his engine sucked.

"Listen in, you bastards!" Radio Wallner screamed. "You're supposed to be switched on!" And he labored on the kick starter, panting into the radio. "You pricks!" he screamed. "I heard old Wut!"

"*Old* Wut!" said Wut, but my father held him back from the transmit switch.

"Old Wut is around!" Wallner screamed to the radio. "Where are you, Wut?"

"Up your ass," said Gottlob, still tearing grass.

"*Wut!*" Wallner screamed.

And another radio voice said, "Who?"

"Wut!" said Wallner.

"Wut? Where?" the other voice said.

"That's Gortz," Wut told my father.

"Bronsky?" said Wallner.

"No, Gortz," Gortz said, "What's this Wut shit?"

"I heard Wut," said Wallner.

A third radio voice said, "Hello?"

"That's Metz," said Wut.

"Bronsky?" Wallner asked.

"No, Metz," Metz said. "What's up?"

"Wut's around," said Wallner.

"I didn't hear him," Gortz said.

"You weren't switched on!" Wallner screamed. "I heard Wut!"

"What'd he say?" asked Metz.

"Oh, I don't know," Wallner said. " 'Piglet,' I think. *Ja,* 'piglet'!"

"I've heard him use the word," said Metz.

"*Ja,* two years ago," said Gortz. "I didn't hear any-thing."

"You prick, you weren't switched on!" Wallner shouted.

"Hello," said a fourth.

"Bronsky," Wut said to my father.

"Vatch?" said Wallner.

"Bronsky," Bronsky said.

"Wallner heard Wut," said Metz.

"Wallner *thinks* he did," Gortz said.

"I heard him, very loud!" said Wallner.

"Wut?" Bronsky said. "Wut, around here?"

"Around *where,* I'd like to know," my father said to Gottlob.

"It was crystal clear," said Wallner.

"Hello," Vatch said, the last to switch on.

"Vatch?" said Wallner.

"Yes," said Vatch. "What's up?"

"Its very complicated," Gortz said.

"Pricks!" said Wallner. "I really heard him!"

"Heard who?" Vatch asked.

"Hitler," said Gortz.

"Churchill," said Metz.

"Wut!" Wallner screamed. "You're out there, Wut, you piglet yourself! Speak up, Wut!" But Gottlob sat grinning on the grass. He listened to the ragged motorcycles and the mad Wallner, his cronies dropping off the radio, one by one.

Then a voice Wut didn't know came from some further distance—carrying static with it: more numbers. And Wallner answered, "I heard my old commander. Wut, the deserter—he's out here." And the numbers answered him back. "No, really! Wut is out here," said Wallner. And a staticful voice from a further distance said, "Use your numbers, Commander Wallner." And Wallner babbled numbers.

"*Commander* Wallner," Gottlob scoffed. He and Vratno listened longer, until there was no more transmitting; the radio crackled and hummed.

"Where do you think they are?" said Vratno.

"Where are we?" Wut asked. Together, they went over the maps. They were maybe five miles above the Drava River and the Maribor road.

"A movement?" said Wut. "They're pulling out of Slovenjgradec, maybe? Going east to fight the Russians? North to join the Austrians?"

"A movement, anyway," Vratno said. "On the Maribor road."

And that night they listened at the radio again. There were more numbers, staticful and distant. It was after midnight when they heard Wallner again.

"Wut?" the radio whispered. "Can you hear me, Wut?"

And Gortz must have been at his radio, because he said, "Come on, Wallner, take it easy. Get some sleep, man."

"Get off your radio," Wallner snapped. "Maybe he only talks to me."

"*That* I believe," said Gortz.

"Get off!" Wallner said, and said again, "Wut?" in a whisper. "Come in, come in. Damn you, Wut, come in." And was drowned out by numbers.

Then the unrecognizable authoritative voice came back: "Commander Wallner, go to sleep. I must ask you, when you use the radio, to use your numbers, please." Wallner spewed numbers and got no reply.

Vratno whispered to the giggling Gottlob Wut, "When he's alone, now, that's when. When you're sure he's got the radio to himself, give it to him then." And Wut, still leaving the dial at listen-in, flipped on the transmit switch.

Later, Wallner whispered numbers. There was no reply. "Balkan Four," whispered Wallner then. "Balkan Four." And got no reply. Then he said, a little louder, "You old prick, Wut. Wut, come in." Gottlob waited for someone else to come in. There was no reply, and Wallner said, "Wut. You traitor, Wut. Gutless prick, Wut."

Then Gottlob said softly, "Goodnight, *Commander* Wallner." And flipped the transmit switch off, still keeping the dial at listen-in.

"Wut!" Wallner hissed. *"Wooooooot!"* he screamed. and there was more static—and brushing, thumping sounds. Wallner must have had the radio off the motorcycle mounts and in a tent somewhere; they heard the tent flap, they heard radio parts crackle. Wallner must have lugged the radio out of his tent like a football hugged to his chest, because his shouts seemed farther away now, as if his mouth weren't near the speaker hole: "He's around, listen in! You pricks, switch on and hear him!"

And Gortz whispered loudly, "Wallner! For God's sakes, man."

And the unknown authoritative voice said, "Commander Wallner, that's quite enough. Use your numbers or lose your radio, Commander." And almost rhythmically, Wallner came on with his numbers; musically, he crooned his numbers into the night.

Vratno and Gottlob sat and dozed; they woke and hugged each other—laughing down their two-year beards —and dozed again, keeping the radio at listen-in. Once they heard Wallner murmur, asleep or still feebly trying, "Goodnight, Commander Wut, you prick." But Gottlob just grinned in silence.

Before first light, Wut and Vratno packed the bikes and moved four miles north, above Limbus. Then they camouflaged their gear and bikes, and carried the unmounted radio, walked a quarter of a mile, north along a ridge line—caught the sun coming over the right of the church spire at Limbus, and camped themselves less than a mile from, and in full view of, the Maribor road.

They were there the next day and night without a bite to eat or a glimpse of a motorcycle scout. At night they tuned in on Wallner, but heard only numbers—none of them in Wallner's voice. It was the next morning that they heard louder numbers, coming from Gortz, and once, shortly before noon, Gortz said, "It's too bad about Wallner." Bronsky answered that poor Wallner had always been too highly strung.

Then the overhearing, unknown voice said, "Com-

mander Gortz, you'll use your numbers, please." And
Gortz said he would.

It was that afternoon when Gottlob spotted sloppy
Heine Gortz on one of the '38 600 models, without sidecar. Bronsky followed him, with soft tires that Wut could
see all the way from the ridge.

And that night a large force moved through Limbus,
observing blackout conditions. With the tail end of the
movement barely out of town, my father made a raid on
a Limbus dairy and came back with milk and cheese.

They stayed two more days above Limbus before spotting a second, following, German movement—this one,
with unidentified motorcycle scouts. Not Balkan 4, anyway; they were some outfit down from Austria, maybe.
They scouted for a ragged force, a straggling crew—no
panzers, just some trucks and jeeps. And they were preceded by no number series. Some of the soldiers marched
with their helmets off; many sprouted most un-German
beards. It was a likely bet, and my father and Gottlob Wut
took the odds. They joined the movement on the Maribor
side of Limbus, meeting them on the road and saying
they'd had motor trouble which dropped them out of
Balkan 4. They were fed—the bikes had an oil change—
and they wheeled into Maribor, not knowing whether they
were on a retreat or headed for a front.

It didn't really matter. When the barracks' assignments
were given out, Gottlob said that he and his man were
hooking up again with their old outfit.

For a fee, they stashed their motorcycles in an outdoor
prostitute's booth in what was called the Old City; then
they rolled and robbed a German officer in an uptown district—cleverly done, disguised in Borsfa Durd's well-worn
clothes; next they found a *saunabad* which uncurled their
beards and made them glossy. Uniformed now, they
turned out on the town—two soldiers out for a night of
fun.

But oh, dear. In all of Maribor, you'd have thought
Gottlob Wut would have found a night spot that wasn't
the topmost choice for the other remnants of Balkan 4.

Perhaps Wut thought his two-year beard made him unrecognizable. Whatever, he was jaunty among the soldiers
in the Sv. Benedikt Cellar. There was a *Turkish* belly
dancer with the suspiciously Yugoslav name of Jarenina;
her dancing belly was Caesareaned. The beer was thin.

Surprising was this: there were no Ustashi troops in
Wehrmacht uniforms to be seen. But there was a blown-
up photo above the bar, riddled with darts—Ustashi in
Wehrmacht uniform, marching with *partisans!* somewhere
in Croatia.

My father was careful to be accurate with his umlaut
sounds; he felt their beards brought them under suspicion.

It was very late when Vratno followed Wut's wincing
walk to the unheated men's room. The urinal steamed; the
tiles were cracked around the terrible hole for the stand-
up crapper. A man weaved on his heels, pants down to his
ankles, and leaned back over the crapper's chasm—
clutching to the handrail that kept him from falling in.
Four men steamed over the urinal; another two came in
with Gottlob and my father.

Heads bowed over the trough, breath held against the
rising steam and stench, eight men fumbled and peed. One
dropped a cigarette down the sluiceway.

Then the man spanning the crapper gave a cry, and
must have tried to tug himself upright with a wrench on
the handrail.

"Wut!" the man screamed, and Gottlob, turning fast
and peeing down my father's leg, saw sloppy Heine Gortz
rip the handrail fron the rotting, tiled stall's wall and pitch
backward, pants snug at his ankles, fanny-first down into
the crapper's chasm. "Oh dear God!" moaned Heine
Gortz, and feet-up, his pocket change falling down on
him, he cried again, "Wut! For God's sakes, Bronsky, it's
Wut! Wake up, Metz! You're peeing next to old Wut!"

And before my father could stop his own peeing, Bronsky and Metz had spun poor Gottlob around and bent him
backward over the urinal. Heine Gortz clawed himself up
out of the hole. My father fumbled himself back in his
pants, but sloppy Heine Gortz said, *"You!* Who are you
with Wut?" But Gottlob didn't even look at Vratno; they
didn't appear to recognize each other.

My father said—enunciating every German syllable,
perfectly—"I just met the man. We had beards in common, you see. Just a mutual admiration."

And Bronsky or Metz said, "Old Wut! Would you just
look at him!"

"Filthy traitor," said Heine Gortz. And one of them
brought a knee up under him—buckled him—and someone tugged him along by his beard. They moved him into

the stand-up crapper stall. Then they upended him, and
sent him head-first down into the breathless bog. Balkan 4
worked as a team. New-leader Heine Gortz, beshitted
from his spine to the backs of knees, with his pants still
down at his ankles, had Wut by one leg and stuffed poor
Gottlob down the crapper's chasm.

While my father fastened his fly, exchanged shrugs of
shoulder and tilts of head with the perplexed others still
standing at the steaming urinal.

"Wut?" said one. "Who's this Wut?"

"We just had beards in common," Vratno said. "Just a
mutual admiration, was all," he emphasized, although my
poor father could scarcely talk—he was struck so dumb
by the terrible teamwork of Balkan 4—and it seemed to
him that he had to shout to get his words out in front of
his rising stomach.

When my father quietly left the Sv. Benedikt Cellar's
men's room, only the soles of Wut's shoes were showing
above the awful hole; like poor Borsfa Durd, Gottlob Wut
was buried coffinless; like Borsfa Durd, Gottlob Wut could
finally be recognized by no more than the soles of his
shoes.

The Sixteenth Zoo Watch:
Tuesday, June 6, 1967, @ 5:30 a.m.

I recommend that we do it just as I've done up to now.
We get behind this headgerow late one afternoon; we just
sit tight through the first-shift nightwatchman's watch.
When O. Schrutt takes over, we'll let him go through a
round or two. We'll have to be on our guard for the gelada baboon too, although that could be made to work
out in our favor.

I can't decide whether we should drive O. Schrutt bab-
bling mad, subtly; or simply feed him to the Famous
Asiatic Black Bear—at the first possible opportunity.

Handling O. Schrutt in the latter fashion could present
some problems. The Asiatic Black Bear might also get the
keyring, and there'd be no taking it away from him, I assure you. Also, O. Schrutt might just have time enough to
pull his gun and get a shot off. Whether he'd save himself
or not, there'd surely be a policeman in Hietzing with an
ear open for trouble in the zoo.

But even if we used the gelada baboon to drive O. Schrutt over the edge, there's no telling what form his final madness would take. He might run amuck in the zoo.

So this is a problem. I believe we'll have to nab O. Schrutt very neatly, in the Small Mammal House. Disarm him, tie and gag him—lead the frotter along a chute and tumble him into a glasshouse for safekeeping.

We'll toss him in with the giant anteaters! They should keep him still. With what O. Schrutt knows about matchmaking, he should know exactly how quiet and inoffensive he has to be to keep the giant anteaters at ease with him. But then, it would be unfair of us not to share O. Schrutt a little. I'm sure the Indo-Chinese fishing cat would love to babysit with O. Schrutt awhile. I'm sure the ratel and the jaguarundi would love to have O. Schrutt visit their homes, all trussed up like a goose for the roasting pan— cooing dovelike through his gag, his face in the sawdust, saying, "Nice, nice ratel—*ooooh!* Aren't you a nice little ratel, though? And you don't have any hard feelings, do you, ratel?"

Better yet, we could blindfold him and let him guess which animal he's been thrown in with—which snuffling, deep-breathing animal is laying a cold, movable nose against old O.'s ear.

Tit for tat, O. Schrutt.

(C O N T I N U I N G :)

THE HIGHLY SELECTIVE AUTOBIOGRAPHY OF SIEGFRIED JAVOTNIK: PRE-HISTORY II

My father laid low in Maribor. He paid a rather high rent for the prostitute's outdoor booth in the Old City, but thereby garaged the motorcycles safely out of sight. Not that he trusted the prostitute, a witchy thing who wouldn't tell him her name; in fact, one night when Vratno came back to the booth to sleep with the bikes, he found an old Serb siphoning gas out of the sidecar model 600. The Serb wouldn't give himself a name, either, but my father talked to him in Serbo-Croat and the old Serb gave way to senile utterances—choosing a theme of general disillusionment: first, with traitorous King Peter, who, after all, Mihailovich had rescued and sent to London. Did my fa-

ther know the song the Serbs sang? No, since it had to do
with politics; the old Serb sang it for him:

> *Kralju Pero, ti se naše zlato*
> *Churchill-u si na čuvanje dato ...*   —

> King Peter, you are our gold,
> We sent you to Churchill to keep you for us ...

But then, the old Serb ranted, the chicken-hearted King
had been bullied by the British into *what was best for Yugoslav unity.* King Peter announced on September 12,
1944, that support of Marshal Tito's People's Army was
the best chance for Yugoslavia. The King denounced
Mihailovich and Chetniks—called all those "Traitors to
the Fatherland" who wouldn't join the partisan army. Did
the King know, the old Serb asked, that only six days before his betrayal of his people, Chetniks had risked their
lives in the night to honor the King's birthday—bonfires
on every mountaintop and singing aflaunt their love for
the King, under blackout conditions too?

Did my father even know that? And Vratno confessed
he'd been tied up for a time in the mountains himself—
but not in Serbian mountains.

Well, then, did my father know what the Serbs sang
now?

> *Nećemo Tita Bandita—*
> *Hoćemo Kralja, i ako ne valja!*

> We don't want Tito the Bandit—
> We want the King, though he is no good!

So you shouldn't want him, then, my father told the Serb.
But the old man changed in Vratno's face:

> *Bolje grob nego rob!*
> Better a grave than a slave!

"No," my father said. "Anything's better than a *grob*."
Undoubtedly thinking: Especially as fresh a grave as the
one that received Gottlob Wut.

But Vratno didn't kill the old Serb for siphoning. He
made a deal. The sidecar model 600, with twenty-three

leftover grenades, for some of the Serb's underground handiwork—a transit permit, with name and photograph, that would enable my father to cross the Austrian border on the racer. Because he was going to Berlin to kill Hitler, he said.

"Why don't you kill Tito?" the Serb asked. "You wouldn't have to drive so far."

But they made the deal. A certain Siegfried Schmidt was issued German-command special-messenger transit papers by the very undermanned but efficient Serb underground of Maribor. And one cold but bright morning in mid-December of '44, Siegfried Schmidt—formerly, Vratno Javotnik—crossed into Austria and over the Mur River on a 1939 Grand Prix racer, stripped of its warlike fanfare (for special-messenger service), and fled north toward the city of Graz on what is now called Route 67.

And I choose to believe that it was the same cold but bright morning of December '44 when Chetnik Captain Rakovich was finally caught by the partisans and dragged back to Chachak—where his body was rearranged and displayed in the market plaza.

But concerning what happened to my father after the cold, bright morning of his entry into Austria, I can only guess. After all, Siegfried Schmidt was not protected for long by his Wehrmacht uniform, his Grand Prix racer, and his special papers—which were special only as long as the Germans held Austria.

One morning my father fled north to Graz, but he was never clear about how long he stayed in Graz—or when it was, exactly, that he drove north-northeast to Vienna. He wouldn't have stayed long in Graz, for sure, because Yugoslav partisans were crossing the Austrian border quite soon after him, without the need of special papers. And Vienna couldn't have been too safe for Siegfried Schmidt, motorcycle messenger, either; on April 13, 1945—just four months after my father left Maribor—the Soviets captured Vienna with the aid of Austrian resistance fighters. The Soviets were supposed to be liberating the city, but for a liberating army they did a surprising amount of raping and such. The Soviets obviously had difficulty considering Austria as a real victim of Germany; they'd seen so many Austrian soldiers fighting with the Germans on the Russian front.

But whatever the conditions, on the thirteenth of April, 1945, Siegfried Schmidt must have gone underground.

And on the thirtieth of April, French troops crossed into Austria over the Vorarlberg; the following day, the Americans entered from Germany; and when the British came into the country a week or so later, from Italy, they were surprised to find Yugoslav partisans running amuck in the Carinthian and Styrian provinces.

Austria was overrun—and Vienna stayed indoors; learned it wasn't wise to welcome the liberators with open arms.

And there's very little that's clear in my father's account of this. Abandoned apartment houses were the best places —though popular, too often crowded, and not wanting the company of some fool who wouldn't leave his incriminating motorcycle behind. Vratno would remember: quarter-faces slanting through letter slots—"No room for soldiers, you hide somewheres else."

Food would get you temporary entry, but food could get you killed too.

Vratno would remember warm-weather months indoors; recalled a week spent in trying to trap a Russian and get his uniform—for, in Wehrmacht cloth, my father's language abilities wouldn't be convincing enough.

Foremost, he would remember this one summer night. A sector near the Inner City, floodlights caught his flight at every roaring alley end—the Grand Prix racer bolting zigzag and hard-to-hit. He remembered what must have been the Belvedere Gardens—soldiers in the trees with flashlights, and Vratno running the racer almost flush to the high concrete wall, where he must have made a poor target but tore his elbow and knee against the jagged bomb tears in the concrete. He recalled a fountain that wasn't turned on; that would have to be the Schwarzenberg Platz. And remembered being forced to double back when he ran into a daze of floodlights and Russian voices.

Vratno would always remember: Gottlob Wut behind him, whispering into the indigo-blue ear hole—and weaving to Wut's flawless directions, my father jumped curbs and traveled down sidewalks, close to the building walls and dodging the occasional door that jutted out; skidding lightless down darker and darker streets, waiting for the wall or door he wouldn't see coming to smack him head-on.

Vratno always remembered a great lobby door, one side twisted off its hinges—the inner lobby where he skidded to, dark as a cave and marble-cool. He recalled daring his headlight once, and seeing the spiraling staircase going up at least four landings—to what he hoped were abandoned apartments. He remembered, forever: lifting his front wheel to the first step, revving, and jouncing madly up the wide but shallow marble stairs to the first landing, where he popped the clutch of the fierce Grand Prix and battered into the first apartment. And opened his eyes then, killed the engine—waited for the shot. Then he set the lock bolts back in place and closed the sprung door of the apartment.

Remembered then are floodlights coming down the street and into the lobby. Voices in Russian were saying, "There's no bike been ditched in here."

At dawn, cigarettes all over the floor, and what might have been good china was smashed; a rank, bleached corner of the kitchen where other hideaways, from this or an earlier occupation, decided to make their toilet. Cupboards empty, of course. Beds with knifed mattresses—occasionally peed-in beds. And only one of many stuffed animals still had its eyes unplucked—on the window sill of what must have been a young girl's room.

Vratno remembered: how odd it was, in a city apartment, to see an occasional chicken feather lacing the floor. But above all, he would cling to this—for days, the one bright spot on the whole dark street: a brass ball that caught the sun for a while each day; the ball was held in a cupid's hands; the cupid had half of its head bombed off, but still perched angelic above what used to be the Bulgarian embassy—in fact, the only embassy building on the Schwindgasse.

The Seventeenth Zoo Watch:
Tuesday, June 6, 1967, @ 5:45 a.m.

You know, Graff, once before there was a zoo bust in Vienna. Its failure is little-known history now. And the details are not the clearest.

No one seems to know just what went on in the zoo during the late years of the war. There was a time, though—let's say, early '45, when the Russians had cap-

tured the city, but before the other powers had agreed on
the terms of occupation—when there wasn't anything to
feed the people. There's no telling what the animals did
for food. There are some accounts of what the people did
for food, though—since there wasn't the manpower, or
the concern, to keep the zoo well guarded.

But four men, say, even if they were unarmed—and almost everyone who moved about was armed then too—
could do a pretty slick job of making off with a fair-sized
antelope; even a camel, or a small giraffe.

And that happened. There were raids, although some
city-guard outfit was supposedly protecting the zoo; they
had the future in mind—a kind of emergency rationing.

For you, and you and you—you get the left hindquar-
ters of this here kangaroo. And you get this rump steak of
hippo; just remember, you got to boil it a good long while.

But regardless of the city-guard outfit, there were successful raids. One bold, hungry crew made off with a wild
Tibetan yak. One man, all alone, stole a whole seal.

I suppose there were plans for a full-scale raid. I suppose it was only a matter of time, before some well-orga-
nized group of citizens or soldiers, from *any* army, would
decide there was a profit to be made in large meat-locker
operations in a starving city.

But nothing that well organized came off.

There was also in the city a would-be noble hero, who
thought the animals had suffered enough; he foresaw a
grand slaughter and figured a way to thwart the butchers.
No one knows who he was; he's only known by his partial
remains.

Because, of course, the animals ate him. He busted in
one night and let loose every animal he could find. I
think he is reputed to have opened just about all the cages
before he was eaten. Naturally, the animals were hungry
too. He should have thought of that.

And so his good intentions backfired. I don't know if
any animals even got outside the main gate, or whether
they were all attacked within the general confines. I suppose animals ate other animals too, before the mob got
wind of what had happened and swooped into the chaos
with old grenades and kitchen utensils.

The details are cloudy. With so many small mammals
underfoot all over the city, who was going to keep accurate records on animals? But the confusion must have been

really something, and I imagine the Russians got in on it sometime during the long night—thinking, perhaps, from all the fierce clamor, that they had a revolution on their hands, already.

I believe that neither tanks nor planes were used, but everything else must have been fair game.

I hope everyone who ate an animal choked on it. Or exploded when his bowels seized up.

After all, it wasn't the animals' war.

They should have been eating all the O. Schrutts.

(CONTINUING:)
THE HIGHLY SELECTIVE AUTOBIOGRAPHY OF
SIEGFRIED JAVOTNIK: PRE-HISTORY III

The Americans occupied the Salzburger province, which includes Kaprun—such a peaceful spot that it made the few Americans who came all the way into the village very friendly. In fact, about the only unpeaceful thing I was told of—and this, before the Americans came—was the setting afire of my grandfather's brother, the postmaster of Kaprun. In general, though, it was so relatively comfortable in Kaprun that I can't speak too well for the wisdom of my grandfather's taking his family and Ernst Watzek-Trummer back to Vienna. Or at least they should have waited to see how the four-way occupation of the city was going to work out.

But in the early summer of '45, my mother had an interest in returning to the *liberated* city. This was before the other Allies had arrived at a definitive agreement with the Soviets too. Even the reports of the Russian occupation should have been enough to dissuade them from going back so soon.

It had something to do with Hilke's idea about Zahn Glanz. Now that the war was over, she felt that Zahn would be sure to look her up. And my grandmother, of course, wanted to see how her little apartment and her abandoned china might have fared. And Grandfather, perhaps, was anxious to return some fourteen books—seven years and three months overdue—to the foreign-language reading room of the International Student House, where Grandfather had been the head librarian. I can't think of any reason Ernst Watzek-Trummer might have had for going back—other than his protective feelings toward the Marter family, and perhaps to take out more books from Grandfather's library. Watzek-Trummer, living seven years with my grandfather, had begun to value an education.

Whatever—or all things combined—it was very poor timing of them to leave Kaprun when they did, in the first week of July, '45.

Also, Grandfather's trip was made difficult by the deplorable state of Zahn Glanz's old taxi. The trip was made easier, however, by Grandfather's political record—vouchsafes, in letter and visa form, from resistance leaders who knew that the Nazi role of Grandfather's brother had been a disguise, and sympathized with the family for the postmaster's flaming death. Watzek-Trummer, too, had a record of some note—mostly a clever bunch of train derailments and subtle arson jobs at the depot in Zell am See.

So in the early morning of July 9, 1945, Grandfather Marter and his crew made an inconceivable journey through rubble and occupying armies, and entered Vienna in the late evening—having had more trouble with the paper work of the Soviets than with anyone else's red tape.

That was the day the Allies resolved the sectioning of the city. The Americans and the British grabbed up the best residential areas, and the French wanted the shopping areas. The Russians were long-term realistic; they settled themselves in the worker-industrial areas, and crouched themselves around the Inner City—near all the embassies and government buildings. The Russians, for example— and much to Grandfather's uneasiness—occupied the fourth district, which included the Schwindgasse.

And sixteen out of twenty-one districts had Communist police chiefs. And in the Soviet-established Renner provisional government, the Minister of Interior, Franz Honner, had fought with the Yugoslav partisans. Renner himself, however, was a veteran Austrian socialist, and had his own premonitions about the suspiciously forward-looking occupation of the *liberating* Soviets.

So did my grandfather have his anxieties, as he drove down a Schwindgasse darker and more windowless than he'd ever seen.

Watzek-Trummer said, "It's a ghost-town street, like the cowboys are always finding."

Grandmother, in the backseat, hummed or moaned to herself.

When Grandfather drove over the sidewalk and into the lobby, some Russian soldiers in the former Bulgarian embassy put the floodlights on them from across the street. Papers were shown again, and Grandfather spoke a little dated Russian—relying on his experience from the foreign-language reading room to send the soldiers away. Then, before they unpacked the taxi, they went up to the first landing, found the keyhole rusted, and shoved against a previously weakened lock bolt—springing open the door.

"Oh, they've been peeing in here, the bastards," Watzek-Trummer said; in the dark he cracked his shin on a large, heavy metal thing a few feet inside the doorway. "Give a light," he said. "They've left a cannon here, or something."

Grandmother crunched on what must have been her china; she moaned a little. And Grandfather put the flashlight on a very battered and muddy motorcycle, sagged against an armchair because it had no kickstand to hold itself up.

No one spoke, no one moved, and from down the hall, out of my mother's room, they heard someone who'd held his breath too long finally let it go—exhale what might have been interpreted as a last despairing breath. Grandfather put his flashlight out, and Hilke said, "I'll get the soldiers, right?" But no one moved; my mother heard her old bed creak. "In my bed?" she said to Grandfather, and then broke his grip on her arm—bumped the chair and motorcycle, moving down the hall toward her room. "Zahn?" she said. "Oh, Zahn, Zahn!" And bolted in the dark for the open door of her room. Watzek-Trummer got the flashlight from Grandfather and caught Hilke before she reached the doorway. He snapped her back up the hallway, and peeking round the jamb, blinked the light into her room.

On the bed was a dark, long-bearded man—a white paste on his lips, like a man with a thirsty, cotton-filled mouth. He sat dead-center on the bed, held his motorcycle boots in his hands and stared at the light.

"Don't shoot!" he cried, in German—and then repeated himself, in Russian, in English and in some unrecognizable Slavic tongue. "Don't shoot! Don't shoot! Don't shoot!" He waved the motorcycle boots above his head, conducting his own voice more than he was threatening.

"You have papers?" said Grandfather, in German, and the man threw a billfold to him.

"They're not right!" the man cried, in Russian—trying to guess his captors behind the dazzling light.

"You're Siegfried Schmidt?" my grandfather said. "A special messenger."

"Up yours, messenger," said Watzek-Trummer. "You're too late."

"No, I'm Javotnik!" said the man on the bed, sticking with Russian—fearing they were only trying to trap him with their German.

"It says Siegfried Schmidt," my grandfather said.

"Fake!" said my father. "I'm Vratno, Vratno Schmidt," he mumbled. Then he said, "No, Javotnik."

"Siegfried Javotnik?" Watzek-Trummer asked. "Where'd you get your dirty Wehrmacht suit?"

And my father fell to ranting in Serbo-Croat; those in the doorway puzzled at him. My father chanted:

Bolje rob nego grob!

Better a slave than a grave!

"Yugoslav?" said Grandfather, but Vratno didn't hear him; he bundled on the knifed mattress, and Grandfather walked in the room and sat beside him on the bed. "Come on, now," Grandfather said. "Take it easy."

And then Watzek-Trummer asked, "Which army are you hiding from?"

"All of them," my father said, in German—then in English, then in Russian, then in Serbo-Croat. "All of them, all of them, all of them."

"War paranoid," announced Watzek-Trummer, who'd read and remembered a number of things from Grandfather's overdue books.

So they went back to the taxi for their food and clothes, and got water from the inner courtyard well pump behind the main lobby. Then they fed and washed my father and dressed him in one of Watzek-Trummer's nightshirts. Watzek-Trummer slept in the taxi, keeping a wary guard; Hilke and my grandmother slept in the master bedroom, and Grandfather watched over the war paranoid in Hilke's old bed. Until three or four A.M., July

10, 1945, when my mother came to relieve Grandfather at his watch.

Three or four A.M., it was—very scarce predawn light and a light rain, Watzek-Trummer remembered, sleeping in the taxi. Three or four A.M., and Hilke, covering my father's sleeping beard with her hand, notices his forehead is somewhat the age of what she imagines Zahn Glanz's forehead to be—noticed how his hands were young too. And Vratno, waking once and bolting upright in my mother's old, knifed bed, saw a slim, sad-mouthed girl—more the green stem than the flower—and said, "Dabrinka! I told that foolish Wut it would have to be you who wasn't blown up." In German, in English, in Russian, in Serbo-Croat.

Limiting herself to one language, Hilke said in German, "Oh, you're all right now. You're safe here, hush. You're back, you—whoever." And gently shoved my father back down on her bed on his back, and lay over him herself—it being a damp, chilly, light-rainy night for both their summer nightshirts.

Many languages were whispered; though the rain was light, it lasted long, and many drops fell. Tireless Ernst Watzek-Trummer, sleeping light as the rain, remembers the rustling on the old, knifed bed that sent me giddily on my long way into this scary world. In very scarce predawn light. With a light rain falling. At three or four A.M., July 10, 1945, when Ernst Watzek-Trummer was sleeping unusually light.

Old Watzek-Trummer, historian without equal, has kept track of the details. •

The Eighteenth Zoo Watch:
Tuesday, June 6, 1967, @ 6:00 a.m.

The rarely diseased binturong is coughing; the shambling bearcat of Borneo suffering from his peculiar, unnamable disorder.

And O. Schrutt is waiting to be relieved of his command. His own unmarketable narcotics have finally soothed him. It's peaceful in the Small Mammal House, the infrared is off, and a lazy, docile-appearing O. Schrutt is greeting the dawn with a cigarette—puffed like a luxury cigar. I see great smoke rings rise above the ponds for the Various Aquatic Birds.

And it's clear to me, with it growing so light out—so quickly too—that we'll have to do most of our work when it's still dark. We'll have to have O. Schrutt safely tucked away—have the keys in hand, and some prearranged order of releasing—before it's light outside.

And clearly the chief problem is this: though it's simple enough to unlock the cages, how do we get the animals out of the general zoo area? How do we get them out the gates? Put them at large in Hietzing, and hopefully guide them in the countryside direction?

This is crucial, Graff. It's why, among other things, the earlier zoo bust failed. What do you do with forty or so animals loose within the confines of the whole zoo? We can't lead them out the main gate, or into the Tiroler Garten, one at a time. That way, some cluck in Hietzing would be sure to spot one and give the alarm before we're finished up inside. They have to leave all at once.

Can we expect them to stand in line?

It seems we'll have to divide them in some orderly fashion. We'll have to save all the antagonists till last, and maybe we'll release the bigger ones through the back gateway and into the Tiroler Garten; they can sneak away through predawn Maxing Park.

I think I must admit it will be a case for Fate.

See us now: the elephants are playing water sports in the ponds for Various Aquatic Birds; countless Miscellaneous Range Animals are chomping the potted plants along the paths; all the wild monkeys are teasing the zebras, scattering after the back-and-forth clattering, bewildered giraffe; some of the small mammals could easily get lost.

If it's still around, surely the least auklet will get stepped on.

When they're all on the loose, how do you get their attention? How do you say, "All right, out the gate, and make it snappy"?

Some of them may not even leave.

It's one reason I've always doubted Noah's neat trick of pairing up the gangplank to the ark.

So I think this calls for faith. I think there's no point in discussing further the possibilities for chaos, because it's a matter of the mass frame of mind. We either convey the spirit to them or we don't.

And you can't draw the line anywhere, either. Not this time.

(CONTINUING:)
THE HIGHLY SELECTIVE AUTOBIOGRAPHY OF
SIEGFRIED JAVOTNIK: PRE-HISTORY III

On August 2, 1945, my mother had her suspicions confirmed by a Soviet Army doctor; she was married to Vratno Javotnik in St. Stephens, in what was a small but noisy ceremony—throughout which my grandmother hummed or moaned, and Ernst Watzek-Trummer sneezed; Ernst had caught a cold, sleeping in a taxi.

And there were other noises—the dismantling work at one of the side altars, where a crew of U.S. Army engineers were sweatily removing an unexploded bomb which had been dropped through the mosaic roof of St. Stephens and was wedged between some organ pipes. For some months after the bombing, the organist had been too nervous to play either loudly or well.

As in any other wedding, after the oaths my mother shyly kissed my father's newly shaved face. Then they were clumsily followed up the aisle and out of the cathedral by several burly Americans bearing their bomb like a very heavy, just christened child.

The wedding party was held in the newly established American hamburger spa on the Graben. The young couple were most secretive. In fact, most of what I know of their relationship is a sparsely documented tale—relying on the interpretations, if not actual witness, of Ernst Watzek-Trummer, Ernst maintains that the most he ever heard the couple say in public was the discussion concerning Hilke's wish that Vratno shave for the wedding. Which was very shy talk, even for such a domestic matter.

Nevertheless, the record has it. August 2, 1945, Hilke Marter was given in marriage by her father, an ex-librarian with fourteen books overdue for seven years and three-plus months; Ernst Watzek-Trummer was best man for the groom.

Record also has it that August 2, 1945, was the last day of bickering at Potsdam, and the only day in which Truman and Churchill slumped a bit off their mark: The British and Americans had come prepared to Potsdam—

this time aware of Russian means and motives of occupation, as observed in the Balkans and in Berlin. But
Churchill and Truman had been thinking hard since July
17, and Potsdam's last day marked a slacking off. It was
on the issue of *war booty*, and Russian claims in Eastern
Austria—the Russians declaring that they had been most
heavily damaged by the war and that Germany would
have to make it good. Russian statistics are always staggering; they claimed 1,710 cities and 70,000 villages destroyed—a loss of 6,000,000 buildings, making 25,000,000
homeless, not to mention the damage to 31,850 industries
and enterprises. The losses to be made good by Germany
were losses for which certain Austrian *war booty* could be
seized. A language confusion was operative; the Russians
spoke of Austria's liberation in the same breath as they
spoke of Austria's co-responsibility with Germany for the
war.

Later, Soviet representative of the Potsdam Economic
Commission, Mr. I.M. Maisky, confessed that *war booty*
meant any property that could be moved to the Soviet
Union. But aside from letting this vague phrase slip by,
Churchill and Truman were prepared for Stalin's aims,
this time.

Vienna herself was not unprepared, either—by the time
of the Potsdam conference. She'd simply been caught by
surprise before then, but made some strongly independent
gestures thereafter.

On September 11, 1945, the Allied Council had their
first meeting in the Soviet-occupied Imperial Hotel on the
Ringstrasse, under the chairmanship of Russia's Marshal
Koniev.

And Vratno Javotnik was not unprepared, either—even
for pending family life. My grandfather got him some
legitimate refugee papers and a job as interpreter-aid to
himself—Grandfather having landed fat work as a docu-
mentor for the supposedly kept-up-to-date minutes of the
Allied Council meetings.

Just fourteen days after the first meeting, Vienna held
its first free parliamentary elections since the Anschluss.
And much against the grain of all previous Soviet efforts,
the Communist party won less than 6 percent of the total
vote—only four seats out of one twenty-five in the National Rat. The socialist and People's parties about split
even.

What Vienna really wasn't prepared for was what bad losers the Soviets could be.

What Ernst Watzek-Trummer was totally unprepared for was the recorded assumption of the Hacking district police who had listed Watzek-Trummer as deceased, since March 12, 1938—the victim of a fire which consumed his henhouse. I doubt if Watzek-Trummer could seriously have been offended by the lack of faith shown in him by the Hacking district police. But whatever, Ernst refused to find a job, and at Grandfather's suggestion, made himself busy with apartment repairs and modifications on the Marters' Schwindgasse home.

In the daytime, then, Watzek-Trummer and the women-folk had the Schwindgasse to themselves. When laundry ladies would chide him for his laziness, his puttering-about at home, Trummer would say, "I'm legally dead. What better excuse for not working is there?"

The first thing Watzek-Trummer did was to partition a section of the kitchen into his private bedroom. Next he took the fourteen overdue books underarm and went to find the foreign-language reading room of the International Student House, which was no longer operating— which had, in fact, been bombed and looted. So Watzek-Trummer tore all the library labels out of the books and took them home again—giving up the idea of trading them for fourteen he hadn't read. Grandfather did bring him new books, but books were very scarce, and the bulk of the literature in the Schwindgasse apartment was Grandfather's and Vratno's homework—the minutes of the Allied Council meetings, which Watzek-Trummer found evasive and dull.

But despite Watzek-Trummer's discontent with his read-ing material, he did a most charitable thing—as a wedding present for Hilke and my father. He scraped all the camouflage off the 1939 Grand Prix racer, and stripped it further—of all warlike insignia, traces of radio mounts and obvious machine-gun creases—and painted it glossy black; thereby he made it a private vehicle, not so easily subject to Russian confiscation as *war booty*, and gave my mother and Vratno a luxury. Although fuel was precious, and travel between the sectors of occupation was tedi-ous—even for an interpreter-aid with a paper-work job on the Allied Council.

So Watzek-Trummer provided the shy newlyweds a

means to get off by themselves, where they must have relaxed and talked more easily to each other than they ever did in the Schwindgasse apartment. Watzek-Trummer insists that they were always shy with each other, at least in public or on any occasion Trummer had to observe them. Their talking was done at night, with Ernst Watzek-Trummer sleeping characteristically light behind the light walls of his partitioned bedroom in the kitchen. Watzek-Trummer maintains that they never raised their voices—nor did he beat her, nor did she ever cry—and the rustling that Watzek-Trummer heard through and over his thin partition was always gentle.

Often, after midnight, Vratno would go into the kitchen and serve himself a sandwich and a glass of wine. Whereupon, Watzek-Trummer would pop out from behind his partition and say, "Blutwurst tonight, is it? What is there for cheese?" And together they'd hold a conspiracy of snacking, silently spreading bread, cautiously cutting sausage. When there was brandy they'd stay up later, and my father would speak of a highly fantastical motorcycle genius, with whom he once had beards in common. And much later, when there was both wine and brandy, Vratno would whisper to Ernst Watzek-Trummer. "Zahn Glanz," Vratno would say. "Does the name ring a bell for you? Who was Zahn Glanz?" And Watzek-Trummer would counter: "You knew a Wut, you said. What was it about this Wut you knew?" And together they'd politic into the night, often interpreting the Soviet-sponsored newspaper, the Österreichische Zeitung of November 28, 1945, for example, which told of Nazi bandits in Russian uniform bringing disgrace to the Soviets by a series of rural rapes and murders, not to mention a few isolated downtown incidents. Or the edition of January 12, 1946, which told of a certain Herr H. Schien of Mistelbach, Lower Austria, who was arrested by the Soviets after he'd spread false rumors about Russian soldiers plundering his home. Or, occasionally, they would discuss my father's and grandfather's homework, the minutes of the Allied Council meetings—one in particular, dealing with an incident on January 16, 1946, which occurred on the U.S. military "Mozart" Train that ran American troops between Salzburg and Vienna. A United States Army technical sergeant, Shirley B. Dixon, MP, turned away a Russian train-boarding party, including Soviet Captain Klementiev and

Senior Lieutenant Salnikov. The Russians went for their
guns, but Technical Sergeant Shirley B. Dixon, U.S.A.,
MP, quick-on-the-draw, shot both Russians—killing Captain Klementiev and wounding Senior Lieutenant Salnikov.
In the Allied Council meeting, the Soviets claimed that
their men had been victims of a language confusion, and
Marshal Koniev demanded fast-gun Shirley B. Dixon's
punishment. Dixon, however, was said, by a military
court, to be doing his duty.

Watzek-Trummer, who'd indulged himself in a rash of
American Western movies, claimed that the name Shirley
B. Dixon rang a bell for him. Wasn't that the gunfighter-
turned-deputy in the one about poisoning water holes in
Wyoming? But my father thought that Shirley was usually
a girl's name, which prompted Watzek-Trummer to
remember the one about the great-breasted lady outlaw
who straightened- or flattened-out in the end, by marrying
an effeminate pacifist judge. So they concluded that Shirley B. Dixon, the fastest gun on the Mozart Train, was actually a Wac.

And Vratno would ask again, "Zahn Glanz? You must
have known him."

But Watzek-Trummer would counter: "You never said
what happened after you and Gottlob Wut got to
Maribor. Did this Wut have a lady friend there? Why
didn't he come with you?"

And Vratno: "Which one of you was this mythical eagle? Frau Drexa Neff, the laundress across the street—and
she's Muttie Marter's friend, I've talked to her—why is
she kept in the dark about it? She's always talking about
this great bird, and all of you get funny faces. Who was
the bird, Ernst? Was Zahn Glanz that eagle? Was he? And
what happened to this Glanz?"

Then Watzek-Trummer, historian without equal, keeper
of every detail—Watzek-Trummer would ramble on: "All
right, all right, I'm with you, to a point. But after all those
Slivnicas were blown up, minus one, and after the bit with
the radio in the mountains—when Borsfa Durd was already dead and buried, in his way, I mean—and after you
let Balkan Four go by and you'd marched to Maribor with
that other outfit. When you were in Maribor, Vratno—is
what I mean—what happened to this Gottlob Wut?"

On and on they went, a snacking merry-go-round, until
my mother would rustle from the other room and my fa-

ther would eat up, drink up, talk up and leave Ernst
Watzek-Trummer to keep track of the rest of the night.
Which he did, with increasing insomnia—perhaps owing to
the growing discomfort of my mother's pregnancy, because she tossed about rather loudly from February into
March. And Ernst gave up his partitioned bedroom; he sat
by the kitchen window instead, poured my mother a glass
of milk whenever she came sleeplessly waddling into the
kitchen; otherwise, he watched the nightwatchmen on the
Schwindgasse—the hourly floodlights from the former Bulgarian embassy, and the hourly check of the house doors
along the street.

A Russian officer who carried a revolver walked flush
against the buildings—a poor target for flower vases or
boiling pasta pots; he tried each lobby lock. He was covered by a Russian infantryman, a machine gunner, who
walked just off the curb in the street—himself a poor target for heaved windowboxes, because it would take considerable determination to launch anything very weighty
that far into the street. The machine gunner watched windows; the officer first felt his hand around the jambs before stepping into doorways. The floodlights from the
former embassy moved in front of them. There wasn't a
curfew, exactly, but even a light left on after midnight
was suspicious, and therefore Watzek-Trummer settled for
a candle on the kitchen table and kept the windowshade
drawn to an inch above the sill. So Watzek-Trummer had
his window inch for watching Russian watchmen; Ernst
insists he kept a kind of peace on the Schwindgasse by
casting a hex, a pox, a jinx, a trance or even blessing over
the machine gunner as he passed. Because the first thing
Watzek-Trummer noticed about the machine gunner was
that he was too nervous; he watched the windows behind
himself more than he watched those coming into the moving floodlight ahead—and he clicked on and off the safety
on his gun. So Ernst contends that his duty at the window
inch was to keep the gunner calm; and be available for
the morning exodus of the laundress Frau Drexa Neff, another nighttime window-watcher, who would bob up from
her cellar cubby and holler across the street to Ernst,
"How's her coffee look to you, Herr Trummer? Low
enough, is it, so I should pick up hers with mine?" And
Watzek-Trummer would usually say, "No, the coffee's fine,
but we could use some fancy almonds, or the best French

brandy the rations man has today." And feisty Drexa:
"Ha! You need some sleep, Herr Trummer. Ha! That's
what, all right."

So that was February and most of March, 1946, with
Drexa—as March came on and on—asking Watzek-Trummer if Hilke had had me overnight, and with no other incidents except this: on Plösslgasse, two blocks south of
Watzek-Trummer's window inch, a man was machine-
gunned for peeing out a window into an alley (because,
it turned out, his toilet was stopped up), after midnight.
The noise of which, had the Schwindgasse machine gunner
wheeling himself around and around in the street, clicking
his safety on and off—checking the night sky for hurtling
windowboxes, kitchen utensils and wet, wadded socks.
Which never came, or he'd have surely opened up.

And this incident too: the Soviets seized the entire
Danube Shipping Company assets under the heading of
war booty. Which was disputed in an Allied Council meeting or two.

But nothing else until I was spectacularly born.

Watzek-Trummer remembers a bit of light snow, recalls
my mother waddling to the kitchen sometime past midnight and not being pacified by her usual glass of milk. He
remembers Grandfather and Vratno getting dressed and
calling out the lobby door to the Russian hangout at the
former Bulgarian embassy. And three of them, then, in a
Russian squad car, batting off to the Soviet-sector clinic.

That would have been early morning, one or two A.M.
of March 25, 1946. It was three or four, Ernst remembers, when Grandfather phoned back to the apartment to
tell Watzek-Trummer and my grandmother about me—a
boy! Nine pounds, nine ounces, which was big, I might
add, considering the diet of that occupied year. And my
grandmother took up the candle and whirled across the
kitchen to the windowshade drawn to one inch above the
sill—and she flung up the shade, candle in her hand, and
cried across the street to her friend the laundress, "Drexa!
It's a boy! Nearly ten pounds too!"

Watzek-Trummer recalls: he was midway from the
phone to Grandmother, off his feet, he believes—spread
out in the air and reaching to put out the candle—when
the floodlights came into the kitchen and Grandmother
was propelled toward him and right past him. Their paths
crossed; he recalls looking over his shoulder as she was

flung by him—her very surprised face, not even bleeding yet. In fact, Watzek-Trummer doesn't remember *hearing* the machine-gunning until after he recrossed the kitchen to her and tried to sit her up.

It's Drexa Neff who has told Watzek-Trummer the details, really. How the gunner was a few feet past the window and looking over his shoulder, as he would do forever, when Grandmother Marter scared the wits out of him with her ghostly candle and her screaming in a language the Russian didn't understand. And after he shot her—Drexa is very clear about this—the whole street was floodlit, but you couldn't see the faces that were in every window, just inches above the sill. At least not until Watzek-Trummer started screaming, "They killed Frau Marter! She was just saying she was a grandmother now!" And how the street rained kitchenware and bits of pottery; how it was downstreet, only a few doors from where Frau Marter was shot, that the machine gunner caught in his neck the first piece of well-aimed crock or lead or silver; and down on one knee, weaving a downed boxer's weave, he opened up his machine gun again and took out a row of third-story windows from the Argentinier corner of the Schwindgasse halfway to Prinz-Eugen-Strasse. And would have gone the whole block length if the Russian officer hadn't got in the way—or had not been able to get out of the way; whatever, the gunner blew his officer down the sidewalk and stopped his sweep shot then. He covered his head with his arms and made a ball of himself in the street; everyone's kitchenware—some of which Drexa could identify, and even told Watzek-Trummer where it was bought and for how much—covered the Russian gunner, lying kitty-corner across from the former Bulgarian embassy, out of which no one ran to try and fetch him.

So I was born on March 25, 1946, and my birth was overshadowed not only by this aforementioned mistake. Because although I weighed nine pounds, nine ounces, and my mother had a short labor and smooth delivery, no one would ever remember. Although there was even a significant argument concerning my name—whether I be a *Zahn*, but my father asked, "Who was *Zahn*?" and got no answer, or whether I be a *Gottlob*, but my mother asked, "What was he to you?" and got no answer, so that Grandfather's suggestion was approved, because no questions and answers were necessary concerning a *Siegfried*, the name that carried Vratno to safety—even though there was this pertinent discussion, hardly anyone would associate me with the date of my birth. Because not only was my grandmother machine-gunned within moments of my delivery—which wouldn't be remembered by many, either—but because on the twenty-fifth of March, 1946, Tito's partisans finally hunted down and captured the Chetnik general Drazha Mihailovich, the last honest and stupid liberator or revolutionary left in the world.

The Nineteenth Zoo Watch:
Tuesday, June 6, 1967, @ 6:15 a.m.

Well, I know, Graff, I may seem to you to be turning my back on old principles. Well, there are some things, I see now, that you just can't split the hair over.

I mean, you always end up arbitrating in the end, don't you? What's the good of being so selective if you end up with more animals left in the zoo than animals that make it out? Now I'm certainly not advocating any slaughter, and I think we ought to save the bigger, rougher ones for last. But what kind of zoo bust would it be if you kept everything big or a little bit dangerous in its cage?

I tell you, I understand these animals—they know what the whole thing's for; or they *will* know, if you just point the way.

Now I don't mean to apply this to other things, but it's the liberators with unswerving principles who never get the revolution off the ground.

I'm sure. If you let these animals know you're for *all* of them, even the gelada baboon, even if we have to save him for near the end—I mean, *all* of them get let out of the cages—they'll be up at those gates, one hundred percent. Nobody trusts favoritism!

I really mean it; even the frotting gelada baboon. I'm not going to be the one to let a little personal experience run my mind amuck.

(CONTINUING:)
THE HIGHLY SELECTIVE AUTOBIOGRAPHY OF
SIEGFRIED JAVOTNIK: MY REAL HISTORY

Nothing was done about Grandmother Marter's death. The minutes of the Allied Council meetings are full of incidents much less understandably accidental than that one. The obviously premeditated ones, for example, were thought to be the work of hirelings for the Upravlenye Sovietskovo Imushchestva v Avstrii, or USIA—the Administration for Soviet Property in Austria. Which, under the label of *war booty*, made off with four hundred Austrian enterprises; foundries, spinning mills, factories for machinery, chemicals, electrical equipment, glass and steel, and a motion picture corporation. Hired killers made off with the Austrians who resisted the USIA.

The majority of these weren't killings of my grandmother's type. Wild shootings, rapes and bombings were more up the alley of the Russian soldier. It was the abductions that bothered the Allied Council, and these seemed to be carried out by the notorious Benno Blum Gang— a cigarette-smuggling ring, also black-marketing nylon stockings. For the privilege of operating in the Russian sector, the Benno Blum Gang deftly did away with people. Benno Blum's Boys would waylay people all over Vienna, and skulk back to the Russian sector when the heat was on—although the Soviets claimed to be hunting down Benno Blum too. In fact, about twice a month some Russian soldier would shoot someone and say that he'd thought it was Benno Blum. Although no one ever saw Benno Blum, to know what he looked like—or if he existed.

So there was a rather general illegality about the Soviet-sector operations in Vienna, which diverted any interest the Allied Council might have taken in my grandmother's commonplace machine-gunning.

But Watzek-Trummer helped my grandfather. He varied his nights between his kitchen partition and the master bedroom—going from time to time to sprawl beside Grandfather on the master bed; head-by-head, they indulged each other's anger—sometimes ranting so loudly that the floodlights from the former Bulgarian embassy would linger at the remembered kitchen window and blink, as if to say: Go to sleep in there, and stop your complaining. It was an accident. Don't plot against us.

But there were enough incidents that clearly weren't accidents to bring about the New Control Agreement on June 28, 1946, which eliminated Soviet veto power over the elected Parliament. This dissolved the Russian Booty Department, although Benno Blum, perhaps revenge-bent, appeared to be more active than ever, snitching a third of the anti-Soviets in Vienna—and causing Chancellor Figl to say, in a sad speech in Upper Austria, "We have had to write down against a very long list of names simply the word 'disappeared.' "

"Like Zahn Glanz, huh?" said Vratno. "Is that what happened?"

And irritable Watzek-Trummer said, "Ask your wife, or do you only talk bed talk in bed?"

Not that they had soured on each other, really. It was only that it had been hashed out so much before, they'd come round to this so many times.

But they did have it out once, all right—although I've no right to remember it as well as I do, since I wasn't quite four months old at the time. I guess Ernst Watzek-Trummer has remembered it for me, like most important things.

Anyway, one night in the summer, the seventeenth of July, 1946, my father came home in a drunken babble, having heard the news that Drazha Mihailovich had been executed by a partisan firing squad. And Watzek-Trummer said, "What about this Mihailovich? What was he, really?" But Vratno cried, "He was abandoned!" And began to describe a ghastly vision for Watzek-Trummer, concerning a fantastical motorcycle mechanic who was gulped down a stand-up crapper in Maribor, Vratno talked not about Mihailovich but about Gottlob Wut, with whom my father once had beards in common. Vratno called to mind the sloppy Heine Gortz's question "Who are you with Wut?" And speculated how he might have kicked Heine Gortz down into the crapper, and then grabbed Bronsky, or Metz, or *both*, bending them back over the urinal while Gottlob freed himself and cracked their skulls with his concealed Amal racing carburetor.

And suddenly Watzek-Trummer said, "You mean you *didn't* do all that? You didn't even *try* to do any of that?"

"I said we just met," my father told him, "and Gottlob was a good enough sport to go along with it."

"Oh, he *was*, was he?" Watzek-Trummer roared.

"Well, I told you now, Trummer!" Vratno said. "Now you tell me, O.K.? Tit for tat, Trummer. Who was Zahn Glanz?"

But Watzek-Trummer stared at my father and said, "I don't consider the information equal."

My father screamed at him, "Zahn Glanz, damn you!" And the floodlights came on across the street, scanning windows near and far.

Then my mother was out of her room, with her nightgown open so wide that Ernst Watzek-Trummer looked away from her. She said, "What was that? Who's here?"

"Zahn Glanz!" Vratno shouted at her. "Zahn Glanz is here!" And with a flourishing gesture to her room, he said, "Zahn Glanz! What you call me in there sometimes—and they're usually the *best* times too!"

So Watzek-Trummer sent a blow across the kitchen table—with his former cleaver hand, his chicken-chopping hand—and belted my father up against the sink, where his elbow struck a faucet and started the water running.

Grandfather Marter came out of his master bedroom and whispered, "Oh, please, don't any of you get near the window. You know it's very dangerous this late at night." He looked at all of them, perplexed; they all sulked, eyes down. My grandfather added, "Better not run the water so hard. It's summer, you know, and there's probably not an awful lot of water."

Then Watzek-Trummer remembers that I started to cry, and my mother went back to her room to me. Funny, how wailing babies bring people to their senses. Even the floodlights went out with my crying. Babies cry; that's perfectly all right.

But that was when it all came out, one way or another. On the seventeenth of July, 1946, when Drazha Mihailovich was shot as a traitor. Which prompted the *New York Times* to suggest that the Russians build a statue of Mihailovich in Red Square, because Drazha Mihailovich was, among other things, the ironical Saviour of Moscow.

Watzek-Trummer, who still read everything he could get his hands on, tried to make peace in the kitchen by remarking, "Isn't it amazing? The Americans have so many good afterthoughts!"

Which was true enough, of course. Very like the Russians in this respect: they react best to statistics and have little interest in details.

For example, it happened—was even witnessed—that one twenty-nine-year-old Viennese social worker, name of Anna Hellein, was dragged off her train by a Soviet guard at the Steyregg Bridge checkpoint on the United States–Soviet demarcation line, where she was raped, murdered and left on the rails. She was decapitated by a train shortly thereafter. But this in no way produced action by the Allied Council so much as did Chancellor Figl's *list* of eleven recent murders by men in Soviet uniform. Now, you see, it was the *numbers* that impressed them. But Figl's request that the Austrian police be armed, and be permitted to defend themselves and other citizens from men in uniform—of *any* army—was postponed a bit because the Soviets produced a *list* of their own; from some anonymous source, the Soviets counted thirty-six hundred "known Nazis" within the police force. *Numbers* again, you see.

Actually, the problem with the police was *decommunizing* it, which went on slowly for about five years. Actually arming the police—or, that is, making the police worth having—was a somewhat slower process. As late as March 31, 1952, when I'd just had my sixth birthday, the Soviets prevented the police chief in their sector from sending any armed force to quell a horde of rioting Communists attacking the Greek embassy—protesting the recent execution of Beloyannis and three other Greek Communists. In fact, the rioters were brought to the scene in Soviet Army trucks.

Even later, when there was a riot due, the Soviets disarmed the police in their sector, taking away their rubber truncheons—which proved too effective in quelling riots, even though they were never quite what Chancellor Figl had in mind by "arming" his policemen.

But the Soviets were losing Vienna, and that made them unreasonable; in fact, there were setbacks all over.

In June of '48 the Yugoslav Communist party was expelled from the Cominform—Tito didn't need his crutches any more—and in November of '48, Soviet soldiers attempted to arrest someone on Sweden Bridge in downtown Vienna and were beaten back by angry crowds, rushing to the defense. Angry crowds were doing the Russians harm, even in their own sector.

And because of their tiff with Yugoslavia, the Soviets withdrew their support of Yugoslav claims in Austria's southland, Carinthia and Styria, and consequently, the Yugoslavs had to drop the whole idea of expanding into Austria.

This brought an odd number of Yugoslavs to Vienna, by the way; strange Yugoslavs—some Ustashi, I'm told, who were in the thick of plots and counterplots along the Austro-Yugoslav border when they were cut off. And the implication is that they found work with Benno Blum, who still had use for good abductors and roughies in general. Even though the records claim that Benno Blum was virtually washed up by March 10, 1950, when gangmember Max Blair was the subject of an Allied Council meeting, there's some evidence that a bit of Benno survived thereafter.

At least Ernst Watzek-Trummer claims so, and I take my history from him.

Ernst was there, anyway—March 5, 1953. When I was twenty days short of being seven, Joseph Stalin died. My grandfather and Watzek-Trummer had a celebration of their own, a little brandy round the kitchen table and spirits higher than their portions. But my parents were out, so I have to rely on Watzek-Trummer's account of their affairs. Not that I wasn't usually with my parents, only not for this celebration. And even I must admit—though Watzek-Trummer has certainly influenced me in this—that my parents had a relationship which struck me, at best, as being shy and unspoken. I was out with them from time to time—most memorably, sunny drives on the Grand Prix racer with my mother's arms around my father and myself, locking me against his stomach and pushing my knees tight against the gas tank I straddled. My father whispering Wutlike maxims of motorcycle-riding in my ear.

But on March 5, 1953, Joseph Stalin died, and Vratno and Hilke took a night out together, to celebrate, and they left me behind—to the old men's celebration at the kitchen table. I don't even remember my mother coming home, though it certainly must have been startling.

Because she came home alone, more puzzled than upset, and sat round the kitchen table with my grandfather and

Watzek-Trummer (and maybe, with me too), wondering out loud whatever could have possessed Vratno.

Because, she said, they were comfortably wined and dined and sitting in a Serbian restaurant that Vratno frequently enjoyed, somewhere up by the Südbahnhof—still in the Russian sector—when all at once, in comes this man, dark-skinned, beared, small but fierce-eyed. Though he was friendly, Mother insisted to Watzek-Trummer. This man sat down with them at their table.

"The killer is dead!" he said to them, in German, and they toasted one with him. Then the man pinched Vratno's arm and said something my mother said sounded like this:

Bolje grob nego rob!

Better a grave than a slave!

And Vratno looked startled, but not very—only a little; perhaps because he hadn't thought that he looked very much like a Yugoslav of any kind, sitting talking German, as he was, with a Viennese lady.

But the man went on: a little Serbo-Croat, and a little German now and then—he was being polite to Hilke. He also put his arm around my father and, my mother guessed, wanted him to come for a drink somewhere, alone. But Vratno said, in German, how he didn't really want to leave his wife, even for a short while, or for a drink or two—or even to meet some more homelanders. But the whole thing was very gay until the man said something my mother said sounded like this:

Todor.

Just that, once or twice—all by itself, or in sentences of Serbo-Croat. Vratno looked startled again—this time, even very startled. But the man kept smiling all the time.

It was then that Vratno very rudely tried to whisper to my mother without the other man hearing; it was something about how she should go to the ladies' room, find an open phone and call Watzek-Trummer just as quick as she could. But this man kept laughing and slapping Vratno's back, leaning over between my father's face and my mother's—so they couldn't really whisper with success.

It was then, my mother said, that the *other* man came in.

Hilke Marter-Javotnik has maintained that he was the biggest man she ever saw, and that when he came in, my father leaned across the table and kissed her hard on the mouth; got up, then, looked down at his feet, hesitated—but the first, smaller man said in German, "Your wife is very lovely, but she'll be safe—with me." And Vratno looked up at the huge man and walked past him, right out the door.

The big one, whom the little one called Todor, went right out after my father.

The worst thing about the big one, my mother said, was that his face was lopsided—sort of chewed or blown off—and flecked with bluish scars; some, jagged, stuck like gum on his face, and some were of sliver thinness, deep enough to tug and wrinkle the surrounding skin.

There wasn't anything wrong with the little one. He stayed and had a drink with her; then he went to bring back Vratno, he said, but never came back himself. And neither did my father.

My mother said that the Grand Prix racer was still parked in front of the Serbian restaurant, so Ernst Watzek-Trummer and Grandfather walked up to get it, chatting with Russian soldiers along the way.

"A big man," Grandfather said to the soldiers. "I think his name is Todor Slivnica. He's got bad scars, was grenaded in a car once. He's with my son-in-law, and maybe with another man too." But no one had seen a soul—except, earlier, my mother walking home with a Russian soldier, the most gentlemanly-looking one she ran across; she'd dared to ask that he walk her home. He was a young one; in the last block, he'd held her hand, but I guess that was all he wanted.

The soldiers along the way had seen no one else all evening.

And when Grandfather and Trummer got to the Serbian restaurant, there was the racer outside, and inside there was a singer singing Serbo-Croat, and couples or dark groups of men clapping and singing along from their tables. Very gay.

But Watzek-Trummer thought the whole Serb joint was in league. He shouted, "Todor Slivnica!" And the singer stopped; she wrung her hands. No one accused Watzek-

Trummer of being rude; the waiters just shook and shook
their heads.

They were about to leave when Grandfather said, "Oh
my God, Ernst." And pointed out an enormous man sitting alone at a table by the door; he was beginning to eat
a custard out of a little glass dish. They'd walked right by
him when they came in.

So they moved in on the man, whose face the candlelight made as multi-colored and multi-shaped as a semi-
crushed prism.

"Todor Slivnica?" Watzek-Trummer asked. The big man
smiled and stood up—an awesome yard, it seemed, above
Grandfather and Ernst. Todor tried to bow, as if he were
little.

My grandfather, not knowing any Serbo-Croat, could
only say, "Vratno Javotnik?"

And Todor let the blood flush his scars, made his whole
face blink neonlike; taking up the little glass dish, he
scooped the jiggling custard into his paw and spread his
fingers out flat, with the custard quivering like a rare gift
under Grandfather's nose, and then brought his other fist
down on it—*fop!* and *squeech!*

Then Todor Slivnica sat down and smiled, a dollop of
custard sliding into one of his deeper-grooved scars. And
he gestured—to the custard on the walls, to the custard all
over the table, all over Grandfather and Ernst, and even
smoking on the pulled-low overhead lantern. Everywhere
there was custard, Todor Slivnica pointed and smiled.

*Where is Vratno Javotnik? Why he's here, on your nose,
and here, on the lantern overhead—and even here! In
space.*

So Watzek-Trummer has remembered that, has kept it
all straight in his mind, to interpret—the riddle of where
my father went is tied up in Todor Slivnica's symbolic gestures. Todor, among other things, was known for his sense
of humor.

The Twentieth Zoo Watch:
Tuesday, June 6, 1967, @ 6:30 a.m.

An interesting thing. O. Schrutt has changed his clothes!
Or not changed them, exactly, but he's disguised them.
He's got a rain slicker on; it covers his nametag and

epaulettes. And he has neatly, purposefully untucked his pants from his combat boots. It almost looks like he's wearing regular shoes—or, at least, just lifters.

O. Schrutt is getting ready for full daylight, and for the keepers who'll relieve him. O. Schrutt is not stupid; he takes good care of his indulgences. O. Schrutt will not likely be appearing as an addict in public. He's had his fix; he can outwardly endure a nonviolent day.

At the risk of sounding polemical, I'd like to say that there are two ways to live a long time in this world. One is to trade with violence strictly as a free agent, with no cause or love that overlaps what's expedient; and if you give no direct answers, you'll never be discovered as lying to protect yourself. But I don't exactly know what the other way to live a long time is, although I believe it involves incredible luck. There certainly is another way, though, because it's not *always* the O. Schrutts who live a long time. There are just a few survivors of a different nature around.

I think that patience has something to do with it too.

For example, I'll bet there are a few survivors among O. Schrutt's previous small-mammal charges. If they've been patient enough to *live*, they'll finally get to see the fellow they've been so patient for. They'll jar their trancelike faces over a newspaper, they'll twitch their old bashed hands in their exhausted laps—a spasm will fling them out of their TV-watching chairs: O. Schrutt is news again, they'll see—recognizing him through twinges in a scar that's been numb for twenty years or more. Their crippled feet will uncramp enough to stagger them to a phone; they'll lose their speech impediments, talking to the operator; they'll breathe twenty back years of patience into the mouthpiece.

That's right, dear Franz, it's him, I seen his picture, and for God's sakes, call Stein right away—to cheer him up, at last. O. Schrutt it was, I'm sure—kicking and screaming with a bunch of wild animals; their keeper, of course. And of course he had the night shift, and his uniform on too. Yes, the nametag still—right on the TV! I got to go tell Weschel, he's got no phone—and with his eyes, no paper or TV. But you call poor Stein, quick as you can. Oh, he'll be tickled to hear!

Because nobody stops looking for the disappeared. It's

only the surely dead who flatly can't end up as you'd want
or expect them to.

It's got to be my good faith, O. Schrutt; it's got me believing that some of your small-mammal charges will survive even you.

(CONTINUING:)
THE HIGHLY SELECTIVE AUTOBIOGRAPHY OF
SIEGFRIED JAVOTNIK: MY REAL HISTORY

March 25, 1953. For my seventh birthday, my mother
took me on the train to Kaprun—just twenty days after
the death of Stalin, and the custardlike disappearance of
my father. Ernst Watzek-Trummer and Grandfather met
us in Kaprun on the Grand Prix racer, which had slowly
and inexpertly made a nervous trip from Vienna.

And so what was left of us settled in Kaprun, a village
very small at the time; this was before the hydroelectric
power dam in the mountains, and before the big ski lift
brought less-hardy skiers to the town.

My grandfather became the postmaster of Kaprun;
Watzek-Trummer became the town handyman, and he delivered the mail—in the winter, towing it in rough brown
bags on a sled that was mine when there wasn't any mail.
I would occasionally ride the mailbags on top of the sled
and allow Ernst to skid me over the steep winter streets.
My mother made red cord tassels to tie up the bags, and a
red cord tassel with a ball of wool on the end was attached to my stocking hat.

In the summers, Ernst Watzek-Trummer delivered the
mail in a high two-wheeler cart that was mounted to the
rear fender of the Grand Prix racer. Which must have
made Gottlob Wut roll over in his grave, if you could call
it a grave.

We were quite happy in Kaprun; we were in the American sector now, of course, and within broadcasting range
of Salzburg. In the evenings we listened to the American
station that played all the Negro music—with rich-voiced
women wailing, and yodeling trumpets and guitars: groin-
blues. I remember that music without Watzek-Trummer's
help, I really do. Because once at the Gasthof Enns, in the
village, an American Negro, a soldier on leave, accompa-
nied the radio with his harmonica, and sang, like a great

iron bucket left out in the rain. It was winter; against the
snow he was the blackest thing in Kaprun; people touched
him to see if he felt like wood. He walked my mother
home from the Gasthof Enns, and pulled me behind them
on the mail sled. He sang a line or two, then he signaled
to me and I honked his harmonica up from the sled—
through the little Y-shaped village, quite late at night, I
think. Grandfather could talk English with the soldier,
and later the Negro sent Watzek-Trummer a book of photographs about civil rights in America.

Much else, I don't remember, and Watzek-Trummer's
selective memory hasn't found anything important in these
years—when I was eight, and then nine. There's just this:
when the last Soviet soldier left Vienna on September 19,
1955, my grandfather suffered a small stroke—pitching
backward into a stack of loose mail. People saw little
squares of him falling through their side of the mailboxes
in the post-office cage. But Grandfather recovered quickly.
Only one thing: his eyebrows wĕnt from gray to white,
overnight. And that's another one of those details which I
may have remembered myself, or which Watzek-Trummer
may have remembered for me—or, more likely, it was
some combined, repetitive remembering from the two of
us.

I remember the only important thing, though—all by
myself, I'm sure. Because Watzek-Trummer either finds
this hard to remember himself, or at least hard to remember out loud to me.

I was ten and a half on the twenty-fifth of October,
1956—Flag Day, the first anniversary of the official end
to the occupation. Grandfather and Ernst had been nine
steady-drinking hours at the Gasthof Enns when they started going through 'old trunks in the post-office basement—our family storage center too. I don't know whatever could have possessed him, but my old grandfather
found (or was looking for, all along) the eaglesuit—completely featherless, because the lard had long ago given
out: a slightly greasy, gleaming suit of partially rusted pieplates; the head, and beak in particular, was solid rust.
But my grandfather put the thing on, insisting to Watzek-
Trummer that it was his turn to be the eagle, since both
Ernst and Zahn Glanz once had a crack at it. And what
better day for the Austrian eagle than Flag Day?

Except that this Flag Day was somewhat marred. At

least for my mother. Only two days before, the streets of
Budapest had been suddenly bled; fortunately, the Hungarians at least had a cleared route of escape, because
Austrian officials, after the Russian withdrawal from Vienna, had removed the barbed wire and picked the mine-
fields along the Austro-Hungarian border. A good thing.
Because the Hungarian political police and the Soviet
Army had driven more than 170.000 refugees across the
border, where Vienna—sympathetic to occupied peo-
ples—had taken them under her eagle's wing. And they
were still coming across on Flag Day.

I can only guess that why this affected my mother so
strongly was rooted back in March of '38, when Zahn
Glanz either crossed the Hungarian border at Kittsee or
he didn't cross at all. And if you choose to think of Zahn
as crossing, then you might think of him as crossing
back—with, perhaps, 170,000 other refugees from Hungary.

I only think this because such things must have been on
Hilke's mind to make her react as she did, to Grandfather—striding, magnificent, into our Kaprun kitchen, and
shrieking under his bald bird helmet. *"Cawk!"* he cried.
"Austria is free!"

My mother moaned; she dug her fingers into me, where
I was being made to model for a knitted sweater. Then
she was up and charging the surprised, featherless eagle in
the doorway, and caught him there, up against the jamb.
She ground her knee between his legs, lifting the hem of
his chainmail dress; she tugged and tugged to get his helmet off.

"Oh God, Zahn," she whimpered, so that Grandfather
pulled roughly away from her and took the eagle head off
himself. And couldn't look at her straight, but sort of
turned his face away and mumbled, "Oh, I just found it in
the P.O., Hilke. Oh, I'm so sorry, but my God, Hilke, it's
been *eighteen years!*" But he still wouldn't meet her eyes.

She stayed sagged against the doorjamb; her face was
ageless, even sexless—showed nothing at all. She said in a
radio-announcing voice, "They keep coming in. More than
one hundred seventy thousand now. All of Hungary is
coming to Vienna. Don't you think we should go back
now—in case he tries to look us up?"

"Oh, Hilke," Grandfather said. "No, oh no. There's
nothing back in the city for us."

Still radio-announcing, she said, "Editor Lennhoff *did* successfully escape to Hungary. That's a fact."

Grandfather tried to stand still enough so his pieplates wouldn't rattle, but she heard his noise and looked up at him; her real voice and face came back.

My mother said, "You left him there once, you know. You made him stay behind for your bankbook, when he could have come with us."

"You watch it, girl," said Watzek-Trummer, and caught her hair in one hand. "You just get hold of yourself now, you hear?"

"You left Zahn in Vienna!" my mother screamed at the bird, who rattled under his pieplates and turned away from her altogether. Watzek-Trummer yanked my mother's hair.

"Stop it!" he hissed. "Damn you, Hilke, your Zahn Glanz didn't have to stay so long as he did. He didn't *have* to drive any editors to Hungary, did he? And what makes you so sure he *did*, anyway?"

But my mother tore her hair free of him and weaved back to me, where I balanced on the modeling chair, somewhat crucified in a thus far unseamed sweater, fastened on me with pins.

Watzek-Trummer took the huddled eagle back to the post-office basement, and that night my mother woke me very late—rubbed her cold, wet face across my own and tickled me down under the covers with a fur-collared coat she only wore for trips. And then she took one. Leaving behind no symbolic gestures to be interpreted—that we might guess, for example, how long she would be gone, or how and with whom she would end up.

Leaving us not so much, even, as custard on the walls, or soles of shoes to be recognized as final.

Although my grandfather didn't need any evidence to know she wouldn't be back. Less than two weeks later, in November '56, Kaprun and the surrounding Salzburger mountains had their first snowfall—a wet, heavy storm that turned to ice at night. So after supper, Grandfather took the mail sled and—although no one saw him—put on the eagle's pieplate armor; he hiked two miles and a half up the glacier field toward the summit of the Kitzsteinhorn. He had a flashlight with him, and when he'd been gone several hours, Watzek-Trummer got up from our kitchen table and looked out the window up the mountains. And saw a faint light, almost motionless, blinking midway up the glacier, under the black peak of the Kitzsteinhorn. Then the light came down—the sled must have been careening, because the light shot straight down, leapt, zigzagged, steered to a route more roundabout than it had climbed: a logger's swath cut across the lower mountain, below the glacier field. The old skiers called it the Catapult Trail. It bent very steeply through fourteen S-curves, three and one quarter miles down to the village.

Now, of course, there's an aerial tramcar that takes you up there, and the new skiers call the trail the Suicide Run.

But Grandfather took the mail sled down what was then called the Catapult, and Trummer and I followed the light of his descent from our kitchen window.

"That's your grandfather, boy," said Ernst. "Just look at him go."

We followed him through eight, then nine S-curves in the timber—he must have been sitting up and steering with his feet—and then his flashlight-headlight became so blurry it looked like a whole line of speeding traffic on the freeway. Though Watzek-Trummer claims he counted that Grandfather made one more S-curve before we lost sight of him altogether. That would have made ten out of fourteen, which isn't a bad percentage for a mail sled at night.

Ernst told me I wasn't to come and shut me up in our kitchen, from where I watched a tiny band of flashlights combing the mountain under the Kitzsteinhorn until dawn. When they found my grandfather, who'd been catapulted off the Catapult by striking a log the new snow had almost hidden. The mail sled, by some mystical steering I'll never understand, made it back to the village all by itself.

In fact, when they got Grandfather out of the forest, it was the mail sled Watzek-Trummer wanted found. And when they'd found it and brought it up to him, Watzek-Trummer laid my grandfather on it and eased him down the mountain and through the village to the Gasthof Enns. Where Ernst drank four brandy coffees and waited for the priest. Who was upset that Trummer refused to remove the eaglesuit. Watzek-Trummer vowed that Grandfather would be buried just as was, in armor—featherless but masked. Ernst was given little debate. Grandfather had made his point clear some time ago, that the Catholics would never have their way with his body after what that traitorous Cardinal Innitzer did in '38. So to end all discussion, Watzek-Trummer said, "You remember Cardinal Innitzer, Father? He sold out Vienna to Hitler. He encouraged all his flock to endorse the Führer."

And the priest said, "But the Vatican never endorsed it."

"The Vatican," said Watzek-Trummer, "has a history of being fashionably late." Because old Ernst was still reading, all he could get.

Then I was sent for, and together, Ernst and I, we straightened poor grandfather's pieplates and packed snow around him—so he'd keep cool while the coffin was being made.

Watzek-Trummer said to me, "It was a stroke, of sorts; it was his heart, one way or another. But at least this is a better burial than some I've heard of."

After which, we went home, Ernst and I. I was a confident ten; if I felt at all abandoned by my family, I at least felt in good hands. You couldn't have much better than Ernst Watzek-Trummer. Keeper of the family album—egg man, postman, historian, survivor. Responsible, finally, for seeing that I would survive to understand my heritage.

The Twenty-first Zoo Watch: Tuesday, June 6, 1967, @ 6:45 a.m.

The cage-cleaners were admitted a little after 6:30. O. Schrutt opened the main gate for them, and he left the gate open. He put a chain across the entrance, though; there's a sign hung on it, probably a NO ADMITTANCE sign—although it's hung in such a way that I can't read it.

The cage-cleaners are a sour, shaggy lot; they went in the House of Reptiles and came out with their paraphernalia, and then went en masse to the House of Pachyderms.

Then I thought that if O. Schrutt would only move away from the gate, I could leave straightaway. I wanted to be casually outside the zoo when O. Schrutt left. Perhaps I could see where he went!

Does O. Schrutt eat a *normal* breakfast?

But some sort of morning watchman met O. Schrutt at the gate. There were very few words between them. Perhaps the new watchman chided old O. about wearing the rain slicker in so much sun. But O. Schrutt simply vanished; he stepped over the chain across the gateway, and I didn't even see which way he turned.

I had to wait for the new watchman to slowly make a half-hearted round. When he finally went into the Small Mammal House, the cage-cleaners were still in the House of Pachyderms. But before I left my hedgerow and made it out the main gate, I saw the new watchman turn on the infrared! Funny, but I can't remember when O. Schrutt turned it off. This watch has worn me out, I guess.

And when I got outside the gate, I couldn't see a trace of O. Schrutt. I went across Maxing Strasse to the café. I sat at a sidewalk table and was told I'd have to wait till seven to be served.

My interesting Balkan waiter was setting ashtrays out on the tables. He must work mornings and afternoons—takes the night off, for cooking up sly reports to make the next day.

He eyed me with immeasurable slyness. He let me catch his eyes, and then showed me, with a side glance, that he noticed how my motorcycle was parked in exactly the same place it was yesterday afternoon. That was all; he just showed me he knew *that* much.

And suddenly I began to get a little nervous about coming back to Waidhofen—about this frotting waiter recognizing me on the day of the bust. I should have a disguise! So I decided to cut all my hair off.

But when this waiter brought an ashtray to my table, and sort of dealt it across the tabletop like a playing card, I got a little bolder and asked him if he'd been around Hietzing when they had a zoo bust—twenty years or so ago.

He said he hadn't been around.

So I said, "You must have heard about it, though. They don't know who it was that had the idea. He was never identified."

"I understand," he said, "that whoever it was ended up like a lamb chop."

See? Sly frotter. He knew it all along.

So I asked him, "What sort of fellow would ever try such a thing?"

"A madman," he said. "A real psych case."

"You mean," I suggested, "someone with inherited flaws? Or someone who had a background heaped with insecurities and frustrations—a type from a broken home?"

"Why sure," he said—still humoring me, the frotter. "That's what I meant, all right."

"A case of transference," I added.

"An error of judgment," he pronounced.

"A lack of logic," I said.

"A total *loss* of logic," said the waiter; he beamed at me. His armload of polished glass ashtrays threw little sharp triangles of sun up to his face.

But I have my own idea of who the mad zoo buster might have been. After all, it's perfectly fair to have your own theory on this matter; it's an open question. And I can think of the perfect man for the job; at least, from all I've heard about him, he would have been ripe for it— both for the divine idea and the flaw in his youthful foresight that caused him to be eaten. He was somehow related to me too; he was rumored to have driven a hunted newspaper editor to Hungary, and rumored not to have gotten back. But everyone knows that the editor was saved, and so it's possible to assume that the driver might have gone to Hungary *and* gotten back—at a time when those he most wanted to see were unavailable. Well, it's possible. This person *did* love animals. I happen to know he once expressed grave concern over a park squirrel who'd been tattooed—so deeply that its mind could only dance in circles.

It could have been him, as easily as it could have been another—say, some guilt-ridden relative of Hinley Gouch.

Then that sly Balkan waiter said, "Sir, are you all right?" Trying to make me think I wasn't, you see; suggesting that I'd been doing funny things with my hands or mouth, maybe.

You have to watch out for these Balkans. I once knew of one who failed to recognize his best friend over a urinal.

But I wasn't about to let a frotting Balkan trick me. I said, "Of course I'm all right. Are you?" Seeing, already, what would happen to his armload of ashtrays, one morning soon, when he'd raise his sly eyes and lose his smug composure—in the face of a charging Rare Spectacled Bear from across Maxing Strasse.

"I only thought, sir," the waiter said, "that maybe you wanted some water. You seemed to be dizzy, or at loose ends—as they say."

But I wasn't going to let him get the best of me. I said:

Bolje rob nego grob!

Better a slave than a grave!

Then I said, "Right? That's right, isn't it?"

Incredibly sly, like a stone, he said, "Would you like anything to eat?"

"Just coffee," I told him.

"Then you'll have to wait," he said, thinking he'd fix me good. "We don't serve till seven."

"Then tell me where's the nearest barbershop," I said.

"But it's almost seven now," he said.

"I want a barber," I told him, nastily.

"They won't cut your hair till seven, either," he said.

"How do you know I want my hair cut?" I asked him, and that shut him up. He pointed round the Platz off Maxing Strasse; I pretended I didn't see the barber's striped pole.

Then, just to confuse him, I sat at the table past seven o'clock—doodling in my notebook. I pretended I was sketching his portrait, keeping my eyes on him and making him nervous while he served a few other early people.

At seven o'clock they open the zoo. There's no one who goes that early, though. There's just a fat man with a gambler's green eyeshade, smug as a sultan in the ticket booth. Over the booth, from time to time, the giraffe's head looms.

THE HIGHLY SELECTIVE AUTOBIOGRAPHY OF
SIEGFRIED JAVOTNIK: EPILOGUE

I grew up in Kaprun, a well-read child because Watzek-Trummer knew the value of books; a child with historical perspectives too, because Ernst filled me in as I went along—leaving gaps here and there, I assure you, until I was properly old enough to hear it all.

Before he sent me to the University of Vienna, Watzek-Trummer saw to it that I learned to drive the Grand Prix racer, 1939—suggesting to me that the bike was an almost genetical inheritance. So I was certainly deprived of nothing; I had my hot rod. First thing I did was to strip it of that degrading mail cart.

But after I'd done some thinking about Gottlob Wut, I

began to consider the Grand Prix racer as something really too special for me to waste on my adolescence, and getting all the details from Ernst, I made my first trip out of Kaprun. That was in the summer of '64. I was eighteen.

I drove the Grand Prix racer to the NSU factory at Neckarsulm, where I tried to speak with one of the manager types concerning the prize-worthy motorcycle that had been my inheritance. I told a mechanic first, as that was the first type I met in the factory—how this had been the bike of Gottlob Wut, the masterful, mystical mechanic of the 1930 Italian Grand Prix. But the mechanic hadn't heard of Wut; neither had the young manager type I finally found.

"What you got there?" he said. "A tractor?"

"Wut," I told him. "Gottlob Wut. He was killed in the war."

"No kidding?" said the manager. "I heard that happened to a number of people."

"The Grand Prix of Italy, 1930," I said. "Wut was the key man."

But the young manager only remembered the drivers, Freddy Harrell and Klaus Worfer. He knew no Wut.

"Well, get to it," he said. "How much you want for that old thing?"

And when I mentioned that perhaps it was a museum piece—and did NSU have a place where they honored their old racers?—the manager laughed.

"You'd make a great salesman," he told me, only I didn't tell him that I'd planned to give it away—if they had a nice place for it.

The bike shop was full of awful, spiteful motorcycles that made spitting sounds when they were revved. So I started up my racer and—in my mind—loosened all their frotting aluminum parts.

I drove back to Kaprun and told Watzek-Trummer that we ought to keep the motorcycle in storage somewhere, and drive it only for emergencies. Of course, with *his* historical perspective, he agreed.

Then I went to Vienna and attempted to join in the university life. But I met no one very interesting; most of them hadn't even read as much as I had, and none of them knew as much as Ernst Watzek-Trummer. There was one student I remember fairly well, though—a Jewish kid who was a part-time spy for a secret Jewish organization that hunted down old Nazis. The kid had lost all eighty-nine members of his family—disappeared, he said—but when I questioned him as to how he knew, then, that he even belonged to this family, he confessed he had "adopted" them. Because as far as he really knew, he had no family. He remembered no one, except the RAF pilot who flew him out of the Belsen area after the camp was busted. But he "adopted" this eighty-nine-member family because on the records he's seen, that looked like the largest single family who had vanished without a leftover. It was for them, he said, that he made himself the nineti-eth member of the family—the survivor, at least in name.

He was fairly interesting, with his part-time apprentice spying, but apparently he became very good at his job and was so boastful that his picture got in one of the Vienna papers, as being single-handedly responsible for the discovery and arrest of a certain Richter Mull, a Nazi war criminal. But that publicity made the kid nervous, and his secret Jewish organization disowned him. He used to sit around in the university Kellers; remembering what had happened to America's Wild Bill Hickok, he never sat back-to a window or a door. When I told Ernst Watzek-Trummer about him, Ernst said, "A war-paranoid type." It was something he'd read.

And then there was my good friend Dragutin Svet. I met him on a ski trip to Tauplitz my second year at the university. He was a Balkan studies fellow, a Serb by birth, and we did a lot of skiing together. He always wanted to meet Watzek-Trummer.

But we had a falling out. A silly thing. I went with him once to Switzerland, skiing again, and while we were there, we overheard a group of men speaking Serbo-Croat in our gasthaus lobby. It turned out there was a sort of convention of exiled Serbs, a mean-looking crew of old folk, for the most part, and a few young, idealistic-look-ing, soldierly chaps. Some of the old ones—so the word was—had fought side by side with the Chetnik general Drazha Mihailovich.

We got to go in their dining room, though our age and nervousness put us under suspicion. I was trying to remember some witty Serbo-Croat when this one old fel-low said, in German—nastily leering at me the length of their table—"Where are you from, boy?" And I said, truth-

fully, "Maribor, by way of Slovenjgradec." And several
men put down their cocktails and said severely, "Croat?
Slovene?" Since I didn't want to embarrass my friend
Dragutin Svet, the Serb by birth, I blurted the only
Serbo-Croat I could remember:

Bolje rob nego grobl

Better a slave than a grave!

Which, as Watzek-Trummer later explained, was precisely the opposite of what I should have said; it was my
own father's unheroic improvising that got me in trouble
with the diehard Chetniks. Because there was a deeply insulted man at the head of the table who leaned over a
long way toward me; he had only one hand and used it remarkably well, to toss a shot glass of Scotch in my face.

My friend Dragutin Svet refused to understand the accident, and he thought me in bad taste for making such
word play with a slogan the Serbs take so seriously. And I
didn't see much of Svet thereafter.

I got a job with a certain Herr Faber, to keep my hand
in—and my eyes open for—motorcycles. Also, I needed to
finance my education, which appeared to be taking longer
than it should have. All because my thesis project was re-
jected by a certain Herr Doktor Ficht.

This thesis was to be my HIGHLY SELECTIVE AUTOBIOG-
RAPHY, as I thought it was well enough detailed, and
even creative. But this Ficht was furious. He said it was a
decidedly biased and incomplete picture of history, and flip-
pant besides—and there were no footnotes. Well, in trying
to calm him down, I discovered that Herr Doktor Ficht
used to be Herr Doktor Fichtstein, Jew, who'd lived a
wharf rat's life on the Dutch coast during the war—having been caught only once; escaping after they'd injected
his gums with some tooth-mortifying chemical too new
and experimental to be safe. The previous Fichtstein was
enraged that I should be so pretentious as to dash through
the war with so little mention of the Jews. I tried to explain that he should really look at my autobiography as
what is loosely called fiction—a novel, say. Because it's
not intended to be *real* history. And I added, besides, that
I thought the Doktor was making a rather Russian-Ameri-
can value judgment by claiming that no picture of atrocity

can be complete without the millions of Jews. Numbers again, you see. Ficht, or Fichtstein, seemed to miss my point altogether, but I confess, statistics have a way of getting the best of you. They can make almost anything, all by itself, seem not in the least atrocious.

But that run-in made my university career look a bit long-term. That is, I'd have to stay around until I mastered some academic subject or other—rather than show them what I already knew and have done with it.

Watzek-Trummer, of course, doesn't understand universities at all. He declares that they all must have read too much before they were interested in anything, which prevented them, later, from becoming interested in anything they read. He's rather perplexing on this issue. Self-educated men, you know, are unbudging.

Ernst still reads like a demon. I see him every Christmas, and I never come without a stock of books for him. Unlike most old people, though, his reading has become more selective; that is, he no longer reads everything he can get his hands on. In fact, he's often unimpressed with the books I bring him. He begins, he browses, he stops at page ten. "I know it already," he says, and lays it aside.

Actually, I go home for Christmas more to read the books Trummer has than to flatter myself into thinking I'm bringing him any favors.

Watzek-Trummer is a retired postman now, and very venerable in the town. He keeps three rooms in the Gasthof Enns; he's even something of a tourist attraction, when he permits it.

One of Trummer's rooms is all books; one room stores the Grand Prix racer, 1939; one room has a bed, and a kitchen table—even though Ernst eats all his meals in the *Gasthof* now. The kitchen table is for sitting at, leaning on and talking over—a habit he says he can't break, even though he's alone now.

Whenever I'm home, I sleep in the room with the 1939 Grand Prix racer. And I enjoy my Christmases very much.

Believe me, Ernst Watzek-Trummer can tell you a thing or two.

The Twenty-second and Very Last Zoo Watch: Tuesday, June 6, 1967, @ 7:30 a.m.

I've stopped for a coffee in Hütteldorf-Hacking, not more than a mile west of Hietzing. There's some country-side here, though it's mostly small vineyards; you've got to go a mile more if you want to see cows.

At the minimum, then, the oryx has a two-mile trip be-fore his first lay.

Hütteldorf-Hacking is taken aback with me. I got a winner of a haircut back in Hietzing.

Following that sneaky waiter's directions, I went round the Platz off Maxing Strasse and was Hugel Furtwängler's first customer.

"Shave or haircut?" said little Hugel Furtwängler. You could tell he wanted to give me both, or at least the hair-cut—since shaves are cheaper.

"Just a shave," I said. "But a *total* shave."

And pretentiously nodding as if he understood me, he packed some hot towels around my cheeks. But I said, "Get the eyebrows too, won't you?" And that stopped him from looking so know-it-all.

"Eyebrows?" Hugel said. "You want your eyebrows shaved?"

"A *total* shave, please, Hugel," I said. "And no nonsense now."

"Oh well," he said. "I worked at the hospital once. We'd get them sometimes after fights, and you'd have to shave their eyebrows then."

"Everything," I said. "Just shave my whole head, please."

And that threw him off again, although he tried to pre-tend he wasn't baffled.

"You mean you want a haircut," he said.

"Just a whole shave," I insisted. "I don't want my hair *cut*, I want it shaved off altogether—smooth as the end of my nose." And he gawked at my nose as if it would help him to understand me.

"If I'm going to *shave* your head," he said, "I have to *cut* the hair first. I have to cut it down close *in order to* shave it."

But I wasn't going to have him talking to me as if I

were a child, or a madman to be humored along. I said,
"Hugel, you do whatever you think is necessary to get the
job done. Only, no gashes in my head, please. I'm a
bleeder, you know—there's been a touch of hemophilia in
our family for years. So no cuts, please, or I'll be bled like
a steer in your chair."

And Hugel Furtwängler gave a phony laugh—humoring me again, thinking he was in control.

"You're a real laugher, aren't you, Hugel?" I said. And
he kept right on.

"Such a sense of humor you have," he said. "And so
early in the morning!"

"Sometimes," I told him, "I laugh so loud that I bleed
through my ears." But he still kept up his giggle, and I
could see he was set in his ways of belittling me. So I
changed the subject.

"Lived in the zoo long, Hugel?" I asked. And he
harumphed over that.

"Did you ever see a zoo bust, Hugel?" I asked. And he
snuck down behind my head in the mirror, pretending he
was trimming the base of my neck.

"There *was* one, you know," I said.

"But they didn't get out," he said—knowing all along,
the frotter.

"You were here, then?" I asked.

"Oh, such a long time ago," he said. "I don't remember
where I was."

"Were you always a barber, Hugel?" I asked.

"It runs in the family," he said, "—like your bleeding!"
And he thought himself so funny that he almost cut my
ear off.

"Watch it," I said, going stiff in my chair. "You didn't
break the skin, did you?" And that sobered him some; he
worked with great care.

But when he'd given me no more than what looked like
a normal haircut, he said, "It's not too late. I can stop
here."

"*Shave* me," I said, staring stonefaced at the mirror.
And he did.

He was starting up his giggles again, while I inspected
my head front-and-back in the mirror, when his second
customer came in.

"Ah, Herr Ruhr," said Hugel. "I'm ready for you right
away."

"Morning, Hugel," said heavy Herr Ruhr.

But I leapt back from the mirror and stared at Herr Ruhr. He looked a little alarmed, and I said, "This barber's a laughing fool. I ask for a shave and look what he gives me."

Hugel gave a little pip of a cry, razor in his tiny hand—shaving cream on the backs of his knuckles.

"Watch out for him, Herr Ruhr," I said, running my hand over my gleaming head. "He's a dangerous man with that razor." And Herr Ruhr stared at the razor in little Hugel's hand.

"He's crazy!" cried Hugel Furtwängler. "He *wanted* me to do it!" But dancing with his razor, and his face so bright red, Hugel looked a little crazy himself. "And he's a bleeder too!" Hugel shouted.

"Hugel's got blood on his mind this morning," I said to Herr Ruhr. Then I paid Hugel for a shave.

"Shave *and* a haircut!" cried the flustered little Furtwängler.

But I turned to Herr Ruhr and said, "Would you call *this* a haircut?" And again I slicked my hand over my dome. "I only asked for a shave."

Herr Ruhr looked at his watch and said, "I don't know where the time's gone to this morning. I'll just have to skip it, this morning, Hugel."

But Hugel waved his razor and made an awkward attempt to block Herr Ruhr at the door. Herr Ruhr dodged quickly into the street, and I followed him out, leaving Hugel Furtwängler bespattered with shaving cream and waving his razor after us.

In somewhat the same condition, I thought, that poor Hugel will be in when he sees the stiff-bristled aardvark come lumbering across the Platz for a shampoo.

Then I snuck up on the motorcycle without that plotting Balkan waiter spying my new head, and quickly put my helmet on so that when he did notice me pumping the kick starter, he wouldn't realize I was much changed. But I only rode as far as Hütteldorf-Hacking with the helmet on, because it was very irritating—not fitting me any more, and bouncing all over my stinging head; Hugel had not rendered my dome absolutely cut-free.

I tied the helmet by its chin strap to the waist cord of my jacket, because I don't need a helmet any more. I have one of my very own.

Then I had a coffee, smelling the sun cooking the little grapes in the vineyards across the road, and trying to figure out exactly where it was from here that a certain fellow I know once had a henhouse; a laboratory, actually, wherein a much talked-about bird was invented. But I lost my bearings among so many buildings that look new, or at least rebuilt.

And it would be hard to spot the property I have in mind now, because the henhouse was burned down long ago.

It doesn't matter. There's an important issue at hand right now.

I'm on my way, Graff, and don't you worry. I'll be careful. I'll come into Waidhofen a sneaky new way; I'll leave the bike a bit out of town and walk in without my duckjacket, and without my old recognizable head. Thinking all the time, see.

And don't you worry either, Graff—about going to Italy. We'll go, all right. Maybe some of them will follow us!

We'll get to see your frotting beaches, Graff. We'll get to see the sea.

In fact, there's an interesting place I know of in Naples. They've a big aquarium where they keep all the wondrous fishes, in stale sea water under glass. I've seen pictures. The place is just off the harbor.

In fact, it would be an easy job. We wouldn't have to wriggle the fishes very far, or keep them out of water too long. Just across a street or two—and maybe there's a small park before the sea wall, if I remember rightly. And then we'd launch them free in the Bay of Naples.

In fact, Graff, it will be even easier than the Hietzinger Zoo.

Part Three

Setting Them Free

P.S.

Of course, there's more to the notebook than that. And, of course, the zoo watches and the autobiography don't appear together in the original; it was my idea to interleaf them. Because, I felt, it was almost impossible to endure either the verbosity of Siggy's souped-up history or the fanaticism of his frotting zoo watches—if you were to read them whole. At least, it was for me; I found myself skipping back and forth, though part of that may have been due to my discomfort at being forced to read in Auntie Tratt's bathtub, where I spent a week, or almost that long, soaking my bee stings.

But I still feel the two journals demand separation, if only for literary reasons. And certainly Siggy made some obscure connections between his awesome history and his scheme for busting the zoo; though, for my own part, I can't speak too well for the logic in that.

Again, if only for literary reasons, I couldn't see the sense in reproducing the other memorabilia in the notebook. All those frotting poems and proverbs. All his exclamation points, addresses and phone numbers, reminders of due dates for library books; and what constitutes his ill-kept bibliography.

I'm afraid that Doktor Ficht was at least right in griping about poor Siggy's failure to footnote. He obviously drew as heavily from Watzek-Trummer's library as he did from old eyewitness Ernst himself.

To mention a few of Siggy's jottings:

I'm quite pleased with Brook-Shepherd's *Anschluss*.
B-S really knew what was the matter.

D. Martin goes to the heart of it in *Ally Betrayed!*

Poor L. Adamic is a hopeless propagandist in
My Native Land.

All the info is in Stearman's *The Soviet Union
and the Occupation of Austria.* But his footnotes
are longer than the text.

There's a lot of emotional writing in Stoyan
Pribichevich's *World Without End* and G.E.R.
Gedye's *Fallen Bastions.*

And other entries, without his pronouncements:

Kurt von Schuschnigg's *Austrian Requiem,* and
Sheridon's *Kurt von Schuschnigg.*

The Schmidt Trial Protocols, esp. the testimonies
of Skubl, Miklas and Raab; and *The Nuremburg
Testimonies,* esp. of Göring and Seyss-Inquart.

*The official Minutes of the Meetings of the
Allied Council and Executive Committee, 1945–55.*

Plamenatz's *The Truth About Mihailovich.*

Vaso Trivanovich's *The Treason of Mihailovich.*

Colonel Zivan Knezevich's *Why The Allies Abandoned
the Yugoslav Army of General Mihailovich.*

And countless references to:

What Ernst Watzek-Trummer said.

It was some days, however, before I could read any of
this—confined to the bathtub as I was. Epsom salts, with
the tub water changed hourly.

Of course, they brought me all of Siggy's honey-covered
things. I was some time separating the pages of the notebook; I had to steam them open, over my bath water.
And then I had to wait a few days before I could see
clearly to read—until my bee swellings had come down
enough to let me hold my eyes open. I ran a fever too,
and vomited a bit—the poison in my system excessive as it
was.

But if my bee dose was excessive, I wouldn't have wanted any part of the overdose that must have been poor
Siggy's lot. And no one would tell me if it had been his
head I heard go THANG!—and put him out before the
bees filled him up—or if I'd only imagined his struggling
under the flatbed, after he'd toppled the hives.

As the notebook says:

God knows. Or guesses.

But when I did get down to reading, I can assure you there were spots that gave me twinges more considerable than my bee wounds. There was this:

Today I met and bought a motorcycle with Hannes Graff.
He's a nice person. At loose ends, though.

And despite his countless recovering baths, I can tell you that Hannes Graff was at loose ends still.
And there were more twinges from the notebook:

What Drazha Mihailovich said at his trial: "I wanted much . . . I started much . . . but the gale of the world blew away me and my work."

Well, Siggy, I'm not so sure. I don't think it was the gale of the world that got *you*. Like so many other unfitted parts of your history and your scheme, I'm not convinced by any logic to your comparisons—only hinted, or leapt to, and not clear.
It was no gale of the world that got you, Sig. You made your own breeze, and it blew you away.

LOOSE ENDS

The honeybee, polliniferous: Any of certain socially-minded, honey-producing bees (genus *Apis* and allied genera), especially the species *Apis mellifera,* native to Europe, raised for their honey and wax and pollinating services in much of the world.
The honeybee has several parts.
Most of which, in varying mashed and torn conditions, I discovered—as Siggy might have put it:

In my trouser cuffs
And socks.

In my underwear
And armpit hair.
Little bee bits,
Here and there.

A thorax part in the spiral binder of Siggy's notebook; a
hairy pair of posterior legs on the bathroom floor—where,
I guess, I was shucked out of my clothes and dunked for
the first time in soothing salts; antennae, eyes and heads,
nasty abdomens and lovely wings, in countless folds and
pockets of Siggy's honey-ruined duckjacket.

I found whole bees too. One of which I slowly drowned
in the bathtub, but I think it was already dead.

For a few days, Hannes Graff soaked all his loose ends,
and was not allowed visitors. Frau Tratt tended to me.

Ironic, I thought, that she who'd taken such great offense to Siggy's startling nakedness should be at ease with
mine. Insulting, I thought. But Auntie Tratt excused herself on account of her age.

"Someone's got to tend to you," she said. "Could you
afford a doctor? There's already some debt outstanding to
me, you know. And I could be your grandmother, you
know. It's just another little bare bottom to me."

And I thought: There couldn't have been so very many
little bare bottoms for you, at any time.

But she was daily there, with soups and sponges; my
general puffiness going down under her eyes.

"They took a liking to your neck," she said—the cruel
old bitch—and she evaded my questions about what they
were doing with Siggy. If they were treating the body or
anything.

Of course, I didn't need to be told he was dead. There
was just this endless bringing back of his parts to me. His
duckjacket, his pipes, his notebook.

Formally, Frau Tratt would inquire, "Where is he to be
sent?"

This before I'd read enough of the notebook to have
visions of his relatives.

Later, when I could read, I pictured a weary Watzek-
Trummer, tired of burial responsibilities. In one way or
another, on hand for two generations of deaths in a
family—endings direct and absolute, and endings only implied.

Siggy certainly had to go to Kaprun, but I couldn't

imagine him there—for a few days beflowered, resting in the room with the Grand Prix racer, 1939.

"Well, anyway, you're lucky," the old Tratt said. "This kind of thing can be expensive, but Keff's building the box for him."

"Keff?" I said. "Why Keff?"

"I am sure I don't know," said Frau Tratt. "It's just a box, though—real simple. You don't get much for nothing, you know."

Not from you, surely, I thought. But I said, "Where's Gallen?"

"What do you care where she is?" said Auntie Tratt.

But I wouldn't give her the satisfaction. I sat hunched-over on my bed of towels, drying off from my last bath of that day and trying to prepare myself for the old Tratt's rough hands going over me—tingling me, in spite of myself, with that good, nut-scented witch hazel.

The Tratt said again, "What do you care where she is? Is Gallen a part of your plans now?"

But I told her, "I just wondered where Gallen was keeping herself. She hasn't once come to see me."

"Well," the good Frau said, "She won't be visiting until it's comfortable for you to wear some *clothes* again." And when she said *"clothes,"* she splashed that icy witch hazel on my back, and as I gasped half upright under her hand, she ground down her forearm on my neck and shoved my head down between my knees. She slopped some down my shoulders, and slicking her hands over me in her slaplike fashion, she got some witch hazel in one of my ears. Then her voice came at me, half underwater, prying, as if I were an eel to be coaxed out from under some rock—for the final stew. "But you don't have any plans for the moment, Herr Graff?" she snooped.

"No plans," I said quickly, and realized that this was the first hopeful thing to come into my head since the frotting bees. Remembering, of course, what Siggy had once said about plans. He had once had *the way not to spoil it. No planning, Graff. No mapping it out. No dates to get anywhere, no dates to get back.* And in a grating sort of way, I started laughing—really, it was so funny; that this should be his foremost, solemn ingredient for a good trip between us. How funny, really, his crazy and elaborate scheme for the zoo bust looked alongside that previous notion.

"Am I hurting you, Herr Graff?" said the Tratt, who must have felt my odd quivers even through her gross, insensitive calluses.

But I just laughed out loud at her. "No plans, Frau Tratt!" I said. "I don't have any. And I won't! No plans. Frot plans! Frot me!" I bellowed at her, "if I so much as start to make any plans."

"Well, goodness," the rare old Tratt said. "I only asked to make a little conversation."

"You lie," I told her, and she backed off—the sweet witch hazel drying on her hands so fast you could see it disappear, like the white under your thumbnail goes back to pink as soon as you unclench your fist.

WHERE GALLEN WAS

Evenually, by my bath- and bedside—after I'd healed sufficiently to wear at least a loincloth equivalent, and after I'd adequately insulted the Tratt, to make necessary someone else's waiting on me—Gallen cared for me, again.

I was permitted to show her my less-private bee welts, still a bit reddened, even after my tedious treatments. Because, I'm told, my poor antibodies had fled my bloodstream on the thirty-fifth or -sixth sting, leaving my general resistance rather low.

"How are you, Graff?" Gallen asked.

"My resistance is low," I told her, and we discreetly discussed my poor antibodies.

She said, "What are you going to do now?"

"I've not made any plans," I said quickly, and she hung by my bed, hands folding and unfolding, in a mock-casual stance. She was growing too tall and forcing too much shape in her little-girlish clothes. Puffed shoulders and frilled cuffs on this outfit—a high-buttoned and forbidding blouse. The old Tratt's choice, I could be sure. A further, plotting defense of hers against me. May she rot.

"Sit down, Gallen," I offered, and slid over for her.

"Your resistance is low," she reminded, saucily; as if she were so old and frotting worldly—a favorite guise of hers—under the clothes.

"What have you been doing?" I asked.

"Thinking," said Gallen, and pulled down her chin with her hand. As if she'd just started this minute, to convince me.

"What about?" I asked.

"About what you're going to do now," she said.

"No plans," I repeated. "But I've got to do something with Siggy."

"Keff built a nice box," said Gallen.

"How thoughtful," I said. "How does he seem to you?"

"Oh, Keff feels very bad," said Gallen.

"I meant, how's Siggy?" I said. "I couldn't care less about Keff."

"Keff's very sorry, really," she said. "He keeps asking about you."

"How's *Siggy*?" I asked. "How's he look?"

"Well, I haven't *seen* him," she said. But the way her shoulders shook when she said *"seen,"* I believe she'd taken a peek.

"All puffy?" I said, a bit nastily. "Like two of me?" And I pinched up a fair-sized welt on my bare, witch-hazeled stomach.

"Keff wouldn't let anyone see him," said Gallen.

"Frotting Keff!" I said. "What's he taken an interest for? Does he enjoy it that much?"

"He's been very nice, Graff," she said.

"And seeing a bit of you too," I said. "No doubt."

So she told me about the aftermath. How the armored beekeeper had finally been the one to extricate poor Siggy from under the flatbed. They'd all taken him for the doctor to poke—and see if he'd deflate—and then the mayor had pronounced over the body. Afterwards Keff had asked for him, and said he'd build the box.

"Where's he going to be sent?" said Gallen. "Keff says to ask you that."

"To Kaprun," I said, "if Keff can tear himself away from the body."

"It wasn't Keff's fault, Graff," she said. And added how she thought that Siggy must have been crazy. So I told her about the mad notebook, and the ultimate, unreasonable scheme; and all the conclusions leapt to, concerning O. Schrutt and the Famous Asiatic Black Bear. I said I agreed with her, that poor Siggy had perhaps gone off his rail somewhere. Then I sat up in bed and pulled her down to sit beside me.

Since we were closer and I'd got her talking about it, I asked her what the doctor said he'd died of. "Cause of death," I said stiffly. "Precisely what?"

"A heart attack," said Gallen, "which could have been the shock."

"Or too many bees," I said, thinking that too much bee gunk went inside him and sent a sort of thrombus to clog his heart. Then I got dizzy, sitting upright; I began to itch all over.

"Witch hazel, Graff?" said Gallen.

But feeling the need for at least an immediate sort of plan I said—as quickly and officiously as possible, "Tell Keff there's to be no fanfare, and no flowers or anything. And the coffin should be sealed. Just the name, no engraving. And put him on the train to Kaprun—to a man named Ernst Watzek-Trummer. Who'll pay for it, I'm sure. Then you bring me a telegram form. I'll send off something to precede the body."

"Keff wonders if you want anything to read," said Gallen. As if I hadn't read enough.

She spread the witch-hazeled washcloth over my eyes, which made it easier for me to answer her back—not being able to see her bent over me. "Just some sex book or other," I said. "I'm sure Keff knows where to find that sort of thing, if he's not too busy—fiddling so much with Siggy and you."

When I took the washcloth off my face, and caught an unscented breath, Gallen had left me alone in the room. With my doubts of her. And with my horror thoughts of Keff's possible necrophilia.

WHAT KEFF WAS DOING

Keff bought a book and sent it to me with Gallen, though it was an honorable, scholarly sort of sex book—the wholesome teamwork of a pair of Danes—called *The ABZ of Love.*

"It's got drawings in it," said Gallen, not looking at me. Probably afraid I'd turn into one of the sketches before her eyes.

"Read it cover to cover already, have you?" I asked.

"I have not," she said distinctly, and left me with Keff's odd gift.

Actually, it's a very sane, clean book, concerned with potting the old taboos, and encouraging us to have good, healthy fun. But I just randomly flipped it open, and was given a misleading picture of the book at first reading— because of this queer anecdote.

During the last century a lady woke up one night, feeling she was being pushed. Somebody went in and out and hands touched her every now and again. As she was not expecting anybody and had fallen asleep alone, she was so terrified she fainted. Much later she came to her senses and by the light of the dawning day saw that her butler (who, incidentally, was a genuine sleepwalker) had laid dinner for fourteen people on her bed. But of course this sort of thing is rather unusual, especially nowadays when so few people have servants.

Which totally puzzled me about Keff and his intentions. But I read on and momentarily rid my mind of a certain planless dark. I put off further the empty telegram form for Ernst Watzek-Trummer. These startling lines were my distraction:

Letting off a thoroughly good sneeze is a natural, spontaneous, frank action of which some people really are a little afraid in the same way that they are afraid of being spontaneous and letting themselves go in their sex life.

It had been contended that there must be a direct connection between a person's ability to have a thoroughly good sneeze and the ability to have a satisfying orgasm.

Which was so fascinating to me that I made a point of not falling asleep until Gallen came back to see if I needed more witch hazel.

"Like your book?" she mumbled.

"It's lowered my resistance even more," I said, feeling nice and playful. And just waiting for her to come near me with that nut-scented washcloth. But she handed it to

me to do for myself, and sat herself down on the edge of
my bed, at the foot. She crossed her nice legs, kicking
up—for just a second—her long apron-like skirt.

So I saw her burns—two perfect fist-sized burns on the
insides of her legs between each ankle and calf, just where
mine had been from the bike.

"How'd you get those?" I said, sitting up fierce and letting her know I frotting well knew what they *had* to come
from.

"Keff fixed the motorcycle," Gallen said. "He's teaching
me to drive." And when I stared at her, she said, "I can
do it very well, except the starting. I don't have enough
kick, Keff says." But I gaped at her, so she went on. "I
just stalled it, Graff, and when I tried to start it again, I
pulled it over on me. While I was kicking you know."

"Gallen," I said. "Just what's going on, please?"

"Well, that's how I was burned," she said. "Really!
When the pipes touched me, you see."

"What is rotting Keff teaching you to drive for?" I
shouted.

"So somebody knows," said Gallen. "So one of us can,
when you take me with you, when you go—if you want
to, Graff."

And she didn't jump up and go this time, when I sat
forward to touch her.

"Only if you *want* to take me with you, Graff," she
said. But when I leaned so far forward that I could tuck
her head down in the crook of my neck, Keff's sex book
slipped off my lap to the floor. Where both of us stared at
it and broke our kind of trance over each other.

When she was still looking down at *The ABZ*, I reared
up in bed and gave out with a tremendous sneeze—
harumphing so, it snapped her eyes back up to my face.

Well, she blushed so much I knew she'd read the book
before giving it to me. Anyone would have remembered
the sneezing part. And when she flashed out of my room,
I only hoped I hadn't scared her away from her plan.

Well, it wasn't really a *scheme* sort of plan—or hardly
more of a plan than Siggy and I had started off with. Ra-
tionalizing, and welcoming it, I thought it was at least so
much better and less defined a plan than the one I'd just
read about. And would, I hoped, lead my mind out of
poor Siggy's zoo notions.

Anyway, it was a pleasure to let Gallen run through my

head that way. It was pleasure enough to keep me another night from composing Watzek-Trummer's telegram.

I even slept, and dreamt the coward's dream of impossible isolation. The landscape unidentified, and no wildlife other than our own—Gallen and I, in daylight lasting only as long as we'd care to have it, in weather of our whim; on forest floors, not damp, and lakeshores free of biting insects. Unbelievably uninterrupted, we danced through the poses I remember from the faint, indistinct sketches in *The ABZ of Love*.

While Siggy, in Keff's box, couldn't intrude on us with his awesome details. And all beasts threatening my perfect peace were snug in the Hietzinger Zoo.

WHAT ERNST WATZEK-TRUMMER RECEIVED BY MAIL

In Keff's sealed and simple box, Siggy left Waidhofen for Kaprun on the Saturday evening train, June 10, 1967. My telegram preceded the body by hours enough for Ernst Watzek-Trummer to be warned to meet the train on Sunday noon.

I wrote several drafts of the telegram. I began:

Herr Watzek-Trummer/ I am informed that you were the guardian of Siegfried Javotnik/ a friend/ who was killed on a motorcycle/ and who arrives in Kaprun on this Sunday noon/ Hannes Graff/ who will write you at a later date/

And rewrote, to this:

Dear Herr Watzek-Trummer/Arriving Sunday noon is your charge/ Siegfried Javotnik/ who was killed on a motorcycle/ He was my friend/ I will get in touch with you/ Yours/ Hannes Graff/

And this:

My Dear Watzek-Trummer/ I am grieved to say that your charge and my friend/ Siegfried Javotnik/ was killed in a freak motorcycle accident in Waidhofen/

He will arrive in Kaprun on Sunday noon/ I will see
you myself soon/ Hannes Graff/

And finally decided on this:

Dear Ernst Watzek-Trummer/ I am very sorry to tell
you that my very good friend and your relation/
Siegfried Javotnik/ was killed on a motorcycle while
performing a secret mission/ the details of which I
will explain to you when you hear from me soon/
You may be proud of his work/ My condolences/
Hannes Graff/

And sent that, not hopeful of much better coming from
me, and not daring to think further of when I must go
meet this Trummer, to whom, I was sure, it would be
hard to lie. But at the moment, I simply couldn't have
faced another of Watzek-Trummer's sort of funerals.

And I was thinking how Ernst would be dimly impressed with me—as someone who couldn't possibly have
the remotest idea of what family griefs of his kind were
like. Because if Siggy ever got anything right, he was right
about this one thing: my family and I *did* miss the whole
war, which, strangely, I felt a bit guilty about.

I remember one thing from the war. In Salzburg, at the
close of the American occupation, my mother, who was
something of a bopper for her time, remarked on how sad
she was that Salzburg would have to go back to the *old*
music now—since the Americans took their Negro-horn
radio station with them.

I believe that was the only thing my family lost from
the war. And my mother wouldn't have had it in the first
place, if there hadn't been a war.

So I couldn't very well feel at ease with Watzek-Trummer, with such scanty horrors of my own. Frot me if I
wasn't thinking that my unwillingness to go with Siggy's
body had to do with my belief that I didn't have nearly
enough calamities on record to hold a candle to Trummer—and his ghastly burial duties, direct and indirect,
certain and implied, one by one.

So I left it all to Keff and said I'd go see Trummer
someday soon; but I made no *plans*. I wouldn't. I'd seen
what schemes for things could do.

Frotting Siggy! What really got me was how, for all his

scheming, he would have doomed himself if he'd ever had
the chance to go through with it. He'd gone so totally paranoid at the end, what with his prying the Balkan waiter
and little Hugel Furtwängler, that if he'd really tried the
zoo bust, those two would have put the word on him. Asking so many smart questions about the other zoo bust, he
was practically confessing before the crime. And shaving
his head was a dumb disguise, to say the least.

We simply mustn't call attention to our extremities, I'm
convinced.

And frot me if we ever would have gone to Italy, simply
to play on the beaches—planless, as he'd promised first. If
there's an aquarium in Naples, there's probably a zoo in
Rome. And wouldn't that have been the total, flying finish
—knocking over all the animal pens on the continent, until
the Regent Park in London would be laying on extra
keepers, waiting for the notorious zoo busters to strike
there?

But sitting up in my room on the bed, looking out
through that nighttime forsythia, I really missed him not
popping up on the window ledge any more. For it was a
little bit like sitting there waiting for him to come back
from that reconnaissance mission. And I began to think
that if he *had* gotten by the roadblock, or if I'd just left
with him when he first came crawling in over the ledge, I
guess I *would* have gone along with it. I mean, it was a
doomed idea, and bad that he lost all reason to the
plan—deciding *all* the beasts would get the open door,
even the eaters—but I don't think I could have let him try
it alone. I would have gone along to introduce my strain
of caution, my vein of limitless common sense—to see if
there wasn't some way I could get *him* safely out again,
unclawed, and maybe even spring an antelope or two in
the process.

That was the funny feeling, that came hazy and yellow
to me from the forsythia garden, clinging with spray from
the falls: I *would* have gone with him, but only because
he obviously needed looking after.

I mean, thinking coldly, it was a brainless, impossible
plan.

But I'd go along with Gallen right now, for virtually the
same reasons that I would have indulged Siggy. Though, I

had to admit, there hadn't been much in that for me. So far. And, I confess, knocking over Gallen seemed to me as impossible as my knocking over the Hietzinger Zoo.

WHAT KEFF ALSO DID

Keff did all the planning. I would have nothing to do with it, and Gallen told him as much.

So I was still sitting on the bed, Saturday evening, the tenth of June, 1967. I was trying to guess where Siggy was, but I didn't know the way the train lines ran. Whether Siggy would ride in Keff's box to Salzburg, before turning south, or whether he'd be turning south as soon as Steyr—in which case, he would be turning south by now, since Steyr was just a bit west of Waidhofen and Siggy had left an hour ago.

I imagined a most melodramatic race. Siggy, riding rigid in his box—a determined traveler—and I wondered if they'd sent my telegram out of Waidhofen yet, although it didn't matter; it would, at some point along the way, leap over Siggy wherever he was and be the first of them to touch down in Ernst Watzek-Trummer's rooms at the Gasthof Enns.

Trummer, of course, would be sitting at his unnecessary kitchen table. While Siggy was hurrying prone.

And then I heard the crawling, clawing sounds in the vines under my window, and I think all my bee stings stung me over again. I saw the paws come groping over the window ledge; I heard grunts. Backing out of my bed, I screamed, "All right! I'll go with you! We'll let them out, if that's what you want!"

But it was Keff. Looking very surprised at my shouting. I couldn't move to help him in, and he appeared to take that as a rebuke; he looked shyly away from me when he swung his thick legs in.

"I didn't mean to scare you," he said sadly. "But we're ready, smarty."

"Why go?" I said, finding it hard to trust enormous Keff.

"Because they've got you on the spot now," he said. "You're good for taxes. The more you stay, the more you

owe—for your room, for one thing. And then there's the
accident. Windisch says you owe him for the bees, you
see. They're going to take it out of you, smarty. They'll
fine you to death if you don't go." And he wouldn't look
at me; he swayed his lowered ape's head.

"Where's Gallen, Keff?" I said.

"In the orchard," said Keff, "on the town side of the
mountain."

"With the bike?" I asked.

"It's registered new, in my name," said Keff. "So they
won't know how to trace it, if they care enough to look
that hard. I'll stay here after you're gone. If old Tratt
comes, I'll hold her here till morning. That gives you some
distance, you see."

"What's in it for you, Keff?" I said, and watched him
knot his eyebrows; tennis-ball-sized, they welted out from
his head.

"Aw, smarty," he said. "Please, I do mean it good for
you." But then he looked at me—a faint menace in his
eyes. "Your nice girl's waiting now, and you're going to go
if I have to lug you, smarty."

"You don't have to," I said, and packed what there was.
Notebook, sleeping bags, helmets—in the rucksack or tied
on top. There was nothing worth saving the duckjacket
for, and I gave Siggy's pipes to Keff. Then I gave him
back *The ABZ of Love*.

"Aw, smarty," he said.

"It wasn't your fault, Keff," I said, and actually gave a
squeeze to the bit of his arm I could get my hand around.

Then Keff caught me under my shoulders and lowered
me by the armpits, half down the castle wall—so I
wouldn't have so far to drop, and plop so loud in the garden when I landed. For a moment, I thought he wasn't
going to let me go. He held me straight down and a little
away from the wall; I couldn't even hear him breathing.
Hanging, I said up to him, "Keff, it's too bad you never
knew Todor Slivnica. Because I'll bet you could have
taken him."

Then I looked straight up above me and saw him giving
down his puzzled little *O*-shaped grin, above his three
thick chins.

"O.K., smarty," said Keff, and he dropped me. I fell
softly in the garden and broke straightaway for the forsythia. In the grove still in the courtyard, I peered out the

gate and all around me. Waiting for an absolutely empty
landscape, and not a sound on the cobblestones.

But before I made my break for the road, I threw a
look back to my previous window and saw Keff pressed
against the grate—the enormity of his shadow blotting out
whole shrubs and garden plots below. His shadow, segmented by bars, loomed so much bigger than Siggy's had,
and although the great Keff had turned so gentle to me,
his caged shadow struck me as even more violent and determined than what Siggy once had cast.

And the Gallen I was headed for now seemed altogether different-promising, too, than the girl of the first
evening, when I'd lightly held her; whom I'd left standing
in the spray of the falls while I hurried to my Siggy's
room to inquire why he aped caged animals at the window
grate.

So I jogged up the dark orchard road with this clutter
in my skull, doing my fighting best to keep the slightest
plan from taking the slightest root in my stung head.

While Siggy, unresisting, was being carried further and
further away from the scene of his schemes—while, I
imagined, O. Schrutt's watch had not yet begun, and the
Famous Asiatic Black Bear, taking his brief rest when he
could get it, slept as stonily as Siggy.

But I cut the imagining there. I broke out of my jog
and ran full-out on my bathtub-tired legs, digging for Gallen, with no more in my head than the most immediate of
plots. Only the essentials.

Would she be there—where Keff said? Would the bike
start? And since she'd had the lessons to make her be our
driver, where would I put my hands when I held her as
she drove us away?

THE FEEL OF THE NIGHT

I had to be careful where I put my hands. This girl was
skittish of them, and a nervous driver anyway. Gallen had
been well enough taught the mechanics of it—the gearing
and leaning—but she had this caution about her that was
carried a little too far. She startled easy, at stuff in the
road that wasn't there.

"Well, Keff didn't teach me at *night*," she said—the helmet so funny, high up on her head, and her braid whipping side to side, as she kept looking for *things* off the road. About to leap out at us, I guess.

So I didn't want to add to her nervousness any, and I was moderate about my hands; I stayed around her waist—except when we were coasting, when I'd let them rest, just lightly, on her hips. She wore her brown leather ladies' jacket, with an old belt Keff gave her to sash it shut. Around her waist, I let my hands go under the jacket and flattened my palms against her warm blouse. But they were the tightest tummy muscles I'd ever felt, so I didn't move against her any.

I once said, in her helmet's ear hole, "Gallen, you drive very well."

But she startled at that too. Turning her head around, she said, "What?" And almost dumped us.

When we slowed for the little towns, I could talk more easily. I said, "It's getting late. We could find a campsite." But she was convinced we should ride through the night and get out of the Waidhofen vicinity—well up in the mountains to the southeast. So if they did care enough to look very hard for us, we'd be hard to find.

But I don't think she wanted to sleep out that night with me. In fact, I wondered if she'd make a travel plan that would have us never sleeping in the dark. For as long as we were together, I foresaw, we'd be nervously driving every night, throughout the night; even if we liked a place well enough to stay awhile, we'd still go off and drive in circles—until the dawn.

But then she surprised me. She stopped in the biggest town we'd come to so far, still before midnight. Mariazell, it was—big and touristy. The whole place was a sort of summerized ski lodge, and the loudest club still open had a young, dancing crowd of smart dressers—rock-and-roll music mashing down the flowers in the windowboxes.

My Gallen kept us idling awhile, out in front of the place; she just stared in the open windows and looked over all the couples, smoking on the outside steps. They looked us up and down, as well.

It was then I realized that Gallen von St. Leonhard hadn't been out of Waidhofen, ever; this was city life to her, and awesome. *Attractive* to her.

It was killing, really, though unnerving, that there was such a world lust, even in her.

And when we were out on the road again, I dared to let my fingers dig at her tummy; just a little kneading, you might say. I thought her muscles weren't quite so tensed. I kissed her, awkwardly, through her helmet's ear hole, and she let some of her weight rest back against me.

Out of town, she pulled the bike into a flashy lay-over on a corner and scared me so much that she had me digging into her tummy harder, which she felt, of course, and knew she'd had the edge on me for a moment. I felt her belly chuckle.

But still she wouldn't stop. We drove straightaway south now, and every coming town was darker. She even developed a feel for speed. And the whole night was wondrously eventless, as if we had stepped out of the gale of this world, as Siggy's old Chetnik hero would have claimed—out in limbo—and were moving nowhere.

Present, somewhere in my mind, was the unnecessary and elbow-worn kitchen table, and Siggy hurrying prone in the box. But I got through most of the night without actually seeing them. It was only when we headed east, through Stübming, that my peace was jarred.

Another drunken town frotter peeing in another town fountain, as if someone had arranged it: that I would always be the one to catch them at it. Only this one didn't dive for cover; perhaps Gallen drove not quite so bomb-like as Siggy. This one simply gawked, his cold part held out in his hand. We struck him numb in our headlight and then batted past him; I felt Gallen's tummy tighten, just a bit.

But the memory was enough to spoil my last hour of traveling darkness. For the next hour before daylight, it was my turn to see *things* off the side of the road—like the night Siggy had called the blackout to mind, and we saw *things* come to the roadside to watch us.

Once, I thought I saw—standing motionless in the deep vines—an old bull oryx, with moss on his horns. Once, more startling, an eagle in a chainmail suit of pieplates— standing as if he'd grown there, or had fallen down wingless and taken up roots, years ago.

We crossed the Mürz River at Krieglach, with the daylight hitting us, and a suddenly strong wind came off the river and blew the bike out over the centerline of the road. Gallen lurched us back to our side of the crown, and the wind fell in behind our backs.

But it's the frotting gale of the world, I thought. If it's not blowing against you, head-on, it's behind you and shoving you faster than you want to go. It even does the steering, maybe.

But I kept it to myself, and let Gallen think she was our pilot.

WHAT GALLEN DID, FINALLY

She stopped us for a long and gluttonous brunch at the top of the Semmering Pass. Somehow she'd wound us south, then east and even a little north, so that although we now were southeast of Waidhofen, we were far enough east to be almost straightaway south of Vienna, and straightaway north of either Italy or Yugoslavia—though we had no plans to leave the country; or, that is, *she* had no plans as such. I made it clear I had no plans at all, when we discussed our money—we had maybe two weeks' worth, of traveling as we were. I did figure that much of our plans. That if we bought no more than one meal a day, and stayed far enough in the country to fish for another—slept out and never bought a room—we'd make it two weeks, fuel and food, and then there'd have to be a job.

And jobs meant not leaving Austria. What with the problems of working permits for foreigners, which we'd be if we went out.

That talk was good for mind-occupying, and I'd have gotten along all right if we hadn't been up on the pass at noontime, when the church bells all through the Semmering Valley so formally announced it was noon.

When Siggy gets to Kaprun, I thought—where most of his family retreated to, at one time or another. And I saw old Watzek-Trummer with the crude, prone box.

"Don't you want another beer, Graff?" Gallen said.

And I said. "He's there now. I should be too."

"Come on, Graff," she said.

But I could only think that the old Trummer had been

in on too many burials to take on the last one alone. And
that was just too sickish-sweet a thought to have in the
touristy Semmering Pass Motel and Restaurant, where
they piped in the Old World music—to quiver us over our
soup.

So Gallen suggested that I learn to drive the bike, since
both of us should know. And she led me out of the restaurant, and wound us northwest into the valley. Then we
climbed up higher than the Semmering Pass, to Vois,
where I bought two bottles of white wine and a butter
pat.

We found a pine-needled bank of the fast black Schwarza
River, out of tiny Singerin Village. There was room to
practice driving; there was running water to chill the
wine, and get some fish for Freina Gippel's pan; and we
were well off the road, to be sure of a private night.

I started driving down the bank—with Gallen up behind
me, saying, "Keff said it's the feel for the gears that comes
first." But I wasn't really listening to her. All of a sudden,
it was broad Todor Slivnica beneath me, and worldly
Bijelo was saying, "Corner sharp left, Vratno, my boy."
And then I was pelting up and down the bank, with Gallen meekly saying something, but it was Gottlob Wut who
was doing my driving, dictating loud and clear: "See?
Like this!" And then I was mounting a marble staircase,
when I was the hunted Siegfried Schmidt, special messenger and alley traveler of Old Vienna. But I hit some root
that jarred me forward on the gas tank, with poor Gallen
sliding up snug behind me—and I had to stretch my toes
back to reach the gear lever. Then I saw again the down-
falling orchard road, and Siggy said, "First-gear work,
here, Graff. You've got to work it."

I was aware of my knees up under the handlebars,
hooking me forever on the old beast—and a honey-gunked
crown of bees settling on my smarting head—when I went
tearing through our unmade campsite and rode right over
our rucksack.

"God, Graff," said Gallen. "You're a bit out of control."

But when she got off behind me and came around front,
probably wondering why I hadn't shut the engine off, she
must have got a look at my dreaming eyes. "Oh, now,
Graff. Come on. That's enough," she said.

And when I didn't answer her, and just kept raising the
idle higher and higher—letting the bike scream itself silly

beneath me—she tapped the kill button and shut me off.
The noise died. "Show me," she said, "how you catch fish,
Graff."

So I did, though the river was too fast here—with no
good bank to get off, and get down in the water. I was
hooking and losing them for a while, before I eked out
three smallish trout—light enough to jerk right up on the
shore.

"Well," I said, "it's always a good thing to go to bed a
little hungry."

"Why?" said Gallen.

"And on two bottles of wine too," I said, and grinned.

But she pouted away from me, skittish again.

They were good trout, though. They made Gallen
sneeze—a *snit* of a sneeze, half caught in her hand. And I
said, "Ha!"

"What do you mean, '*Ha*'?" she said.

And I reminded her: " 'Letting off a thoroughly good
sneeze is a natural, spontaneous, frank action of which
some people really are a little afraid.' " And stopped there,
to see what she'd do.

She said, "Graff." And spilled her wine.

"There's more," I said. "There's a second bottle in the
river."

"Thought of everything, didn't you?" she said, but not
angrily.

So I thought a bit more, in my way—an immediate sort
of plotting. Remembering how Siggy had bought the two
sleeping bags at the same place, at the same time; how
they made a pair, and zipped either separate or together.
They could make a double.

It's the double for you, Gallen, I thought. But it wasn't
even dark yet, and we still had a bottle to go, in the river.

So I said, "Gallen, fetch us that second bottle, and I'll
build up this fire. It cuts down on mosquitoes, you know."
But there weren't any mosquitoes, anyway, thanks be. We
were too high up; it was cold.

And would be colder after dark, I knew, looking at the
winter sort of river, that even in summer was hard to
imagine without frills of thin ice on the outskirts of the
current, and shuddering deer coming down off the bank
for a lick, picking their hooves up high and shaking them,
as if deer could get cold-footed. Though maybe they can.

Anything's possible, Siggy said somewhere. And I had a sort of seizure at the fire, bending down.

If anything's possible, Siggy could get lost on the train; they could send him to Munich or Paris. I saw Siggy stacked upright in a warehouse in Paris.

Or, I thought, there could be trouble in Ernst Watzek-Trummer's tiny rooms. Surely, he'll put Siggy in the room with the racer; and there's sure to be candles. A candle was burning too close to the Grand Prix racer. And they surely left a bit of gas in the tank, to prevent the tank from rusting. I saw the Gasthof Enns blow up.

But I had no feelings about any of the things I saw, seeing them all in the time it took an ash to rise from the fire, or in the time it took Gallen to fetch the wine. I was just numb to reacting to any of it, even to the ashes I tossed in the air. They floated down straight; there wasn't any wind.

So the gale of the world dies down at night, I thought. And I thought: So what if it does? Because I had totally benumbed myself with either too many related or unrelated things.

And all this happened in the time it took ashes to rise, or Gallen to get the wine—or it seemed to; although it was somehow dark before I was aware that Gallen had brought back the wine, and drunk half of it herself. And dark by the time I said, "It's time to fix the sleeping bag." *The bag,* singular, I said—because I was plotting for us in the double.

"I've already done it," said Gallen. *It,* she said—singular. And I realized how she'd zipped them together—perhaps, to make things easier for me. Out of pity, I hoped not.

I went down to the river and washed the fish off my teeth. Then I crept to the bag, which Gallen was warming. But she was dressed. That is: still the corduroy slacks, and her blouse. At least she'd taken her bra off; I saw where she'd tried to hide it under her jacket, just outside the bag.

Little things make a difference, I'm sure.

But when I slipped in beside her, she said, "Goodnight, Graff." Before I'd even stretched out! And I'd been discreet enough to leave my miserable, sagging boxer shorts on.

The river was so fast it made a racket. And frog tones

came up, across the river. There's always a swamp where you least expect it.

I was thinking like that—little philosophies popping up all by themselves. Gallen had her back to me—balled, with her knees drawn up. "Why, you must be tired, Gallen," I said, bright and snappy.

"Yes, very, goodnight," she said again—faking a groggy voice, as if she'd fallen into an instant sleep. So I just pushed toward her, my shoulder against the warm back of her blouse—and she stiffened. "You took your clothes off," she accused.

"I've got my hangies on," I said.

"Your what?" said Gallen.

"My hangies." I told her. "My boxer shorts."

For a moment I thought she'd call for a light to look at my miserable hangies; I would have expired for the shame. She sat up in the bag.

But she said, "Isn't it a lovely night, Graff?"

"Oh yes," I said, crouching back in my corner of the bag—just waiting for her to lie down again.

"And isn't the river loud?" said Gallen.

"Oh yes," I said, in my bored way. I just lurked in my part of the bag for her. I watched how her blouse was fluffled by the wind.

And I remember waiting a long time for her to lie down, and finally getting myself sleepy because she sat up so long. I thought: She's probably going to put her bra back on.

So I let myself be carried away with the water in the fast, black, winter river. I dozed downstream; I woke for short spurts and swam against the current. But always restfully, without any struggle. I let myself be coaxed into letting it carry me—past towns brightly lit over the water; paddling past a typical sort of sawmill, with pitch-smelling logs jamming up along the bank; past young girls doing their sheer laundry. And then I was traveling, muffled, through steep riverbanks of snow, and it was almost dark, or almost light, and the deer were coming down to drink. A great buck with a harem of does all meekly herded after him; the buck looked, I admit, a bit like the oryx. He dared walking out on the thin frills of ice offshore. He eased down his great weight; lightly, he placed his carefully aimed, sharp hooves. The herd of does brushed warmly together. I stopped floating by; I treaded water in place.

The does brushed too loudly together, I thought. But it was Gallen, sitting up above me—getting into her frotting bra, no doubt. Except that her legs behaved foolishly beside me in the bag. She is bicycle-pedaling in this bag, I thought. What next? She's getting into her chainmail pants, which are padlocked. This girl takes no chances.

But then she slipped into the bag, out long alongside me, and I felt her knee draw up and lightly touch my hand.

She'd taken *off* her clothes! I faked sleep.

"Graff?" Gallen said, and her feet clapped like hands round my ankle.

I squiggled a little toward her, still sleeping. Of course.

"You, Graff," she said. "Wake up, please." But except for our feet touching now, she held off my tummy with her hands. Then she moved; she was touching me nowhere. And then she came down from the roof of the bag on top of me; it was her hair, unbraided and falling loose, that fell over me first. Our skin touched very hot or cold; we were flush in a moment. I felt the ice frill break from the bank and cast the great buck adrift.

Gallen said, "Wake up now, please," And hugged herself so tight to me I couldn't move.

"I'm awake," I said, down in my throat. But I gurgled so meekly, I tried to get my neck off her shoulder bone so she'd be sure to hear me.

But before I could croak again, she crawled down on me a bit and kissed over my mouth. So I gurgled again. Her face was wet against mine; she was crying down over me, of all things.

I was confused, I confess. I said, "Don't do me any favors—if it's just because you feel sorry for me."

"I don't at all," she said—fierce for her.

"You don't?" I said, hurt—and held her at elbow's length off my chest. Her hair covered her face and mine. Then she kneed me and I doubled up into her, where her body seemed to know I'd be coming—because she caught my shoulders and swung herself off me, and brought me down over her.

Now she was crying out loud and I kissed over her mouth to stop it. We rolled to get leg room in the frotting bag.

I felt obliged to—I said, "I love you, Gallen, really."
And she told me the same.

It was the only part that felt at all forced—or seemed
remembered from a history of necessary prefixes that we
didn't use quite naturally between us.

She tied her hair around my neck; she bound my head
on her chest—so high and thin and fragile. I thought I'd
break through it and fall inside her. I closed one eye on
the pulse in her throat; it was running light and fast.

Like the winter river, bearing downstream the daring
buck, who rode the ice flow that melted beneath him; his
does ran apace with him, safe on the shore.

And Gallen said, "What are these? What did you call
them?"

"Hangies," I said, but softly. I wouldn't, for this world,
have interrupted her pulse.

"Well then," she said (and her hip bone jabbed me; she
was turning under me), "these of mine are called
huggies." No more tears, but she was stalling. Then she
said, "Take them off."

I thought: If only a poor soul could see in this frotting
bag.

But when I looked, I saw the buck, in the balance—his
ice cake almost gone beneath him.

And if I hooked my thumbs just over the front of Gallen's waist, and touched down the heels of my hands
where her hips began—and if I squeezed, hard—my middle fingers touched, or seemed to, on her backbone. So I
lifted her.

And she babbled, as if she were blurting it out in mid-
stream of the running, winter river, "You, Graff, where
did you put my huggies, you—they're bought new for this
trip."

Then she lifted herself when I lifted her. The does ran
in step.

Gallen said, "You Graff!" And something squeaked in
her throat, an inch behind her pulse and stepping it up.

I saw the buck's hard forehoof break through the ice;
his chest fell first and split the lace-thin cake in two. He
floated down; he passed towns brightly lit over the water,
and sawmills smelling thick with pitch—the river dark and
musty with slabs of bark. He emerged between spotless
banks of snow, saw his does wanting him ashore. He took

an easy stroke or two, in no hurry, brushing the frills of ice that fingered out into the current.

I was confused again, I held my breath, for I'd stopped treading water and had sunk too long ago. I got my footing on the blanket-soft river bottom. As I pushed off, the buck reached shore.

Then I sneezed, of all things. I had surfaced.

From out of the sawmill smell of the bag, Gallen brought her hands against my ears and rang my head. The buck staggered, dizzy, up the bank. Gallen kissed over my mouth, and my head cleared. Solidly ashore now, the buck loped for the warm does.

Then Gallen let her hands fall lightly away from my ears, my pulse came down, and the only real sounds came back to me.

The river storming along. And frog tones from the swamp that you'd least expect to find here.

WHAT GALLEN DID, AGAIN

I woke up early, feeling guilty that I'd slept at all. Because I knew that Ernst Watzek-Trummer had spent the night at elbow height above his kitchen table, had even outlasted the dishwashers downstairs in the Gasthof Enns.

Gallen was already awake, inching about for her huggies and trying to snare her bra, outside, without my seeing any of her. Thanks be, she took my guilty look for herself. Because she said, "Graff, it's all right. I feel fine." And she tried to look very gay—but not at me; her eyes shiny and shying away.

So I said, "Just so you're fine, then." To keep her thinking I'd been thinking of her. Then I did think of her, and kissed her, and started to hunch myself out of the bag, very lively.

But Gallen said, "Wait, your hangies are right here." She turned her back so I wouldn't have to contort myself down deep in the sweet, pitch-smelling bag.

"This bag could stand some air," I said.

"Is that me?" she said. "Do I smell like that too?"

"Well," I said, and we both looked around. I was hoping for some small, unusual animal to come on the scene, or a wild-colored bird, about which I could say, "Heavens, Gallen. Would you look at that." And thereby change the subject neatly. But I saw nothing except the dew-covered motorcycle and the river, heaped in fog. The morning air was cold.

"Let's have a swim," I said bravely.

But she didn't want to get out of the bag until I'd fetched her the bra. Which she wouldn't ask me for, either, so I popped out and groped around for it, finding it and holding it aloft. "Why, what's this odd article?" I said.

"O.K., give it here," said Gallen, hair over her eyes. Then I went down to the river and waited for her.

Lord, the water was fierce; it made my teeth tinkle like glass, and nearly tugged my miserable hangies off. Gallen didn't swim; she just dunked in and out. With her hair wet, I saw how sleek her head was. Her ears were a little funny—too long, and even pointed, slightly. Her jaw was trembly from the cold. When she climbed out, her bra was full of water. In such the nicest way, she squeezed herself; she sort of wrung out her breasts and made her bra cling to her. Then she saw me watching her and she danced over the bank, back-to me, conscious of how tightly her huggies hugged her.

I came up the bank, forced to walk somewhat apelike because my frotting hangies were stuck all over me, almost down to my knees. And when she saw what a figure I cut, she laughed at my vain bones. "I think you need smaller-sized hangies," she said.

Then I leapt toward her, hooting self-conscious, and danced around her, pointing. "Look!" I shouted. "You've got two schillings in your bra."

Because that's just what her nipples looked like, size- and color-wise—a lovely off-brass color, just glorious. Two schillings, for sure.

So she stared at herself and then spun away from me. I thought: Please laugh, Gallen—even at your own parts. A little humor is essential, I'm convinced.

"Do you have a shirt I could wear?" said Gallen, seriously worried. "My blouse would wet through, and I didn't pack any towels."

And when I brought her my fabulous red-and-white-striped soccer jersey, she was hiding her schillings with her hands—but smiling wide, with a slash of hair in the corner of her mouth, stuck wet against her cheek; she pushed it away with her tongue.

"Breakfast?" I said. "If you can make a fire, I can ride to Singerin for eggs and coffee."

"I can," she said, laughing at something funny to her now, "if you can help me with this first," and I came around behind her to help unhook her bra, under the soccer shirt. She wiggled, sliding the wet thing down to her waist; behind her, I just came up with my hands for a moment—around her wet, cold, hard breasts. She was like a statue just hosed down.

"Let me brush my hair," she said, but she didn't try to get away. She leaned back into me.

The river rose; it seemed to wash over us. But it was only a wind that came up and moved the fog our way. I saw deer in the forest, docile as sheep. Except the forest was hemmed in by something. Rivers on all sides, maybe, or even a fence. And standing off to one side of the deer, like a shepherd—though he didn't have a staff—Siggy was saying, "Sit tight, my deer. I'll have you out of here, don't you worry."

Then Gallen said, "You're hurting me, Graff—just a little." I'd bitten a ring-shaped, fire-bright spot on her neck, through a strand of her hair. And when she saw me looking guilty again, she thought it was just because I'd bitten her.

"Well, I'm all right," she said. "Graff, I'm not so delicate, really."

I went along with it, letting her think I wore my odd look for her sake. She brushed her dark wet hair, bringing the red back into it. So I ducked into the woods to change out of my impossible wet hangies.

Then I drove to Singerin for eggs and coffee. And when I came back, she had a fire going, with too much wood to cook on. But she'd also spread open the sleeping bag and dragged it back up into the woods, way above the water. Embarrassed, I saw she'd hung my hangies on a stick—a spear stuck in the ground and the hangies waving, as if the wearer lay buried under this crude marker.

We ate a lot. I found a very old loaf of bread too—in the rucksack, where it must have been stashed a week or so ago. But it toasted very well in the grease in Freina's pan. Because I make it a policy never to really clean the pan. That way you remember all the good meals you've had.

Gallen still dried her hair. She brushed it down over her face, then she gave a puff and blew a strand of it away from her—baring just her mouth and nose. Her hair danced alive by itself; she played with it across from me, and I gave several fake moans and crawled up in the woods, plopping down on the bag. Bigger than any bed-spread, set better than any tablecloth—with trees all around it, and pine needles packed under it. Soft as water; you sank in it.

But Gallen went futzing around with the fire, and wash-ing her hands in the river. She'd changed back in her cor-duroys again, and hadn't been so bold as to fly her huggies in the same way she'd chosen to immortalize me.

I faked some more exhausted grunts from my great bed in the woods. Then I shouted down to her, "Aren't you sleepy, Gallen? I could sleep all day, myself."

"But you wouldn't," she said, "if I came up there with you."

Well, such conceit seemed to demand some firm resolve on my part, so I bolted out of the woods and charged her on the riverbank. She raced into the field. But I never knew a girl who could really run. It's their structure, I'm convinced; they're hippy, whether there's much flesh or not, and that structuring forces their legs to swivel out sideways when they move.

Besides, I'm tireless in short bursts. I caught her when she tried to double back to the woods to hide. She said, all out of breath and as if she'd been thinking on it all along, "Where do you think we should go next? Where do you want to go?" But I wasn't to be that easily thrown off. I carried her back to the sleeping bag; she tied me up in her hair again, even before I set her down. But I noticed how she genuinely winced when I rolled over her.

"Gallen, are you sore?" I said. She looked away from me, of course.

"Well, a little," she said. "It's not anything wrong with me, is it?"

"Oh no," I said. "I'm sorry."

"Oh, I don't hurt a lot, anyway," she said. Meaning it, because she didn't untangle her hair from around my neck.

Lord, in the daylight, I thought—embarrassed, myself. But she surprised me.

"You don't have any hangies on under," she said.

"I've just got one pair," I said, sheepish.

"Graff, you can wear mine, you know," said Gallen. "They stretch."

"These are blue!" I said.

And Gallen said, "I have a green pair, a blue pair and a red pair."

But she only had that one bra, I knew—having seen some of the packing.

"You can have my soccer shirt," I told her.

And seeing the shirt off to the side of our spread, I remembered a loon of a boy who was on my old soccer team in high school. He hated the game as much as I did, I'm sure, but he had this special knack in that awful situation when you're running to kick the ball and the other man is running toward you, to get the ball first. You don't know who'll get to kick it, but if he does he'll probably kick it in your face or you'll catch his toe in your throat. But this loon I knew would always start yelling when he got in that situation. He wouldn't shy off, he'd dig hard for the ball, very serious—but yelling as he ran, *"Yaaii! Yaaaiii!"* He'd scream right in the face of the fellow opposite. He terrified everyone, just by showing them how scared he was.

He was a very good player because of it, I'm convinced. He beat everyone to the ball. It sort of took your edge off to have him blubbering like that, as if he were charging a machine gunner's nest.

And I thought: That's true. We should all be loudly afraid when we are—just so no one confuses the hero with the loon. It's the loon who makes you laugh, and makes you think he's crazy. But it's the hero who's stupid. He's full up with platitudes and vague notions, and he doesn't really care if he gets to the ball first. Now take me—I'm the loon, I thought.

And Gallen said, "Graff?" Probably embarrassed that I *wasn't* looking at her, having prepared herself to have me see.

She was no statue; she was soft, despite the bones around. Someone shouted, above the river:

Bless the green stem before the flower!

It must have been Siggy, speaking prone—droning in the candlelight by the Grand Prix racer, '39.

"Why do you have hair there?" said Gallen.

There's always a swamp where you least expect it, I thought. And I lay my head down quickly between her high, small breasts. This time, I wanted no distractions. No frotting deer by the winter river, or tended to by a shepherdlike Siggy. I thought—and surprisingly, not until now—I might be going mad. Or just bizzare.

It frightened me so, I wouldn't close my eyes. I looked down her long waist; I saw where her pelvis moved, if that's a pelvis. I looked up her neck—saw the pulse beating at the thin-skinned spot, but didn't dare to feel it. Her mouth opened and her eyes looked down at me—still surprised, no doubt, at where I had hair and where I didn't.

Then I was over her mouth and so close to her eyes I could count all her lashes; saw her squeeze water down over them, but not crying, really.

And I didn't have any inappropriate visions—only her face and her flooding hair. The hands over me were absolutely the hands of Gallen von St. Leonhard; there were no distractions. No sound effects, either, except what I caught of Gallen's breathing.

Her eyes closed; I nipped a tear off her cheek. She covered my ears in her fashion again. My head rang, but I knew precisely what caused it.

I had sneezed. This time she had too. Because her eyes opened very frightened. She said, "Graff?" I thought: No, that wasn't anything wrong. That was perfectly proper. But she said, "Graff, did you feel that? Did I hurt myself?"

"No, you just sneezed," I said, making light. "That's good," I said, like a frotting doctor. But this time I heard her every word and breath, and I knew I hadn't traveled beyond the bag. I was sane: I knew Gallen and I were alone there together, and everyone or everything else was either dead or not with us. For that moment.

"It was something that fell out of me, though," she said. "Graff? It was, I think."

"You simply sneezed," I said. "And nothing fell out that won't be back."

I thought: A sense of humor is essential, Gallen. This is so important. Please smile now.

But Gallen said—still nervous, and I hadn't left her—
"Graff, do you think of other things when you do this? Do
you ever?"

"How could I?" I said. And I didn't dare take my eyes
off her, or dare to close my eyes, either—because I knew
that the woods around us were full of deer and oryxes and
shepherds, just waiting to catch my mind. Frot them.

Gallen smiled; she even laughed a little, under me. "I
don't think of anything, either," she said. "I can't even get
anything on my mind right now."

Well, you're a very healthy girl, I thought. But you'd
better watch out for me. Hannes Graff is known for his
loose, straying ends.

NOAH'S ARK

Later that afternoon, Gallen said, "Do you think it's
come back yet? It still *feels* gone."

"What does?" I said, and because she was talking, I
dared to close my eyes.

"What I thought fell out of me," said Gallen. "You
know."

She was a little too glum about it, I thought.

"Look," I said. "Some girls never sneeze all their life.
You're lucky."

"Will I ever again?" she said. "Is what I mean."

"Of course you will," I said.

"When?" said Gallen, more brightly—even playful.
With her one wet bra still drying, she certainly tossed my
soccer shirt around when she moved.

"Hannes Graff needs time to recover," I said.

And that's true enough, I thought—my eyes still closed.
I could move my head back and forth—into a spot where
the sun hit my face and changed my darkness from black
to red. Then back to black, with the frame of my darkness
edged in red and white stripes, like the soccer shirt.

Keep talking to me, please, Gallen, I thought.

But she must have been imagining the degrees of my
recovery—a silent wonder, I've often thought myself.

My eyes still closed, I moved my head, black to red, red
to black—a simple trick, with lighting effects—but the

core of my darkness was opening like the shutter-eye of a camera. It was really premeditated; I could have stopped it by just opening my eyes wide and talking fast to Gallen. But I compromised, to test myself. Eyes still shut, I said, "About where we'll go. Have you given it any thought yourself?"

"Well, I've been thinking," said Gallen.

But my shutter-eye opened wider now, on the frotting winter river—like a movie beginning, with no titles and no characters yet onstage. Please *think* out loud, Gallen, I thought. But she didn't say a word, or if she did, it was too late for me to hear her—for the speed of my traveling.

This river went everywhere; it passed every place in the world. But I was just a camera-eye, not in the picture. In spots, there were crowds on the banks, all with their suitcases. And there were animals too—on the ark, that is. I neglected to mention it: a rather poorly put-together raft. Someone ran a collection service; he wore an eaglesuit and was in charge of the ship—or he ran about, breaking up squabbles on board, thrusting an oar between cats and wombats, separating the bears and shrieking birds. *People* tried to swim out and board the ark. They tried to hold their suitcases above water; their children were sinking.

The ark and the river went through a city. The man in the eaglesuit welcomed strange animals aboard. Cows huffed alongside—escaped from the slaughterhouses. A taxi drove into the river.

Siggy said to the cows, "I'm terribly sorry, but we already have two of you. This is an arbitrary business."

The taxi was still afloat. An impossible number of passengers unloaded, treading water in place. Someone tipped the driver, and he sank with his cab.

And then I was watching myself, making my way through the water with my suitcase overhead; my fellow-passengers from the cab were chatting.

One said, "There's no proof at all that the driver was actually Zahn Glanz."

"Whoever he was, you overtipped him," said a woman, and everyone laughed.

When I came alongside the ark, Siggy said, "I'm sorry, but I believe we already have two of you."

I said, "For God's sake, Sig, a sense of humor is essential."

"If you're really with us, Graff, you may board," said Siggy. But a vicious Oriental bear was protesting. "I mean *really*, Graff," Siggy said. "We can't give up the ship."

Then Gallen put her arm around my waist, dragging me under. "I've been thinking where we should go, Graff," she said.

"All right! I'm with you!" I screamed, and bolted upright off the sleeping bag, into her arms and the movable soccer shirt.

"Graff?" she said. "Graff, I just said I thought about where we could go."

"Well, I've been thinking too," I told her, and clung to her.

I had my eyes open as wide as they'd go. I counted the stripes on the soccer shirt. They were nice, broad stripes—two white and one red, from the collar to where her breasts began and unstraightened the striping; five red and four white, from her breasts to the hem on her thigh. I lay my head on her hem.

These stripes were more restful than counting sheep.

"Or walruses, Graff," said Siggy, somewhere. "Wallowing, frolicsome walruses."

"All right, that's enough. I'm with you," I said.

"Well, of course you are, Graff," said Gallen.

PLANS

Just before nightfall, I reenergized myself and took a long walk upstream to a good fishing spot, where I could wade out within easy casting range of the rocky pools on the far bank. I pulled them in very handily there, while Gallen rode to Singerin for beer.

Before she was back, I had a fire going and six trout cleaned for Freina's super-flavored pan.

My head was clear. It's always good to have a few money plans forced on your mind; it keeps you from having notions of other, vaguer plans.

We'd talked over where we should go next, and Gallen thought that Vienna might be best—because I knew my way around the job spots there; but mainly, I think, since her glimpse of Mariazell, Gallen had her eyes on the city life—as she imagined it. I was worried it might make her stickish, but I had to admit that Vienna did seem the likeliest place for either of us to get a job. Now, what I'd argued with her, though, was this: you'd also *spend* more money in Vienna than anywhere else around us, while you were *looking* for a frotting awful job. And what would keep us fed and well slept for two weeks in the country wouldn't hold us for five or six days in Vienna—if we wanted to eat. We could still drive out past the suburbs each night and camp in the vineyards—if we weren't eaten by watchdogs. But you couldn't catch your meals in Vienna, for sure.

On the other hand, in the wilderness we were in, there were too many places for *things* to hide—and be popping out at me. There's less daydreaming in a city, all right, and Hannes Graff could stand to have less of that.

So Sunday evening, after we'd eaten, we sat with our beers and talked it over again.

"I've been thinking," said Gallen.

Well, thinking's good for you, I thought—at least, this fussy kind. Also, this business at hand seemed to have taken her mind off her first sneeze. And no one should ponder on that subject for very long, I'm convinced.

"The trouble is, Graff," she said, officiously, "—as I seem to understand it—we need more money than we have now, if we're to give ourselves enough job-hunting time in the city. Until the first pay check."

"That's precisely what the trouble is," I agreed. "I think you've got it."

"Well then, it's solved," she said, and brought her long auburn braid over her shoulder—holding it out to me, the way a vendor shows you his vegetables and fruit.

"Very nice hair," I said, puzzled.

"Well, I'll sell it," said Gallen. "There's good money in selling your hair for wigs."

"Sell it?" I said. It struck me as a perverse sort of whoring.

"We'll just find some classy *friseur* in the suburbs," said Gallen.

"How do you know about wig makers?" I said.

"Keff told me," said Gallen.

"Frotting *Keff?*" I said. "And just what does he know about it?"

"He was in Paris for the war," she told me. "He said it was big business, even then—ladies selling their hair."

"In Paris for the war?" I said. "I understood they were snatching hair, not buying it."

"Well, some maybe," said Gallen. "But it's a very classy business now. And real hair makes the best wigs."

"Keff told you he was in Paris?"

"Yes," said Gallen. "It came up when we were talking about my hair."

"Oh, *were* you?" I said, and tried to imagine Keff in Paris. It wasn't a pretty picture. I saw a very young, swaggering, bullish Keff—in the ladies' hair business, or somehow connected with hair. In his off-duty hours.

"Well, we were talking about money too," said Gallen. "That's when he mentioned my hair."

"Did *he* want to buy it?" I said.

"Of course not," said Gallen. "He just said I'd get a good price for it, if we were short." And she stroked her hair, as if she were petting a cat.

"Gallen, I love your hair," I said.

"You wouldn't love me without it?" she said, and snatched it up above her head, showing off her ears and the long back of her neck. She made her face sleeker, and her shoulders more slight; she seemed even more fragile. I thought: Frot Hannes Graff—the girl would cut off her hair for him.

"I'd love you without any hair," I said, but I was sure I wouldn't. I saw her bald, gleaming at me; she had her own helmet, spotted with speed-struck insects, pitted as a peach stone. I took Gallen's braid in my hands.

Then Siggy snapped at me, out of the fire, "No nonsense now. Just a total shave, please." And I dropped Gallen's hair.

She must have noticed my faraway-traveling eyes, because she said, "Graff? It's not that you don't want to go to Vienna, is it? I mean, if you'd rather go somewhere you've never been before—if you don't want to see any old stuff you remember, or might, you know—I wouldn't care, Graff. Really, if Vienna's a bad place for you now. I just thought it would be easier for money—in the long run."

In the long run? I thought.

"You know," said Gallen. "It would just probably give us enough to get someplace to stay, indoors. Just a room, maybe, at first."

At first? I thought. Oh, frot me if she doesn't have some overall plan.

"Wouldn't you just like a room with a great big bed in it?" she asked, and blushed.

But this girl's schemes were sounding dangerous to me—this vague, long-term stuff never works. This was too much planning in front of ourselves—for sure.

I said, "Well, let's just to to Vienna and get one or both of us a job, at first, Then maybe we can do whatever we want. Maybe we'll want to go to Italy then," I said hopefully.

"Well, she said, "I thought you'd like the room with the bed."

"Well, let's just see what heppens," I said. "What's the matter? Don't you like our sleeping bag?"

"Well, of course I like it," said Gallen. "But you can't sleep outside forever, you know."

Maybe *you* can't, I thought. And who said anything about *forever?*

"Well, just thinking practically," she said, sounding too much like her frotting Auntie, "it will be cold in a few months, and you can't sleep outside and drive a motorcycle in the snow."

Well, the truth of that was startling. *A few months?* I'll have to get the bike down south *before* it snows, I thought. And suddenly *time* was involved in any plans you made or didn't. For example, tomorrow was Monday, June 12, 1967. A real *date*. And one week ago tomorrow, Siggy was leaving Waidhofen in the rain—past the fallen horse and milkwagon, headed for the Hietzinger Zoo. And today was Sunday, Siggy was in Kaprun with old Trummer; they were respectively prone and sitting, above the dinner guests in the Gasthof Enns.

"Well, we'll leave for Vienna, early tomorrow," I said. And I thought: Maybe it will rain like a week ago.

"Do you know the suburbs?" said Gallen. "Where we might find some classy *friseur*."

"I know *one* suburb," I said. "It's called Hietzing."

"Is it hard to get to?" she said.

"You go right through it on your way downtown," I said.

"Well, that's easy then," said Gallen.

"That's where the zoo is," I told her, and she was very quiet.

"Fate shapes the course!" Siggy popped from the fire.

Frot that myth, I thought. I'm doing this all by myself.

"Oh, Graff," said Gallen, making light. "Come on, now. We don't *have* to see the zoo."

"Well, you shouldn't go to Vienna," I said, "without seeing how spring has struck the zoo."

And although the first-shift watch was the only chance the animals had to sleep, I saw them all wake up and cock their various ears to this talk.

But you animals misunderstand me, I thought. There's no point in getting your hopes up. I'm just coming to look. But they were all awake and staring through their bars, accusing me. I shouted aloud, "Go to sleep!"

"What?" said Gallen. "Graff? Do you want to think or something? I'll go up in the woods, if you want to be alone—if you don't want to talk to me or anything."

But I thought: You're giving up your hair for me, for Christ's sake don't do anything more. So I tackled her when she tried to stand and leave me. I burrowed in her lap, and she lifted her soccer shirt to tuck my head under it, face-down on her warm, ribby tum. She hugged me; she had little, alive pulses everywhere.

I thought: Hannes Graff, gather up your loose ends, please. This living girl is vulnerable to being let down by just about everything.

MORE PLANS

Just out of Hütteldorf-Hacking, in the outskirts of Hietzing, we found a first-class *friseur*, name of Orestic Szirtes—a Greco-Hungarian, or a Hungarian-Greek. His father, he told us, was Zoltan Szirtes; his mother was the former beauty Nitsa Papadatou, who sat and watched us from her throne in the best barber chair.

"My father's gone," Orestic said, and not just out for lunch, I gathered—by the way the former Nitsa Papadatou shook her glossy black mane and rattled the bright gems on her long black robe; lowly V-necked, her jeweled robe exposed her fierce cleavage and the rump-sized swell of her mighty, unfallen breasts. A former beauty, for sure.

Gallen said, "Do you buy hair?"

"Why should we buy it?" old Nitsa said. "There's no need—it's all over our floor."

But it wasn't, really. It was a spiffy place—a light, tasteful perfume hit you when you walked in the door. But the air turned more to musk the nearer you got to Nitsa. And the only hair on the floor was under Nitsa's chair, as if no one were allowed to sweep under her while she was enthroned.

"The girl means for wigs, Mama," Orestic said. "Of course, yes, we buy hair." And he touched Gallen's braid, sort of flicked it to see how it behaved when provoked. "Oh, lovely, yes," Orestic said.

"I think so," I said.

"Young hair is best," he said.

"Well, she *is* young," I said.

"But it's *red*," said Nitsa, shocked.

"All the more in demand!" I claimed. While Orestic stroked the braid.

"How much?" said Gallen, world-wise and tough as cork.

Orestic pondered over her braid. His own hair was as thick and shining-clean as damp black saw grass in a marsh. I wandered to the rows of speared heads in the window; each head, wigged and necklaced, had an upturned nose without any nostrils.

"Two hundred schillings," said Orestic. "And for that I trim her after—any kind of cut she wants."

"Three-fifty," I said. "Your window sales start at seven hundred."

"Well," said Orestic, "I have to do a bit of work to make a wig out of it, you know. She's got scarcely more than a hairpiece here." And with that, he swished her braid away.

"Three hundred, then," I said.

"Two-fifty," said Nitsa, "and I'll pierce her ears for free."

"Pierce her ears?" I said.

"Mama pierces ears," said Orestic. "How many ears has it been now, Mama?"

Probably all saved in her chest of drawers, I thought.

"Oh, I lost count long ago," old Nitsa claimed. Then she

looked at Gallen. "So how's two-fifty and your ears in with it?"

"Graff," said Gallen, "I always did want to—especially since I'm in the city."

"For God's sake," I whispered. "Not here, please. You might lose them altogether." I said to Orestic, "Three hundred, without ears."

"And you'll fix my hair up after?" said Gallen. "All right?" She tossed her braid over her shoulder; it teased poor Orestic like a charming-snake.

"All right," he said.

But the former Nitsa Papadatou spat on the floor. "Weak!" she told her son. "Just like your miserable father, you've got no spine." She straightened up in the best barber chair and whumped her backbone with her hand; Nitsa had a spine, all right. She huffed out her frontispiece at us; her wondrous cleavage opened wider, closed tighter, opened wide and closed again.

"Mama, *please*," Orestic said.

But when Orestic ushered my Gallen into the vacant, lesser barber chair, Nitsa was a welcome distraction. Because it pained me to see Orestic feverishly undoing Gallen's braid, then brushing—crackling her hair out full and over the back of the chair, nearly to the seat. Then he snatched it up above her head and with sure, heavy strokes brushed it upward, stretching it—as if he were coaxing it to grow another inch or two before he claimed it. I was sitting directly behind Gallen, so I couldn't see her face in the mirror, thanks be; I didn't want to see her eyes when Orestic gathered up a great horsetail of hair and sheared it off at the roots—it seemed. I looked slantwise at the mirror, down the full, reflected cleavage of Mama Nitsa.

Orestic swished the auburn tail around; then I had a sudden shiver, as if I'd just watched a beheading; Gallen held both hands to her scalp. Slick Orestic put her hair on a cushion in the windowseat, and came back, dancing round her—his razor *tzik*ing over her ears and up the back of her long, bare neck.

"Now! What to *do* with it!" he said. "Leave you bangs, or none?"

"No bangs," said Gallen. He cut a little, but left enough to brush back; he trimmed off her forehead, swept it over only the points of her ears, left it fairly full on the back of

her head, but brought it up close on her neck. Near the
roots, though, the auburn shone richer.

"No thinning," he said. "We'll leave it nice and thick."
And he seized up a handful, as if he were going to tear it
out. "Oh, it's thick as a *plet!*" he cried excitedly. But Gallen just stared at her new forehead; she sneaked a look,
now and then, round the sides of her head to her startling
ears.

It was the turning in the swivel chair that disconcerted
me, I guess. I was just thinking how it wasn't so bad, really; how she was spared disgrace by very nice bones in
her cheeks and jaw, and by her neck being so nice naked—when Orestic began swiveling her around in the
chair, taking his finishing looks.

"See?" he said proudly to me. "How even? All around."
And spun her a little faster, so flashes of her caught the
mirror and flashed back at me double, on both sides of the
chair, as if we were suddenly in a full barbershop—with a
spinning row of dizzy customers, and madmen barbers,
conducted by the old fortunetelling woman in the best
barber chair. It was funny; I relaxed my eyes.

But then he shampooed her and—before I knew how
long I'd watched the row of customers spin themselves
bald—he stuck her head in a large chrome hair dryer; he
tipped her head back in the chair, back toward me, and I
watched the humming dome gleam.

"I only asked for a shave," someone said. "Would you
call *this* a haircut?" And somehow, Nitsa's cleavage,
spreading everywhere, was reflected on the back of Gallen's domish hair dryer.

"Would you like *your* ears pierced?" Nitsa asked me.
"But I know, the men usually like just *one* ear done."

"Not in *this* country, Mama," Orestic said.

And little Hugel Furtwängler, with a barbers'-union
flag, leered over the wigged heads in the window. He said,
"He's a lunatic! He *wanted* me to do it!"

Oh, I'm off, I thought—just because this hair dryer is
steaming up this room, unhealthily.

Nitsa Szirtes plucked her robe a bit away from her
stuck-together breasts and blew a thin-lipped jet of breath
down her cleavage.

Then I asked Orestic, "Have you been here long—in
this country? Or just since the war."

"Since and before," said old Nitsa. "His father, Zoltan,

took us back and forth to Hungary—a wretched place, if I ever."

"My father's gone," Orestic reminded me.

"He was a cruddy, hairy man," said Nitsa.

"Mama, *please*," Orestic said.

"I should never have left Greece," said the former girl-Papadatou.

"Oh yes, we've been here awhile," Orestic told me, and lifted Gallen's dried and shrunken head out of the shiny dome. He made her keep her head thrown back while he brushed, furiously. An odd angle, I had, looking over the back of Gallen's tilted chair; I could see no more of her face than the sharp bridge of her nose. Except what I caught misreflected in the hair dryer—her enlarged ear.

Which blushed when it heard me ask Orestic, "Then were you here when that man broke into the zoo?"

"Ha! He was eaten!" said Nitsa.

"Yes, he was," I said.

"But we weren't here, Mama," said Orestic.

"We weren't?" she said.

"We were in Hungary," Orestic said.

"But you've heard about it, obviously," I said.

"We were in Hungary," he said, "when all those things were going on here."

"What *other* sort of things?" I said.

"How do I know?" he said. "We were in Hungary."

"Then we must have been wretched," said Mama Nitsa, "with that cruddy, hairy man."

"Hair's done," Orestic said. Gallen nervously touched the top of her head.

"Well, two-fifty we owe you," said Mama Nitsa.

"Three hundred," I said.

"Three hundred," said Orestic. "Be fair, Mama."

"Weak!" She snorted. As weak as the cruddy, hairy man, no doubt. Poor blasphemed Zoltan Szirtes must have rolled in his grave to hear her—if he had a grave or was in it yet; or if those in their graves can roll.

"Anything's possible!" Siggy called, out of the hair dryer's gleaming dome—or out of Keff's box, alongside the Grand Prix racer, 1939.

I checked my watch. Time was a part of my life again. It was nearly lunchtime, Monday, June 12, 1967. Which would put us perfectly on schedule, if we left straight-away, parked the motorcycle off the Platz, down Maxing

Strasse; went to the Balkan waiter's café; went into the zoo that afternoon.

We'd be sure to find the same conditions that were written down, one week ago this Monday.

"I like your hair, Gallen," I said. She was sort of sheepish, but trying to be proud. Her new hair was tufted close to her head, like a bobcat's.

And trying to be casual—not thinking about her choice of words—she asked me brightly, "What's the plan now?" Which forced my cluttered mind to admit, if only to myself, that I *did* have one.

HOW THE ANIMALS' RADAR
MARKED MY REENTRY

I drove far enough down Maxing Strasse to park opposite Maxing Park.

"Is this the zoo?" said Gallen.

"No," I said. "It's up a block or two, off the Platz."

"Then why are we parking so far away?" she said.

"Oh, it's a pleasant walk," I told her. And while she was fussing with her new hair in the side-view mirror, and pressing against her head to try to make her ears lie flat, I unloaded our pack and sleeping bag and tied everything all together in a gross lump, with our helmets strapped on top. Then I crept off in Maxing Park's deep hedges and stashed the whole mess out of sight.

"Why are you unpacking?" Gallen asked.

"Well, we don't want to be robbed," I said.

"But we won't be gone long, will we? Graff?"

"Everyone's out to rob you, these days," I said, and I didn't let her see me tuck the notebook under my shirt and jacket.

It's just common sense. If there's an available instruction manual for a job you're doing, you should certainly bring it with you.

"Oh, it's lovely here," said Gallen.

We passed the Tiroler Garten, and I said, "There's a mile of moss and ferns in there, and you can take off your shoes."

"But that's just like the country," she said, disappointed. She was much more impressed by the overhead maze of

tram wires, when we got to the Platz. "Is that the café
you mean?" she said.

Of course, it was, but we were on the zoo side of the
Platz, and from there I couldn't distinguish the Balkan
waiter among the other white coats round the café.

We were about to cross over when I heard a Big Cat
behind us, starting an uproar in the zoo.

"What's that?" said Gallen.

"A lion," I said. "Or a tiger, a leopard, a puma or
cougar—a jaguar, cheetah or panther."

"God," said Gallen. "Why don't you just say *cat?* A
large cat."

But I was suddenly too impatient to bother with the
frotting Balkan waiter. Knowing what a sly one he was, I
also thought he might make me tip my hand. So I said,
"There's a better place inside the zoo. It's a *Biergarten,*
and much better than this café."

Then maybe I turned her around too fast, and set off at
too quick a clip, because Gallen said, "Graff? Are you all
right now, really? Do you think you should come back
here?"

I just dragged her on; I couldn't look at her. I think I
would have seen her with all her guards down, and I was
sure there'd be a better time to break my plan to her.

"Well, yes," I said. "The Hietzinger Zoo."

Still gated by stone. Admission still granted by the man
with the gambler's green eyeshade. Over whose stall the
giraffe's head loomed.

"Oh, Graff!" said Gallen. "Oh, look at him! He's beautiful!"

"Well, look at his chin," I said. "It's all scraped up from
the fence."

"Oh, look how he *moves!*" said Gallen, not even notic-
ing that the poor giraffe's chin was damaged on account
of his captivity. "Oh, what's in *here?*" she said, and darted
off for the walrus's pool.

What really *is* here? I thought. She was much too gay; I
couldn't watch her tottering so happy on the edge of that
belching giant's slimy tub.

"Does he talk?" said Gallen, and flashed her new, sharp
face back to me. "Do you talk?" she asked the walrus.
"*Grrumph!*" she said. And the walrus, an old hand at
doing favors for fish, rolled his great bulging head and
belched for her.

"BROP!" said the walrus.

"He talked!" Gallen cried.

And said more than I have to say, I thought.

I felt the notebook go clammy against my stomach; when I moved, it scraped me. The pages of zoo watches pressed against me. It was as if I'd eaten a whole magazine; and the paper, in shreds, was wadded in my belly.

"Oh!" said Gallen—a general statement, while looking around for what came next.

Hannes Graff, I thought, please do get rid of your stomach disorder. This zoo is a place to enjoy. Nothing more.

Not ten feet away from me was an iron litter basket. I rapped my belly with my knuckles. I took a light step, my first. Then something happened with the giraffe.

He began to canter; he loped along, his great neck arching his head over the top of the storm fence like a live antenna, a kind of radar.

My God, he's recognized me, I thought.

"What's happening?" said Gallen.

The giraffe clattered excitedly. The walrus raised his head up above the rim of the pool; for just a second, he held his mass erect and goggled at me. I heard nearby skitters from pens and cages throughout the zoo. My presence, and my step toward the litter basket, was passed along the animals' grapevine. From half a zoo away, I heard the bar-slamming, roaring Asiatic Black Bear.

"What's happening?" Gallen said again.

"Something must have startled one of them," I answered, defeated.

"BROP!" said the walrus, rising again.

BROP yourself, I thought.

"BROP!" he repeated, his throbbing neck straining to keep himself up—and in sight of me. While the great cantering giraffe zoomed his neck in on me.

"Where's the *Biergarten?*" said Gallen, so frotting eager.

And down by the *Biergarten* that my Gallen wanted to see, the terrible Asiatic Black Bear deafened the zoo.

"God, what's *that?*" said Gallen.

"BROP!" said the endlessly belching walrus. "That's our terrifying leader. That's who that is."

The giraffe now transfixed me with his neck. "How could you?" his radar asked. "How could you have even considered it?"

"BROP!" said the tiresome walrus. "Weren't you forgetting O. SCHRUTT?"

Gallen tugged my arm. "Come *on*, Graff," she said.

And as I stumbled, half-blind, toward the *Biergarten*, I saw again my loon of a soccer mate on my old high-school team. Down the path was the ball, and ahead of it, coming full tilt, the Famous Asiatic Black Bear, who wouldn't allow O. Schrutt to be forgotten, appeared to have a step or two on me; he was going to get to the ball first.

Past the Monkey Complex then; my eyes were blurred by the frotting bear's speed. I began, low down in my throat: *"Aaii, aaii,"* I cried softly, *"Aaaiii!"* I screamed.

"Graff!" said Gallen. "What's the matter with you?"

"Aaaiii! Aaaiii!" wailed a monkey or two, old hands at mimicry.

And Gallen laughed, with all her guards clearly down, even more vulnerable than I'd imagined—to my inevitable surprise.

"I didn't know, Graff," she said, taking my arm, "that you knew how to talk to monkeys."

But I thought: It's clearly a matter of them knowing how to talk to me. And make me one of them.

HOW, CLEARING THE DITCH, I FELL IN THE GORGE

The Rare Spectacled Bears sat upright and stared, seeing me ensconced in the *Biergarten* with a new partner. Gallen shone a rich wine-brown, her new neck pale and perhaps prickly in the sun bearing straight down on her. She sat outside the fringe of our Cinzano umbrella; she pushed herself back from our table—the better to view me at a distance, with awe.

"You mean, you've been thinking you'd do it all along?" she said. "Then you *tricked* me into coming here with you."

"No, not exactly," I said. "Not at all, really. I don't know when I really *knew* I was going to go through with it."

"You mean, Graff," she said, "you're going to creep around in here all night? You're going to let them out?

And it was *you* who told me it was a crazy idea! You *said* so, you *did*, Graff. You agreed he must have been crazy to even think of such a thing."

"No, not exactly," I said, with the frotting notebook rising up under my shirt and against my belly, like a gorged feast I couldn't possibly keep down. "Not at all, really," I said. "I mean, yes, I think it's a crazy idea—I think he lost his sense over it, sure. But I mean, I think there's a proper way to go about it. And basically, I think, it's a sound enough idea."

"Graff, you're crazy too," she said.

"No, not exactly," I insisted. "Not at all, really. I just think there's a *reasonable* way to go about it. I think his error was to even imagine that he could get them *all* out. No, this is the point, you see: *reasonable selection* of animals, Gallen. Naturally, I agree, you'd have to be mad to let them *all* loose. That would be unmanageable, I agree."

"Graff," she said. "Graff, you're even *talking* like him. You are, really. More and more. I've noticed. You sound just like he did."

"Well, I haven't noticed any such thing," I said. "And so what if I do? I mean, he went too far—I'd be the first to admit. But there's a proper perspective to put this in, I think. What I mean, Gallen, is let's put it in a new light. It *could* be kind of fun, if it's done with some taste."

"Oh, *fun*, yes," said Gallen. "Oh, with *taste*, sure. All these lovely animals out biting people and each other. That's fun, sure. And that really has taste, Graff, I have to admit."

"*Reasonable selection*, Gallen," I insisted; I wasn't going to let her bait me into a fight.

"Oh, you're out of your head, Graff," she said. "You must be." And she stood up. "I'm not staying in here for one minute more," she said.

But I said, "Oh, fine. Just where will you go?"

"Oh, Graff," said Gallen. "We're fighting already." And she held her ears—remembering, no doubt, that I was the cause of them being so exposed. I went round the table and squatted down next to her; she crouched, sniffling in her hand.

"Gallen," I said. "Just think of it, please—just for a minute."

"I wanted to go *shopping* with you, or *something*," she said. "I've never been."

"Gallen," I said. "Just a *few* animals, really. Just a few of the gentle types. And just a little scare for old O. Schrutt." But she shook her head.

"You're not even *thinking* of me," she said. "You just *took* me!" she whispered, fierce and dramatic. "You have *had* me! I was just taken along," she accused, with ridiculous flourishing of her pointed elbows.

"Oh, frot," I said.

"You're crazy and mean," she said.

"All right," I said. "Frot me, I am." And then I whispered these fierce dramatics of my own: "Siggy's dead, Gallen, and I never took him seriously—we never even got to talk about anything at all." But that didn't sound like what I meant, really, so I said, "I hardly got to know him. I mean, really, I didn't know him at all." But that led to nothing logical either, so I said, "it all started out very light and funny—just easy, going nowhere in particular. We were never very intimate, really—or serious. We'd only gotten started." And I saw no conclusions leaping at me out of that, either. So I stopped.

"How could *anyone* take Siggy seriously?" she said.

"I *liked* him, you bitch." I stopped. "It was his idea and it's crazy, maybe. And maybe, so am I."

But she took my hand, then, and sneaked it under the soccer shirt to her hot, hard tummy; she sat back down in her chair, holding my hand to her. "Oh no, you're not crazy, really," she said. "I don't think you are, Graff. I'm sorry. But I'm not a bitch, either, am I?"

"No," I said. "You're not. And *I'm* sorry." She held my hand against her a long while, as if she were telling my fortune on her tummy.

Anything's possible.

"But what will we do afterwards?" she asked.

"I just want to get this over with," I said.

"And then what?" said Gallen.

"What you want," I said, and I really hoped so. "We'll go to Italy. Have you seen the sea?"

"No, never," she said. "Really, though—what I want to?"

"Whatever you want," I said. "I just want done with this business here."

And she sat so frotting trusting in her chair, my hand snug in her lap.

The Rare Spectacled Bears relaxed too. They slumped

in their fashion, against the bars and each other, as if they'd been not so much interested in that outcome as in any, even over-simple settlement of our squabble.

Oh, don't fight among each other, their sighs implied. Never fight among each other. We know. In close quarters, it's not wise. You'll find there's no one else. Passively, they hugged each other.

But I thought: This is strange. This isn't quite right. It's the wrong mood for it. I want to restore this idea to its proper larklike light. But I saw too many alternatives to be fair to either Siggy or Gallen.

The *attitude* for zoo-busting wasn't right yet. It was just something I was getting over with—I'd even said so—and Siggy wouldn't approve of the unhappy tone in that: such a piddling, compromising gesture.

The Big Cats roared. But I thought: No, I'm sorry, Big Cats, but I'm not here for you. Just for a harmless, trivial few. Thus the notebook warns:

Most decisions are anticlimactic.

So, oddly, after all, it hardly seemed worthwhile, at least as I had rearranged it—the reasonable selections of Hannes Graff. That only seemed of any consequence when I looked across the table at my Gallen. Who deserved, at least, a *little* reason.

Passively sad but accepting anything, the Rare Spectacled Bears repeated their sighs: At the very least, we must get along with each other.

But there was one to refute them. The Famous Asiatic Black Bear wasn't familiar with compromise.

I thought—with considerable surprise: Why, they're all *different*—these animals! Just like people, whose sad history shows they're all impossibly different too. And not equal, either. Not even born that way.

About that, the notebook says:

How incomplete. How funny. How simple. And also, a great pity.

I stood up from the table; on the facing of the service counter, the *Biergarten* staff had hung an old funhouse mirror, salvaged somewhere; if you were weary of animals, you could look up skirts at unidentified bits of bloomer and thigh. Remarkable, I caught myself in it—or caught part of myself, weirdly segmented, and parts of other people and things. Legs of unassociated chairs, and unmatching shoes. In the strange mirror, I was generally unfitted; my parts didn't go together, at all.

While the sweaty notebook on my belly made such a unit—a solid bulk of perfect lunacy.

"Oh, look," I said to Gallen, or to anyone. "How nothing goes together."

And she stood in the mirror with me, her parts no more together than mine, but easier to pick out—from chairs and more people-pieces. Because all her parts were simply beautiful; a mirror fragment of broad, thin mouth and long, downy throat; crease of blousy soccer shirt between one breast and a half. She laughed. I didn't.

She said, "How do we start?" Whispering, so frotting eager and trusting me, all of a sudden. "Do we let them out in the dark? What do we do about the guard?" And when I kept looking for my scattered self in the mirror, she said, with mock stealth, "No good attracting attention like that, Graff. Shouldn't we slip off somewhere and go over the plan?"

I watched the mirror-section of her mouth, talking all by itself. I didn't even know if she was baiting me, or if she was serious. I squinted. Somewhere in the frotting mirror, I had lost my head and couldn't find it.

FOLLOWING DIRECTIONS

It was easy. We poked about till late afternoon, and scouted out the hedgerow by the long pen for Miscellaneous Range Animals; the hedge was every bit as snug as Siggy said it was. Shortly before we ducked behind it, and listened to the cage-cleaners and sweepers calling for stragglers, I showed Gallen the Small Mammal House—and noted, for myself, the closed door of the room that had to be the watchman's lair. In fact, we had time to look at everything—before we went in hiding behind the hedgerow.

I was only disappointed that the oryx had been thinking

in his shed—travel plans, perhaps—and Gallen hadn't seen him and his fierce balloons.

But the skulking part was easier than easy, and we got to feel quite cheery about it—lying close against the fence line, peering through the hexagonal holes at the shuffling Assorted Antelopes and their miscellaneous kin. I'll admit, though, I didn't totally relax until all the daylight had left us.

By eight-thirty or so it was dark, and the animals were dropping off—breathing more evenly and making those comfortable, unconscious noises. A paw flapped in a water dish, and someone briefly complained. The zoo dozed.

But I knew the guard was due for another round at a quarter to nine, and I wanted us to do it just as Siggy had—and be down on the ponds for the Various Aquatic Birds, when the guard started out.

It was very easy getting there too. I dipped my fingers over the pool curb; sleeping ducks floated by, heads tucked, webbed feet dragging. Occasionally, a foot would paddle in sleep. Unaware, the duck would turn like a row-boat pulled by one oar, and bump the pool curb; wake and squabble with the cement; churn off, doze, paddle and sleep again. Oh, the rhythms of that first-shift watch were lovely.

Gallen's heartbeat was no more than a flutter on my palm, as if some elf inside her were blowing softly on the pale skin under her breast.

"It's so quiet," said Gallen. "When does Schupp come?"

"Schrutt," I said, and woke a duck. He croaked like a frog.

"Well, when does he get here?" said Gallen.

"Not for a while," I said, and watched the casual first-shift guard stretching and yawning in the good, white light coming out the Small Mammal House door.

"This is the good guard?" said Gallen.

"Yes," I said, and immediately had kindly feelings toward him—seeing him go off through the zoo, softly clucking his tongue to special friends. The boxing Austral-ian, and his cherished zebra horde.

"This is the one who leaves the red off?" said Gallen.

"Infrared," I said. "Yes, this one's all right."

And when he was being considerate enough not to wake anyone in the House of Pachyderms, we went back to our hedgerow and snuggled along the fence line, legs scissoring—with each other's elbows for pillows on the roots.

"Now," said Gallen, "this guard has another watch at eleven?"

"Quarter to eleven," I said.

"All *right*," she said, and lightly bit my cheek. "Eleven or quarter to. What's the difference?"

"*De*tail," I said. "*De*tail is the difference." Knowing myself that details are, of course, essential to any good plan. And, of course, knowing the need for a plan.

I was working on one; like every good plan, I was taking first things first, and first was O. Schrutt—the nabbing and stashing thereof. After which, I do confess, my thinking was still a little too general. But under the hedge I was calm again, and Gallen seemed so much in this anticlimax with me that I at least had an easier conscience toward her.

In fact, after the guard's round at a quarter to eleven, with the zoo sleeping heavily around us, I initiated suggestive nuzzles in Gallen's rich, thick hair—patted her behind, and attacked with suchlike ploys—because I thought our hedgerow was just too snug to abuse, or not use at all.

But she turned away from me and pointed through the hexagonal holes in the fence, indicating the sleeping, overlapping mound of Miscellaneous Range Animals huddled in the center of the pen. "Not with *them* there, Graff," she said. And I thought: Really, this animal business has been carried far enough.

I even felt foolish, but I got over it; Gallen was all of a sudden climbing on me with nervous ploys of her own, and I thought she'd changed her mind. But she said, too sweetly, "Graff, don't you see how nice it is in here? What do you want to do anything for?" She performed disgusting nibbles on my chin, but I wasn't to be so easily fooled.

I admit I was a bit defensive; I drew back in the hedges. She whispered after me, "Graff?" But I kept backing down the fence line from her, on all fours, getting all bushed over in the hedge. So she couldn't see me, and she said, too loudly, "Graff!"

There was a violent clubbing sort of sound from the Monkey Complex, and some heavy, hooved animal clattered back and forth. One or two Big Cats cleared their throats, and Gallen said, "All right, Graff. Come on, it was just an idea."

"Been your idea all along, hasn't it?" I said, peering from deep in the hedge. "You just stayed with me to try to talk me out of it."

"Oh, Graff!" she said, and what was left of the range herd picked themselves up and cantered down to the opposite fence line.

"Shut up, Gallen!" I whispered, hoarse.

"Oh, Graff," she whispered back, and I could hear her take her little catch breath, setting up a good sob. "Graff," she said, "I just don't know what you *want* to do, even. Really, I can't imagine why."

Really, I can't either, I thought. It's hard to make any decisions when you're as reasonable as I am. But for decision-making, little helpful things, like swamps, come when you least expect them.

I was suddenly aware that the zoo was awake—and not, I thought, from Gallen's slight blurting. I mean, it was *really* awake. All around us, creatures were balancing in frozen crouches, three-legged stances, anxious suspension from the squeaking trapezes in the Monkey Complex. I checked my watch and realized I'd been too casual for the occasion. It was after midnight. I hadn't heard the bell for the changing of the guard, but the first-shift watchman was gone. The zoo was poised. I listened to the footfall on the patch along our hedgerow. I saw his combat boots, with pants tucked in. And the truncheon in the sheath that's stitched so neatly in the left boot.

There wasn't time to warn Gallen, but I could see her silhouette up tight against the fence line, hands over her ears; I could see the profile of her open lips. Thanks be, she saw him too.

And when he'd passed by us, spinning his light once or twice and jolting himself off balance so his keyring jangled under his armpit, I dared a headlong look out in the path, through a root gap, and saw him strutting robotlike—his head and epaulettes above the horizon line the hedgerow made against the night. He turned a military corner on the path; I waited, and heard his keyring ringing in the empty *Biergarten*.

"Graff?" said Gallen, in her accomplice voice again. "Was that Schupp?"

"His name is *Schrutt*," I said, and thought: So that sudden phantom was old O. Schrutt.

Whose reception was instantly flung through the zoo, in echoes bouncing off the ponds; the Famous Asiatic Black Bear's nightly rage. Gallen scurried down the hedgerow to me, and I held her through this second phase of zoo-watching, on this week-old anniversary of poor Siggy's unreasonable conclusions; in the Hietzinger Playhouse with everyone playing his own separate role, of not living very well with each other; where I was decision-making—there were just these three choices: the anticlimax; no climax at all; or the raging, unreasonable but definite climax demanded by the Famous Asiatic Black Bear.

FIRST THINGS FIRST

When O. Schrutt finished his first round, he went back to the Small Mammal House and turned on the infrared.

"Graff," said Gallen. "Please let's get out of here." And I held her behind the hedge. Coming through the root gaps, far down the fence line, there was a purple light reflected on the wire hexagons.

When the first muffled complaints from the Small Mammal House came to us, Gallen said, "Please, Graff. Let's just get the police." And for a moment I thought: Why not? How easy that would be.

But I said, "How would we explain our being here?"

"They'd understand, Graff," she said. And although I'm not absolutely sure they wouldn't have, I didn't consider it further. My own variations on the theme were anticlimactic enough.

And besides, I remembered, if one was to even come close to Siggy's absolute faith, the idea for the zoo bust existed before O. Schrutt.

O. Schrutt was simply an added feature. Who happened to come first in any overall plan.

"O. Schrutt comes first," I said to Gallen, and going over the plan once more, I sent her on her way to the Monkey Complex while I passed by the complex myself, and took a stand behind the children's drinking fountain.

The geleda baboon didn't see me. Unlike Siggy's eve-

ning, on this occasion the baboon was not on guard for
anything. So when I waved back to the corner of the complex, Gallen began her business in the brush just outside
the trapeze terrace. I listened to her, shaking the bushes
and making low, girlish grunts of an inappropriately erotic
nature. Perhaps, though, not inappropriate for the old gelada male and his fiery red chest, which suddenly flashed
between the dark terrace bars—catching a bit of the
blood-lit reflections coming out the Small Mammal House
door.

Then I couldn't see the old primate; I could hear him
huffing and wrenching down on the trapezes, one by one,
which he used to swing himself from one long end of the
terrace to the other. Where Gallen must have had some
fright, thinking he'd sail right through the bars and get
her.

The trapezes tangled and clanged on the wall. The gelada baboon wailed his frustration; he ranted, doglike and
crowlike—all sounds of all animals were compressed and
made one in this frotting baboon.

And, of course, the zoo joined in. And Gallen slipped
out of those bushes; I saw her—just a bit of her nice leg
flicking out in the doorway path of blood-purple light
from O. Schrutt's research center.

Then there was old O. himself, his scar stretched over
his face like a worn-thin spot on a balloon. And when he
went bleating past me, flashlight aimed at the gelada baboon's corner, I ducked behind him and ran the other
way, into the Small Mammal House. And in lurking fashion, hid myself behind the door of his office room.

Around me, I surveyed: the gaffing-hook thing, the
electric prod, the zoo ledger open on the desk.

The binturong was still rarely diseased; the ocelot was
still expecting; the giant forest hog still suffered from his
ingrown tusk. But there was nothing entered concerning
the bandicoot who had been dying—who was either dead
or better.

Most likely dead, I thought—as I heard O. Schrutt curs-
ing the gelada baboon, his voice on a pitch with the shriller monkeys, his key loop ringing the terrace bars like a
gong.

I took up the electric prod and waited for Schrutt's
surly footfall coming down the aisles of the maze.

When O. Schrutt came in his room, I stepped up behind

him and snatched his revolver out of the handy open holster, and as he turned round to me, grabbing for the truncheon in his boot, I zapped him with the prod across the bridge of his nose. He fell back, blind for a moment. He threw his flashlight at me; it hit my chest. But before he could go for the truncheon again, I zonked his wet lips with the neat, electric prod. That seemed to buzz him properly; he spun around and tripped himself; he was down, sitting on the floor, his arms wrapped round his head, making a spitting sound—as if he were trying to get that electric fuzz off his gums.

"O. Schrutt," I said. "If you open your eyes again, I'll clean out your sockets with this electricity. And shoot off your elbows with your own gun." And I clicked the safety on and off, just so he'd remember that I really had it.

"Who?" he said, his voice furry.

"O. Schrutt," I said, in a deeper and older voice than my own—an ancient voice, I attempted. "At last I've found you, old O. Schrutt," I droned.

"Who are you?" he said, and went to move his hands off his eyes. I just skittered the prod over his fingertips. He howled; then he held his breath, and I held mine. The room was tomb-still; down the maze, even the small mammals were hushed.

"It's been a long time, O. Schrutt," I said, in my creaky voice.

"Who?" he said, in a little huff. "Zeiker?" he said, and pressed his eyes so hard that his blotchy knuckles whitened.

I laughed a low, gritty laugh.

"No. Beinberg?" he said, and I held my breath for him. "Who are you?" he screamed.

"Your just reward," I said, with pomp. "Your final justice."

"Final?" said old O. Schrutt.

"Stand up," I said, and he did. I snatched the truncheon out of his boot and lifted his chin up with it. "Eyes closed, Schrutt," I said. "I'll guide you with this beating stick, and see you don't move odd or I'll bash you. In the old fashion," I added, not knowing what that might be but hoping it might ring bells for him—or have him imagining an old fashion of his own.

"Zeiker!" he said. "It *is* Zeiker, isn't it?" but I just poked him through the door and out in the maze. "Is it Zeiker?" he screamed, and I bopped him lightly on his head.

"Quiet, please," I said, tapping his ear with the truncheon.

"Zeiker, it's been too many years for this," he said. I said nothing; I just led him through the aisles, looking for a cage.

Empty was the biggest glasshouse of all, the home of the giant anteaters—missing, off on a Schrutt-sent mission of terror. I found the chute behind the cage rows, opened it and prodded old O. Schrutt inside.

"What are you doing?" he said, feeling his hands along the chute. "Some of these animals are vicious."

But I just poked him along until the label on the chute door said: GIANT ANTEATER, PAIR OF. Then there was the problem of cramming Schrutt down into the pitlike cage, where he groveled in the sawdust, covering his eyes and throat. And when nothing attacked him straightaway, he sat up for me so I could lash him all together in a lump—in his thick, multi-buckled ammunition belt, I crossed his arms and feet on his rump, and trussed him up, face-down in the sawdust.

"Keep those eyes shut, Schrutt," I said.

"I'm sorry, Zeiker," he moaned. "Really, that was a terrible time for us all, you know." And when I didn't answer, he said, "Please, Zeiker, is it you?"

He was still asking me when I crept back in the chute and locked the door behind me. He could yell all night in there, and as long as the glass frontispiece wasn't slid back, no one would hear him. His cries would be as muffled as his mistreated neighbors'.

Out in the aisle, then, I paused to watch him under infrared. He peered at the blank glass; he must have known I stood there, watching him. His scar pulsed double-time, and for that moment I might have pitied him, but across the aisle I noticed a new sadness. The expectant ocelot was wary of her forced company, the frightened wombat, *Vombatus hirsutus*—a small bearlike creature with a rodent's sort of nose, or a huge hamster, looking like a toothy bear's runt cub.

First things first, again, I thought. And ran into the doorway aisle of the Small Mammal House.

"Gallen!" I cried, and the zoo responded—thumps and outcries bolder than my own. "All clear!" I shouted, and the monkeys mimicked. I could almost sense the Big Cats purring.

And when I said. "The ocelot is a waiting mother," Gallen was helpful and unwary about the delicate business of separating O. Schrutt's luckless charges. She even paused at O. Schrutt's cage and stared at him awhile—her eyes the closest they could come to hating, a sort of horror-struck glare through the one-way glass. While old O. flopped nervously about in the sawdust, anticipating company.

But Gallen got her caution back, once the mother ocelot was bedded by herself and somewhat relaxed in her crib of straw. "Graff?" she said. "Don't you think it's illogical of you to separate these animals now, because they scare or even hurt each other, and then to let them all loose in the same mess, when they're sure to *really* hurt each other?"

"I said I wasn't going to let them *all* go," I told her, and felt a little let down by that reminder to myself.

Perhaps as an added gesture, then—after Gallen had left the Small Mammal House to scout down the paths for me, to see if our disturbance had brought anybody snooping around—I thought I shouldn't leave old O. to himself in the cage. And having no place to put the giant anteaters, anyway—having removed them from the cages of ratel and civet, respectively—I allowed O. Schrutt to *know*, before the chute door was opened, just who was returning home.

The giant anteater measures seven feet from nose to tip of tail; it's sort of two-fifths tail and two-fifths nose, and one-fifth hair. With no body to speak of.

And O. Schrutt surely knew them by their peculiar grunts—and how they sent their long noses inquiring into the cage, before they allowed me to budge them with a shove down into their rightful home. Which was not trespassed in by old O. Schrutt, whom the anteaters regarded distastefully from the other side of the cage. And seeing, I suppose, that Schrutt was without gaff or prod, and had himself trussed up in a lump, they were not afraid of him. In fact, they clawed up a little sawdust and grunted at him; they began to circle him—although the anteater is no meat hunter at all and wouldn't be interested in eating people, preferring bugs—while old O. said, "No! I didn't *mean* to come in here. I'll leave you alone. Please don't you feel threatened by me, oh no, sir!" And then whispered, a different pitch, "Here now, isn't this cozy, sort of? Wouldn't you say so? Oh, I would." But they shuffled around and around him—now and then a long tongue flying out and testing his cheek, tasting how sacred he was.

When I left, he might have been saying, "Here now, did you have a nice visit with ratel and civet? All for fun, I hope you know—and exercise, which you need. And there's no harm done, now, is there?" But I assured myself that the anteaters wouldn't eat him, or even pound him very severely with their leaden tails; or claw through him, the way they can claw through trunks of trees, or at least thigh-thick roots.

I *could* have left him with the Chinese fishing cat, I thought. And if you're not a good O. Schrutt, I will.

Then I walked out of the Small Mammal House, going over again in my mind just what few animals I would select as safe. But I saw Gallen looking rather frightened outside the door, and when I entered the real night again, I heard the din the zoo was making. The Big Cats sputtering like barges on the Danube, the monkeys reeling, thumping loud against the bars, the birds all calling their praise of me; and over it all, in a low-voiced monotone, the Famous Asiatic Black Bear.

All of them greeted me as I stepped out in the zoo I now had total charge of. *All* of them. Every different, frotting one of them—awaiting Hannes Graff's decision.

MY REUNION WITH THE REAL
AND UNREASONABLE WORLD

"Graff," Gallen said, "someone's sure to hear all this." And I wondered if perhaps there were loud nights in the zoo, anyway; if the conditioned suburb folk of Hietzing wouldn't just roll over and mildly complain: the animals are having a restless night. But I couldn't convince myself that there ever was a clamor like this. They were stomping, shaking the bars and bellowing delirious. And my frotting fellow-primates were the worst.

I'd left the infrared on because I didn't want anyone sleeping now; they had to be ready; and I wanted O. Schrutt kept in the dark, you might say. So I stayed a mo-

ment in the pathway of purple light from the Small Mammal House and I tried to read the key labels off the keyring. Finding the Monkey Complex key, I skirted the outside terrace, where shriveled and savage faces poked
through the bars, ushering me inside with wails. I didn't
dare an overhead light, thinking some passer-by outside
the zoo might notice something different and report. I
went from cage to cage with O. Schrutt's flashlight, glimps-
ing the rows and rows of black, leathery hands clutching
the bars. I was being careful; I read the names of animals.

Monkeys: howler, lion-tailed, proboscis, rhesus, spider,
squirrel and woolly—all small ones, so I let them out.

Then the ·snarling baboons: smiling, snowy-haired
hamadryases, and the dog-faced geledas; my red-chested
male, now forgetting his grievances. And the chacma baboons, the biggest; and perhaps I shouldn't have let out
that old hundred-twenty-pound male.

Then gibbons, a whole horde. And chimpanzees, all
six—one potbellied, who shoved the other and bit a spider monkey's tail. But I passed over, ashamed, the male,
two-hundred-pound orang-utan, and the quarter-ton lowland gorilla from the Gulf of Guinea. They couldn't believe it; they let me get almost to the door before they
cried out, enraged and very envious. The orang-utan tore
his swinging tire off the rope and crammed it through the
bars, squishing it up as thin as a bicycle tube. The lowland
gorilla folded his tin water dish, as neatly as an envelope.

And the primates I released were not quiet, the frotting
ingrates. I could hear my primates smashing ashtrays off
the tables in the *Biergarten*.

"Graff," said Gallen, "you've got to calm them down or
get us out."

"These antelope types are safe enough," I said, "and
they might distract the monkeys." So I bolted for the
pens—stretching from the Monkey Complex to the Australian's Little Colony—turning loose the aoudad, the anoa
and the addax; letting go the gerenuk, the gemsbok and
the gaur. I should have thought twice about the frotting
gaur—tallest of wild oxen of the world—but I just read
the name and didn't see him lurking in the dark. This bull
stood six-foot-four at the shoulders, and I *thought* the
gaur was a sort of diminutive goat. When he thundered
out the fence gate past me, Gallen screamed, "What's
that, Graff?" And it tore by her, smashing down hedges,

frightened blind. "What was it, Graff?" said Gallen, pinned down alongside the waiting zebra. "You promised, Graff!" she cried.

"My mistake!" I cried. "You let out those zebras now!" While I promptly loosed the sleek impala and the knobby Siberian ibex; all the Australians, and selected others.

But the zoo wasn't getting any quieter. The elephants blatted their brassy notes—resounding in the ponds of squabbling birds.

What harm would an elephant do? I thought. Just one, of course. And I could pick a docile one, certainly.

So I was off, scattering a conspiracy of gibbons cowering by the house for Big Loud Cats, and by the mysteriously silent hippohouse, where the hippo, I could only guess, was underwater and oblivious to this activity. Just as well, for sure, I thought—with his great plant-reeking mouth.

Inside the House of Pachyderms, the elephants were swaying, lifting their leg chains and thudding their trunks against each other's sides. I selected an old, large and chewed-eared African, and set my key in his shackles. He was so nice; I had to lead him by his trunk, out the Pachyderm House door, through which he barely fitted and where his presence scattered those conniving gibbons. But apparently, the elephant was a little deaf and had appeared so docile inside because he hadn't *heard* the rumpus. Because, outside, he jerked his trunk out of my hand and moved off at a steady, sideways trot, gathering speed, crushing shrubs and flattening down the iron rails along the paths.

I thought: Please don't let Gallen see him, God. And heard more ashtrays crash in whatever game the scheming monkeys played at the *Biergarten*.

Then I passed the tall, screened ruins where the giant birds of prey were perched, and thought: Not you. You'll eat the smaller monkeys. And for a second, thought: Which would at least keep them quiet.

But I went on back to the Small Mammal House, to collect my thoughts and see how old O. was doing with the anteaters. I met Gallen on the steps; she crouched in the purple light.

"I saw an elephant, Graff," she said. "I want to leave right now."

"Just one elephant," I said, dashing inside to spy O.

Schrutt rumpled in a corner, his eyes watering with saw-dust. The giant anteaters sat happily in the center of the glasshouse, spiraling their tongues around their long snouts, calmly watching over old O.

This will never do. I thought—O. Schrutt must be kept on his toes. And I crawled back in the chute again, enticing and prodding the anteaters out of there—telling Schrutt, before I opened the chute door, that if I saw his eyes looking at me, I'd bring in the Chinese fishing cat.

Of course, I didn't. I exchanged the anteaters for the ratel—a surly, snarling badgerlike oval of hair and claws, with a long memory concerning Schrutt, I was sure. But the ratel was too small, I knew, to ever initiate a full-scale assault on old O.—even in the lumped and trussed condition.

I just popped open the chute door and called down to Schrutt, "Here's little ratel!" And nudged the fat snarler inside. I watched them from the glass front; they respected each other from opposite corners, before the ratel grasped the situation Schrutt was in and boldly began a strutting show of himself, across the center of the cage.

But when I began lifting glass fronts elsewhere in the maze—releasing small and reasonable animals—I had to contend with Gallen again.

"You're not going to do a thing to that mother ocelot," she said.

"Of course I won't," I said, displaying my common sense for her to see—turning loose the casual sloth and the dour wombat, but passing by the lean, low, liver-colored jaguarundi. And letting go the zippy coati-mundi.

Of course, the anteaters were a nuisance—just blocking traffic in the aisle where they sat, watching the ratel and old O. Schrutt.

Gallen said, "Please. Graff. Can't we leave now?"

And I said. "We've got to muster them together, at one gate or another." Then I turned the mongoose loose, of which Gallen disapproved, and freed the reluctant slow loris and the ring-tailed lemur, feeling more reasonable every minute.

Just to show you how reasonable I was, I did not free the poor binturong—the bearcat of Borneo—not wanting other animals to catch his rare disease.

And I gave a silent bow to the empty glasshouse of the bandi-coot, already escaped this world.

But when I shook off nagging Gallen and emerged on the steps outside again, I was greeted by those animals I hadn't selected. And they weren't cheering me now. They were tyrannical; they raged their envy. Forever present gibbons were sitting at the step bottom, shrugging shoulders and spitting. When I reached the path, they chattered accusations. They threw stones at me; I threw some back. I swung at one gibbon with the keyring, and he danced to the path rail and flung himself into the brush. Then I was assaulted with weed clods, sticks and general earth.

"You're free to go!" I screamed. "Why don't you? Don't ask for too much!" And responding to my voice was what sounded like the utter demolishment of the *Biergarten*. I pelted down there, through a crunchy dust of littered ashtrays. This was a primate sort of destruction, for sure; a vandalism of a shocking, human type. They had shattered the one-time funhouse mirror; chunks of it lay all over the *Biergarten* terrace. I kept looking down at my puzzlework reflection, looming over myself.

"Just one more and that does me." I said. And moved to the reeking cage of the Rare Spectacled Bears, who were hiding behind their drinking-and-dunking pool when I opened their cage. I had to shout at them to make them come out. They came shoulder to shoulder across the floor, heads lowered like whipped dogs. They turned circles through the destroyed *Biergarten*, running too close together and butting themselves into umbrellas and hissing monkeys.

This is enough, I thought. Enough, for sure. And I was winding through the other, roaring bear cages when Gallen screamed. Schrutt's out! I thought. But when I squinted through cage corners and down the dark paths toward the Small Mammal House, I saw a man-shaped figure, loping more or less on all fours, turn the corner by the Monkey Complex—followed by another just like him, though not as thick in the chest. The orang-utan and the lowland gorilla, in cahoots.

I thought: But how the frot did *they* ever get out? And saw then—cantering sideways behind them—the house-sized blur of the African elephant, carrying a cage wall in his trunk; a great rectangle of bars bent every which way.

When he flung the cage wall down on the path, it rang off the cement—as if the bell in St. Stephen's had broken loose and dropped straight down the steeple, striking the organ pipes behind the center altar.

Then all running forms stood still: I stood trying to hold my breath. The zoo was church-still; a new hope brings silence. And I started up slowly, past the polar bears and brown bears and American grizzly; I turned up the path by the Famous Asiatic Black Bear, who stood like an assassin in his cage. But I was forced to leap over the Oriental's safety rope and crash against his wrist-thick bars—when the elephant blurred up in front of me on the path and charged on by me after I'd crumpled against the terrible bear's cage door; the elephant tore through the *Biergarten*, squashing umbrellas and grinding up fallen mirror-bits under his mammoth feet. And I was almost up and away again, when the Famous Asiatic Black Bear seized me round the chest and hugged me back against his bars. I took a breath and held it; I was back-to him and could feel his foul breath stir my hair. I thought, calmly: When he realizes he can't fit his great head through the bars to eat me, then he'll rake up my belly with his claws and gobble me innards-first. But instead, he turned me to face him; his head seemed buffalo-sized. But when I dared to look him in the eye, I saw that he eyed the keyring looped over my shoulder.

"Oh no!" I told him. He hugged me; I was chest to chest with him, the bars grooving my ribs. I felt the claws plucking at my spine. "Squash me, then," I grunted at him. "Just get your eyes off that keyring, because I'm not ever letting *you* out." He roared all over my face; he bellowed up my nostrils, so loud I almost choked. "Never!" I squeaked. "You have to draw the line somewhere!"

But then Gallen screamed again. I thought: That elephant has loosed O. Schrutt! Or: That virile orang-utan has got my Gallen—surely, the best he's ever had.

I moved my hand for the keyring; the Asiatic Black Bear let my spine move out a notch. I fumbled, reading in the dark for the key I thought would probably be labeled: NEVER USE! But it said simply: ASIAN BEAR. Such understatement, but I fitted the key to latch; the bear held me, unbelieving. I felt the door swing into me; the bear and I swung out together on the opening frame of bars. And for a moment, he still squeezed me, not really believing he was free. Then he let me go; we both plopped to all fours.

Now he'll run around this door and eat me whole, I

thought. But both of us heard the Big Cats then, a brief upcry noticeably louder than before, as if—at the very least—their general house door had been opened. And then I heard the *terrible* Big Cats, purring close-by. The Big Cats were *prowling*, on the loose. I crept backward from the door. But the Oriental took no notice; oddly, he crouched very still, his nose lifting up now and then— salivating, and quivering the long, coarse hair on his flanks.

The Famous Asiatic Black Bear is *thinking!* I thought. Or plotting.

And I didn't wait a moment more—for him to make up his awful mind. I bolted round his open cage and back to the path, past the ponds, to the Small Mammal House. Where I found my poor Gallen huddled in the doorway aisle of the maze, watching down the blood-bathed path to where a tiger, his stripes tinted crimson and black in the infrared, was squatting over a large and tawny, deep-chested antelope with spiraled horns; with a large brain-shaped mass of intestines spilled over his side. And with a hind hoof bent or drawn up under his thigh, over which sprawled his unmistakable, familiar balloons of volleyball size.

"Oh, Siggy, it's the oryx," I said.

"It's a tiger," said Gallen, colder than the winter river. "And I'm *not* Siggy."

And just as coldly, I said, "You screamed?"

"Oh, you heard?" she said, with a demented brightness to her voice. "Well, I got over whatever it was, without you."

"Where did the apes go?" I asked. But she sat mum and hard-faced, so I didn't press her.

Down the maze, a muffled voice was naming names. I went to see: old O. Schrutt upright against the glass, the ratel almost playful with his odd snarls—boastful in the center of the cage. And old O. was naming names, or asking them.

"Zeiker?" he called. "Beinberg? Muffel? Brandeis? Schmerling? Frieden?" Name by name, O. Schrutt was leaving his mind behind.

So I went back to Gallen, just in time to hear the final thunder: the Famous Asiatic Black Bear's deciding roar. At last, adjusted to the surprise of his freedom, the bear had made up his mind. The zoo pitch of the other creatures hit hysteria, as if this bear were a griffin and what they feared was more his myth than his reality—all of them knowing what he thought for so long about Hinley Gouch, and how that had warped his mind.

"You let that bear out too," said Gallen.

"No!" I said. "I mean, I *had* to. He caught me. He wouldn't let me go. I had to make a deal." But she stared at me as if I were as foreign to her as the fallen oryx, whom she'd never seen when he was so wondrously whole and upright.

"Oh, Graff," she whispered. Her eyes glazed.

I looked out the doorway of the Small Mammal House and saw the Asiatic Black Bear mounting the stairs, four at a time. Gallen was benumbed; she never even flinched when he rushed at us, and by us, echoing through the maze. But he stopped, silent, when he saw O. Schrutt. Who was saying: "Weinstürm? Bottweiler? Schnuller? Steingarten? Frankl? Little Frisch?"

And I thought: Why not Wut? Javotnik? Marter? Trummer? Or loose-ended Hannes Graff too?

Having found what he came for, the Famous Asiatic Black Bear sat down at the glass front, perplexed, and rapped the hopefully foot-thick frontispiece once or twice, with a curious, pecking sort of claw. O. Schrutt stopped reciting. "Who's there?" he said. "I know it's Zeiker!" But the Asiatic Black Bear was not one to further endure O. Schrutt's yelling at him. He reared up and thudded against the glass; backed away; thudded again; then sat down, puzzled.

And O. Schrutt said, "Come on! Who are you? I know you're out there!" And the Asiatic Black Bear began to roar. A gathering din that gained force through its own echo in the maze. O Schrutt flopped backward in the sawdust, rolling into the ratel, who snapped, but who backed away himself—at the chute door, the two of them quaking at the close-range roar familiar to all the inmates of the Hietzinger Zoo.

O. Schrutt screamed, "No! Not *you!* Don't let him in! Not him! Not ever! No! *Please!* Zeiker? Beinberg? Frankl? Schnuller? Schmerling? Little Frisch? *Please!*"

And I hustled Gallen out the door—the roaring seemed to shove us out—into a zoo that was bolting; hearing, no doubt, the rage of the animal no one dared to challenge. Not Big Cats, and not the elephant, either; nor apes run-

ning somewhere—for the main gate, it seemed. Along
with everyone else. They were organized; the zoo was
mustering. The Asiatic Black Bear was out, and nobody
wanted his unreasonable company.

But when Gallen and I turned round the ticket taker's
booth and headed for the main gate, I saw outside the zoo
a daze of headlights, parked in rows—and heard the
blurry, human sounds of a crowd in waiting. And saw a
stream of animals, hooved, padded, clawed and dashing,
splashing through the ponds for Various Aquatic Birds,
setting the night aflight—all of them making for the rear
gate that opened to the Tiroler Garten. Where there's
moss and ferns, all the sweet way to Maxing Park.

There was a jam at the gate, but the elephant had obliged
and left a passable hole for all but himself. He'd managed to spring one hinge, but the bottom corner of the
gate had held, and the bottom hinge had swung the whole
gate crosswise in the exit.

Gallen and I sneaked by the elephant's trapped and
blundering shape, plunging through little mustering teams
of monkeys.

But in the Tiroler Garten there was also a crowd, a predawn army of more citizens than police—of suburb folk
in nightwear, blinking flashlights. We were not noticed in
the mayhem; we jogged alongside housewives, shriller than
monkeys.

It was only when we reached the larger, darker shrubs
of Maxing Park, that a sense of outcome loomed clearly
in my mind against his chaos. Through the shrubs, I saw
them hiding. Anonymous men with ancient weapons—with
fireplace tridents, grub hoes and gleaming bucksaws; pitch-
forks, sledges and moon-shaped sickles. And *people's*
voices, now, were raised above the Asiatic Black Bear's
din—left behind me.

And when I'd dragged Gallen as far as she could go, I
knelt over her, sobbing on a stone park bench, and saw
how the hiding men seemed uniformed and old and starving; an army of diehard meat-eaters, all these years of
nights in the parks round the Hietzinger Zoo. Ever since
Zahn Glanz, or whoever he was, was eaten.

I heard a shot or two; the trees shook with birds and
monkeys. Beside us, on the park bench, a comfortably
seated gibbon ate a candy-bar wrapper.

I said to Gallen, "Will you promise me to stay here

with this gibbon?" Her face was as calm, or numb, as the gobbling primate's.

I dashed for Maxing Strasse, tracing down the curb for the bike, and spotted the bush where our lumpish rucksack was stashed.

It was still dark, but all the houses were lit along the street and headlit cars tore by; cabs unloaded customers carrying *things*—sticks, brooms, mops and shish kebabbers. Men stepped out into the battle sound. A din like they hadn't heard in years.

I lashed the pack on the motorcycle and drove down Maxing Strasse, yelling for Gallen. I didn't know if I could be heard above the clamor—the wailing police-green Volkswagens sounding behind me in Maxing Platz. And over the trees of the Tiroler Garten, their blinking-blue bars of light. Streams of people pouring into Maxing Park, and streams of animals pouring out.

I saw Gallen on the curb, standing as if she were catching a bus she always caught at this hour, in this customary traffic. Mounting numbly behind me, she was slightly bumped by a Siberian ibex, stumbling blindly and goatlike over the curb—a chunk of his hide torn open and flapping down over his shoulder; the gash was sort of hoe-shaped.

And I listened and listened for him—the Famous Asiatic Black Bear—for some final roar of despair or satisfaction. But I could never have heard him above the din the *people* made; not even him.

Gallen sat like a puppet behind me, and I pulled us out in the traffic of Maxing Strasse. The police were now cruising Maxing Park; I saw the bobbing, single headlights and pearl-white fairings of their BMW's—weaving through the shrubs, trying to rout the mob. Inside a fast-closing circle of motorcycle headlights, the great gray boomer was beating up a man, who'd lost his grip on his garden shears; they shone in the grass, pinned under the boomer's hunting claw.

The mob was around us for five suburb blocks of driving. In a doorway on Wattmann Gasse, I saw the snow leopard panting and licking one paw. And in Sarajevo Platz, I saw a team of five successful hunters trying to crouch down out of my passing headlight, thinking I was a police cycle; behind them, they attempted to conceal the dragged, bloodied and unprotesting gaur. Who, when he was upright, was six-foot-four.

The low, sturdy zebra herd came in a noiseless wave across the lawns, weaving through shrubs—shifty, and able to fool the three-some of hunters with a net and two-man saw. The zebras came out over the curb in front of me, their hooves sparking off the cobblestones. Their own clatter startled them; they veered and zigzagged between parked cars, crossing the far sidewalk and bolting down tiny Wolter Gasse, where onrushing headlights turned them back—again across Maxing Strasse—and once more drove them into Maxing Park.

Then Gallen and I were in the Lainz suburbs, in the eerie outlying hospital district. We passed them altogether—the Old People's Home, the Invalids' Home, and City Hospital; the floodlit lawns, and stark, beige stucco. On the balconies, rows of wheelchairs gleamed; on the lawns and in the windows, cigarettes and pipes were glowing. The old and sick and maimed were listening to the clamorous zoo, like people in the country watch the lighting effects in a city being bombed.

And for a moment I idled low, listening with them, and watching, as they were, for the one brilliant animal who might any second appear—having run the best possible obstacle course. For the one superb gibbon, maybe, who would come handspringing over the hospital grounds—be surrounded by nurses, showered by wheelchairs off the balconies; be finally snagged in rubber breathing tubes, and strangled with a stethoscope. A capture for which all the hospital staffs and patients would take proud credit.

But no one made it that far. Gallen slumped more heavily on my back; I felt her start shaking against my neck. So I turned us past the waiting hospitals, toward the country west of the suburbs, with Gallen's wet cheek sliding against my own, and her hands plucking at my shirt; and her teeth in my shoulder, biting me fierce.

But I didn't mind it, and wished for all this world that she could bite much deeper and hurt me more. While I alternated driving fast with driving slow; fast so the din would fade behind me, and slow so that if there were any who successfully escaped, they might overtake me and lope before me in my headlight—serve me for that moment kindly, as guides I would be happy to believe in.

But no one overtook me; there was no traffic headed in

my direction. All the traffic I met was going the other way. Family autos, farmers' wagons, clattering with tools and weapons—in the early morning dark, the people poured eagerly into the calamity area.

For every headlight I met, I saw again my old soccer-ball situation. And I was beaten to the kick, every time.

MAKING NEW PLANS

The beginning daylight found us out of the city, in the countryside above the Danube, south of Klosterneuburg. Where there still were monks.

I don't know how long I'd been pulled off the roadside, sitting down in the ditch, before I noticed the country folk coming wearily back from the wondrous, city-type excitement in the Hietzinger Zoo. Truck- and whole wagonloads of them, mostly; some of the loutish younger farmers whistled at Gallen, who sat in a ball on the other side of the road from me.

We hadn't spoken. I thought: It's not wise of me to let her do so much thinking by herself. But I had nothing to say, so I kept the peace of the road between us. Until these farmers started coming back.

Then I thought: We look suspicious. Although O. Schrutt never got a look at us, and probably would never be coherent again, there was that Balkan waiter and little Hugel Furtwängler who might have had something to say about a big, ragged motorcycle, and a madman who spoke zoo talk.

O. Schrutt, I thought, at least was found with his name-tag on—and his epaulettes buttoned down sharp. That's something.

But it wasn't enough, for sure. Because the last of the pickup trucks to pass us had a load in the back—a lump under a tarp, hanging down off the tailgate. I saw a bit of leg and hoof protrude; I recognized the brownish-red and creamy-white striping, running from hock to shank. Heavens forfend all evil from the previous bongo, handsomest of antelopes—about to be eaten and have his rack mounted over the mantle of the humble peasant dwelling. For later generations of hunters to ask: Was he once native to Austria?

Oh yes. A slave boat to Austria brought the first of them.

But extinct now?

Oh yes. They were a damaging lot—to the gardens. And dogs were gored.

By *them?*

Oh yes.

But he has such a thin, gentle face.

Oh yes. But he was actually fat and very tasty.

Him?

Oh yes.

And when the last of the caravan had passed us, I thought I should try to salvage Gallen out of this. She sat across the road from me and stared over my shoulder, or through my chest. But I couldn't face her; I looked down my pant leg and discovered, wadded and clinging to my sock, a little mesh of fur.

Oh, I *am* sorry, Siggy, I thought. But you were more than illogical. You were wrong.

Then Gallen crossed the road to the bike and stood over the lumpish rucksack, for a moment, before she began to take her things out.

She'd done entirely too much thinking, for sure.

And since I had nothing to say, I said, "Well, what do you want to do now?" She just gaped at me. So I said, "We'll do whatever you want." But she just pulled her things out faster; she made a sack of her ladies' leather jacket; I saw her stuff her silky blue panties up one sleeve. And that hurt me.

I thought: She's going to give me back my soccer shirt. But she gave no signs of taking it off. At least, she was sparing me the little gestures.

"Where are you going?" I said.

"To Vienna," she said. "May I have my hair money, please?"

"To Vienna?" I said.

"Aren't you interested in going back and reading all about it?" she asked. "Don't you want to know, *exactly*, just what happened? Aren't you interested in all the *details*, Graff?"

But she wasn't going to get a rise out of me; I had no place to come up from. And casualty statistics were of no interest to me, for sure. After the oryx, there was no need to keep count of disasters.

I said, "Really, please. Why is it Vienna?"

"Because," she said, "it's the one place I can think of where you wouldn't try to come along with me."

And I got some footing, suddenly—to rise from. I said to her, "You won't ever sneeze again, I hope you know." And she just glared at me. "Well, you won't," I said. "Whoever gets you."

"It was *my* hair," said Gallen. "You give me the money now, please." So I did. She took it like suspected bait, as if she were afraid I'd touch her.

"Wherever will *you* go, Graff?" she said, in a bright, cold, clear-sky voice. But I wouldn't allow myself to be taunted.

I said, seriously, "To Kaprun." And she looked away. "When I come back," I said, "how can I find you?"

"*If* you come back," she said, still turned away.

"I will," I said. "And where will you be?"

"Oh, I'm very fond of *zoos*," she said, in the cold, bright voice again. "I expect I'll visit the zoo often. You might find me there, when you decide to try it again— with a *new* plan."

But I wasn't going to have us go out this way. I said, "I'm going for a while to Kaprun, and I know I'll want to see you again."

"You mean, when you're all better?" she said, mock-sweet. "When you're all done with it?" But I knew that wasn't the way it worked, and was the wrong attitude to carry off with me. You can't rush getting over anything. Even the notebook is clear on this:

The figures make a certain sum,
no matter how you add them up.

Officious, as ever. Another half-truth, as always.

I said, "Gallen, I'm sorry. And I won't forget about you."

"Then come to Vienna with me, Graff," she said, and I couldn't tell what kind of edge her voice had now.

"I have to go to Kaprun," I said.

"Then how will you find me?" she asked—my question. And it was her unsharp, thick and natural voice again—a genuine query.

"Kahlenberg," I said, "is a place you'll hear about when you're in the city. Take any Grinzing tram and a bus up through the Vienna Woods. Go there Wednesday evenings," I said. "There's a view of the Danube, and all Vienna."

"And you'll come some Wednesday, I suppose," she said.

"You be there every Wednesday," I said. But this was pushing her too hard, and roundabout from where she'd first taken a stance.

She said, "Maybe." With a touch of that bright coldness in her voice.

"I'll take you to the buses in Klosterneuburg," I said. "The first outlying tram stop is in Josefdorf."

"I don't want to ride with you," she said. "I'll just walk."

And because I felt I was losing again, I said, "Well, sure. You're a strong-legged girl, I know. It won't hurt you."

"You said *Thursdays?*" she asked.

"*Wednesdays,*" I said quickly. "Any *Wednesday night.*"

"You'll come then?" she asked.

"For sure," I said, and she started to go. I said, "*Wednesday.*"

"Maybe," she said, and kept her fine legs strutting away from me.

Trying to make light of it all, I said, "I'm going to watch your sweet behind till you're out of sight."

But she wasn't exactly smiling when she turned round to me. "Not a long, *last* look, though?" she said. "Or is it?"

"No," I said—so quickly that her mouth came close to smiling. She kept walking away from me; I watched her almost to where the road turned.

Then I called *"Wednesday!"*

"Maybe," she called, in an uninterpretable voice, and didn't turn around.

"For sure!" I hollered, and she was gone.

I sat in the road ditch, letting her get all the way into Klosterneuburg; I didn't want to pass her on the road.

Around me the morning was coming on stronger. The domestic life of the trimly hedged and fenced fields. The borders separating cows from corn; the property lines orderly and unmistakable in the sun. All cows were belled; all sheep were ear-notched.

All men have names, and specific places where they're allowed to go.

A wind picked up and blew the roadside dust in my face. I watched the motorcycle brace against the little gale and shudder on its kick stand. I saw the mirror mounted on the handlebars, reflecting some anonymous patch of tar-smeared gravel of the roadside—and a petal-part of a flower, grown too close to the road. But when I looked behind the motorcycle, I just couldn't say, for sure, which flower lent its part to that reflection. Or just which stretch of tar-smeared gravel.

Things didn't piece together any better than before.

And that should have been no surprise to me. I knew. All the figures in your frotting column make the sum, but the figures are in no way bound to be otherwise related. They're just all the things you've ever paid for. As unfitted to each other as toothpaste and your first touch of warm, upstanding breast.

Gallen was in Klosterneuburg. Where there still were monasteries. And monks making wine.

And Gallen, who might some Wednesday meet me in Kahlenberg, was not of the nature of Todor Slivnica's custard—to be interpreted from wherever it all lay spattered.

CONGRATULATIONS TO
ALL YOU SURVIVORS!

Hannes Graff, I thought, is too split-haired and loose-ended to ever rise up out of this road ditch and ride his beastly motorcycle out of this deceptively ordered countryside.

And orderly, too, were the towns I'd go through. If only I could get myself started.

An easy plan. Through Klosterneuburg, Königstetten, Judenau and Mitterndorf; through Hankenfeld or Asperhofen, Perschling, Pottenbrunn and wee St. Hain; to the big town of Amstetten and three hours west on the Autobahn—where you can easily drive faster than the frotting wind. Then there would still be an hour south of Salzburg, through the little Lofer Range; and I know a place to eat in Fürth. And after-dinner coffee in Kaprun, across that well-worn kitchen table—a second pair of elbows, speaking. Now, at least, with something to say. Something needless and lunatic enough to hold the attention of doughty Watzek-Trummer. Surely, I thought, Ernst Watzek-Trummer has had enough experience with pointless schemes to be sympathetic.

But I thought, too, that I wouldn't rise up from the road ditch, just yet. Or if I did, there was no need to hurry my visit to Kaprun.

Let the grave mound grow a little grass, I always say. Grass is nice, and it will not hurt you, Siggy.

So I'd move along in the general direction of Kaprun, for sure. But I'd creep up on it slowly, you might say; I'd have myself more familiar with this frotting memorabilia I was trucking to Trummer.

But what deadened me in the road ditch was that *none* of my ideas was very stirring, and there seemed to be no excitable planning called for—for *this* trip.

Something new to get used to, I thought. How Hannes Graff was rendered inert. What worse awareness is there than to know there would have been a better outcome if you'd never done anything at all? That all small mammals would have been better off if you'd never meddled in the unsatisfactory scheme of things.

And I surveyed once again this unalterable countryside around me—namable and controlled. A pasture down the road with three white fences and one brown; with nine ewes, one ram and one watchful dog. A pasture up the road with one stone wall, one briar hedge, one wire fence, and one forest—the boundary at the rear; with one horse, and six splotched dairy cows—and, conceivably, an old bull in the woods behind. But not an oryx, surely.

Across the road was a forest, through which the old wind tunneled, furrowing the pine needles.

Then the watchful sheepdog barked over the road at the forest. So, someone's coming, I thought, and I got on the motorcycle—thinking I'd better leave, ready or not, because I looked pretty foolish, just sitting there.

The dog barked more. At someone coming on a well-walked path through the tidy forest, and probably someone who'd come this way, at this time, for years and years—and for years and years, this dog has always barked. A domestic chore, connected to wagging the tail. Which the dog will do next, I thought—at any moment

now, when this farmer's wife or daughter breaks out of
the forest and up on the road. And shouldn't see me here,
suspiciously inert.

But when I tried to pump the kick starter, my legs were
spongy; the heel piece of my boot wouldn't grip the lever.
And I forgot to open the gas line. I leaned over and sniffed
the carburetor, filled my mind with woozy thoughts of
fuel sloshing loose in my skull. I had all I could do to keep
the bike upright; I tottered back and forth.

So whoever it is will just have to see me here, I
thought; I'll be a non-routine blob on the landscape.
Someone will sick the dog on me. Or perhaps the dog is
really barking *at* me; only he's got this crazy habit, de-
rived from sheep, of looking in another direction from
what he's barking at.

But the dog was barking furiously now. And I thought:
Whether it's me or not he's barking about, why didn't he
bark at me before now? If that's the sort of dog he is—
given so easily to woofling at the slightest thing.

The dog was berserk; he snapped around his sheep and
drove the flock into a tight circle. He's lost his head, I
thought—familiar with the symptoms. The sheepdog is
going to eat his sheep!

He was the most unreasonably behaving dog I have
ever seen.

I was still watching him, and shaking on the motorcycle, when the shoulder-to-shoulder pair of Rare Spectacled
Bears tumbled out of the forest and huffed across the
road, not more than twenty yards from me. The dog
dropped flat down on his belly—paws spread, ears tight to
his head.

But the Rare Spectacled Bears were not looking for
sheep, or dogs—or cows in the next field, or a possible
bull in the woods. They were running steadily together;
they came down in my road ditch and up over the fence,
into the sheepdog's field. He howled by the huddled flock,
and the bears pushed on—not at unreasonable speed; not
even hurrying, really. They just headed for the woods at
the far end of the field—where, more than likely, they
would still keep running. The inexhaustible, remarkable,
and very Rare Spectacled Bears, running back to the Andes in Ecuador. Or at least to the Alps.

But when they reached the end of the field, they stopped
and cocked their heads back toward me. I wanted to

wave, but I didn't dare. I wanted them to go on. If they'd
ever waved back to me, or had shouted "Hello!"—if
they'd said "Thank you!" or "Frot you!"—I wouldn't have
been able to believe they were really there. They just
paused, though, and went on again; they ran shoulder to
shoulder into the woods.

I was so thankful that their escape didn't take on the
custardlike quality of too many other endings.

And I suddenly didn't dare stay there any longer. In
case, I thought, the Famous Asiatic Black Bear comes
next. Or even gibbons. Or Siggy astride the oryx—the remaining flesh and ghosts of the Hietzinger Zoo. That
would have spoiled this little token offered me by these
Rare Spectacled Bears. That would not have allowed me
to believe in them, either.

So I worked the kick starter this time. The bike made a
ragged, suffering idle under me. I was still shaky. Even so,
I couldn't stay there—until, perhaps, the Rare Spectacled
Bears passed by me again, this time followed by some
more of those who had temporarily escaped. Vratno
Javotnik on the Grand Prix racer, '39—leaving Gottlob
Wut behind. And other selected mammals.

I looked nervously to the woods behind the field, and
was happy to see that the Rare Spectacled Bears were
gone—leaving the pastures at least not quite the same, at
least not for this moment. Cows fretted; the sheep still
obeyed the panting dog. A little something had been
harmlessly disrupted, and I certainly don't imply that it
made things all frotting rosy. Only that I was able to sincerely imagine coming this way again, some Wednesday.
And meeting someone from the area, who would tell me:
There are bears in Klosterneuburg.

Really?

Oh yes. Bears.

But they've done no harm?

Not these bears. They're strange bears.

Rare Spectacled Bears?

Well, I don't know about that.

But they're multiplying?

I don't know about that, either. But they're very
friendly with each other, you know.

Oh yes. I know.

And that was a little something to know, anyway. And
enough to get the motorcycle running under me. I listened

to my idle coming smoother; it still had rough edges, of course. But I braced my feet on each side of the old beast, and it sat steady; it waited for me, now. Then I identified all its parts in my head; there's a certain confidence in having names for things. I called my right hand Throttle, and turned it up. I called my left hand Clutch, and pulled it in. Even my right foot responded to the gear lever, and found first—and it's not a particularly impressive right foot.

The point is, everything worked. Oh, sure, for a while I would have to be careful, and keep a sharp eye on the mechanics of things. But for that moment, at least, everything was functioning. My eyes too; I saw no more bears, but I could see the grass they'd bent down for a path across the field. Tomorrow the grass would be sprung back in place, and only the watchful dog might remember them with me. And he would forget before I would, for sure.

As for those casualties back at the Hietzinger Zoo—even for old O. Schrutt's mind, left behind, name by name and roar by roar—I will admit to being responsible. For sure, I will turn myself over to Ernst Watzek-Trummer. Historian without equal, and the keeper of details. He should make a fine confessor, for sure.

So I felt the clutch in my left hand; I controlled the throttle and front brake with my right. I put myself in gear and was properly balanced when I came out of the gravel at the roadside. I was steady, shifting up, when I rode into the full-force wind. But I didn't panic; I leaned to the curves; I held the crown of the road and drove faster and faster. I truly outdrove the wind. For sure—for the moment, at least—there was no gale hurrying me out of this world.

For sure, Siggy, I'll have to let your grave mound grow a little grass.

For sure, Gallen, I'll look you up some Wednesday.

For sure, I expect to hear great things of the Rare Spectacled Bears.

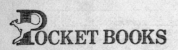

Bestselling Novels from #1 POCKET BOOKS

_____83649   THE CRASH OF '79, Paul Erdman $2.95

_____82388   GOOD AS GOLD, Joseph Heller $2.95

_____43200   LOVE KILLS, Dan Greenburg $2.95

_____43665   THE ROGUE, Janet Dailey $2.95

_____83531   WIFEY, Judy Blume $2.75

_____43996   THE WORLD ACCORDING TO GARP, John Irving $3.95

_____42377   GHOST STORY, Peter Straub $3.50

_____42851   BLOOD WILL TELL, Gary Cartwright $3.25

_____82155   FEVER PITCH, Betty Ferm $2.75

_____81638   WAR AND REMEMBRANCE, Herman Wouk $3.95